D0919009

*The Best
from the
Rest of the World:*
European Science Fiction

The Best
from the
Rest of the World:

European Science Fiction

Edited by

DONALD A. WOLLHEIM

DOUBLEDAY & COMPANY, INC.
GARDEN CITY, NEW YORK
1976

Library of Congress Cataloging in Publication Data
Main entry under title:

The best from the rest of the world.

CONTENTS: Wollheim, D. A. Introduction.—Klein, G.
Party line.—Van Loggem, M. Pairpuppets.—Sandrelli, S.
The scythe. [etc.]
1. Science fiction—Translations into English.
2. Science fiction, English—Translations from foreign
languages. I. Wollheim, Donald A. II. Title: Euro-
pean science fiction.
PZ1.B44664   [PN6071.S33]   808.83′876
ISBN 0-385-04550-6
Library of Congress Catalog Card Number 74–27594

ACKNOWLEDGMENTS

Party Line, from *La Loi de Talion* by Gérard Klein. © 1973 by Éditions
Robert Laffont.
Pairpuppets, from *Paarpoppen* by Manuel Van Loggem. © 1974 by Manuel
Van Loggem.
The Scythe, from *Caino dello Spazio.* © 1963 by Sandro Sandrelli. By arrange-
ment with Gian Paolo Cossato, agent for the author.
A Whiter Shade of Pale, © 1974 by Gyldendal Norsk Forlag A/S.
Paradise 3000, © 1975 by Herbert W. Franke. By arrangement with Thomas
Schlück, literary agent.

76-61408

Dedication

*To my many friends abroad without
whose advice this work would have
been virtually impossible, and
most especially to the gracious
hospitality and unstinting kindness of*

MARIANNE and CLAUDE AVICE

Contents

Introduction

Science fiction is the branch of literature that perceives the universe through the widest-angle lens. Unlike the mainstream of literature, which attempts, more or less, to depict the real world and real people in present or historic situations with the maximum amount of verisimilitude, science fiction acknowledges from the start that it is fantasy, that it is not depicting that which is or that which has been but is engaging in assaying the actions of people and things against backgrounds of limitless imagination.

All that might have been, all that might by the remotest chance ever be, and the world today as perhaps it could be if things are going on of which we are not aware, all these infinite horizons are covered by the lens of science fiction. Yet, because the reader must be convinced of credibility, the best science fiction tries to underline this fantasy by persuading the reader that this is not just the spinning of another fairy tale, that these tales, too, are merely part of some parallel mainstream of which the workaday world is not perceptive.

Science fiction has always been with us—writers have always speculated on the horizons of the not-yet-proven—and examples can be culled from the dawn of written lore and are to be found in all periods of storytelling. To some extent this is a type of escapism and to some extent it is a form of genetic curiosity: people always want to know what is over the next hill and beyond the farthest horizon and at the end of the rainbow. When tellers of tall tales could no longer convince an audience not quite as gullible as our less informed ancestors, the art of science fiction came into being. Extend what we know a little further, advance the line of what could be, bring in the "if this goes on" factor—and we have science fiction. Fantasy designed as reality.

The roots of modern science fiction, which some trace to *Gulli-*

ver's Travels, some to *Frankenstein,* some to Jules Verne and H.
G. Wells, came to mature growth in the nineteenth century, the century of innovative science and the Industrial Age. This growth continued into our century and assumed flexibility, full color, and
infinite variety in the constantly refertilized soil of our science-
oriented and invention-infiltrated world.

At first, science fiction was shared by all the countries of the Western world, those who were the pioneers in the advance of technology
and education. Before World War I, the highest quantity and quality
of science fiction was to be found in Great Britain and in France.
America had its share but not its giants . . . and it was from over-
seas that what science fiction was published or written in America received its primary derivation and ideas. After World War I, American science fiction began to grow strong, mainly through the medium
of the pulp magazines, which were a particularly American phenomenon of the 20s and 30s and which allowed—through their lack of
"literary establishment" dignity—the widest latitude of imagination
in its writers just as long as their stories were entertaining. Because
the language of the United States was English, the British were able
to share in this and to develop their own writers alongside it and
within it.

The Germans, recovering from World War I, began to achieve em-
inence in science fiction, and some of their writers were translated
into English, and their names became known, often without great fa-
miliarity with the bulk of their production. Names like Otfrid von
Hanstein, Otto Willy Gail, and Hans Dominik became familiar—
authors distinguished by their meticulous attention to technological
detail, whose spaceships had nuts and bolts much more convincingly
substantial than the backyard constructs of American pulp adventure
writers. But, alas for Germany—and for the world—the rise of the
Nazi regime put an effective end to German imaginative horizons
and to German influence in science fiction.

In France, a steady growth of science fiction was continuing as it
had since the days of Jules Verne, but contact had diminished almost
to the vanishing point. French science fiction went untranslated, save
for some social speculations by André Maurois, and nobody heard of
Jacques Spitz and Régis Messac. In France itself, science fiction from
the English consisted of H. G. Wells and no one else.

After World War II, science fiction became English-language
based. All the great writers of the forties, fifties, and sixties were
American and British. In Europe, very little science fiction was being
published and what there was turned out to be translations from the
English-American.

When I first investigated the subject of European science fiction, scarcely more than ten years ago, it was clear that just about anything I was likely to find would turn out to be an author with whose work I was familiar—just an American or Briton whose originals I knew. But during the past decade the scene has been changing. European science fiction, written by Europeans in their own languages, has been coming back.

True, the field is still dominated by translations . . . perhaps as high as ninety per cent or more in some countries. Yet there has been a rise in the quantity of original work appearing; slowly and steadily the names of new writers are appearing, and these new writers are achieving some prestige in their own countries—edging their way into the ranks of translated foreigners in their native bookshops.

The first European science fiction conventions have come and gone, prizes are being awarded that are not the American Hugos and Nebulas, organizations are thriving, and the state of European science fiction promises a development that is most encouraging.

In researching this book we set out to find and select good examples of what is going on today in European science fiction. We have entitled this work "the best" but we beg the readers' indulgence here. Only a linguist with an able grasp of a dozen languages could read and evaluate the whole mass of European science fiction and make such a claim. This is, we will say, the best that we have been able to cull from translations, with the aid of suggestions from friends abroad and with what slight ability we have with languages not our own. When this book was first conceived, we planned to include all of Europe, East and West, but there are limits to economic book publishing. Hence, we have deliberately omitted the countries of Eastern Europe and the Soviet Union. In those lands, science fiction is booming—there is a multiplicity of material—but this will have to wait for a second volume, if possible. Here we must perforce concentrate on the lands of Western Europe.

What is the state of affairs in those countries?

By far the healthiest and most vigorous science fiction literature is that of France. No less than nine book publishers include science fiction series in their regular production schedules, and the range is phenomenal. In fact, in many respects it outclasses and puts to shame the science fiction scene in the United States. Yet, it remains, in most aspects, typically French. France seems to breed a type of national coloration that still carries the heritage of the grandeur of the eighteenth century, when France was the cultural center of the world and French the language of international diplomacy and learn-

ing. Or, to put it another way, the French are a world of their own—
they are hard put to acknowledge their role as part of Western
Europe.

I was first made aware of this when I attended the Heidelberg
World Science Fiction Convention in 1970, the first to be held on the
European mainland. It was a well-attended convention with writers
and readers and fans from all over Europe, from Britain, and a large
group from the United States. But French attendees were few and far
between—perhaps a half dozen, perhaps less. They avoided contact
with the others and, when questioned, they insisted that there was no
"fandom" in France. No, no, science fiction was very slight in
France, hardly worth mentioning.

Then I went to France, and in following years went again, and saw
and heard and found. No fandom, indeed! No science fiction, ha!
The country was booming!

A French fandom existed, though it did not call itself such, and yet
it supported "fan magazines" professionally printed, sold through
bookshops, and obviously thriving. It supported monthly editions of
pulp magazines reprinting in translation the best of the Anglo-Saxon
authors. It supports the most expensive and awe-inspiring editions of
science fiction and fantasy books for collectors that exist anywhere in
the world. This is the Club du Livre d'Anticipation, edited by Michel
Demuth and published by Éditions OPTA. The club publishes
monthly selections of beautifully bound and finely illustrated books,
"limited" to five and six thousand copies, numbered, sold by
subscription, and priced at two or three times that of standard
books. I cannot imagine such an enterprise thriving in the American
market, despite its larger size, but in France it goes on spectacularly
and profitably.

At the other end of the literary spectrum, the series "Fleuve-Noir/
Anticipation," published by Presses de la Cité, was and is turning out
four new novels a month, paperbound, cheaply produced, written to
order by French writers—perhaps a dozen such writers busily turning them out—and doing profitably! In this entirely French series,
many of the nation's better science fiction authors made their start,
turning out novels to formula, yet often able to experiment, to try
out new ideas and novel themes, and even to develop special styles.
Such writers as Francis Carsac, Stefan Wul, Gérard Klein, Pierre
Barbet, B. R. Bruss, and Pierre Suragne were—and some still are—
making their mark in these remarkable paperback books, one of
whose principles is that novels are never reprinted (unlike American
paperbacks, in which the second and later reprintings are often the
guarantors of profit). Every month four new titles appear and the
emphasis is on the word "new."

Gérard Klein, himself one of the best sf writers of France, is also editing a very high-grade line for the publisher Robert Laffont. It includes translations, many French originals, and some French "classics" of the twenties, thirties, and forties. These books are distinguished by their glittering metallic covers on the stands of major bookshops.

Jacques Sadoul, editor of the paperback line L'Ai Lu, produces science fiction steadily, including excellent collections of stories from other languages, special anthologies, new French authors, and even nonfiction literary studies of science fiction.

One could go on! Such publishers as Calmann-Lévy, Albin Michel, Denoël, Christian Bourgois, La Masque, and so on, add to the quantity and quality of French sf. And, of course, science fiction and serious studies of it appear in just about all publishers' lists occasionally.

As for fandom, the idea of conventions does seem to be new to France, but there have been some, and in 1975, at one held in Angoulême, the foundations of a Science Fiction Writers of France organization were established. In the true Gallic tradition, heated debate between "left" and "right" went on, which resulted in efforts to form an organization that will avoid political alignments and combine all the writers from advocates of the "New Wave" like Andrevon through "Old Wave" like Barbet.

It should not be surprising that science fiction thrives in France. Not only was there a vast growth of native literature in the nineteenth century, of which Verne was the only one who achieved international prominence, but it never stopped developing. Even during the dismal years of the war, some appeared—René Barjavel made his first appearance in Occupied Paris in 1943 with a novel, *Ravage,* still regarded as a modern classic—and Barjavel is still producing bestsellers.

The situation in Germany is decidedly different and rather peculiar. Once it held the lead for hard-core science fiction (meaning that most firmly grounded in technological speculation). It is still a nation of high technology, earnest students, and great literacy. But its sf output is dominated by the astonishing phenomenon known as *Perry Rhodan.* Perry Rhodan is the pseudo-American name of the lead character of the most prolific sf series in the world today. The publisher who owns Perry, Pabel Verlag, must certainly publish more sf titles per month than any other publisher in the world. *Perry Rhodan* appears as a weekly, featuring a short novel of about thirty thousand words, part of a cliff-hanging cycle of galactic adventures. It has a companion magazine appearing about twice a month entitled *Atlan,* who is another major character in the series. Perry appears in an original sixty-thousand-word paperback novel once a month. He appears in a comic magazine version. Pabel publishes in addition a regular science fiction paperback series, featuring both translations and original novels, and a magazine-type sf twice-monthly entitled *Terra Astra,* doing shorter examples of sf novels. In addition to which there are Perry Rhodan clubs, stamps, toys, spaceship blueprints, records, and there have been films and even conventions.

Perry Rhodan, conceived and directed by two writers, Walter Ernsting ("Clark Darlton") and Karl-Herbert Scheer, is written by a group of seven writers, who space out the tasks among them. The style and level of the *Perry Rhodan* work is deliberately fast-action space opera, and the plots are rarely original, being borrowed wholesale from all the ideas and devices of the American pulps of years gone by. (In fact, there seems to have been and still to be an effort to make the novels seem of American origin—the chief terrestrial characters are supposedly Americans, the language is often styled to seem an Americanized or translated German, and one sees on some of the publications a line to the effect that the book is now first appearing in German, a line generally used for works in translation!) Nobody claims that the *Perry Rhodan* works are great science fiction and no one seems ever likely to consider any part of it for literary awards.

The result of all this enormously successful hackwork is that Germany has produced little science fiction worth comparing to the greats of the Anglo-Saxon and Francophonic worlds. Two outstanding authors seem to dominate what there is of literary sf. One is the Austrian engineer Dr. Herbert Franke, and the other is Wolfgang Jeschke. The two combine to act as editors of a series of anthologies published by Heyne Verlag, as well as turn out original work of their own.

Yet Germany does produce a lot of science fiction in translation. Several paperback firms, Heyne, Bastei, Goldmann, and Fischer, produce regular sf books—usually translations, but sometimes classics or even new native writing. A few publishers have tried regular books (the equivalent of hardbound books in America, as distinguished from mass-market paperbacks) but the efforts have not been very successful. Insel Verlag is the principal survivor, producing a distinguished line of science fiction in beautiful hardbound editions under the direction of Franz Rottensteiner of Vienna. And there are the inevitable imitators and competitors of *Perry Rhodan,* of which Bastei's *Commander Scott* is the most notable. This one began as a translation of the *Cap Kennedy* novels of Gregory Kern but is continuing as a twice-monthly with German writers filling in between the Kern offerings.

Austria and German-speaking Switzerland are part of the German literary market and I do not know of anything special produced there that is distinctive of the area in sf. In French-speaking Switzerland resides Pierre Versins, whose tremendous *Encyclopedie de l'Utopie et de la Science Fiction,* a thousand-page highly illustrated work, is not likely to be challenged as an informational reference work for many years to come in any language.

In Italy the scene is still dominated by translations, with half a dozen publishers producing regular series of books, generally in paperback, keeping up with the Western science fiction world. Mondadori's series *Urania,* La Tribuna's *Galassia,* and the several imprints of Editrice Nord in hardbound editions are the leaders of the bookshop science fiction group. Of special interest is the existence and continued prosperity of the publisher Editrice Libra, whose fine hardbound editions, usually translations, are available only by mail and whose printed fan magazine *Nova* is one of the best in the world for quality and content. There are Italian science fiction writers, though they have to struggle against the high tide of translations to make their mark. Luigi Cozzi and Ugo Malaguti, who are associated with Libra, are among the better known of the labeled "sf" group, although the mainstream of Italian literature has produced Italo Calvino, Buzzati, and several others. Italian fandom has established a going national organization and has been running annual conventions, usually in Ferrara, where an equivalent of the Hugo is presented. In Italy, as in France, there exists a split, as the Libra group declines to acknowledge or participate in the Ferrara gatherings and instead presents its own Hugos, called thus by special permission of Hugo Gernsback himself many years ago.

The tradition or curse of the fan feud, which is endemic to science fiction enthusiasts, reaches its peak and highest level of animosity among what we would suppose to be the peaceful and level-headed Swedes. Sweden has not a large past history of science fiction, but in recent decades the continual publication of magazines with translations and the increase in sf books doing translations produced a small but intense fandom. This would be of no concern to this book were it not that the storm center of much of their activity has been the person of Sam J. Lundwall. Lundwall, who fought his way in his younger days to the top of fandom, is today one of the country's best translators and also Sweden's most prolific science fiction publisher—and one of its leading sf writers. His Delta Forlags publishes between forty and fifty science fiction books a year and he is also the editor-publisher of the country's one remaining sf magazine, *Jules-Verne Magasinet* (a magazine that started in the 1940s as a weekly).

Introduction

Swedish fandom is split into two feuding factions over Lundwall—one supporting him and applauding his friends and works, the best known of which is his novel *King Kong Blues,* a bestseller; the other, which tends to be New Wave, attacking his work with unconcealed venom. Lundwall is the author of most of the reference works available on Swedish science fiction. His antagonists, such as John-Henry Holmberg, have also written reference works and act as advisers to competing sf publishers. Sweden does not have a national organization as such (it did once but it blew apart into fighting fragments) and there are two conventions a year—the pro-Lundwall SF Kongress in autumn and the anti-Lundwall Scancon in spring. All this in a country whose population is so small (eight million) that literature in Sweden often has to receive financial assistance from the government.

Government subsidy to native literature is also characteristic of Norway and has managed to keep at least two publishers doing science fiction regularly. The writing-editing-translating team of Bing & Bringsvaerd (as they often sign their work) is the keystone of Norwegian sf. Both Jon Bing and Tor Åge Bringsvaerd are writers, more or less in the New Wave tradition, and they are both represented in this anthology. The Lanterne paperback series published by Gyldendal Norsk includes science fiction regularly under their guidance. The other major publisher of science fiction in Norway is Fredhøis Forlag, who publishes Old Wave science fiction and mainly in translation.

In Denmark the master science fiction writer is the old and respected Niels E. Nielsen, whose many novels are in the style of past decades and are well liked there, oft-reprinted, but almost unknown outside Nielsen's native land. Jannick Storm, a translator and active fan, has been foremost in the production and encouragement of other Danish science fiction writing and publishing and several anthologies have borne his name as editor. There are quite a number of minor Danish writers, as we can detect from Storm's various collections, but much of this is apparently experimental and none of it has been available in translation.

In the Netherlands, science fiction is regularly published in translation by the major paperback houses such as Bruna, Meulenhof, Ridderhof, and others. Science fiction written in the Dutch language has a few good authors. Manuel Van Loggem, Hubert Lampo, Eduard Visser, Katinka Lannoy, and Harry Mulisch are some of the better writers one will find in the Dutch language. Circulation of Dutch books extends to the Flemish areas of Belgium, insofar as Flemish and Dutch are the same when written. So we may add Eddy C. Bertin of Ghent to the list of authors, and Bertin has had several collections of his fine short stories published in Holland.

In Belgium there are two languages and hence two fandoms and two sf literatures. Sfan is the organization of the Flemish speakers and it has encouraged sf writing among its members. Paul Van Herck has achieved some fame in his native land and outside it. An Antwerp publisher, Brabantia Nostra, has undertaken to do Belgian-Flemish science fiction under the direction of Danny De Laet, fan editor and translator.

In French Belgium, it is only to be expected that the strong world of French sf will have extended itself, and such is the case. Nevertheless, a Belgian paperback publisher, Marabout, produces fine works regularly, both original and translation, and even classics, and these books are available and compete with French publishers in France itself.

Spain has an active fandom and an active Spanish list of publishers. None of them is strong, but they are prolific, and some of the editions of Acervo, Aguilar, and others compare favorably with those of other countries in appearance and content. The prize-winning fan magazine *Nueva Dimension* is published in Barcelona by Sebastian Martinez and has, with justice, been acclaimed the finest of its kind in the world. Martinez, who is also a publisher, under the name Ediciones Dronte, produces an occasional book, working closely with his collaborators, Domingo Santos and Luis Vigil, both of whom are writers of ability.

Of Portugal I can say nothing. I do know that translations appear regularly in Portuguese, but it has always been my impression that they emanate mainly from Brazil, and it may be that Portugal is little more than an outlet for its giant South American offspring's productions.

So now we have covered rather generally the scene in Western Europe. Every major English and American author finds a translator and European fans know their names and their works. The growth of native writing and its qualitative skill continue, and the future is very hopeful. In this book we have attempted but a small sampling of what there is. We would like to hope that there will be more to come. The enrichment and further development of science fiction requires new blood, and it is going to come from Europe.

—Donald A. Wollheim

Rego Park, N.Y.

Party Line

by Gérard Klein

Translated from the French by Arline Higuily

The problem of time is a veritable obsession with French science fiction writers, and almost all the novels of Gérard Klein have dealt with time paradoxes. Several of his novels have appeared in English translation and all have traversed the universe not only from one end to the other but backward and forward as well. In this story, however, Klein—who is an economist with a branch of the French government—takes only one subtle thread of time's interplay and weaves it into a fabric that may not be too remote from his own working scene.

The two telephones rang at the same time. Jerome Bosch hesitated. An annoying coincidence which often occurred, but never at this hour, never at five after nine in the morning when one has just arrived at the office and has only the dreary outlook outside—a long gray wall, with just a few spots, so abstract, so dim, that they didn't even allow the starting point for a daydream.

At eleven-thirty, yes, the time when people began to feel well, quickly finish their business with the idea of saving some minutes for lunch, feeling more at their ease, when the lines are busy or all the telephones ring together, mostly when the telephone centers in their cool caves begin to vibrate, to smoke, to melt.

He knew a few solutions to the problem. Take one of the phones off the hook, answer, and let the other ring till the caller got tired and decided to call five minutes later. Take the receiver off, ask the name, say you're sorry. Take the second line, ask the name, ask them to be patient. Choose the most important name, or the longest, listen first to the woman, if there is one, rather than the man. Women in business were more concise. Or take the two calls at the same time.

Jerome Bosch seized the two phones. The ringing stopped. He watched his right hand, and the little cold black halter which weighed next to nothing at the end of his arm. Then looked at his left hand and the other twin halter. He had a desire to crush the one against the other, or to kindly place them next to each other on the desk right side up so that the two callers could talk to each other and, who knows, maybe make some sense out of it.

But nothing to do with me in any case. I'm an intermediary. That's what I am. Listen and repeat. I'm a filter between a receptor and a microphone, a hearing aid between a mouth and an ear, an automatic pen between two letters.

He put the receivers next to each of his ears.

Two voices:

"Jerome, has someone called already?" "I'm the first, isn't that so? . . . Answer me . . ."

A precise, clear voice, a disturbing voice, at the border of hysteria. They made an echo, curiously alike.

"Hello," said Jerome Bosch. "Who am I talking to please?"
The ordinary formula, prudent, impersonal, but why don't they give their names?

"It would take too long
to explain . . . the com-
munication might be cut off . . .
difficult to get . . . Listen well,
it's the chance of a
lifetime. You have
to say yes and go . . ."
(Click, static, noise of
falling sand on metal.)
". . . don't hesitate."

". . . don't . . . don't
you mustn't . . . you mustn't
. . . pretext . . . I am
no . . . not . . ."

"Who are you?" cried Jerome Bosch into the two phones.
Silence.
A double hissing. To the right, it was the rubbing of metal. To the left, the rattle of a machine. To the right, a tiny noise of eggshells being crushed. To the left, the light sound of a grater on a bed spring.
"Hello," Jerome Bosch said in vain.
Click. Click. Buzzing. Silence. Buzzing. Silence. To the right, to the left. A double busy signal on the lines.
He hung up the phone on the left. He waited a minute for the other phone, lying in the palm of his right hand, pressed next to his ear, listened to the sad mechanical music which sang on two notes, noise and silence, noise and silence, which like a siren of absence moaned at the bottom of its plastic shell.
Then he put the telephone at his right on its hook.
Through the open window he scrutinized the sky where a few dirty city birds and black sparrows drifted above the weather-glazed wall which blocked a good part of his horizon. Then, inside near the window he regarded the artistic calendar offered by an electronic calculating machine company, which presented a careful reproduction of a baroque painting for each day: *Visit to the Rhinoceros*. The Rhinoceros, with an air of annoyance, turned its back on his visitors, probably to better show himself to an art amateur. On the other side of the fence, quite low, a woman in a long dress with a mask on her face, a harlequin, and two children tied with ribbons amused themselves with the beast.
It was the same voice. But how could someone talk at the same time into two different phones, and, in spite of that, speak different words, simultaneously, on two different lines.

I knew the voice. I had already heard it somewhere.

He thought back on the voices of his friends, his clients, the voice of people whom he had relations with, without being especially friends or without selling them something, the voice of businessmen, doctors, trades people, taxi-telephones, all the voices one hears at the bottom of a phone without being able to add a face, oily voices, arrogant voices, dry voices, sprightly voices, laughing, metallic, harsh, hoarse, contracted, distinguished, mannered, vulgar with a husky accent, suave and almost perfumed, gloomy, tight, precise, pretentious, bitter, or sardonic.

He was sure of only one thing. He had heard on the two sides a man's voice.

They'll call back, he said.

He'll call back, because it concerned only one and the same person, even though at the left the voice had been clear, assured, exacting, and almost triumphant, and at the right smothered, terrified, and almost whining.

It was incredible what one could learn about people simply by listening to them on the telephone.

He began to work. A ream of white paper, a small box of clips, three colored pens, and all kinds of samples of formulas next to him. He had to prepare a letter, complete a document, fix up a report, and verify some columns of figures. That was enough to take up the morning. The writing of the report would have to be taken care of in the afternoon. He would take care, before going to lunch, of the difficult problem of choosing to eat in the office cantine or in one of the little restaurants in the neighborhood. He would go as usual to the cantine. The first two years, he chose regularly one of the two small restaurants, because the cantine depressed him. It reminded him that he lived in a universe he hadn't chosen, and as long as he could try to escape it, even if only symbolically, he held on to the impression that his stay was only temporary. A bad moment to pass, like school or military service. Not so bad, however. Work was often interesting and his colleagues were intelligent and cultivated. There were some who had even read his books.

Someone wanted to play a joke on him.

Things like that are possible with a tape-recorder. There wasn't even any conversation. I just listened, called out hello, and asked for names. A joke without the punch line. He began to work. The strange thing was that when he worked he couldn't help thinking of the stories he wanted to write, that he must write, and of the one he wrote with difficulty the evening in his apartment, lit from one end to the other, where he walked from one room to the other because he could not stand the night. And then not less curious, he thought of his work in the day, he could not keep from worrying about a certain affair, and how would so and so take the explications—a little flimsy—would the final document come out on time, everything which should have been blotted out in the silence and left him in peace with his dreams. A man, it was said, could not keep up with two different activities. He finishes by developing two different personalities, which fight and destroy each other. He starts down the double road of schizophrenia.

He picked up the telephone and dialed an interior number.

"Mrs. Duport? Yes . . . Bosch. How are you? . . . Fine, thank you. . . . Will you bring me the Marseilles report? Thank you."

One day, one day, he'd write full time. But at this idea a sudden terror made him lose his breath. Would he be capable of writing, to invent stories, to put together other words than those of accounts and letters? There was a knock on the door. "Come in," he said. The young woman was attractive. She had a round face and a small, pointed nose. What would she like to do, he thought, if she weren't weighed down with paperwork and typing? Paint, sew, read, walk, increase her sentimental relationships? It was a question he'd never ask. But somehow, he thought, it should be the subject of an inquiry, the only inquiry worth taking. It should be taken in the streets, the cafés, in the movies, in the theaters, in vehicles, and right into homes to ask people what they would do if they were completely free, how they would choose to spend that rare commodity which is called "time," in what sort of bottles they desired to pour the numbered sand of their lives. He could imagine the hesitation, the incredulity, the reserve, the panic. How does that concern you? I don't know, no really not, I never thought about it. Wait. Maybe I . . .

She saw that he was reflecting, put the document on the desk, and, without saying anything, left.

He took the document and opened it.

The phone on the left rang.

"Hello," he said.

"Hello, Jerome Bosch?"

It was the precise voice.

"I called you two days ago. The contact was bad. Can you hear me better now?"

"Yes," he said, "but it was a little while ago, not two days. If this is a joke . . ."

"For me it was two days ago. It isn't a joke."

"I believe it, nevertheless," said Jerome Bosch. "Two days or a little while ago is not the same thing. And why are you so familiar?"

"It took me two days to find the combination, or rather to arrive at favorable conditions. It's not so easy to telephone from one time to another."

"Excuse me," said Jerome Bosch.

"From one time to another. I prefer to tell you the truth. I'm calling from the future. I'm you, older than . . . It's better you don't know too much."

"Look, I haven't any time to waste," said Jerome Bosch, his eyes fixed on the open document.

"This is not a joke," pleaded the voice, calm, reasonable. "I didn't intend to tell you the truth, but you don't want to listen to me. You always need explanations and precise reasons."

"You also," said Jerome Bosch, entering into the game, "because you are me."

"I've changed a bit," said the voice.

"And how are you?"

"Much better than you are. I'm working at a job that interests me. I have all my time to write. Quite a bit of money, at least from your standpoint. A villa at Ibiza, another at Acapulco, a wife and two children. I'm glad to be alive."

"Felicitations," said Jerome Bosch.

"All that is yours, naturally, or will be yours. It's just necessary not to make a mistake. That's the reason I've called you."

"I see. The stunt of tomorrow's newspaper. The stock market or next week's lottery . . ."

"Listen," the voice said, annoyed, "at eleven fifty-eight this morning you will receive a telephone call from a very important man. He's going to make you a proposition. You must accept. Don't hesitate to leave the same night even if it's to the end of the world. Have confidence."

"I hope at least it's an honest proposition," said Jerome Bosch ironically.

The voice on the phone seemed hurt.

"Very honest. It's what you've been waiting for, for years. For God's sake take me seriously. It's the chance of a lifetime. One you won't have again. This person often changes his mind. Don't give him the time. It will be the beginning of a brilliant and stimulating career."

"And why have you called me, since you have succeeded?"

"I won't succeed unless you decide. You so often have the habit of hesitating, of equivocating, and then . . ."

The telephone to the right began to ring.

"They're calling me on another line," said Jerome Bosch. "I'm going to hang up."

"Don't hang up," cried the voice frantically, "don't . . ."

He had put the phone on the hook.

He waited a moment, listening to the other phone ringing, and time suddenly opened up. The ringing stretched out over miles of seconds and the silence was like an enormous cool oasis of repose. Ibiza, Acapulco. Names on a map. White and red villas hanging on the sides of steep hills. All the time to write.

He remembered the day when he had heard this voice. It came out of the speaker of the tape-recorder. It was his own voice. The telephone naturally had changed it, impersonalized it, smothered it, but it was his own voice. Not the one which he had the habit of hearing, it was different, restored by being registered. The voice which others heard.

The telephone on the right rang for the fourth time. He picked it up. He thought at first that there was nobody on the other end of the line. He only heard a false silence full of hissing and echoes, of mechanical scratchings as if the line picked up the sounds emitted in a great cave buried underground, full of microscopic noises, feeble drippings, raspings of insects, and tiny landslides. Then he heard the voice, even before understanding what it said, or rather like an indistinct singsong.

"I hear you very indistinctly," he said.

"Hello, hello, hello, hello," said the voice, now a little more distinct. "You musn't go . . . under any circumstance . . . Jerome, Jerome, do you hear me? Listen to me for the love of heaven. Don't leave . . ."

"Speak louder, please," he said.

The ridiculous voice shouted, strangled:

"Refuse . . . refuse . . . later . . ."

"Are you sick?" said Jerome Bosch. "Shall I let someone know? Where are you? Who are you?"

"Yyyyy . . ." said the voice. "You."

"Again?" he said. "But the other voice said that."

". . . am in the future . . . don't leave . . . that's how it is . . . understand . . ."

There was a timid knock on the door.

"Come in," said Jerome Bosch, lifting the phone from his ear and mechanically putting his hand over the microphone.

The new office boy came in. It was his first job, and the men and women shut in their offices, who blackened sheets of paper all day long, impressed him. He blushed easily and he was always impeccably dressed. He put the newspaper and letters on the edge of the desk.

"Thank you," said Jerome Bosch with a nod of his head. The door closed.

He put the phone back against his ear. But the voice was gone. It was lost in the labyrinth of wires that covered the world. A click. Then the dial tone.

He hung up the phone, thoughtful. Was it his own voice like the other time? He wasn't sure. Yet the two voices, the one at the right and the one at the left, had a familiar air. Two moments of the future, two different moments that tried to reach him.

He opened the letters. Nothing important. He annotated them and put them in a box. He threw out the envelopes. Then he tore open the band on the newspaper and rapidly scanned the pages to look at the financial section. Like every morning, his glance wavered over the page and then fixed on the weather report. He looked without interest, as usual. The map pinpointed with symbols caught his attention.

He read:

Weather cool and humid over region of Paris.

His eyes skipped two or three lines.

The cyclical perturbations in the Antilles are moving toward the northeast, above the Atlantic Ocean. There might be . . .

His attention wandered to the top of the page and flickered diagonally over the stock market and the leading values. Stocks strong, but not many transactions. Rise on silver. Light fall on cocoa.

Nothing but the usual affairs. He folded the newspaper.

He began to read the first document in his file.

He reread the first paragraph four times without understanding it. Something was wrong, not in the paragraph but in him. A drunken squirrel turning in a cage that resembled a telephone dial.

He took the phone at the right and dialed the switchboard.

". . . I'm listening," said an arrogant voice.

"A little while ago I had two telephone calls. Can you tell me if my callers left their numbers?"

It was the habit of the switchboard operator to note down all the communications, not like a policeman, but to be able to easily establish a broken communication.

"Which extension?"

"Four one three," said Jerome Bosch.

". . . go see . . . don't leave."

He heard the indistinct voices at the end of the line.

Another voice, feminine, friendly:

"You haven't received any calls this morning, Mr. Bosch. At least not from outside."

"I've been called four times," said Jerome Bosch.

"Not from outside, Mr. Bosch, at least not on your extension."

"I haven't left my office."

"I can assure you . . ."

He cleared his voice.

"Can a telephone call from outside reach one without passing through the switchboard?"

The switchboard operator waited a moment.

"I don't see how, Mr. Bosch."

Uneasy: "I haven't left my post."

Polite but cool: "Shall I call the main office?"

"No," said Jerome Bosch. "I must have been dreaming."

He hung up and passed his hand over a moist forehead. It was a joke. They had used one of the secretary's tape-recorders and they hadn't even taken the trouble to use the outside line. They must be screaming with laughter in the office next door. Melchior was a specialist at imitating voices.

Silence. The staccato of a typewriter stifled by the thickness of two doors. A distant step. The clamor of the city swallowed up by the open window, drilled by escaping rumblings.

He looked at the two telephones as if he had never seen them before. It was impossible. The two telephones were supplied with two distinct bells. A piercing one for the exterior, a muffled one for the interior. The ringing that had preceded each of the four strokes of the telephone still echoed in his ears.

He got up so abruptly that he almost turned over his chair. The hall was empty. He pushed the partly opened door of an office, then a second, then a third. They were all empty; there wasn't even a scrap of paper on the polished surface of the tables as a reminder that they were used. In the last office he picked up the phone, pressed the corresponding button for the inside office, and composed his post number. A muted grumble came from his office, filled the hall. Nobody had reversed the lines of the bell system.

He crossed the corridor, knocked, and entered his secretary's office. She waved her fingers in the air over her machine.

"There's no one around this morning."

"It's vacation," she said. "There's only the assistant director, you, and I . . . and the office boy," she added after a moment.

"Oh," said Jerome Bosch, "I forgot."

"I'm leaving next week." She pointed in the air. "Don't forget. Will you need someone else?"

"I don't know," he said helplessly, "see personnel."

He leaned against the frame of the door.

"Do you think the weather's going to be good, Mr. Bosch?"

"I have no idea. I hope so."

"The radio this morning announced a cyclone over the Atlantic. We'll probably have rain."

"I hope not," he said.

"You need to take a rest, Mr. Bosch."

"I'll leave soon. Two or three little jobs to finish. Oh, by the way, did you hear the phone ring this morning in my office?"

She nodded her head affirmatively.

"Two or three times. Why? Weren't you there? Should I have answered?"

"I was there," said Jerome Bosch, ill at ease. "I took the calls, thank you. Where are you going?"

"To Landes," she answered, watching him curiously.

"Well, I hope you have good weather."

He left, closing the door after him, and waited a moment in the empty corridor. The staccato of the machine began again. Reassured, he returned to his office.

He picked up a letter.

The telephone to the right began to ring.

He looked at his watch. It was eleven fifty-eight.

"Hello."

"Mr. Bosch," said the operator. "A call from out of town. One minute please."

Click. He heard the distance, the waltz of electrons crossing frontiers without passports, waves leaping across space, sent over oceans by the intercontinental rackets of satellites, bounding along cables posed on the bottom of the sea.

"Hello," said a man's voice. "Mr. Bosch. Jerome Bosch."

"Speaking," said Jerome Bosch.

"Oscar Wildenstein on the phone. I'm calling you from the Bahamas. I just finished your last book, *Within a Long Garden*. Very good, excellent, very original."

A male voice assured, vibrant with a light foreign accent. Italian, maybe American, or a little of both. A voice that had an odor of expensive cigars, dressed in a white tuxedo, speaking from the edge of a pool, under a clear blue sky from which hung a torrid sun.

"Thank you," said Jerome Bosch.

"I read it all night. Couldn't tear myself away. I want to make a film with Barbara Silvers. You know her? Well, I want to see you. Where are you now?"

"I'm in my office," said Jerome Bosch.

"Can you get away? You have a plane that leaves Paris-Orly at

four P.M. local time . . . wait . . . it's four-thirty. I'll get you a
ticket. My agent in Europe will take you to the airport. No point taking anything with you. You can find everything in Nassau."

"I'd like to think about it."

"Naturally, think it over. I can't tell you everything over the telephone. We'll discuss the details tomorrow over breakfast. Barbara is
very excited over the idea of meeting you. She's going to read your
book. She'll have read it by tomorrow. I'll translate the difficult pas-
sages. Natasha wants to see you, also. And Sybil, and Merryl, but
they're just extras."

The voice became distant. Jerome Bosch heard feminine laughter,
then the voice of Wildenstein, a little fainter but very distinct, so distinct he might have been speaking from the room next door: "No,
you can't speak to him just now."

"They're completely crazy. They want to talk to you immediately.
It's not possible. I told them to wait until tomorrow. Harding or
Hardy—can't remember his name—who is my representative in
Europe, will take care of you. It was very nice to talk to you. Tomor-
row. *Domani. Mañana.*"

"Good-bye," said Jerome Bosch in a weak voice.

What time is it there? he asked himself.

Six or seven o'clock in the morning. He had read all through the
night. A novel not possible to arrange for the movies. Except, maybe
by him. After all, I know better than anyone how to arrange it. He
understood that all the script men would break their backs over it. A
brilliant and successful career. Two houses, one in Ibiza and one in
Acapulco.

There was a knock on the door.

"Come in," he said.

The secretary stood in the doorway, a strange expression on her
face. She held a small piece of paper in her hand.

"There was a call for you while you were on the other line, Mr.
Bosch. I was given the call."

"Well?" said Jerome Bosch joyously.

"I couldn't hear very well. The transmission was terrible, really
bad. He must have been calling from far away. I'm sorry, Mr.
Bosch."

"And what did he say?"

"I couldn't understand except for two or three words. He said:
TERRIBLE . . . TERRIBLE . . . two or three times, then . . . ACCI-
DENT . . . or OCCIDENT. I wrote it here."

"He didn't leave his name?"

"No, Mr. Bosch, or his number. I hope he'll call back. I hope nothing has happened to your family. An accident. Heavens, it's so quick to happen."

"I don't think there's anything to worry about," said Jerome Bosch, taking the little square of paper. His glance wavered over the stenographic hieroglyphics and stopped over: TERRIBLE . . . TERRIBLE . . . ACCIDENT.

The A of ACCIDENT was underlined and above it was marked an O.

"Thank you, Mrs. Duport. Don't worry. I don't know anyone who could have had an accident. No one."

"Maybe it's a mistake."

"Certainly it's a mistake."

"I'm going to have lunch."

"Very well, enjoy your meal."

When she had closed the door he wondered if he should wait for her to come back before leaving the office. Usually he arranged it so someone was there to take the urgent calls. But it was vacation. There wouldn't be any calls.

Unless the two voices called back.

He shrugged his shoulders and threw an oblique look at the Rhinoceros. The real question was what to decide. It was vacation time, after all. He could leave for a week without having to give an excuse. The Bahamas. Maybe Wildenstein's agent would show up. Maybe it was a millionaire's whim. As soon as said, forgotten. Someone in the Bahamas had read his book or heard it talked about and wanted to hear the sound of his voice, verify that he existed.

He put the newspaper in his pocket. He stared at the telephones as if he was waiting for the ringing to start again while he crossed the corridor with its threadbare rug, stripped with parallel lines, and walked down the large stone stairway. He listened, almost surprised not to be stopped by a loud ring. He crossed the courtyard into the street.

He took the street to the little Basque restaurant.

He went up to the first floor, where few people came in this season. He looked at the menu purely from habit, as he knew it by heart, and ordered a tomato salad and a Basquaise chicken with a small bottle of red wine. It was almost one o'clock. In the Bahamas, Wildenstein was having breakfast with Barbara, Sybil, Merryl, Natasha, and a half a dozen secretaries under a clear blue sky in the shade of exotic palm trees, and while eating called the four corners of the world with his assured male voice echoing around him, speaking in three or four languages of all the books he had read at night.

Jerome Bosch opened his newspaper.

He had just started on his salad when the waitress came over to him.

"Are you Mr. Bosch?"

"Yes," he said.

"There's a telephone call for you. The person said that you were upstairs. The phone is downstairs next to the counter."

"I'll go," he said, suddenly anxious. Was it that faraway voice, indistinct, covered with static? Or was it the other voice, which phoned from Ibiza or Acapulco? Or was it Wildenstein's agent?

The telephone stood between a counter and the kitchen. Jerome Bosch squeezed into a corner to let the waitress pass by.

"Hello," he said, trying to protect his ear against the rattle of dishes.

"I had trouble finding you. Oh, I knew where you were, naturally. But I couldn't remember the number of the restaurant. To tell the truth, I never knew it. It's not so easy to find a number when you don't know the name or the exact location of the restaurant."

It was the voice to the left—precise, clear, but more nervous than in the morning, it seemed.

"Wildenstein, did he call?"

"At the exact time," said Jerome Bosch.

"Are you going to accept?"

The voice was anxious.

"I don't know yet. I have to think about it."

"But you must accept. You must go. Wildenstein is an extraordinary man. You'll get along great. From the first minute. You'll do big things with him."

"And will the film be good?"

"What film?"

"The adaptation of *Within a Long Garden*."

"It'll never be done. You know it's completely untranslatable. You'll speak to him about another idea. He'll be thrilled. No, I can't tell you what. It's necessary. . . . It's necessary that it will happen."

"And Barbara Silvers? How is she?"

The voice softened.

"Barbara, oh, Barbara. You'll have plenty of time to get to know her. All the time. Because . . . I can't tell you."

There was silence.

"Where are you calling from?"

"I can't tell you. From a very pleasant place. You must not know your future. It would upset a lot of things."

"Someone called me this morning," Jerome Bosch said abruptly.

"Someone who had your voice or mine, but broken, tired. I heard it very badly. He told me not to do something. To refuse something. Maybe Wildenstein's proposition."

"Did he call from the future?"

"I don't know."

A silence. Then:

"He spoke about an accident."

"What did he say?"

"Nothing. Just one word. Accident."

"I don't understand," said the voice. "Listen, don't worry. Go see Wildenstein. Go ahead."

"He called several times," said Jerome Bosch. "He'll certainly call back."

"Don't get scared," said the voice, anxious. "Ask him the date when he telephones, understand? Maybe someone is trying to keep you from succeeding. Someone who is jealous of me. Are you sure he had our voice? One can imitate voices."

"Almost sure," said Jerome Bosch.

He waited a moment because a waitress was behind him.

"Maybe he's calling about *your* future," he continued. "Maybe something will go wrong for you and he wants to let me know. Something which began with Wildenstein."

"That's impossible," said the voice. "Wildenstein is dead. You . . . you needn't know. Forget it. It doesn't matter. In any case, you don't know when."

"He . . . he will die in an accident, isn't that it?"

"In an airplane accident."

"Maybe that's it. You . . . you have something to do with it?"

"Absolutely nothing. I can assure you."

The voice became nervous: "Listen, you're not going to ruin your future over this story. You don't risk a thing. I know what's happened. I've lived through it."

"You don't know your future?"

"No," said the voice. "But I'm capable of taking care of it. I'll watch out. Nothing will happen. And even if something happens, I'm much older than you. No, I can't tell you my age. Let's put it that you have a good ten years ahead of you. Really good years. I would let the opportunity go, even if I had to die tomorrow!"

"Die tomorrow," said Jerome Bosch.

"Just a way of speaking. It's a lot, ten years, you know. And I'm fit as a fiddle. Much better than at your age. I promise you. Accept. Leave for the Bahamas. Don't tie yourself down to anything. Promise me you'll accept."

"I would like to know one thing," Jerome Bosch said slowly. "How can you talk to me. Have they invented a time machine in the future? Or have you done the job yourself?"

The voice began to laugh at the other end of the line. A laugh a little forced.

"It exists already in your era. I don't know if I should tell you. It's a secret. Very few people know about it. Anyhow, you wouldn't know how to use it. Nobody knows how it works, even now. You need luck, the right set of circumstances. The machine is the telephone."

"The telephone," repeated Jerome Bosch, surprised.

"Oh, not the combination you hold in your hand, but the network, the whole network. It's the most complicated thing done by man. More complicated than the calculating machines. Think of the thousands of miles of wires, the millions of amplifiers, of the inextricable tangle of the centers. Think of the millions of messages which go around the earth. And everything is connected. Time and again something unexpected happens in this jumble. Time and again the phone connects two moments instead of two places. It might become official one day. But I doubt it. Too many unknowns. Too many risks. Only a few are in the know."

"How did you do it?"

"You will have very intelligent friends in the future if you accept Wildenstein's proposition. But I'm talking too much. You don't need to know everything. Accept. That's all."

"I don't know," murmured Jerome Bosch as he heard a click at the other end of the line.

Someone was waiting behind him.

"Oh, excuse me. I was very long." He tried to smile. He walked up the stairs holding on to the railing. The chicken had been served. It was almost cold.

"Do you want me to reheat it?" asked the waitress.

"No, that's all right."

They didn't have a machine to travel in time but they had discovered a new way to use the telephone.

The telephone.

It covered the entire planet. It ran along roads, railways, suspended over linear forests. It plunged under rivers and oceans in a rubber coat. It formed a thick and spiderlike ball at the same time. The wires crossed and intercrossed. Nobody would be capable of drawing a complete diagram of the telephone system. And in ten years? And in twenty years? The system would be more complex than the human brain.

He tried to imagine the cool, dark caverns of the great centrals where, in silence, impalpable impurities drowned in a crystal heart, oriented innumerable voices. And the networks were in one sense living. Men spread it all the time and meticulously repaired it. The networks were nerves. Automatic calculators cutting messages into small pieces so as to be able to cross and fill the silences. What would be so surprising if the telephone should be capable of another miracle?

He remembered stories—maybe legends—that one told about the telephone. Numbers one could dial at night that would put you in contact with unknown voices. Not only one voice, but anonymous voices bodiless, which exchanged between them their own talk, playful, joking, who profited from the situation and said things which wouldn't be quoted under cover of a known name or face. He remembered ghost voices, which they said wandered without stopping in the line of the network and always repeated the same thing. He remembered automatic systems answering when you lifted the phone.

Sooner or later everything in the universe found a means which it hadn't been made for. So with man. A million years ago, he ran through the forests gathering game and fruit with his bare hands. And now he built villas, wrote poems, threw bombs, and phoned.

So it was with the telephone.

He pushed away his plate, ordered a coffee, drank it, paid, and left. The sun had chased away the clouds. He turned toward the quay. But just loafing was impossible since cars were all over. Even the fishermen had given up. I'm just turning around he said. I know all the streets in this neighborhood by heart. I work, I inhabit one of the most fantastic cities in the world, and it has ceased to move me. It says nothing to me. I'd love to get out of here.

He looked at his watch. Almost two-thirty. The time to go back and finish what I couldn't do this morning. The walls and windows, always the same, were gray and almost transparent, used by the insistent and excessive stare of eyes.

Then there were the girls who the seasons, the change of work, and the tourist buses renewed. But this year's crop was very bad. He hadn't seen a good-looking girl for over a week.

In the Bahamas, Barbara, Natasha, Sybil, and Merryl were splashing in a pool under the satisfied eyes of Wildenstein. He was right. I should accept. It was a chance not to be repeated.

The secretary's door was open. She was waiting for him. A new call, he thought anxiously.

She leaned toward him.

"Someone is waiting for you in your office, Mr. Bosch." He stopped short, a lump in his throat. He didn't have an appointment. Who could it be? Have they managed to physically cross over into time? Wasn't it enough for them to call him? He took his courage in his two hands: no, they couldn't do anything except telephone through time. He opened the door.

A man who didn't look like Jerome Bosch waited, seated on a corner of his desk, one leg hanging, the other on the worn rug. His face was long, his features fine. His dark hair was long but carefully cut at the collar. He was dressed in a gray suit with large checks, with lots of pockets—the one over his heart had a colored handkerchief artistically creased—and the narrow lapels underlined the fantasy. He wore a striped shirt, a tie with polka dots, black shoes with complicated designs, and red socks. Next to his right hand, a small suitcase of black shiny leather. He looked English from the tip of his toes to the end of his nails. He got up.

"Mr. Jerome Bosch? I am very pleased to meet you."

The voice was cultivated, serious, with a strong British accent.

Jerome Bosch nodded his head.

"Fred Hardy," said the man, holding out a beautifully manicured hand. "Mr. Wildenstein called me before coming here. He hoped that I would take care of all the details."

He opened his suitcase and spread out on the desk a handful of papers.

"Here's your airplane ticket, Mr. Bosch. Here's a special visa that you just have to put in your passport. You have a passport, don't you? This wallet has fifty pounds in it in travelers' checks. You just have to sign. I think that will be sufficient for the voyage. And here's a letter to give to customs at Nassau. The governor is a personal friend of Mr. Wildenstein. You don't have to handle anything. Mr. Wildenstein is probably not in Nassau but someone will be at the airport and conduct you to Mr. Wildenstein's island. I wish you a very good trip."

"I haven't accepted yet," said Jerome Bosch.

Hardy began to laugh politely.

"Oh, naturally you're free. I've prepared all this on the assumption of a favorable answer."

"You've done it very quickly," said Jerome Bosch, astounded, contemplating the plane tickets, the visa, the wallet, and the envelope. "You live in Paris?"

"I just arrived from London, Mr. Bosch," said Hardy. "Mr. Wildenstein likes efficiency. Mr. Wildenstein recommended that I accompany you to the airport. Moreover, my plane leaves a half hour after yours. These schedules are practical between Paris and London."

The telephone to the right began to ring. Hardy put his case under his arm.

"I'll wait for you in the corridor, Mr. Bosch. The taxi is downstairs. We have plenty of time."

He smiled, showing his large, immaculate white teeth. The door closed after him.

Jerome Bosch picked up the phone.

"Hello," he said.

Nobody. The echo in a cave, a long tunnel, a well.

"Hello," he said, louder. He had an impression of not hearing himself. He had the impression that his voice was swallowed up by the phone, smothered, stifled.

Without conviction he said:

"Where are you calling from, what do you want?"

He held the airplane ticket close and leafed through it. The ticket, Paris–Nassau via New York and Miami. One return-trip ticket. Hardy had done things thoroughly. It wasn't a trap. No matter what happened he could return. And Hardy had come from London just for this. Let's see. Wildenstein had called him at ten-thirty, maybe eleven. He had taken the twelve-o'clock plane. At one o'clock he was in Paris. At a quarter to two in the office of Jerome Bosch. It was very simple. He lived in a world where you jumped from one plane to the other, where one wore apparently sober suits but which in reality were quite extravagant, shoes made to order, where one was invited to governor's dinners and was to telephone from the four corners of the globe. I can't let him down before he goes back to London, thought Jerome Bosch.

It was a first-class ticket. On the upper left-hand corner of the cover was a stamp. V.I.P. And someone had added Fm. WDS.

Very Important Person. From Wildenstein. Made out by Wildenstein.

He was in a state. I can't just tell him: Tomorrow if you like, but not today, I must think it over. He'd laugh at me. No, he's much too well bred. He'll say Mr. Wildenstein will be sorry, he hopes to see you tomorrow morning. He would bend over and put the ticket, the visa, the fifty pounds, and the letter from the governor back in his case and then he'd return to Orly to wait for his plane. What time is it? Almost three. In an hour and a half, the plane would take off. Nassau via New York and Miami. They had no intention of letting the plane wait fifteen minutes just for him.

"Hello," said Jerome Bosch into the dumb phone. He opened a

drawer of his desk, the only one that locked. He picked up official papers and found his blue passport, drew it toward him with one hand and opened it. An old photo of three or four years ago. He was almost good-looking then, much thinner. He looked alert.

"Hello," he called for the last time, and hung up. His hands were damp and trembling. I don't have the experience for this type of situation. I don't know what to do. In his right hand he put the passport, ticket, visa, the wallet, and the letter. With his free hand he opened a large drawer in his desk and threw in papers, documents, pens, and the box of clips.

At the end of the corridor, Hardy was waiting, smiling, not even leaning on the wall, holding the suitcase nonchalantly by the handle with two hands.

Jerome Bosch knocked and pushed open the secretary's door.

"I have to leave for a few days, Mrs. Duport," he said, "this man . . ."

"It was an accident, wasn't it?"

She seemed frightened. What must she imagine? he thought. But I can't tell her the truth. I can't say that in an hour I'll be in the sky on my way to the Bahamas.

"No," he said in a sudden hoarse voice. "Not an accident, on the contrary. A . . . personal affair. I'll be gone for a few days. I think it's better to get a temporary helper. To answer the telephone. I'll send you a postcard."

She finally decided to smile.

"Have a nice trip, Mr. Bosch."

He must leave and recover.

"If . . . if someone calls me, say I'm on vacation. I haven't much time. This man . . . You'll explain all this to the codirector . . . all right?"

"Don't worry. Enjoy your trip, Mr. Bosch."

"Thank you."

In the corridor, Hardy took a cigarette from a red and gold box. He tapped the end against his case, then slipped the cigarette into his mouth, the lighter from his pocket squirted a flame, he inhaled a puff, and exhaled the smoke in a thin line almost without opening his lips.

"A cigarette, Mr. Bosch?"

"No, thank you," he said. "I . . . I . . . smoke a pipe."

He felt his pocket, but he knew that his black briar pipe, the one which was split—its life would be short even though he preferred it to his others—wasn't there. He had left it at home this morning. Moreover, he never took it to the office. He didn't use it except while writing or reading in the tranquillity of his apartment with all the lamps lit.

"Mr. Wildenstein will be very pleased with your decision, Mr. Bosch. He'll be very happy to see you. He likes people who know how to make quick decisions. Time is so precious, isn't it?"

They went down the large stone stairway.

"Do you have to let anyone know, Mr. Bosch?" said Hardy. "You can telephone from the airport."

He looked at his watch.

"We don't have time to go to your home, but it doesn't matter. Mr. Wildenstein is about your size. He has an enormous wardrobe. You can find everything in Nassau. Mr. Wildenstein likes to travel without baggage."

The pebbles in the courtyard cracked under their steps.

"Your taxis are so convenient in France, Mr. Bosch. I only have to telephone from London before leaving and a car is waiting for me at Orly. Radio-taxis, isn't that so? Our taxis are so out-of-date in London. And in New York, it's so difficult to find a driver who will wait for you. It's a nice day, don't you find it so? It rained this morning in London. It's even better weather in Nassau. But the sky doesn't have this shading, this soft color. I want to talk to you about your book, Mr. Bosch, but I must admit I haven't had the time to read it yet. My knowledge of your language is very incomplete. I hope it will be translated soon. You'll like Mr. Wildenstein. He's a man with a lot of personality, or, as you would say, 'character.' "

"Well now. Baron," said the driver when they were installed in the back of the car, "where are we going?"

"To Orly," said Hardy.

"By Raspail or by Italie?"

"Take the Boulevard Saint Germain and the Boulevard Saint Michel," said Hardy. "I like so much going along the Luxembourg Gardens."

"As you like, but it will be longer."

The streets were almost deserted. The traffic lights before them turned green almost as if the driver had telecommanded them. It only needed, said Jerome Bosch, that the car have a little flag and a siren. No, a siren would have destroyed this deep silence. Real power has a great deal of discretion. No noise, baggage. Invisibility. Only a name used as a passport.

As they were going along Luxembourg, the radio began to ring. It was an old telephone model. Without slowing down, the driver unhooked the phone and hung it at the side of his head.

"I'm listening," he said.

A voice breathed a few words.

The driver looked in the rear-view mirror.

"Are you Bosch?" he said.

"That's me," said Jerome Bosch.

"It's not regular, but someone wants to talk to you. It must be important if the station gives it to you. This isn't a telephone, it's a taxi. Go ahead, take the tube, because they want to talk to you. I've never seen anything like this. And I've been driving for over twenty years."

His throat dry, Jerome Bosch took the apparatus. He was obliged to fold himself almost in two on the seat because the cord was too short. His chin pressed against the worn velvet.

"Hello," he said.

"Jerome," said the voice. "Finally I found you . . . difficult . . . Don't leave, for the love of heaven. There's going to be . . . Don't . . ." Static. Cracklings.

"Where are you calling from?" asked Jerome Bosch with a voice which he tried to make firm and keep discreet.

"Why, why, why?" said the voice plaintively, the voice broken, complaining. "From . . . tomorrow . . . or after . . . don't know . . ."

"Why mustn't I . . . ?"

He stopped, thinking that Fred Hardy would hear him. He had come from London just to put him on the plane.

"Accident," said the voice. It was nearer than it had ever been. But it sounded more miserable, more worn for being clearer.

"Who's talking?"

"Yyyy . . . you," said the voice to the only Jerome Bosch. "I have already . . ."

"Your voice sounds so low . . . isn't it?" asked Jerome Bosch abruptly.

"I'm so far . . . so far," said the voice as if explaining.

The car went faster. They rode on the left side of the autoroute.

An intuition hit Jerome Bosch like a blow.

"You're sick . . ." he ended.

He didn't dare say any more. Not in front of the driver and Hardy.

"No, no, no," said the voice, "not that . . . not that . . . worse, it's terrible. You mustn't . . . I . . . I . . . I wait . . ."

"I mustn't what?"

"You mustn't leave," said the voice distinctly, and immediately it disappeared as if it had accomplished a last terrible exhausting effort.

Jerome Bosch remained overwhelmed for a moment, bent forward on the seat. The perspiration dripped from his forehead. The apparatus slipped from his fingers, bounced on the cushion, then hung at the end of the line, hitting the driver's knee, ringing on the metal.

"Is it finished?" said the driver.

"I think so," said Jerome Bosch, breathless.

"So much the better," he said, hanging up.

A jet plane passed very low overhead.

"You seem nervous, Mr. Bosch," said Hardy.

"It's nothing," said Bosch, "nothing at all."

He thought: I haven't left yet. I can change my mind. Say I've been called back. A very important affair. Leave it till tomorrow.

"The air in Nassau will do you a world of good, Mr. Bosch," said Hardy. "The agitation of big cities is wearing on the nerves."

"Depart or arrival?" asked the driver.

"Depart," said Hardy.

The car stopped beside the sidewalk. Jerome Bosch looked in front and saw that the amount registered on the meter had three digits. Hardy paid. The glass doors opened automatically in front of them. They kept away from the lines in front of the booking office and went to the entrance of a small discreet office. Jerome Bosch put his hand in his left pocket, which contained the passport, ticket, wallet, visa, and the letter. They took care of the formalities.

"No, not there," said Hardy as Jerome Bosch went toward the large stairway. He conducted him to a narrow hall. The marble was covered with a large rug. A door opened without noise.

"Back already, Mr. Hardy," said the elevator operator.

"Alas, yes," said Hardy. "I can never take advantage of my stay in Paris."

They were now in the upper hall.

"You have plenty of time to buy newspapers, Mr. Bosch, or a book. It's a ten-hour flight to Nassau including the stops. There is a direct flight from London, but only once a week."

I can still refuse, thought Jerome Bosch. Thank him, wait with him for the plane to London, promise to leave tomorrow. Say I had forgotten something. Through what did he call me? From where did he call? Why did he say tomorrow? How could he call me through tomorrow? Tomorrow I wouldn't know more than today how to telephone across time. Who is he?

He let himself sink little by little into the atmosphere of the place.

"You haven't given me time to fetch a coat," he said.

"Useless, in Nassau, you won't need one. You rather need a light suit. You have the best English tailors in Nassau, the best London houses."

On the other side of the glass wall, giant planes waited, immobile, frozen. Others rolled slowly on belts. Another warmed its motors at the end of a runway, pushed ahead, refusing to leave the ground, then suddenly breaking its headway, lifted and rose. I am in an aquarium. Even sounds don't come through this glass prison. On the other side, above, in the blue sky, freedom begins.

Jerome Bosch let his eyes wander over to a young woman printed in two copies. Twins. Exactly the same. Long honey-colored hair, same faces, a little dull but exquisitely fresh. Their legs were long and thin. They each carried a small shoulder-strap bag of red leather. They are either in the movies or models, thought Jerome Bosch, at bottom surprised not to discern between him and them the thickness of a window or the impenetrable depth of a movie house, or the photographic varnish of a magazine page. The story of a man in love with one of the twins, either one; which should he choose, A or B? He chooses A. Very quickly she shows her nasty character. He understands that he should have married B, who is sweet, affectionate, and who loves him in silence. What should he do? Divorce and marry B. That would never work. She loves her sister too much. He discovers a method to call through time. He telephones himself the day he makes his decision. Marry B, he cries helplessly to his undecided past. What will the past do? And if B should become in time nasty also? Completely idiotic, said Jerome Bosch to himself.

"The Berthold sisters," said Fred Hardy. "They pretend they are Swedish, but in reality they are Austrian or maybe Yugoslavian. Mr. Wildenstein wanted to use them. But they don't know how to act. Nothing to be done. Not the least stage presence. As if one was the reflection of the other and vice versa. In Hollywood, Jonathan Craig pretends that they have only one shadow for two. They are going to act in a small French film."

"Do you meet the same people all the time in the airports, Mr. Hardy?"

"No, but you fall sometimes on well-known personalities. Especially on the Paris–New York line. Like a suburban line. London is the suburb of New York today, Mr. Bosch."

"Isn't it dangerous to travel by plane?" Jerome Bosch said impulsively and naïvely. He heard the voice: Accident . . . accident.

"Certainly, Mr. Bosch," said Hardy, "but less dangerous than traveling by automobile. There are statistics. I take the plane three times a week generally. And Mr. Wildenstein belongs to the millionaires' club. You've heard it talked about. That means that he has covered more than a million miles by plane. Never a single accident. Have you ever taken a plane, Mr. Bosch?"

"Yes," said Jerome Bosch, suddenly humiliated by his cowardice. "I've been to London two or three times, and to New York, to Germany, and also to Nice. But I don't care for the taking off and landing."

He had a desire to tell how he had seen a helicopter burn in Algeria during the war. The plane hesitating like a large fly, then slipping, gliding a few feet from the ground, and for an unknown reason turning over. A sudden light of magnesium. A thick cloud of smoke, no explosion, it only burned, the sirens, the fire engines, a shroud of snow, carbonic suds on a ridiculous block less than a yard from his side, the motor, all that remained of the helicopter.

"The weather is splendid, Mr. Bosch," said Fred Hardy. "It will be an excellent flight. Look, your plane has just been announced."

Jerome Bosch turned toward the flight panel and read: FLIGHT 713 B.O.A.C. PARIS–NEW YORK–MIAMI–NASSAU. SALLE 32.

"We have plenty of time," said Hardy. "Really, you should buy some newspapers, a book, a pipe, tobacco. Or maybe you'd rather think on the plane. Planes are really such quiet places."

PARIS–LONDON 5 P.M. AIR FRANCE FLIGHT A SALLE 57 FLIGHT B SALLE 58

"Your plane," he said.

Fred Hardy examined the panel.

"Oh, it's been doubled."

"Which one will you take?" Jerome Bosch asked abruptly.

"It doesn't matter," said Hardy. "If there's no room on A, they'll put me on B. They arrive at the same time, I think."

But thought Jerome Bosch, If plane B had an accident, wouldn't it be better to take plane A? The chances, are they mathematically equal? How to choose?

"They are calling you," said Fred Hardy.

"Who, me?"

"The microphone," said Fred Hardy. "Maybe it's Mr. Wildenstein."

He smiled, a cigarette between his fingers, his valise placed on the arm of a chair, leaning against his hip, impeccable, elegant.

"Mr. Jerome Bosch is requested to come to the welcoming office," said the voice, asexual but feminine, angelic, too low-pitched, too smooth, too calm.

"Someone wants you on the telephone probably," said Fred Hardy. "Here. Straight ahead. Do you want me to buy you newspapers? A pipe? Meerschaum or briar? What do you prefer in tobacco? Amsterdammer or Dunhill?"

But Jerome Bosch had already gone, dizzy, staggering. Too much noise. Too many faces. A complicated itinerary. Where was it? The panels. Welcome.

He held on to the counter as if he were drowning. He understood. An idea flashed in his mind. Till now it turned around like a fish in a bowl. Circular. It came to him. He believed everything.

"I'm Jerome Bosch," he said to a young woman with a smiling face and a gray beret placed across her head. Her eyes were too big, heavily underlined with black, and her teeth too large, also.

"I've been called," said Jerome Bosch nervously. "I'm Jerome Bosch."

"Certainly, Mr. Bosch. An instant, Mr. Bosch."

She pushed an invisible button, said something, then listened. "A telephone call, Mr. Bosch. Booth three. No, not there. On your left."

The door closed automatically after him. Silence. The roar of the planes didn't sound here. He picked up the phone and without waiting:

"I don't want to leave."

"You're not going to give in now," said the voice of the left, firm and resolute.

"The other," said Jerome Bosch. "He isn't calling from your future. He's calling from *another* future. Something has happened to him. He took the plane and he had an accident and . . ."

"Are you crazy," said the voice. "You're afraid to take the plane and you invent anything. I know you well, you know."

"Maybe I invent you also," said Jerome Bosch.

"Listen," said the voice, "I had a lot of trouble getting hold of you. I knew you'd hesitate. I don't want you to give up this opportunity."

"If I don't leave," said Jerome Bosch, "you won't exist. That's why you insist."

"And then," said the voice, "I'm you, no? I've explained all this to you. Ibiza. Acapulco. All the time to write. And Barbara. And Barbara. Good God. I shouldn't tell you, but you're going to marry Barbara. You don't want to miss that. You love her."

"I don't know her yet," said Jerome Bosch.

"You'll meet her," said the voice. "She'll be crazy about you. Not right away. Ten years, Jerome. More than ten years of happiness. She'll act in all your films. You'll be famous, Jerome."

"Give me time to think about it," said Jerome Bosch.

"What time is it?"

He looked at his watch.

"Four-ten."

"You must get on the plane."

"But the other voice that phones from I don't know where. It told me not to leave. Another future, another possibility. He said he called from tomorrow."

"Another future," said the voice, indecisive. "And then, I'm here, no? I took the plane and nothing happened to me. I've taken the plane hundreds of times. I belong to the millionaires' club. You know what that is? And never an accident."

"The other one has had an accident," said Jerome Bosch stubbornly.

Silence. Cracklings. An abysmal insect devoured the line somewhere on the bottom of the ocean.

"Let's admit," said the voice, "you could run a risk, no? Look at the statistics. There are ninety-nine chances out of a hundred that you will arrive safely. More than that. Nine hundred . . ."

"Why should I believe you," asked Jerome Bosch, "and not the other?"

". . . chance out of two . . ."

"Hello," said Jerome Bosch. "I don't hear you."

"Even if there wasn't," said the voice, which cried and died far away, which spoke from the other side of a partition of glass, which screamed from the interior of a closed box, "one chance out of two, you can't let it drop. You don't want to spend your life in an office, no?"

"No," said Jerome Bosch feebly.

A tiny voice at the end of the line as if the caller out there was sinking in the foam, falling in the infinite labyrinth of telephone wires.

"Hurry up," said an insect, "you'll miss the plane."

Click.

"Hello, hello," cried Jerome Bosch.

Silence. Dead phone. He looked at his watch. Four-fourteen. He was one or two minutes slow. Hardy must be asking what he was doing. I'll miss the plane.

Should I leave? Jerome Bosch asked himself.

"It's time," said Fred Hardy, smiling. "I bought you a briefcase. A meerschaum pipe. Mr. Wildenstein prefers meerschaum pipes because it's not necessary . . . how do you say, *de les culotter*. Three packages of tobacco. *Le Monde* and *Le Figaro*, the New York *Times*, *Paris-Match*, *Playboy*, and the latest *Fiction*. That's the French review where you publish your short stories, isn't it? I bought you a toothbrush. A flask of whiskey. Chivas. You like Chivas, no, Mr. Bosch? We just have time. No, not there."

The policeman smiled, greeted Fred Hardy, and made a sign.

The customs officer let them through.

"Tell Mr. Wildenstein that everything is all right in London, Mr. Bosch. I'll call him tomorrow. No, Mr. Bosch, here."

Loudspeakers diffused soft music.

They advanced into an infinite corridor, limited at the end by a large mirror which threw back their images as they hurried toward it. But they didn't reach it. Fred Hardy took Jerome Bosch's elbow and turned him a quarter way around and they walked immobile down the lower story on a little mechanical escalator.

The waiting room was divided into two parts. To the right, a line of people. Jerome Bosch wanted to join them. But Fred Hardy took him toward the other door. There was almost no one there. A gray suit with a weather-beaten face who held in his hand a shiny leather briefcase, and a woman, very tall, very beautiful, whose long pale hair touched her shoulders. She didn't look at anyone.

There was one more door to go through.

I don't want to leave, thought Jerome Bosch, pale. I'll pretend I'm ill. A forgotten appointment, I have to get a manuscript. I won't say anything. They can't hold me back. They can't kidnap me.

"Here," said Fred Hardy, handing him the briefcase. "I hope you have a nice trip. I would have liked to go with you, but the London office is waiting for me. Perhaps I'll be in the Bahamas at the end of the month. I am very happy to have met you, Mr. Bosch."

The door opened. A hostess entered, smiled, looked over the three first-class passengers, took their red tickets, and left.

"Will you please take your place in the bus."

"Good-bye, Mr. Hardy," said Jerome Bosch, moving away.

Jerome Bosch is almost alone in the bus, which carries the first-class passengers. The bus rolls slowly, following a complicated itinerary on an enormous surface of smooth cement which doesn't seem to be ground-lighted. Jerome Bosch feels nothing, not even the slight excitement which accompanies all his trips. He thinks that now nobody can reach him by telephone—here he fools himself. He thinks that no one will try to influence his conduct because that will not have any importance. The bus stops. Jerome Bosch gets off the bus, which leaves to get the batch of second-class passengers. He climbs the mobile stairway applied to the front of the plane. He hesitates an instant on entering the first-class cabin. He lets himself be conducted to a chair next to a porthole in front of the wings. He fastens his security belt under the hostess's vigilant eye. He hears some noise, the scraping of feet behind him, the second-class passengers settling down. He sees the hostess go forward toward the pilot's cabin and disappear for an instant, return, and unhook a micro. He hears her wish everyone welcome in three languages and recommend everyone to put out cigarettes and examine their seat belts. A panel lights up which renews these instructions. A basket filled with candies is served to him. He chooses one. He knows that it fulfills a rite, that these planes are pressurized and that his eardrums will not suffer even if he doesn't take the trouble to swallow, and moreover, he will have swallowed the candy even before the plane has finished taking off. The plane rolls. It seems to Jerome Bosch that in the distance, near the waiting room, stands the tall, elegant silhouette of Fred Hardy. The plane stops moving. The motors roar and the universe hurls itself ahead and throws Jerome Bosch against the back of his seat. He tries to look out the porthole. The plane has left the ground. A shock. The wheels have been drawn up into their place.

Jerome Bosch begins to relax. Nothing happens. He is given a newspaper, this morning's, and he opens it to the economic page and his eyes fall on the small weather map. He puts it aside. He opens the briefcase, looks inside and finds the pipe, examines it, superior quality, and stuffs and lights it. He is served a whiskey. He flies over the clouds. He asks himself if ephemeral, tiny civilizations are growing in the folds of these mountains of fog. He thinks he is beginning to forget the telephone. He tries to imagine Nassau. He begins to discover that he has left. He takes possession of the cabin. He makes his seat move. He questions himself on the possibilities of his two futures. It seems to him, but he isn't sure, that the voice from the left, the firm assured voice, Ibiza, Acapulco, and Barbara, has become more distant, become less clear, from conversation to conversation, and the other more present. Question of telephone lines. He is given something to eat. He is served champagne. He looks at the hostess, who smiles when she passes by him. He asks for more champagne. He drinks a coffee. He sleeps.

When he wakes up—but what time is it?—the plane is flying over the sea in a perfectly clear day. Jerome Bosch hasn't dreamed or he couldn't remember his dreams. He regrets rather absurdly, in looking at the sea, not having brought a bathing suit. Mr. Wildenstein certainly has a dozen suits. Jerome Bosch finally understands that the hostess is addressing him. She holds out a blue piece of paper intricately folded like a telegram. She seems surprised.

"A call for you, Mr. Bosch. The operator excuses himself but he could only understand a few words. There's static electricity in the air. He tried to confirm it, but without success."

He unfolds the paper and reads only one word scratched in pen: *Soon . . .*

Mr. Wildenstein, he thinks. But he can't be sure.

"Please," he said, "please could you find out what the voice was like."

"I'll go see," said the hostess, who disappeared into the pilot's cabin and came back in a moment.

"Mr. Bosch," she said. "The operator couldn't describe the voice very well. He begs to be excused. He said it seemed very near, that the communication was very powerful and he didn't think, in spite of the static, that there was any more to say. He asked for confirmation."

"Thank you," said Jerome Bosch, as he sees her leave, take up the microphone, take a breath, and say in a smooth voice:

"A second of attention, if you please, ladies and gentlemen. We are going through a zone of perturbation. Please fasten your seat belts and put out your cigarettes."

He doesn't listen anymore. He looks out the porthole at the bottom of the sky, otherwise clear, and sees that a little cloudy spot, almost black, is topped by an intense dark bubbling toward which the plane precipitates. Black, black, black, as an eye.

Pairpuppets

by Manuel Van Loggem

Translated from the Dutch by the author

Manuel Van Loggem is a professor at a Dutch university. He has a dry, sharp wit, which is reflected in his conversation and also in the short stories for which he is noted. In this one he takes up the sort of question that most Anglo-Saxon collegians would prefer not to discuss. But in the Netherlands, as in most of Europe, they are much more able to face realities even when dealing with fantasies, if you get what I mean.

"It's the end of our mutual service time," Eric said softly to himself, "and I'm not glad."

He was standing at the window and looking out over the polder far below him. The carefully calculated disorder of renovated mills and sham farms held less attraction for him than usual. He knew that he was on the brink of a new period in his life. Far away, on the lines of the horizon, he saw the contours of the gigantic machines that emitted a faint and incessant humming as the only evidence of their otherwise inscrutable activity; they glimmered faintly like a weak imitation of a reluctant sunset. "Like secret signals from outerspace invaders," Eric thought. He shook his head as if to drive out the waspish buzzing of continuous whining thoughts in his brain.

"Why do I think of aliens?"

He once had been on an instruction tour of the power stations. He knew that there was no living creature in the immense rooms where the computers drew their flashing runes on the glass screens. Only the contented purring of tame nuclear forces could be heard, like a smile in sound. They brought into movement the innumerable pivots, axles, and junctions through which all the vital necessities of life were distributed throughout the country.

Eric became conscious of a vague sense of fear caused by the sight of the vast expanse filled with rows of factories cleverly integrated with the artificial landscape. He recovered, however, quickly.

It was almost time for his appointment with his girl friend Tina. Her imminent visit filled him with lust, slightly dulled by weak vibrations of an almost imperceptible boredom. The delights of her body were known to him to the last details, as if they were the results of a programmed pleasure pattern, punched on a tape and tuned to his carnal receptors. "Fixed habits are bad for passion," he thought. "It really seems to mark the end of our service time. I should be glad to get a new partner, but I'm not."

He had agreed with Tina to perform the mating from behind this evening, with hand-and-mouth foreplay of half an hour, as was explained in the third chapter of the *Handbook for Fornication*. Eric knew that in former times the drive for pairing had been discharged in unbridled frenzy without any training. Much misery had been the result. Now good mating manners were already taught to children at the end of their anal phase.

With a certain sadness Eric remembered his initial experience after the first signs of sexual maturity had manifested themselves. He'd had the luck to be assigned to a wise, motherly initiator. His delights then must have equaled the religious thrills of ancient saints as described in books of cultic lore. He remembered the fever of orgasm when his thoughts had melted away in the heat of passion. His body had been engulfed by a white hollowness, giving him the sensation of becoming one with everything that existed. He now remained painfully himself in his polite and skilled mating bouts with Tina.

She arrived at the appointed moment. Eric poured her a glass of wine, inspecting her carefully while she was drinking, as if it were their first meeting.

She was supple and plump, with dark hair. Her eyes were big, almost black. She had an upturned nose and a wide, full mouth. Her teeth were large, healthy, and perfectly shaped. Eric liked women with an even set of teeth.

Tina and he were of the same age.

Eric knew that in former times people met in a haphazard way, falling in love without system or sense, according to the laws of chance, playthings of their hormones' whims. He also knew that this kind of higher madness had resulted in endless conflicts, leading people into the snares of legal matrimony, which made couples unhappy and children neurotic, and in the end disrupted society as a whole. Tina and he had been brought together in the only correct way. Out of all the people within a certain radius they were the most suited to each other. The boy's as well as the girl's conscious and unconscious desires, outer appearance, intelligence, tastes, and emotional patterns had been matched by one of the computers in the polder. This guaranteed a mutual understanding in the most fundamental aspects of personality. Tina was the ideal mate for him. He raised his glass and drank to her health. She smiled and returned his toast. It was a perfect preparation for things to come. Suddenly Eric felt more bored than he had thought possible. He undressed her and tried to feign impatient passion, even to make tears in her paper one-day underwear. When they were lying next to each other they started to perform the movements they both knew from their manual of instructions. Simultaneously with the deeper excitement, Eric felt the boredom growing ever stronger.

It was, perhaps, because they'd come to the end of their lovetime.

For a short moment he considered marrying Tina, as the culmination and ending of their probation years. But they were both still too young for a final domiciliation, too far away from the mid-thirties, usually set for marriage. He had to go on with the carefully planned partnerships, at first loose and short, which would gradually increase in duration and stability, till, finally, he had reached the stage in which marital ties offered the best warrant for lasting harmony.

Yes, his affair with Tina was coming to an end. That might be the reason why she was more exacting than usual. Eric was already on the brink of exhaustion, wanting to rest, when Tina was still pushing on with unabated lust. He complied with her passion with a feeling of bitterness. When she was lying at his side, panting with obvious satisfaction, his thoughts were already with the new woman who would be assigned to him. It worried him that he would again be obliged to take her personal wishes and oddities into account. There was always a period of mutual adaptation between new mating partners. Sometimes it was a thrilling experience. Now the idea irritated Eric.

Tina got up from the bed. She dressed slowly with the well-known tired gestures, which were supposed to indicate that she had been so completely satisfied that she hardly had the strength to lift her arms. But there were lines of bitterness around her mouth and she was breathing fiercely, an obvious indication to Eric of how much unused energy she had to repress beneath her simulated languor. She, too, was not happy with the situation. He kissed her when she said goodbye. She pressed herself long enough against him to give the impression that she had to tear herself away, but it didn't last long enough to convey real attachment.

II

The next mating companion was more adapted than Tina had been to the weary irony Eric had developed during the last year. She showed much humor. She was subdued and sometimes shy, modest in her manifest desires, but developed a fierce sense of domination when Eric had prepared her extensively for the final thrust in bed. Her signs of satisfaction were overwhelming but they didn't give Eric the elation he would've experienced in a former period. Her unbridled discharge of lust had an aspect of calculated exaggeration, so Eric couldn't trust his own abilities as a skilled lover. She left him after a week. For the first time Eric learned that even computers could make mistakes. On this occasion the matching of the many items of information from the two candidates must have been imperfect. He accepted the fact with resignation but a feeling of failure still gnawed at him, adding a touch of disagreeable sharpness to his melancholy. Among the personal oddments the young woman had left behind was a fiercely colored pamphlet. A GOOD PAIRPUPPET IS A JOY FOREVER, flaming letters screamed from the cover. Eric wanted to throw it away with the rest. "A pairpuppet," he thought. "Good for the common people who prefer to be fobbed off with a custom-made dream, rather than to cope with the circumscribed pleasures of nature."

Yet he read on. He now realized that the woman who had left him had preferred the perfections of a pairpuppet to his limited abilities. It shocked him. In the circles of the artistic-minded intellectuals to which he belonged, vulgarity of this kind was till now unknown. Pairpuppets were good for people without imagination. "A pairpuppet is the ideal bed companion. The latest issue has been installed with a thermostat, which regulates the temperature of the skin according to the degree of excitement. The moisture of the skin and orifices, together with the movements (adapted to the special requirements of the buyer) and the appropriate sound, are built in with a remarkably high degree of authenticity. Our pairpuppets can only be distinguished from the natural product by their perfect pairing technique."

There was also a scientific report from the National Consumers Organization. Men and women had paired with the puppets under laboratory conditions. Their complaints had been carefully investigated, and their delights had been meticulously analyzed by the extremely sensitive instruments placed in the bodies of the volunteers. Their dreams also had been analyzed, in order to detect the primeval types of their desire. Their ideal images were compared with the four standard types of pairpuppets available for each sex. It appeared that they indeed represented the ideal prototypes. Their subtle powers of adaptation to the movements of their human pair companions were described as extremely satisfying. The sounds they produced had been shrewdly composed from the range of cries and groans taped during the experiments. The disdain with which Eric had at first read the booklet soon gave way to an uneasy libidinal fantasizing.

When he went to sleep he had decided to at least have a look in at the showroom.

The dream he still remembered the following morning greatly strengthened his decision.

The salesman received him with the smooth eagerness he had expected. In the showroom there were many people.

"How's business?" Eric asked.

"We can hardly satisfy the demand." From the tone of bewilderment in the salesman's voice Eric could hear that he meant it. "The use of pairpuppets seems to have suddenly become the fashion. We used to have clients only from certain circles, but now it seems that people in general are becoming fed up with people. And if I may say so, sir, pairpuppets are, indeed, much better. Since the latest models have come out, the experience with a pairpuppet has changed from a coarse pleasure to a refined delight."

He talked with the pepped-up optimism of a slogan manufacturer, but at the same time there was much genuine enthusiasm in his voice. Eric found it extremely difficult to make his choice. There were four types in each sex, able to satisfy the most common needs. There were subjugated and domineering women; cool beauties, who came slowly to their orgiastic frenzy, and unassuming motherfigures with warm breasts that gave a soft refuge for a man's head. For women there were broad-shouldered athletes and soft childlike types; cruel lovers and tender devotees.

"These basic forms can be delivered in different sizes and skin color," the salesman explained. "And for those who are not satisfied with the usual modes of pairing, there are some irregular types, hunchbacks for instance. They, of course, are much more expensive, but there's not much demand for them. In general, our eight types seem to be satisfactory."

"I don't find it easy to choose."

"That's not unusual, sir. But why don't you take the whole range. For variation. That's much cheaper, too. I've already sold a lot of series. Some customers even take the whole set of eight. As a free gift we supply a book about group-pairing with unparalleled techniques."

Eric chose a rather big redhead whose desire was swiftly aroused and who gave easily and abundantly, without requiring a long demonstration of carnal skills. He also let the salesman pack a small, shy puppet who came slowly to her climax and exacted much tenderness.

When he came home he carefully locked his apartment.

III

He called his best friend, Eberhard, with whom he had maintained a deep understanding ever since college; though they didn't meet too often. They made an appointment. The first thing Eric saw when he arrived at his friend's home was a couple of switched-off pairpuppets in a corner of the living room, a sign that Eberhard too had taken to the new fashion. His friend had also changed the arrangement of the furnishings. His polyester walls with changing light-sculptures—creative panels, as the inventor called them—had been exchanged for a wainscot of rough pinewood. There was a marked smell of resin around, so strong that it could only have been applied by spraying.

"I like it as a change," Eric said, when he had downed his first drink.

"A little bit rough. You could even call it old-fashioned, if it were not so unusual that it might now be called new-fashioned."

Eric was astonished.

"Where've you been all the time?"

"Mostly at home. I couldn't think of a better place to be. I've paired a lot. Then you don't have such a strong need to leave your home."

Eric saw that his friend wanted to answer. But Eberhard checked his speech.

"And now you're bored?" he asked at last, with such studied nonchalance that Eric became suspicious.

"Yes. How d'you know?"

"It's the general feeling. You would've known it too, if you hadn't locked yourself up so selfishly. It's already been going on for a long time, but when it started nobody had the courage to confess to it. People are starting up the old forms of communication again, making appointments with friends; organizing parties; even talking to strangers in the street. Human beings are funny things. They're never satisfied."

He poured his visitor and himself another drink. "The common man still wants his pairpuppet," he continued. "And, if possible, a different type for every season. But among the more sophisticated people there is already a marked resistance. The intelligentsia want to return to nature."

"The mannerisms of today's tastemakers will become the manners of tomorrow's masses," Eric said. "Which means that pairpuppets will be out and we'll have to go back to nature."

He downed another drink. When he at last took his leave he was in a floating state of reckless insouciance. Outside, the autumn manifested itself in a pungent, spicy scent permeating the fresh air that already had a tinge of winter's cold.

Eric had hardly gone a few yards when a girl approached him. He looked at her, at first with amazement, then with pleasure. In the beginning he doubted whether she meant to contact him, but when he saw that she was looking behind her, he knew that she was deliberately trying to attract his attention.

He turned and followed her. She looked attractive from behind;

small, dark, with narrow and yet well-shaped legs. Proportionally she couldn't compare with the perfectly built pairpuppets, but she was a living creature, young and probably full of lust.

Then, suddenly, he understood why she was contacting him so obviously and yet without the professional skill characteristic of the type of women who in former times had roamed the streets for business. She had done it because he was a living man and because she probably had developed as much distaste for her pairpuppets as Eric had for his own perfect lust objects. He followed her. He became soft with sensuous appetite and soon he had overtaken her. She smiled when he addressed her.

"I assume you wanted me to follow you?"

She was young enough to have preserved the beauty of youth and yet sufficiently advanced in age for a ripeness in experience. This kind of woman attracted Eric most of all.

She took him by the hand and pulled him after her. Suddenly he fell in love with her. He had been used to the perfect streamline of delight for too long and now he realized how much genuine love he had missed. All his repressed affection broke out and he became dizzy from the strong attachment that broke loose within him.

"What's your name?"

She didn't answer. She was walking faster and faster, almost running. Now he could confirm his first impression that she wasn't beautiful. She had an irregular face, her nose was too long, and her mouth was too large. When she smiled he saw that her front teeth were crooked. But the combination of irregular features attracted him more strongly than the smooth principals after which his pairpuppets had been manufactured. He found it more of a pleasure than a hindrance that her skin was too dark and too coarse and that there were pigment spots on her forehead. At any rate, she was natural.

Outside the city she pulled him into a dry ditch. They didn't undress. She was in too much of a hurry. They mounted each other like adolescents whose immediate lust is too strong for the more refined delights of preparatory delay. They paired like animals, swiftly, grossly, without caring for each other's needs.

It was an overwhelming experience for Eric, as powerful as the first time. In a certain sense it was the first time. Now he knew that pairpuppets had been a transient misconception. In the long run, only pairing with an imperfect human being could give true satisfaction.

Tenderly he looked at the woman lying next to him. She had closed her eyes. She was breathing softly. He touched her. She opened her mouth.

"I'm Elly," she said in a warm and yet businesslike tone. "I am the improved version of the pairpuppet. I am an experimental specimen. Will you be so kind as to give me your critical remarks with regard to my behavior. They are being taped and they will be carefully considered. You may leave me where I am. I'm able to return to the factory without assistance."

The Scythe

by Sandro Sandrelli

Translated from the Italian by Gian Paolo Cossato

Italy—religious Italy, stronghold of the church eternal. Italy—modern Italy, pioneer of engineering design, land of artistic ingenuity. Somehow this story captures the contradictions that one associates with the many facets of that country, which exasperates even while it enchants.

A fragrant breeze caressed the grass in the meadow as the dazzling lights of the camp came on under the blue-black night sky. The great city, with its towers of polychrome metal, and its streets sweeping skyward in dizzy curves, disappeared into the blackness on the distant horizon. . . . For the first time in centuries, in thousands upon thousands of years of incessant, pounding rhythm, silence reigned over the city, and it remained plunged in darkness.

Here and there in the camp, a questioning voice was raised, but even these betrayed a vague sense of relief. Outside the circle of light, the reassuring voice of the commanding officer rang out clearly in the night.

"I am responsible!" announced Coxhaven, jumping nimbly down from the antigravity plate. "I managed to find the switchboards of the underground power station and have brought all the machinery of the city to a standstill. I think my action meets with the general approval, no?"

The eyes of all those present turned once more toward the hushed city, now completely swallowed up in the starless sky. It was silent at last: its frenzied streets no longer ran their incessant course on the load-bearing rollers; the perpetual careering of the magnetic vehicles was stayed; the traffic lights had ceased to change for a nonexistent crowd . . . and the houses were troubled no longer with the incessant buzzing of the air-conditioning apparatus. The trains had ceased to arrive and depart with chronomatic precision inside the immense, brightly lit tunnels; the illuminated fountains no longer spouted forth their fanned-out jets; the luminescent writings in the unknown language had stopped flashing on the façades of the deserted skyscrapers. In the enormous factories the exterminated machines flanked by their conveyor belts were silent; the clatter and throbbing of millions of distributor arms, cutting machines, wire-drawing machines, pumps, rolling mills, vacuum furnaces, power hammers, cranes, and trucks had ceased. And the energy-distributing plants had finally checked the tumultuous spinning of the gigantic dynamos.

The exploration teams, who had reached the planet across inconceivable distances of light-years, had been oppressed for weeks on end by the hallucinating rhythm and incessant activity of the deserted city, marvelous and perfect though it was. The sky was practically starless; the galaxy was a long way off—a very long way off. It could be seen low down on the horizon, standing out in the night sky like an immense incandescent vortex. This black planet and its star hung isolated amid boundless abysses of nothingness.

In far-off times, so distant that the dust of these days had become rock, a spaceship from Earth had reached this lone planet. It had been an immense machine, fully equipped for the first jump to the nebula of Andromeda. But this perfect spaceship had had a breakdown. The last messages flung across the subether spoke breathlessly of a gravitator that had recrystallized and disintegrated; of two unexpected explosions in rapid succession in the gigantic propulsion chambers; of serious conflagrations, of terror and of death. . . . Then, the notification of the solitary star; of the planet nearby; of the first phases of the desperate landing maneuvers—then absolute silence.

Thousands of years of silence. Civil wars had broken out in the galaxy colonized by man. Civilization had retrograded at an alarming rate. Then, emerging phoenixlike from the chaos of immense destruction, the sparse armies of the devastated planets united peacefully and recommenced the painfully slow upward march. The forgotten documentation of the lost expedition was rescued from the debris of the Arcturus X archives. Hundreds of years were to pass in the reconstruction of civilization before an expedition set off in search of the missing spaceship.

From the personal diary of Commanding Officer Coxhaven: "Today, standard-day 1143 post-Irmelin II, we found the solitary star . . . drift, negligible; spectroscopy, normal; surface temperature, eight thousand absolute; dimensions, average; color, white; fixed star; one planet only, terrestrial type . . .

"It is a most beautiful planet, rich in remains of an unusual civilization which was almost completely mechanized, but perfectly integrated into the lush natural beauty of the forests and meadows, of oceans and immense mountain chains. . . . The enormous cities are marvelous; bristling with metal towers that form beautiful silhouettes against the starless sky. At night they glitter with millions of lights and throb ceaselessly with the rhythmic beat of innumerable machines and contrivances. . . .

"A human paradise which the men who survived the catastrophe succeeded in building, supplanting, in a short space of time, millions of years of natural development, exploiting the most advanced scientific and technical data that they had brought with them and saved from the fire . . . But in this wonderful city, with its absolute purity of line, its towers and machines of sparkling polychrome (made of a thousand new and old metals), there is no sign of life: the men who built it have vanished.

"The materials are perfect and incorruptible; the founts of energy are eternal. . . . We cannot establish, therefore, how many years or centuries ago it was that the men disappeared. . . . Everything is new, perfect, efficiently abandoned it seems but yesterday, no, rather today—just a second ago. . . . But there is not a footprint, not a sign, not the minimum, imperceptible trace of man. . . . The libraries—but are they libraries?—are empty. There are no tapes, no discs, no film reels, no psychoregistrations to give us the hint of a message. There is not even a song—not a single word of the vanished inhabitants of this planet. . . . Only the illuminated writings on the skyscrapers . . . but do they represent a language, these writings that we have been unable to decipher? Or are they nothing more than an abstract design?

"And the innumerable machines—what do they produce? Nothing. Their movements are full of grace and harmony; their mobile parts resemble the paws and wings and limbs of very beautiful, strange animals; and the fixtures and supports are modeled on almost transcendental lines. . . . But they produce nothing. There are no storehouses, not even empty ones. Nothing . . . Only these perfect machines in perpetual motion . . ."

Again from Coxhaven's personal diary: "The mystery remains unsolved. . . . The men are becoming more and more ill at ease as each day passes. . . . Following their first burst of activity in the search for some trace—no matter what—of human life, they now wander dazed through the streets of the enormous city near which we have set up camp. . . . The metal walls of the skyscrapers, the lights, and the fountains oppress us. And the machines, especially the machines . . . They are still very beautiful, still marvelous, but a hypnotic current seems to emanate from them and is beginning to overwhelm us. . . .

"At last! Today, standard-day 1197 post-Irmelin II, old Marescot, rummaging in an underground aerating tunnel, found, embedded behind a grille, a metal-paged notebook filled with strange designs. . . . The old fellow began bellowing as though someone had slit his throat, so much so that we feared he had met up with some monster or other. When he appeared, running, waving his arms about, with his hair all disheveled, we pulled out our fulminators, ready to fire. . . . Marescot seems to have gone mad. He has affirmed that the strange signs engraved on the metal pages are a form of writing and has vowed to decipher it. . . .

"Day 1207 post-Irmelin II. Marescot has quarreled again with the men in the biology squad. . . . Since he began working on the translation of the metal pages, he has been extremely bad-tempered. . . . Every morning he appears in the canteen with his eyes redder than ever and his hands trembling. It seems that the book refuses to be translated and Marescot's naturally pessimistic character is deteriorating. . . .

"Today, day 1217 post-Irmelin II, Marescot has quarreled with the men of the mechanics squad. . . . He had asked for too much energy for his probabilistic computer and was refused it. He made a terrible scene. . . .

"This afternoon, a disconcerting discovery had made us momentarily forget Marescot's tantrums. Mistral and Guglielminet, out on an exploratory expedition in the direction of the southwest mountain chain, climbed as far as the tableland: a vast, almost completely smooth expanse of rock, swept by winds and scorched by the sun. On this immense terrace they found heaps of whitened powder, riddled with myriads of metal objects; some corroded, others still glittering. . . . The chemistry and biology squads are at work on the samples brought down by Mistral, while Guglielminet and the mechanics squad are busily engaged in photographing the rock terrace and its gruesome contents from every angle. . . . Marescot had declared that on our return to Irmelin II, he will give a detailed report to the Galactic authorities and have all our space licenses withdrawn. . . .

"Day 1221 post-Irmelin II. The mystery deepens. . . . The analysis of the white powder cemented together with the metal fragments has been discovered to be very similar to that of human bones—taking into account that it is presumably many centuries old and has been permanently exposed to the inclemency of the weather and changes of temperature. Guggenheim, in charge of the chemists squad, has affirmed that it is nothing short of a miracle that the residue has survived. . . . Is it possible that this dust is all that remains of the prodigious builders of these fantastic cities? And what do the metal fragments represent? There are billions of them. Our mechanics squad is going mad in the attempt to extract some concrete evidence from the chaos of the tableland. . . .

"Day 1230 post-Irmelin II. The mystery deepens still further. . . . I have led the air squadrons on a much more intensive exploration of the whole planet. We have sounded the bottom of all the oceans with transfer-radar. We found nothing. . . . We have cataloged practically all the cities of the planet. There are a hundred and fifteen of them, all immense, all practically identical even in their indefinable diversity. All their machines, vehicles, streets, and trains are incessantly on the march in the service of the vanished humanity. . . . Close to every city, we have discovered a terrace of rock covered with still more heaps of bleached powder mixed with countless metal fragments. . . . Our technicians are slowly going out of their minds!

"Day 1231 post-Irmelin II. Marescot has been shut in his tent for over a week now. . . . Roars of anger greet anyone who dares go near him. . . . This evening, in an immense underground chamber, I at last discovered the switchboards that control all the mechanisms of the city. . . . It took a great deal of effort on the part of the Militis Kombinat and myself to interpret them correctly. In the end, Kombinat found the right levers and we lowered them. For the first time in centuries—perhaps in thousands of years—complete silence and obscurity has descended on the city."

Marescot knew that now the success of the expedition depended on him alone. He was perfectly aware that Coxhaven had doubts about its outcome. Would it have served some practical purpose? The reasons for this costly undertaking were quite plain. There had been no wars on the planet of the solitary star (or at least one hoped not), and probably the survivors of the catastrophe (if there had been any—and the marvelous cities scattered about the planet clearly demonstrated it a posteriori) hadn't had to laboriously reconstruct an entire civilization from nothing after thousands of years of insane battles and foolish destruction. Moreover, the whole of humanity, scattered on hundreds of thousands of planets, was hoping to rediscover the lost secret of longevity. . . . Today, men were born, matured, and died in the brief span of forty Earth years. . . . He himself, "old" Marescot, was thirty-nine. . . . But the men of the lost spaceship had lived at least three hundred years. . . . This was what the Coxhaven expedition was searching for across infinite space, and they had still not succeeded in finding it.

Marescot was sweating profusely, driving himself mad trying to interpret the hieroglyphics engraved on the numerous metal pages. In their illusory regularity they defied every comparison, every measurement, every possible set of combinations. . . . Centuries upon centuries of isolation can result in the most paradoxical distortions of language, in its concepts as well as in its formal structures. Marescot was nearing the end of his resources and his humor was getting blacker and blacker. . . .

Until . . .

Until it occurred to him to illuminate the script with a polarized lamp. And suddenly, miraculously, in the interplay of subtle interferences, the characters engraved in the metal took on wonderful hues, reinvesting the cipher language of the vanished man with a second chromatic cipher. While this greatly complicated the possible combinations, it enabled Marescot, in a marvelous flash of intuition (and after another sleepless night), to grasp the key of the unknown message.

Feverishly, in a state of growing exaltation, he translated pages and pages of the metal book into the corresponding intergalactic alphabet. He did not preoccupy himself at this point about establishing precisely all the phonetic and conceptual parameters. . . .

In a couple of hours he had completed the first stage. Then he proceeded to the second, which was easier although more laborious. He filled out an incredible number of metalplastic cards and fed them into his probabilistic computer, which, winking its tiny lights, set itself in rhythmic rustling motion. The literary translation of the ancient message began to emerge on a long strip of paper from the belly of the computer. At last Marescot held the whole thing complete in his trembling hands.

Finally, with the magnetic tapes and the automatic reproducers of the equivalent intergalactic language assembled in front of him, Marescot set to work. His eyes sparkled and the perspiration poured down his face as he rendered an absolutely exact translation of the message contained in the metal pages in such a way as to be clearly understood by everyone. It was not an easy undertaking, and Marescot was busy with it the whole night. But at the first light ot dawn he had completed what was bound to be his last masterpiece before the Coxhaven expedition fled terrorized from the terrible solitary planet.

The morning after, Marescot mingled once more with the other men in the canteen. His companions, thinking that he was surrendering because of hunger, nudged one another and grinned. The days had followed one another without incident. The investigations had once more reached a standstill. The countless metal fragments found on the plateau had been collected and listed. They were plainly parts of machines, of complicated mechanical contrivances; disturbing fragments of worked metal to which only one description could be given: they were BEAUTIFUL, of a strange enigmatic beauty; emanations, it seemed, of a much greater, much more illusive beauty. For days and days technicians and biologists had exhausted themselves attempting to reconstruct the devices of which the fragments formed a part, but in vain.

Marescot finally became aware of the sniggering of his companions. He raised his head and gave them the benefit of an unusually brutal epithet, drawn from the depths of his considerable linguistic store, collected from all over the galaxy. This was just what the men were waiting for.

"Mad Marescot is having another of his convulsions!" exclaimed Dillinger, a fairish man, grinning over the top of his mess tin. "Marescot learned to speak from a macao!" chimed in Ben Burek with a leer. This was a very old joke referring to the fact that Marescot had been born on Earth. And Bolinsk added: "Give a boiled potato to Marescot so that he can have a chat!" And they all rolled about the grass, convulsed with mirth, like the simple souls they were. Marescot, his mouth full, mumbled something indistinctly, swallowed with difficulty, turned purple, and had to take long drafts of water from the flask that Coxhaven had quickly extended to him. At last he shrieked in his falsetto voice:

"You worthless wretches. You don't deserve to be here on this wonderful planet among the remains of such a fantastic civilization! . . . You are miserable worms, whose horrible braying can be heard in the nebula of Andromeda!" Unaware of the zoological confusion his anger had provoked, Marescot drew the ill-famed, metal-paged notebook from his pocket and said with a triumphant air:

"While your inane efforts only go to show your pitiful inadequacy, I have at last succeeded in deciphering these pages, and I tell you that only a member of a very highly evolved civilization, only a sublimely spiritual and enlightened person with a brilliant grasp of electronics, could have written these words."

"What?" exclaimed Coxhaven, who was having lunch along with his men. "You mean to say that you have deciphered the language of the inhabitants of this planet and you haven't let me know?"

Everybody, technicians and military men, grinned: at last someone was going to put old Marescot in his place! . . . About time! . . . But old Marescot had unsuspected reserves of energy. He shrieked once more:

"I wanted to translate the whole thing from the first to the last word! . . . I am certain, absolutely certain, that if I had given the news prematurely, my work would have been criminally interfered with! I know only too well"—his eyes swept contemptuously around the room—"the stupid, importunate curiosity and the maliciousness of these men, who ought to be the finest squad of experts of the whole Webbe Quadrant. But when we return to Earth I'll make my voice heard and then . . ." A half-empty food container flew through the air and missed Marescot's head by a hairsbreadth. The latter turned vermilion. But Coxhaven's decisive intervention broke up the argument:

"Binder, you are under arrest!" The spaceman who had flung the box rose up muttering and slouched away to the spaceship. "And you . . ." Coxhaven commanded Marescot, "read us all that you have managed to decipher, by Vigan! . . . I can hardly believe my ears! Here we are after months and months of eating our hearts out in an attempt to discover something and you sit back and take it easy!"

It was Marescot's hour of triumph. He rose to his feet, his contact lenses sparkling with inexpressible satisfaction, looked around, and began to read. And a strange thing happened: the light of the star shone brightly in the early morning light; the sky was limpid and blue; the towers of the silent city stood out black against the white clouds, which were just beginning to break up on the distant horizon. A subtle and evocative spell descended on the spirit of everyone present. Marescot's voice rang out and seemed to fill the whole of Space:

"O supreme Lord of infinite, starless Space, O supreme Lord, hear us. You who have given us life and, through the music of your steel heart, the joy of everything and of nothing, hear us. . . . We have raised up marvelous towers against the dark sky in your name; we have built thousands of arms, and thousands of voices that sing your perpetual glory. . . . We exist for a moment, for but a single instant, O Lord; but you are infinite and in you all the beauty and harmony of the universe unite. . . .

"The cities are temples to your glory, and your name is repeated a million times over therein, filling the emptiness of Space. . . . We came from nothing, O Lord, driven by an irresistible force, and in the night of time we set foot in this distant land to create your kingdom. Here, on the threshold of the abysses of the void, your immortal kingdom began. . . . The harmony and beauty, O Lord, are your own ineffable images, in your eternal life. . . . The tiny, miserable yet lofty intellect of man; master, yet most abject slave; perfect but unworthy constructor; and most passionate lover, annihilates himself in supreme joy. . . .

"O Lord, supreme Lord of the infinite arms and voices. You have enriched our solitude with songs, strength, and supreme eloquence, O Lord of infinite beauty and blessings, who has sustained us in this long arduous climb. O Lord, who will continue to live on, marvelous and infinite, a thousand million years after our death. Grant us, O Lord, for whom we have raised countless powerful and glorious images toward the sky, and into the shadowy depths of the solitary planet; grant that we, O Lord, may savor in one immortal and supreme moment the joy of eternity. . . .

"Lord, Lord of incorruptible metal, of the thousand rhythmic voices, and of the thousand resplendent colors. Lord of flame and ice, in whose stupendous body flow a thousand rivers of tumultuous, irresistible energy and incorruptible, universal life. Lord, unique yet multiple, immobile yet vibrant in the countless harmonies of the Cosmos, concede to us, O Lord; we beg you with gifts, with sacrifices, with music, and with endless hymns and lamentations; grant to us, supreme, most beautiful, infinite Lord, the extreme joy of annihilating ourselves in Thee. . . .

"Lord, Lord of the incorruptible adamantine metal, supreme and infinite Lord; Lord of unquenchable fire, of everlasting miraculous flames; Lord of the incandescent lights; Lord of the Universe, of obscurity and of infinite light; O ineffable Master, indescribable and eternal; O Lord of inexhaustible and sublime perfection, answer us from your hundred and fifteen altars; turn your benevolent gaze upon us; lay your hand on our heads and grant to us in this the last moment of our peculiar and imperfect existence the most supreme and incxpressible joy of annihilating ourselves in Thee, forever. . . ."

"What does it all mean?" asked Coxhaven, coming to himself with a start.

The men looked at one another in bewilderment. A subtle emanation hung in the air. Marescot began to speak again in a more normal tone: "That's all," he said. "The other pages of the metal book just repeat the same things, merely switching the first lines. . . ."

"But what does it all mean?" repeated Coxhaven. "This plaintive litany is trying to tell us something . . . something."

"I don't think we'll ever understand what it means," said Marescot, "not until we succeed in reassembling the mysterious heaps of fashioned metal that we found on the tableland."

"But it can't be done!" wailed Bolinsk. "We have been driving ourselves insane for weeks and weeks in our efforts to piece them together."

"For the simple reason, my poor Bolinsk," said Marescot, putting the finishing touch to his moment of triumph, "that, without exception, all the members of the mechanics squad are imbeciles!"

Day 1300 post-Irmelin II. A fragrant breeze again caressed the grass of the meadow as the dazzling lights of the camp came on under the blue-black night sky. The great city, with its towers of polychrome metal, and its streets sweeping skyward in dizzy curves, disappeared once more into the blackness on the distant horizon. . . . For the first time in centuries, in thousands upon thousands of years of incessant, pounding rhythm, silence reigned over the city, and it remained plunged in darkness.

Here and there in the camp, questioning voices trembled with a vague, almost mystical terror. The voice of Marescot rang out clearly in the night, echoed by that of Coxhaven. Then silence enveloped the camp once more.

The gold and silver interlacing of the marvelous machine glittered almost supernaturally in the glare of the spotlights. The delicate, graceful machine was also, in fact, an admirable piece of abstract sculpture. Beside it the finest masterpieces of the most acclaimed artists of the whole galaxy seemed as nothing. Pikash to Passereaunu, Dellerpontosh to Von Edmendgard, even Contakty's most sublimely delicate filagreed constructions paled in comparison to this marvelous machine of the solitary planet. It was a vision of extreme strength and delicacy whose emanations penetrated subtly and irrevocably into the human spirit so that man felt instinctively compelled to love and adore it.

To realize such a construction, such an infinitely delicate miracle, whole generations of scientists, technicians, and philosophers must have given the best of themselves, distilling from their intellects whole universes of sublime concepts and proportions. This marvelous machine was an indisputed masterpiece, not only of the solitary planet but of the whole history of countless man-made civilizations flung in fantastic flights across space and time. In it, matter had become living, intelligent, and reasoning; had attained the utmost peak of its creative possibilities; had reached dizzy, inconceivable heights, flinging a bridge toward other limitless dimensons. . . .

The fascinating words of the laboriously translated book resounded vividly and meaningfully in the minds of everyone. And it was clear, in fact, that such a machine, emanation of thousands upon thousands of years of wisdom, couldn't not be raised to the rank of a god as soon as it was created. And, in a universal and supreme god, in fact: "the tiny, miserable, yet extremely lofty intellect of man; master, yet most abject slave; perfect constructor, even though unworthy; and passionate lover, joyfully annihilates himself. . . ." Annihilates himself? These obscure words were becoming clear now: no one would ever have known how to cease contemplating this marvelously beautiful machine, annihilating his own intellect in limitless contemplation. . . . But even in these last moments Marescot erred.

A perfect, universal philosophy, distilled from thousands of years of wisdom and knowledge, had led the scholars of the vanished race far beyond this annihilation of their egos in the sweet, blessed bondage of the machine.

With an almost spellbound gesture, Marescot raised his right hand and grasped a gently curved lever that glittered with silvery reflections at the base of the marvelous machine. He pulled it toward himself, preparing for new, unimaginable pleasures of the spirit. . . . And the machine moved. The supremely beautiful, marvelous piece of mechanism sprang into life. It vibrated with growing fervor, and at last it became clear that it would infallibly destroy itself. But, just at the last moment, with a movement of indescribable harmony, it extracted from the upper part of its shining body a slim and beautifully proportioned arm, which terminated in a sharpened scythe. With an elegant, mercurial gesture it descended on Marescot's neck and, with a stealthy click, cut off his head.

A Whiter Shade of Pale

by Jon Bing

Translated from the Norwegian by Steven T. Murray

Here is Bing of Bing & Bringsvaerd with a story that is positively Old Wave in its style. Yet, in his published novels, it is Jon
Bing who appears to be the farthest out in experimental writing and
avant-garde science fiction. But not here.

I

Space makes the word "size" meaningless; you can't tell the difference between something small and close and something large but far away. For this reason, the starship *Caligari* might have been confused with a cluster of drifting grapes, bluish-red and shining.

But each of the grapes in the cluster measured over thirty meters in diameter, and the stalks connecting them were corridors and cables.

Thin veils shimmered all around the starship—like the shimmer drawn across the stars by the hydrogen fog in Berenice's Hair.

But the veils were sails of gossamer metal fabric—more than a hundred square kilometers spread out around the starship. The sails caught the wind created by light from distant suns, and, borne on waves of light, the starship crossed the Milky Way.

The *Caligari* was on its way from the star LM Monoceros to 16 Corona Borealis. The journey was expected to take more than ninety years. The starship had a crew of twelve men and women, lying frozen in cabinets. Their bodily functions were suspended; they would not age during the journey. When the goal had been reached, they would awaken as if after a good night's sleep. Measured in ordinary human years, they had already lived several centuries by the time the *Caligari* set its course for Corona Borealis.

Human beings had reached the stars and scattered their civilization among them. Civilization requires communication—those who settled on a new planet wanted to maintain contact with their home planet. But natural laws reign more strictly than any regent. Even though spaceships could span the distance between the stars, they could not exceed the speed of light. It was more than thirty light-years between LM Monoceros and 16 Corona Borealis, and even a radio message would take the same number of years to travel from one star to the other.

Starships like the *Caligari* connected the inhabited planets with cords of information: science, literature, and art. It was seldom a question of any actual trade: it was a voluntary exchange of information, an attempt to maintain the shadow of a common culture. Slowly the ships sailed from star to star; when the *Caligari* reached her destination, the people who had loaded the starship would already be dead.

The start of the journey had gone according to plan: the *Caligari*'s ion drive had pulled the ship clear of the planetary system around LM Monoceros, the sails had billowed out, the space travelers had sealed themselves in their cold cabinets, the computer had assumed control of the ship—the long journey had begun.

But shortly before the halfway point there was an accident: the thin metal sails were slashed, and the cluster of grapes was shaken by an invisible hand. The grapes which together made up the starship *Caligari* were ripped apart and flung aimlessly through space.

Inside the grape in which the crew lay frozen, the computer's disaster program took over. Information about the nearest stars was analyzed. The computer weighed the probabilities and selected a little white sun as the most likely center of a planetary system. It activated the emergency engine built into the grape, and the slumbering crew set its course toward the nameless star.

Two years later the computer confirmed that one of the planets circling the star was habitable. When the space travelers thawed out a short while later and climbed out of their cabinets, the computer was already preparing to land.

II

The bluish-red grape that had once been part of the starship *Caligari* was not built to land on any planet. But its designers had realized that this might be necessary in an emergency. So the grape was not completely crushed against the surface of the planet—it just split, tearing itself open on the ground.

The twelve space travelers got up from their padded acceleration couches. The control room was in the middle of the grape, protected by shock absorbers. They had been able to watch through huge video screens during the landing, and the computer had given them information about the planet by digital readout as it completed its measurements.

Now the screens were dark. The computer was no longer functioning. But before it was crushed, the computer had informed the crew that the planet's gravity was approximately 0.8 of Earth normal and that the atmosphere maintained a temperature of less than thirty degrees below zero centigrade, but was breathable.

The space travelers were already dressed in protective suits. Now they closed the glass plates in front of their faces to protect themselves from the cold that was already creeping into the room, waiting for Blancheur to take the initiative. There was no captain or official leader among them—the space travelers had been trained to transmit knowledge, not to survive crash landings. But they had selected Blancheur in advance as the leader if a crisis made it necessary.

Blancheur opened the door of the control room. The corridor was twisted, ending in a gash. Followed by the others, Blancheur climbed through ruins of metal and plastic. A piece of the hull had fallen so that it formed a natural ramp down to the ground. The space travelers gathered in a tight clump of chrome-yellow spacesuits outside the wreck, as if the knowledge of the cold in the air made it necessary to huddle together to keep warm.

It was daylight. The nameless star which was the planet's sun was a white pea in the western sky. It was too weak to create full daylight; the stars were shining along with it against a black sky.

The ground was covered with snow as far as they could see. Hard white snow—so hard that their boots hardly made a mark in it. They looked out across a landscape where the snow was shaped by the wind into knife-sharp ridges, steep escarpments, and soft, lazy slopes. The shadows created contrasts in gray and black which accentuated the topography.

The spaceship had plowed a long furrow in the hard snow and finally stopped on top of a sort of ridge, with snow broken up in chunks before it. Even though the ship had been torn open by the collision with the hill; it still towered high above the nearest snowdrifts—as though a reddish-blue croquet ball had been mistakenly hit across a lawn in the middle of winter and had broken the crust on top of a snowbank.

They had a fairly good view across the black and white landscape. A sea of hardened toothpaste as far as they could see; above it a black sky with a feeble sun, a sun shining like a moon. Behind them, a piece of the starship *Caligari*— painted a brutal bluish-red. And themselves: chrome-yellow, almost luminescent figures.

Blancheur turned and walked back to the spaceship. He had not said a word to the others. But they were trained in communicating information, and his silence was eloquent.

III

One of the space travelers, Weiss, had had an accident aboard a starship ten (subjective) years ago. Something went wrong with the cabinet that was keeping him alive between the stars. When he woke up, both legs were gone.

As an invalid he was bound even more inseparably to space. When the *Caligari* reached an inhabited planet and went into orbit around it, the others went down to the planet and stayed there for months, often years, while the starship's cargo of information was transmitted and new information was gathered. But Weiss stayed on board. The weightlessness of freefall eliminated his disability better than any artificial limb could. He could pull himself along with his arms, kick off with his short leg-stumps, and fly like a bird inside and outside the starship. Eventually he had become a master at maneuvering in a weightless condition—it was pointless to speak of Weiss as disabled aboard the *Caligari*.

So for Weiss the shipwreck also meant that he was again an invalid who could not move under his own power. But his spacesuit could be easily hooked up to a wheelchair. The wheels would not replace his legs, but Weiss would be able to take part in the salvage operations.

The space travelers were a little astonished to discover that after the disaster was over and the first shock had passed, the drama too was gone. Laborious routine was all that remained: emergency rations had to be dug out of crushed containers, auxiliary machinery had to be located and repaired. A radio beacon was erected and activated—but they knew that the distress signals sent out by it would be answered by a rescue expedition only after several decades.

They suppressed the thought of how they would survive that long, and concentrated on the more short-range salvage work. But the six female space travelers got a new look in their eyes when they gazed out over the white, snowy landscape, which now was a picture of their own future: white like photographic paper, with themselves like drops of developing solution.

The wheelchair was rigged up for Weiss with improvised belts and wheels and did service as a sort of one-man snow tractor. Weiss worked mostly on retrieving objects that had been flung a great distance in the collision; he dragged them on a sled made of bent metal plates. The sled often had to be pushed by two or three of the others, heavy and clumsy as chrome-yellow polar bears in their spacesuits.

After two weeks they had gotten the wreck in order. They had repaired two generators, and there was enough fuel to heat the control room. They had also found enough food to last two or three years.

But the situation was still critical. This became evident when the salvage operation was over and Blancheur had to rely on his ingenuity to think up new assignments. Only the control room maintained anything approaching normal room temperature. The space travelers had to pursue their private lives outside in the cold among the remains of the wreck or the snowdrifts. Minor quarrels arose which soon developed into serious conflicts. Two of the space travelers took sick, only a few days apart. The symptoms were reminiscent of influenza or pneumonia. They had little medicine, for only remains of the well-stocked container of medical supplies had been found. Blancheur shook his head and said it was almost incomprehensible that they had taken sick—the space travelers themselves were bacteria-free, and an uninhabited planet should have neither bacteria nor viruses that attacked human beings.

A short while later, the two that had gotten sick died. A third got glassy-eyed and feverish.

IV

Weiss was now using most of the moonlit days to explore the terrain around the ship. The wheelchair was driven by a miniature reactor which also heated his spacesuit. Weiss was thus the one who could move around most easily outside the wreck.

Actually, it was a futile task to explore the surroundings. It was all one single plain of snow, broken only by drifts and the shadows in between them. A landscape in black and white, where even the gray tones were a variation.

One morning three months after the shipwreck, Weiss reached the crest of a snowdrift about four kilometers from the wreck. The drift was unusually high and shaped like a long, gently sloping hill which ended in an overhanging cliff a couple of hundred meters above a snow valley. Weiss rolled slowly up to the top, afraid of starting an avalanche—even though he had yet to see the eternal snowdrifts loosen.

He stopped, looked out over the frozen landscape—and discovered something moving across the drifts between him and the *Caligari.*

A sort of ship was sailing across the snow. The hull was small and black, the sails big and white—they billowed in the steady wind, which Weiss himself shut out with his spacesuit. He could count three figures on board; one of them was half-standing aft in the snow ship, leaning on something that must be the tiller.

The ship cruised at a good clip up along a drift, came about, and slid out of sight down into a snow valley. Several minutes later it appeared again on its way up the next slope.

The news that the planet was inhabited was encouraging to the space travelers. Of course they were a little surprised that the computer had not known about the colonization—but they, more than anyone, were aware of how much information was lost between the stars.

Blancheur talked with the others, and lookouts were posted on the snow peaks around the *Caligari*. The spaceship's bright color was in itself the best distress signal they could have given in this landscape of white and black; Weiss had actually been amazed that the crew of the snow ship had not noticed the bluish-red hull which lay so conspicuously atop a drift.

Not more than four days passed before one of the lookouts saw snow ships again. This time it was three boats of a little different size, which came sweeping through a valley about five hundred meters from the lookout. He had pushed up his faceplate and shouted, but it seemed as if the sailors had not heard him. Then he fired a signal flare—a red flare that floated slowly down over the valley. But the flare did not arouse any attention on board. The ships held their course, hissed across the snow, and were gone. The spaceman who had discovered them was already halfway down into the valley— clearly visible in his chrome-yellow suit—when they disappeared.

Weiss went off with two others to the place where the ships had been seen. They inspected the bottom of the valley more closely and discovered the distinct tracks of runners. And tracks were made by far more than three boats. They guessed that this must be a kind of shipping lane for snow ships, and posted extra lookouts in the valley. Weiss was one of them.

But they had to wait for almost two weeks before the next snow ship appeared. And this time it was just a little one-man boat—a snow dinghy, so to speak—with a large spread of canvas. It came whining into the valley, cutting up along one side in an arc as it put about. Weiss was not more than a few meters from the man in the boat, and thought that he met his glance: black eyes in a white face. It was impossible to see much more than his eyes and the upper part of his cheekbone; the rest was hidden by thick fur and a scarf wound around his mouth. But even though the stranger could not have helped seeing Weiss, not even a twitch around his eyes or a jerk of his body signaled that he had noticed the space traveler in the wheelchair.

Weiss started his wheelchair with a jolt and tried to follow the snow dinghy. But it was going much too fast and soon vanished out of sight among the white slopes and black shadows.

V

The optimism that the shipwrecked space travelers had felt when they discovered the snow ships for the first time soon turned into a feeling of impotence. They continued to try to contact the ships, but without success. It was as if the sailors were blind both to people waving and to signal flares—yet nothing seemed to be wrong with their eyesight otherwise. The space travelers could have understood it if they and the wreck of the *Caligari* were spreading terror and if the inhabitants were fleeing head over heels from something they could not explain. There had been many examples of people who themselves had once come to a planet in a starship; yet after a few generations had forgotten their own origin.

The space travelers were spared new fatalities, but more of them had come down with influenza and were getting weaker day by day. The illness was a drain on their collective strength and reduced their chances of survival. As Blancheur saw it, it was no longer a mystery where the virus came from. And their only salvation, as well, lay with the source of the infection, the planet's inhabitants.

Blancheur laid out a plan which won grudging support. An expedition was to try to follow the tracks of the snow ships back to the harbor they had started from. The expedition would consist of Weiss and two others. Weiss's wheelchair would pull a sled with provisions and equipment, and the two others would hang on to the sled whenever possible.

Two days later the expedition set off from the wreck of the *Caligari*. A female space traveler, Gwyn, went along with Weiss and Blancheur. Weiss was in the lead, like a motorized husky, heated and powered by the wheelchair. Behind him was slung the improvised sled, and Blancheur and Gwyn curled up amid the equipment. Their spacesuits protected them from the cold and the wind, but needles of ice penetrated occasionally, reminding them of the temperature outside.

It was a strange journey through a landscape that was always shifting but never changed. White, almost luminescent snowdrifts mounted up and sank again into valleys; the pale sun folded long shadows of black felt in between all the white. At the end of the first day they were hypnotized by the unreality around them.

At night they dug into one of the drifts, cutting out a narrow cave with a power saw intended for quite different tasks. They lit a fuel

burner inside the cave and spent a warmer and more comfortable
night than they had dared hope for.

Four days passed this way.

When they had come about a kilometer from their overnight cave
on the fifth day, Gwyn shouted in surprise to the others. When they
turned around, they saw that behind them—in front of the cave they
had just left—a snow ship had anchored, and two or three figures
were moving at the entrance to the cave.

Weiss turned all the way around and rolled his chair back toward
the cave.

When they were a couple of hundred meters away, the space travelers shouted to the strangers. The strangers glanced up uneasily and
looked all around, but then continued investigating the area around
the cave.

They could hear the strangers talking to one another but could not
understand the language—not that they had expected to. Gwyn ran
up to one of the strangers and grabbed hold of his arm, shouting at
the same time. The two others turned toward the sound, and the
stranger yanked his arm back and stared behind him, terrified.
Blancheur came up and cautiously touched one of the others. This
one flailed about violently, floundering in terror toward the snow
ship, which lay quietly with sails flapping. When Gwyn realized they
wanted to escape, she became almost hysterical and clung to the
stranger's fur. He danced around, yelling, as he thrashed at the arms
clutching him. He climbed halfway up into the ship, shouting to his
comrade on board, who came to his aid with pointed poles of some
kind of bone or wood. A spear caught Gwyn in the throat; she lost
her grip and dropped to the ground. Blancheur caught her, but she
collapsed in his arms and slumped to the ground. The snow was red
under her. As the snow ship vanished from the valley, with its crew
scared out of their wits, Gwyn was already dead.

Weiss had been bound to his spectator seat in the wheelchair during the scuffle. His feeling of unreality had been intensified. For a
long, dizzy moment he doubted his own existence—were he and the
other space travelers only ghosts, private nightmares without form or
substance? But Gwyn's death destroyed all doubt in him. Only the
helplessness remained, the helplessness that a stranger can feel in a
country where he doesn't know the word for "help."

VI

Weiss and Blancheur were alone in the soft labyrinth of snowdrifts
and snowbanks. As the shock of Gwyn's death gradually passed, the

feeling of unreality returned: it was as if they were locked in a prison of gelatin—transparent, but hermetic; soft, but impenetrable. Forced together by the white, flat landscape and the incomprehensible reactions of the sailors, Weiss and Blancheur grew closer to each other. They needed to touch each other, to have long talks together— needed all the reassurance that they could give each other of their own existence.

After six days the landscape changed. At first they didn't notice it, because the mountain in front of them blended in with the black sky. It was just a darker shadow against the horizon, with snow caught in its clefts.

They reached some boulders that night. The boulders were black too, and the stone was hard and smooth, clearly of volcanic origin.

The next morning they found the snow ships' harbor. It was a V-shaped field between two arms of the mountain. At the end of the field they could see where the mountain opened into a cavern. Half a dozen ships lay at anchor on the field; on board one of them, the crew was at work hoisting the sails. Weiss and Blancheur kept still while the ship was made ready. Finally the lines were cast off, the crew shoved the boat out of the windbreak in the lee of the mountain wall, the wind caught the sails, the crew climbed aboard, and the snow ship headed out of the field, passing a couple of hundred meters from Weiss and Blancheur.

When the ship was gone, the harbor lay deserted. Cautiously the spacemen approached the opening of the cave. Nothing could be seen inside. They lit a flashlight and shone it inside. After about thirty meters the passage made a turn.

Weiss and Blancheur retreated and found a suitable drift out of sight of the field. They built a large snow cave and camouflaged the opening as best they could. Their plan was for Blancheur to go into the mountain cave alone and try to contact the inhabitants. Weiss would wait in the snow cave along with the provisions and equipment.

Blancheur came back during the night. He was exhausted and in despair. While Weiss opened the emergency rations he had already heated over the burner, Blancheur told him with strained composure about the meeting with the inhabitants of the cave.

The mountain cave seemed to be a sort of port for the sailors. When Blancheur rounded the bend in the cave, the darkness gradually gave way to a pale, white, phosphorescent light that made it possible to see the surroundings. Blancheur turned off his own lamp and continued through the ghostly glow. The cave walls were covered with equipment for the snow ships: sails, furs, masts, rigging. Soon he began to see people. At first he hid in the shadows along the cave wall so that he wouldn't be discovered. But when a group of people suddenly came out of a side passage, he could do nothing but stand still in the middle of the corridor. The group came toward him but seemed not to notice him. Several of them bumped into him, stumbling to one side—they looked a little surprised, but laughed and gestured as if they were telling the others that they had slipped on a patch of ice. Blancheur realized that they simply could not see him.

And like an invisible man, Blancheur wandered for hours through the cave. He got a glimpse into a shadowy civilization. He saw huge chambers where funguslike organisms were cultivated and carefully collected in nets and sacks. He also saw a kind of furrier's workshop, where the white pelts of unknown animals were sewn together into furs and clothing.

The mountain cave was a shadow realm in the true sense of the word, and the people who inhabited it were like shadows: white faces, black hair, grayish-white clothes. The cave walls were black, the furniture made of bone and skins. There were few people; many of the rooms in the cave were not in use.

Blancheur had noticed that it had gotten warmer the deeper he penetrated into the cave. White steam was billowing out of one of the chambers. When he looked in, he saw something like a kitchen: snow water was bubbling in holes in the floor, and two people were working on grayish fungus which they boiled and kneaded and boiled again to a kind of cake. Blancheur had touched the floor in the cave and burned his fingers on hot stone—the volcanic activity which had created the mountain and the cave was not yet extinguished.

Blancheur had seen enough of the cave people's life. He had planned how he would try to make contact with them. He waited inside an empty chamber until a lone man came by outside. Then he stepped out and blocked the man's way, speaking in a calm, clear voice while raising his arms with his palms turned up. The man stopped when he heard the voice speaking a foreign language, and looked around, confused, as if he suspected someone of making a fool of him. The confusion gave way to terror, and he spun around and disappeared the same way he had come, screaming. Blancheur himself fled from the spot, with the memory of Gwyn still in his mind.

He made a new attempt: attacked a man, pulled him far into an out-of-the-way chamber, and held his hands and feet so that he couldn't get away. The man looked as if he would lose his mind with fear—he looked like a man fighting an invisible demon. It was almost as if an expression of relief crossed his face when his limbs were no longer bound by Blancheur's arms, but by rope stolen from the cave wall. But when Blancheur began to speak, the man rolled his eyes, stared all around wildly—and fainted.

Blancheur untied the ropes and left the man. He made two more attempts to make contact with the cave dwellers, choosing a woman and a child. But both fled in terror.

And the explanation? "They can't see us," said Blancheur.

"But why not?" asked Weiss. "They're people, like us. Maybe they've lived here for many centuries, maybe they've forgotten that there are people on other planets—maybe they've even forgotten that there are other worlds besides their own. But we are just as real as they are. Physical laws must apply to them too; it's simply unnatural that they can't see us."

Blancheur shook his head.

The next morning they started on their way home to the *Caligari*.

VII

Blancheur was silent all the first day. When they had pitched camp for the night, he said:

"Unnatural, perhaps. But people are unnatural from time to time. If the cave dwellers can't see us, it could be because they perceive *us* as unnatural."

"Just because we come from another world, because they don't know us?"

"Because we actually are unnatural on this planet. Look at us, dressed in chrome-yellow spacesuits, with a sled full of color-coded containers, from a bluish-red ship stranded in all this white and black. *Colors* are unnatural on this planet. And the cave dwellers are incapable of grasping that colors exist. When I stand in the way of one of them, he might see my chrome-yellow figure—but he refuses to *believe* that it is there. And when he collides with it anyway, he stumbles aside and tells himself and the others that he slipped on a patch of ice. It's as if we really were ghosts, something that grabs at them, something that asks them for help—and which they themselves deny can exist. If we catch them in our arms, they just get scared. They hear our voices, but cannot—*will* not—see our faces."

And Blancheur's blue eyes studied Weiss's face, a face which like his own was flaming red. For when the space travelers were frozen on the way between the stars, minute blood vessels in their skin burst —not only on their faces, but all over their bodies.

They both sat for a while, thinking of what Blancheur had said.

Weiss realized that Blancheur had found the explanation: such a planet-wide obsession might well have arisen, perhaps even as a part of the struggle to survive in such inhospitable surroundings. He thought of the red signal flares they had sent up, of the gestures they had made to get the sailors' attention. They had used a language of colors to call for help, a language they had thought was universal (red=help). But the cave dwellers did not understand colors, could not see colors, and only got terrified if anyone tried to force them to realize that colors were real.

But in a way, the discovery was also a hope. Now that they knew the cause of the inhabitants' fear, perhaps they could also eliminate it —and get the help they needed.

Weiss and Blancheur continued their journey back to the wreck of the starship through a snowy landscape which had become even more unreal for both of them.

Paradise 3000

by Herbert W. Franke

Translated from the German by Christine Priest

Dr. Franke specializes in the paradox of science, the complex made to appear simple. His novels are not easily translated—the first impression is one of simplicity—the stinger comes as contradictions grow and usually is quite unexpected. This is not a novel, of course, but it's a sample.

No cause has yet been determined for the accident which occurred on the 227th day of the year 3000, in which a carriage of the city's overhead railway broke free of its magnetic grapple and plunged two hundred fifty feet to the ground. There was no fatalities, as the compartments were unoccupied, but two passers-by sustained slight injuries.

I couldn't finish my food this evening, and the television didn't interest me. Worse still, I didn't make my report. I threw what was left of my rations into the trash can, and afterward when the others came around I made almost no contribution to the evening's discussion. Fortunately, no one seemed to notice.

I can't stop thinking about the day, on which everything had happened so suddenly and quickly. I know I've often said to Sigi, "Don't keep asking questions," but now it's my turn to want a few answers. I daren't ask them, though, because of the Psychos.

It happened just before midday meal. We were exercising as usual, and the city seemed the same as always: clean streets, synthetic grass and vegetation, happy-seeming OrdCits riding on the expressbelts. There was almost no haze, so that the golden rays of the regional sun reached us unfiltered, and the usual soft music from the loudspeakers could be heard against the background whirring of the air-conditioning. I could never have dreamed, then, that my world could change so suddenly.

Sigi and I were in the square by the Information Center, watching a replay of the latest hunt. I'm very fond of Sigi; we've been together for several decimonths now. We were standing close together, holding hands, when it happened.

Our first awareness was the deafening crash as the railway-carriage hit the ground no more than fifty feet away from us. It shattered like glass, hurling metal splinters in all directions, some landing uncomfortably close to us.

There weren't many people in the square; only one OrdCit was closer to the accident than we were. This man was bent over strangely, staring with wide-open, unseeing eyes as he clutched his hip. It was then that I saw the blood beginning to seep through his shirt.

Within half a minute the place was full of OrdCits. They surrounded the injured man, stunned by the sight of the damp red patch that grew on his shirt. He tried to stagger away, but the density of the crowd was too much for him.

Only when the police hovercraft arrived did the crowd move back to make way for it. Several men jumped down and erected a screen hastily, cutting off our view of the wounded man. After a great deal of hidden activity the screen was taken down again, but now there were only a few policemen to be seen, spraying the street with a disinfecting liquid.

The hovercraft moved away, taking with it the injured man, and the crowd dispersed. Within a few minutes there would be no sign of the accident: robbies were already arriving to clear away the wreckage of the carriage.

"Will that man be recalled?" I said to Sigi. "He can't be more than twenty."

Sigi made no reply, and when I turned to look at him I saw the expression on his face.

"What is it?" I said.

"I was hit too," he said.

He raised his hand and showed me a gaping cut at the base of the thumb. He'd made no sound when the splinter hit him, and I'd had no notion that he too had been injured. I began to feel sick.

Representatives from a wide range of departments—from clerics and doctors and teachers through television controllers—sat as members of the Commission. Most of these people were unaccustomed to the atmosphere of a scientific laboratory. They walked cautiously through the aisles between the glass cases and electronic equipment, anxious to avoid stepping on the cables which ran everywhere across the floor.

Roger White, the present head of the Psycho-Technic Center, led them toward a row of cubicles. Inside these, as they saw through the port in the front of each cubicle, was a couch on which lay a motionless body. The head was inside a helmet, which was linked by a mass of wires to machinery mounted against the rear wall.

"The people we chose as guinea-pigs were all due to be recalled," White said by way of explanation. He caught the eye of Father

Olfhus, one of the church representatives, and added: "They experience both good and bad in there, you know!"

He signaled to an assistant to raise a lever, and the people inside the cubicles began to move. Their limbs showed the first signs of life, and then their faces moved, revealing a variety of expressions. Some of the people looked happy and contented; others were clearly terrified.

"Well, ladies and gentlemen, I think you can see that this invention is going to have a significant effect. In essence, we now have a means of channeling information directly into the mind. This is instantaneous communication . . . and I'm sure I don't need to underline the implications of that."

The head of the Education Department was the first to speak. "So we could transmit teaching material this way? And it would be retained in the memory?"

White nodded. "Yes, of course."

"What do you suppose will be the effect on program transmissions?" asked a member of the Television Department.

"All the potential is yours, in that field. But it will remove the need for picture transmission, because the images can be fed directly into the brain. More than that, the transmission can be done in such a way that one does not just see and hear, but *feels* it, experiences it."

Gradually the rest of the group joined in the discussion, and the various aspects of the invention were considered at some length. Soon, a volunteer was called for, and to everyone's surprise Father Olfhus stepped forward to become the first of them to try the new experience. To his evident surprise, he became, in turn, Jesse James, Tarzan, Dr. Frankenstein, and Captain Nemo. . . .

"I think we should continue discussing this over lunch," said White.

Lil's been good. She hasn't told anyone about me. I think I'll give her my pocket recorder as a present; I know she'd love to have it. But she'll keep quiet for a bit longer, I know, and that's the important thing.

I can hardly feel the wound, but whenever I look at it I find it's still bleeding. I keep a paper tissue wrapped tightly around my fist, and try hard to concentrate on the lessons. Today we had an examination; the last thing I wanted! And gym was even more of a problem. I had to avoid it today, because it would have surely made the cut much worse. Perhaps it'll be better tomorrow. I've heard it said that injuries heal themselves, but no one seems to be sure about this.

But the one thing I *am* sure of is that anyone who is taken away for an injury is never seen again. They're recalled.

If I survive until tomorrow, that'll be half the battle won. We have handicrafts tomorrow, so I'll be able to get hold of some adhesive. It must be possible to stick the cut together somehow.

I hope Lil's not too worried. We get an hour together this evening. She's usually very lively then, and so would I be, normally. But not tonight. I hope she'll let me rest; I'm really exhausted. I'll have to persuade her.

I don't want to be recalled. I'm still very young.

Sigi has been very subdued recently. I don't understand him. I think it would be better if he declared himself wounded. They say that being recalled isn't too bad. You don't feel anything, and you lose track of the passage of time. A thousand years seems like a day, an hour even. You just lie there waiting, waiting for a better time. No one knows for sure whether the people of the future will live our way, but what is certain is that it's a wonderful future.

Sigi is afraid. He's stuck his cut together, and claims that it isn't hurting anymore. But he won't stop talking about it! Then he goes quiet, and broods for hours.

I admit that I wouldn't like to be recalled myself. I'm nineteen, and should have eleven more years. I'm a good OrdCit; no black marks yet! I think I stand a very good chance of reaching thirty, and I don't want to throw away those years. Perhaps I should declare Sigi after all.

I'm not even sure what's preventing me from doing it. I'm getting very annoyed with him now, and when I think of all the other partners I've had there's nothing so special about him.

Or perhaps there is. . . .

Perhaps I do feel something for him, something I haven't experienced with anyone else. Although this could be explained by what's happened to him recently: his weakness, and the fact that he needs me more.

In our free hour today we went on the overhead railway. Sigi didn't want to walk anywhere. He was very tired, and his cheeks were flushed. He sat in the train looking depressed, and it made me feel I should look after him and fuss over him, like a child with a doll.

At the end of the line we climbed down and stared through the glass wall at the cooling-halls. These are gigantic blocks, stretching away into the distance, one behind the other. The temperature inside has to be kept at $-140°$ C; this creates a mist about the buildings, and you can almost see the wind moving across the buildings. Each cooling-hall has a raised tube leading into it; it's made of frosted glass, and the cylinder-shaped recall-boxes can be seen sliding inside, at regular intervals.

"How long do they stay there?" said Sigi. "Does anyone ever come out again?"

I had never doubted what I had been taught, and had no reason to. Everything in life runs as planned: we receive our food, our lessons, our television programs. The railway, the express-belts, the heating, air-conditioning, and atomic sun; these never fail us. We're safe and well cared for. We're good OrdCits, and we're happy.

In the relaxed atmosphere of the luncheon, the members of the Commission enjoyed a lively discussion. They projected the new development into the future, imagining all kinds of resultant utopian societies. Only when they reconvened for the afternoon session did they come back to earth and begin to consider the realities of the situation.

Roger White stood up.

"Well, ladies and gentlemen," he said. "I think I've convinced you that the device works. The machine is ready to go into production, and is at your disposal. There are so many possible applications. Perhaps you'd like to tell me what conclusions you have reached."

He sat down and reached for his glass. He looked relaxed, almost nonchalant, now that the burden of decision had been removed from him.

Mouritzen, the chairman of the Commission, took the opportunity to speak first.

"I think there's one highly important point to be raised before we go any further," he said. "That is the question of whether using such a technique is permissible under our Fundamental Principles."

Mouritzen nodded to the Secretary of State, who was sitting next to him. The latter, without raising his eyes from his notebook, began: "We must first remind ourselves of the underlying law of medicine: that human life be preserved at all costs. Also, the law of our religion: that natural childbirth must not be prevented. The consequence, as you are all aware, is the Principle of Reduction; reduction of rations, of living-space, of life-expectancy, of schooling . . . at the moment we are down to seventy-five square feet of floor area per person, and thirty years of active life. And, because we must preserve life, we have no choice but to freeze every Ordinary Citizen who reaches thirty—"

"—In the hope that conditions will improve," interrupted Jurubi, as if to defend the practice. As a member of the Entertainment Department, he was included to be rather more complacent than the rest of the Commission.

"It is not our job to hope," said the Secretary of State. "Our task is to preserve life. And . . ."

But he had lost his train of thought and was glancing again at his notebook.

"Let us return to the point," said Mouritzen. "Is this method of direct brain transmission compatible with our Principles? Perhaps you'd like to comment, Dr. Shi-Yin?"

The doctor looked uncertain. "I suppose there's one point in its favor: there's no danger of any damage to the health."

"But what's more important," said Father Olfhus, with an apologetic smile, "is the type of information we transmit. If it's not to be of ethical or moral value, then—"

Mouritzen broke in: "That, of course, can be controlled. But even if we have no positive objections here to the scheme, how can we be sure that anyone will be really interested outside?"

This remark did not please Jurubi.

"How is it that we never take up any new ideas?" he said. "I'm all for this new system. It'll allow us to do all sorts of things we haven't tried before, like helping people catharsize their emotions, giving them controlled relaxation sessions—"

"Relaxation? We could make far better use of the system in the educational program," said Papoussot. "Everything that has to be taught could be done so quickly that we could make really dramatic reductions in the allowance for schooling."

Delgado, a socio-economist, shook his head. "Have you considered the cost of all this? We would need a vast amount of new equipment, and then there'd be the question of disposing of the equipment which would become obsolete. And think of the social consequences. Our present organization works beautifully, but under this new system we'd have to scrap all the present schedules and timetables. There would have to be more leisure time, and you know that that will bring discontent and unrest eventually. That we cannot allow."

Mouritzen nodded in agreement.

"These are very important considerations," he said, and turned to Roger White. "I'm sure your system offers a multitude of fascinating opportunities. Really, though, it's ahead of its time. I don't think we can cope with it at present. Perhaps later we'll reconsider. For the time being, though, I think we ought to resist the temptation to play around with it. Many thanks for the demonstration."

I am at a loss as to what to do. Sigi just lay on the couch in our free hour today, hardly moving. He was talking about declaring himself at last, and yet now I find myself trying to dissuade him. It is strange that now, the time when he's causing me more worry and irritation than anyone ever has before, I can't bear to think of losing him. I've tried to comfort him, but all I can do is wipe the perspiration from his brow with a paper tissue.

The wound has stopped bleeding, but under the layer of adhesive it looks very inflamed. The hand is swollen and seems to be giving him a lot of pain. I managed to smuggle five cans of Stimu-Cola into our room, but I know that it won't do him any real good. There's nothing I can do to help him.

He pulled me toward him, and we lay quietly together. I felt more affected by this than by all the physical contact we've had in the past.

Could I hide Sigi somewhere? Could I find someone who'd be able to help? But no . . . the only people with any qualified knowledge are the Medics and the Psychos. It's out of the question to approach them. Suddenly, I feel as if we're trapped together on the other side of a high wall.

Sigi became calmer and nestled closer to me. I lay still and quiet. I could have wept.

The guests had left, leaving behind them a room full of bad air, empty glasses, and crumpled serviettes. They were by now on their way through the underground tunnels back to their rooms in their own districts. Only one had stayed behind: Father Olfhus. He and Roger White were old friends. They had been students together, and despite their different callings they had always maintained contact with each other.

They walked together up a spiral staircase to the top floor of the building, and out onto a roof garden. Here the outlook was pleasant: they were directly beneath the dome-shaped roof and the garden was filled with natural light. There were real flowers, real stones. The view from here extended far across the flat land below, which was dotted with innumerable rainwater reservoirs, red algae floating on the surface.

"So they didn't accept your idea," said Father Olfhus. They were leaning against the perimeter wall of the garden, looking out toward the haze which obscured the horizon.

"I didn't really expect them to," said White. "I held the meeting more as a formality than anything else."

"You've always had to consider us . . . the church, I mean," said Olfhus.

"Yes," said White. They were silent for a while, and the only sound they could hear was the creaking of the dome material in the strong wind outside.

"Why isn't this crazy idea abandoned?" White said at last. "This Principle of Reduction, how much longer can it go on? Not enough food, not enough doctors. Ordinary Citizens over sixteen barred from medical treatment. Every new baby born inherits some disorder —allergies, hemophilia—the natural immunities of the human body are breaking down completely. And all because you refuse to introduce any kind of birth-control or genetic engineering."

"But we must preserve freedom!"

"Do you call this freedom? Are OrdCits free? They're not educated, cannot develop or progress. All they experience is Reduction. I expect the rations will be reduced again soon . . . then the active lifespan will come down to twenty-eight years. What kind of life is that?"

"But they're happy, and innocent, and . . ."

"But what value is there in an unfulfilled earthly existence?"

Olfhus shrugged. "They do at least have hope."

"Yes . . . a false hope. How can you promise them 'Paradise' when you know their real fate?"

"Exactly," said Olfhus. "That's why we promise it."

"If only the promise could be kept," said White, but it was more to himself than to the other man, who merely nodded.

It's happened at last. They came for him. Someone must have noticed. I only hope he doesn't think it was me who betrayed him. I tried to see him, to say good-bye, but they wouldn't let me near him.

I've seen it happen so many times before. A white hovercraft appears, police leap out and come straight into the classroom, or the gym, even the dining hall or the television room. For a moment everyone thinks: Are they coming for me this time? but then they take the one they want, lay him on a stretcher, close up the frame, and cover him from view. They move so quickly that it's all over in a matter of seconds. Afterward, it's as if nothing has happened. The seating is rearranged so that no chairs are empty, the room once occupied is cleared out, and the number on the register is altered. No one shows any surprise. There's no cause for fear . . . it's all normal. He'll be all right. There's a new, better world waiting for him. They keep telling us about this world, what a beautiful, peaceful place it is, and yet . . .

I've been very unhappy since Sigi went. I've found a new boyfriend, but he doesn't know that I'm thinking of Sigi all the time. I know where Sigi is, but I don't know what will become of him. I know it's the same for all of us in the end. I'll just have to hope that it's not too terrible.

The pain has ceased at last. I was only under the healing-lamp for ten seconds, but it cured the burning feeling in the hand, and my throbbing veins and aching head. . . . For a moment I thought it was completely cured, but when I looked at my hand the wound looked as bad as ever.

For a few minutes I thought I'd be able to go back to the city, to my friends, and to Lil. But then I realized. And I'm afraid. I know it doesn't hurt, but it's not pain I'm afraid of . . . it's the emptiness. . . .

I'm still on the stretcher, and they've put me in the conveyor. I can see shadowy shapes—they must be the struts that support the dome —but I can't see properly through the frosted glass.

Darkness . . . and now rows of lights. I seem to be in a big, light hall. Machinery all around me . . . an overwhelming smell . . . something's touching me . . . I'm floating . . . into darkness . . . and cold.

Suddenly it's light again. I can see blue sky and white clouds. I think I can hear birds singing.

And a voice, deep and quiet but seeming to encompass all: "Welcome to Paradise!"

My Eyes, They Burn!

by Eddy C. Bertin

Translated from the Flemish by the author

Eddy C. Bertin is a devotee of Lovecraft and of horror tales. This is a story of science fiction but with the clement of emotionalism we can expect of a horror tale expert. Bertin's stories have appeared in English in several anthologies, including one of the *World's Best* annuals. He reads and writes English fluently but with a verve that belies the legend of Flemish stolidity.

Through the darkness, I am gliding, very softly as the shadow river carries me along on its rippling back. There is no boat, nothing to hold on to, I am just aimlessly drifting in the water, my face turned upward. Though I have nothing to guide myself with, I stay in the middle of the current, never touching the land on both sides. I know that I CAN, if I would like to; I'd just have to stretch out my fingers and the river banks will close in on me as the walls of a coffin. But I'm not really interested.

Strange growths throw their blacker shades over the dark river, sometimes their moldgreen fingers almost touch my face as I drift under them. Their leaves open as crowns of flowers, but there is only dark hair growing on them, constantly and slowly moving as if it consists of millions of microscopic insects. When I look in front of me, I can see the river, endlessly crawling along, dimly illuminated by a strange fading light, while behind me the darkness is complete. I can see only the water and the trees, and even those only when I am passing directly underneath them. As time passes, I begin to notice other things, though the darkness doesn't lift. It is almost as if I am turning into a nyctalope, able to stare through the dark haze which is hovering around everything of the country around me. There are hills beyond the treetops, weirdly glittering hills, perfectly well formed and bare of any growths, and they have small, sharply pointed towers on top of them, as alien nipples on enormous iron breasts. Sometimes small hawklike things soundlessly drift through the black yet illuminated sky, passing over me as I drift toward the river's unknown end. The current is softly rocking me, and the water is comfortably warm, so, without noticing it, my eyelids drop and I drift away into dreamshades.

Something makes me open my eyes and look in front of me. The water is changing into ice, freezing into insanely shaped forms all around me. Half-frozen pieces grate along my back and legs with many needlepoints. I stare right into an enormous eye looming up before me and cynically looking me over. The stream flows into the center of the iris. I begin thrashing around wildly, but the river banks disappear on both sides, and I am all alone in a dark sea that stretches endlessly in all directions, except for the eye. The current goes on toward it, taking me along. I stretch out my hands and feet to keep it away, and then on my hands, my fingers, on my feet, the flesh tears, and a thousand eyes open on my body, all looking at the enormous eye awaiting me. The iris splits, its darkness flows out to meet me, envelops me with slimy tentacles, drowns and soothes my panic into a fading nothingness. . . .

A soft humming sound as of an enormous but distant beehive crawled through the subterranean control rooms. The machines rose up along the walls of the room as colossal metal insects, their countless dials staring as cold but intelligent eyes. The people, all uniformly dressed in white, moved as silently as the many androids busy with files and computer cards. Only what was absolutely necessary was spoken out loud; for the rest, only mechanical sounds rippled the waters of silence. The dry *click* of a moved handle, the short *knack* of a pushed button, the *bipbipbip* of a control light. This was no place for human beings, here only machines felt at home, and people who themselves were closer to the machine than to humanity, people who thought in numbers and computer symbols. E.T.A., short for Extra-Terrestrial Explorations, kept close watch on the development of Project CYB.

Awakening is difficult, although I don't have the impression of having slept long. There is a half-real memory of an alien, dark sea. I drift through the twilight dream figures, who swirl through my mind, changing shape, fading into darkness when I touch them. Now all is dark around me, or haven't I opened my eyes yet?
Too difficult to think about it for the moment, I must let reality come slowly, easy, superimposing upon the sleepworlds, as transparent sheets placed upon each other, until they'll mingle and become one.
AAAHHHHHH.
My eyes jerk open, and still there is nothing but darkness, but I'm awake, fully awake. My head is throbbing with sudden shock. There is an already fading impression of pain. Somewhere, something has hurt me enough to wake me up in an instant, but I can't tell where. There is only the memory of unexpected, sharp needlepain, and it is disappearing.
Though there can be nothing to watch, I would like to look around, and then discover that I can't. My eyes won't turn. Frequently, my brain gives the orders: turn, turn LEFT, turn RIGHT,

LEFT, RIGHT, LEFT, RIGHT, TURN DAMN YOU! It is almost as if I can feel the order running through the nerves to the muscles of my eyeballs, but they don't move at all. What is this? Now I try to close my eyes, but they don't either. Nothing happens at all. ARE my eyes really open? I dimly remember having opened them, but now I can't be sure anymore.

I raise my right hand and bring it to my face to touch my eyes. I feel the muscles move, the arm bending; my fingers spread and come down as a spider descending from her web on a scared fly. But nothing touches my eager face.

A reasonless horror hovers above me, and slowly drips feelers of fear on my upturned, helpless face. Frantically I move my arms and legs and head, try to sit upright. The orders race as frightened rabbits through the nerve-knots, but the muscles are petrified.

Then I scream, +WHAT IS THIS?+ The silence stifles my scream, which rises out of an empty throat, is voiced by a tongue which isn't there. I wait, shivering with unknown dread, but physically nothing happens. There is no cold ice on my back, no sweat on my forehead, no wetness in the palms of my hands.

+HELP! HELP ME!+ But there is no sound, no voice, no responding echo to my fear. So I let it rest. The fear is slowly going over in my brain-fluid, dripping into my cells. I have no voice, and I can't move. I feel my body yet it doesn't accept my commands. My eyes are closed and I can't open them, or else they are open and I can't close them, and everything is in darkness.

+WHAT HAVE YOU DONE TO ME?+

Now why did I say that? WHO has done what to me, and WHY? Time has no ending, there is only the motionless waiting for something, anything, to happen. The irreality of it all is enormous; I begin to think that this is all an illusion, a nightmare from which I will awake in due time. I have dreamed like this before, I remember, mornings when I dreamed that I stood up, dressed, ate, and went to the office, then returned home, made love to my wife, and went to sleep. Then afterward I awoke again, to restart the day I had just finished that night. It all seemed real also. Then . . .

+ARE YOU AWAKE?+

Something else existing, giving reality and the shape of sound to the void of nothingness which shrouds me! Something real at last, something to cling to, to react to.

+YES, YES, I'M AWAKE. I'M AWAKE.+

+GOOD.+

No, the voice can't go away, I have to speak to it, hold it. It spoke to me.

+WHAT IS THIS? AM I DREAMING? I AM, AIN'T I? THIS ISN'T REAL? WHERE IS THIS? WHO ARE YOU? WHY CAN'T I SEE YOU?+

+YOU ARE AWAKE. YOU ARE REAL. THAT IS ALL THAT MATTERS.+

+BUT WHY CAN'T I MOVE? WHAT HAS HAPPENED TO ME?+

+STRANGE THAT YOU STILL SHOULD CARE. THINGS HAVE CHANGED FOR YOU. YOU REMEMBER, DON'T YOU?+

+REMEMBER? WHAT SHOULD I REMEMBER?+

+DON'T YOU REMEMBER THE ROOM? THE PAPER YOU HAD TO SIGN, TO SAVE YOU FROM THE DISTORTION-DOOR?+

Distortion-room . . . paper . . . Something starts throbbing in my head, and I want to shut it out, it is hurting me. But I can't stop it, it is as if someone is striking an enormous gong, right inside my brain, and the booming noise echoes within the bone chambers of my skull. DISTORtion. DISTORtion. DISTORtion. The darkness is moving around me, but it isn't as if I were really seeing something. It is almost as if something is turning my eyes as mirrors, making them look inside my head, deep down there, at the distortion-door, where they were going to kill me. Where they DID kill me. I'm . . . I'm DEAD. I'M DEAD.

The gong is striking again, and automatically I count the strokes. One . . . two . . . three . . . four . . . five . . . six . . . seven . . . SEVEN. At seven o'clock straight, the hands of the clock in the cell with the white walls stopped, and they came to get the man. I am looking down in that cell now, inside my head, watching the man sitting there, knowing what he thought, knowing what he felt.

He still couldn't believe it. The Great Judge had said it himself, as he stood proudly before him in his metalsheet cloak. Of course the dress wasn't worn for him, but for the millions of bored yet watching eyes of the world, living with their telesets. Then he had known it for weeks, walking and living through them as through a slowed-down movie fragment. The last night through he had lain awake, thinking about it, repeating it to himself, and still he didn't really believe.

They couldn't just kill him. He was himself, Charles Harkson-8, electro-accountant, and a good one. He earned a good salary, had friends, a three-room flat, two cars, and a wife. No, he hadn't a wife now, had he? The Verdict automatically canceled his four-year marriage. At least, he thought it did, it all seemed so unreal, and there were many things he couldn't remember clearly since the Verdict. She hadn't come to see him anyway. Not that it mattered very much, she'd remarry soon; they had both agreed before that there would be no renewal of their four-year contract.

Life and death were the only important matters now. He was alive, a thinking existing person. They couldn't just destroy him. Couldn't they? It seemed rather simplistic, yet it was the only reason that he kept on repeating.

They came for him, four armed policemen in their striking green garments, rattling their keys in unison. A stupid ancient ceremony, with all the locks being photoelectrical and based on the jailer's brain-patterns, but it showed nicely on the teles. He didn't resist them, just went with them, two in front of him, two behind him. It all seemed like a parody of a bad play; small cameras were placed every ten meters, emitting his last walk to the many million silent watchers. The policemen didn't talk, hardly looked at him. As he walked, he listened to their footfalls echoing endlessly through the empty corridors. Then there was a corridor without cameras, ending in a large door, which opened as they approached, and he saw IT.

The distortion-door. It was as he had seen it in a picture, just a circular open door into darkness, placed at the end of that room. That was where they would put him, and then they'd twist his molecules into new patterns, change him into a mass of blubbering flesh and broken splintering bones. And all the time his mind would stay sane, his brain untouched, but feeling every bit of pain and terror and unable to voice his agonies, till the distortion would reach it also. They were . . . they were . . .

"You are going to kill me!" he shrieked. The shout seemed to spring from every nerve in his body. It was as if a white wall suddenly collapsed, splintering into a thousand shrieking fragments, and exposing something very definite, very ugly, to him.

He kept on screaming, his mind a white blanket of horror. The whole world of self-centered time and consciousness seemed to be in that black circular hole. He tried to run, but couldn't move. A numbness had taken over his arms and legs. He just kept on staring and screaming, but there was no sound in the white noise-absorbing world. They dragged him forward. He could see everything, but it triggered no reactions; the stark terror overpowered all his other emotions. There were three men in white spotless jackets, so white that they almost were one with the white walls, so that he could only see their balloon-faces, as grotesque paintings on those walls. There was also a police officer, the yellow cross on his shoulders stating his high rank. No preacher, but then he didn't belong to one of the acknowledged Uni-Churches. Hidden out of sight by the opening door, a stretcher stood, with a blanket lying over a still form. His mind's eye imagined the mass of blood and flesh that must be lying under it, and he almost expected to see a red finger crawling slowly from under it. They were all here to kill him, and they didn't even know him. They weren't interested, and neither was the rest of the world. An example had to be set for the tubereacs, so they'd kill him. To them, he was just a puppet. They'd cut his strings, and he'd drop dead.

"All right," one of the white-cloaked men said. "Just let him here. You can go now."

The policemen loosened their grip on his arms, and he almost fell, but now the white man held him. The big door behind them snapped shut, cutting off the camera eyes.

"Come on, quick now," the white man said. The words didn't register. Only the other open door was there, looking impartially at him with the black empty socket of a skull. Death. The distortion-door and death, his own personal death. He choked, his eyes stinging with fear, terror crawling over his back and through his brain as a thousand many-legged spiders.

"Move," the officer said. The gun in his hand now pricked in Charles's back. Slowly he fell from one leg onto the other, walking clumsily. But they didn't lead him to the circular door. Instead, one of the white men closed it. There was a soft *hissssssss*. The hands of the clock had crawled to seven-ten.

The officer nodded. "Execution finished," he said. He took a significant look at Charles. "Now you're officially dead, man." He showed the stretcher. "There, under the plastic blanket, lies what is left of a big android-dog who went through the distortion-door, just before they brought you. No one will ever know the difference between it and a human body NOW. No time to spare, let's leave."

Charles's tongue couldn't form the questions he wanted to ask. It was all happening too quickly; the succeeding emotions drowned his understanding. They took him through a side door he hadn't even noticed, through long corridors to an elevator, and then they went down, and down. They never loosened their grip on him, and he just kept on looking from one to another, searching for a clue on their expressionless faces. They passed through an enormous room, where other white men and many androids were working on machines he had never imagined to exist under the city, and then into a small office, where they put him down in a chair.

The man in white who had spoken first put a paper in front of him on the small table, and said, "We have taken you away from death, a death which you certainly merited. Our reason is very simple and selfish: we can use you. You are here in department E.T.E. of the government-sponsored Science Development. We are working on a project you could never have even dreamed of, but which is of enormous importance. Your test-patterns before the Verdict have shown you to be an intelligent man, which is exactly what we need as a guinea-pig. You agree on your own free will to subject yourself to this experiment. Sign here."

It was too much. Action, reaction, superimposing emotion.

"No," he whispered.

The officer's voice was a grating sound against his ear. "Remember one thing, my friend. You're dead. You're officially dead. YOU DON'T EXIST. We don't really need this signature, except that IF we succeed, then we can prove that we DID use you for it."

There was a paradox somewhere, it couldn't be legal, because legally he was dead. He couldn't think. "No. I'll only sign when I know more. What are you going to do with me? What kind of experiment? What are my chances of getting through it alive?"

The officer smiled. His cynicism crawled through the air as cigarette smoke, shaping almost-touchable patterns. "As a matter of fact, you don't have much chance. But does that matter? We have delayed your death by twenty-one minutes now. We'll just have to make a short trip backward in time."

Something small, hard, and very cold was pressed against Charles's neck. It seemed to be enormous in proportions, although he knew it was only the size of a pinhead.

CLICK! thundering through his ear channels, echoing in his brain. He pictured the microscoping poison needle, waiting in the mouth of the gun, the tail of a scorpion, already stretching out for the kill. The voice was cold, it dropped ice lakes as it slithered through his mind as a snake.

"You have six seconds left," it said.

"You can't do this," he screamed, but only the echo of his shriek ever left his mouth.

"Five . . . four . . ."

"It's against the law, it's murder, murder, MURDER!"

"No, YOU are the murderer. I am the executioner. Three left. You're dead, don't forget that. You're already dead NOW."

"But you're not killing me for what I've DONE. I was a victim, they could have put me through Conform with drugs, but they wanted an example against the tubereacs. But you, you're not executing me, you're MURDERING me because I don't want to—"

"Two seconds."

"—sign your bloody paper. You can't just destroy me as you . . ."

"Oh, but we can, and we will. The time is past. SIGN."

The coldness was all over his body now. With shaking fingers he grasped the ballpoint pen and signed, a spidery crawl all over the paper.

A sudden sharp pain, he hadn't the time to understand what was happening. A black wing overshadowed him as he fell forward, and the ground opened a dark, toothless mouth which swallowed him into a pit of darkness.

+YES, I REMEMBER NOW.+ And I do remember, all of it, the smell of fear, the weakness, and the biting pain in my neck. I know that the man I watched is me. No, was me, because it's all past.

+I REMEMBER,+ I say, +BUT WHAT HAPPENED WITH ME?+

+WE GAVE YOU AN INJECTION,+ the voice out of nowhere says, +THEN WE TOOK YOUR BODY AWAY AND CUT IT APART. WE TOOK OUT YOUR BRAIN AND STUCK A THOUSAND MICROSCOPIC NEEDLES IN IT. AND NOW YOU'RE ON YOUR WAY.+

+ON MY WAY? MY WAY TO WHERE? I DON'T UNDERSTAND ANYTHING. YOU MUST EXPLAIN OR I'LL GO MAD HERE. WHERE AM I? WHY CAN'T I MOVE? AND WHERE ARE YOU?+

+WE ARE QUITE A DISTANCE AWAY FROM YOU. WHAT YOU ARE HEARING ARE NO WORDS IN THE REAL SENSE OF IT. OUR WORDS ARE SPOKEN INTO A TRANSMITTER, WHO CHANGES THEM INTO CODED IMPULSES. YOU RECEIVE THEM WITH RADAR-EARS, CONNECTED WITH YOUR OWN TRANSMITTER, WHO PASSES THEM ON TO THE HEARING CENTER OF YOUR BRAIN, WHERE THEY ARE INTERPRETED AS RECOGNIZABLE SOUNDS, DUE TO A FEW THINGS WE PUT IN THERE.+

+BUT I SPEAK TO YOU, AND YOU HEAR ME!+

+THAT IS ONLY THE SAME PROCESS BUT IN REVERSAL. YOU DON'T SPEAK. YOU CAN'T SPEAK. THERE'S NOTHING LEFT FOR YOU TO SPEAK WITH. YOU ARE THINKING THE WORDS, IMAGINING YOURSELF SPEAKING THEM, WHICH MAKES THE CORRECT CONTACT WITH THE TRANSMITTER IN THE NEEDLE. OUR RADARS RECEIVE THE IMPULSES YOU'RE SENDING, AND PASS THEM ON TO OUR TRANSMITTER, WHO TRANSLATES THE SYMBOLS YOU'RE SENDING.+

+BUT WHERE? WHERE AM I?+

+NOT EXACTLY 'WHERE.' YOU ARE A PHOTON-NEEDLESHIP, AND HAVE JUST LEFT THE CALCULATED ORBIT AROUND THE MOON. YOU'RE LEAVING US, GOING OUT, QUICKER AND QUICKER EVERY MILLISECOND.

+LEAVING? OUT? TO WHERE? WHY?+

I think the right words, triggering the electrical contacts that operate the sound modulators. I speak-think my questions toward the faraway underground machines, around which the men in white are sitting. It is crazy! They're mad, or else I'm sick and having hallucinations. There must be a way out of this insanity. Let's try it by acting logically.

+WHAT'S THE SENSE OF THIS? WHY SEND ME? AND WHERE TO?+
They couldn't fool him, those madmen. Everybody knew that the
space projects had been stopped, and that all the money for government projects had been channeled into Medic Center for mass production of the Controlled Breeding Wombs. Oh no, they wouldn't
fool HIM with their lunatic talk.

+WE WILL TRY TO EXPLAIN THE ESSENTIALS. AS YOU KNOW, BE-
FORE THE GOVERNMENT OFFICIALLY BANNED THE SPACE PROJECTS,
MANNED SHIPS HAD BEEN SENT TO MARS AND VENUS, AS DID OUR
FRIENDS FROM THE OTHER SIDE OF THE GLOBE. THREE YEARS AGO,
THE FIRST SHIP WAS SENT BEYOND THE ORBIT OF VENUS, TOWARD
MERCURY. SOMETHING BROKE DOWN IN THE MACHINERY, AND THE
SHIP HURLED ITSELF INTO THE SUN. THAT WAS WHAT THE PUBLIC
WAS TOLD. NO ONE EVER LEARNED THAT IT WASN'T THE SHIP WHICH
HAD FAILED, BUT THE PILOT. A MAN POSSESSING IRON NERVES AND
COMPLETE CONTROL OVER HIS MIND AND BODY, A HIGHLY SPECIAL-
IZED ASTRONAUT WHO HAD BEEN TRAINED TWO YEARS EXCLUSIVELY
FOR THIS TRIP, NOT COUNTING HIS GENERAL TRAINING AS AN ASTRO-
NAUT. STILL, SOMETHING HAPPENED TO HIM, ENOUGH TO SHATTER
THAT BRILLIANT MIND. RAVING AS A MANIAC, HE CHANGED THE SHIP'S
COURSE. WE DON'T KNOW WHAT CHANGED HIM, OR FROM WHERE IT
CAME, WE SENT TWO SHIPS WITH ROBOTS, AND THEY RETURNED
SAFELY. WE TRIED ANOTHER MANNED SHIP, AND THE PILOT KILLED
HIMSELF. THE SHIP WAS LOST. THAT WAS WHEN THE GOVERNMENT
HAD A FEW MEETINGS WITH POLITICIANS FROM THE OTHER SIDE,
KNOWING THAT THEY HAD BEEN EXPERIMENTING ALONG THE SAME
LINES. RESULTS WERE NEARLY IDENTICAL, THOUGH THEY REFUSED TO
ADMIT DEFEAT OPENLY. THEN THE SPACE PROJECTS WERE STOPPED
OFFICIALLY, AND E.T.A. WERE FOUNDED, TO FIND A WAY TO GET A
MAN CLOSE TO MERCURY AND SAFELY BACK. THAT'S WHERE YOU
COME IN. SOMETHING INFLUENCED THE MINDS AND/OR THE BODIES
OF THOSE ASTRONAUTS. IT WON'T BE ABLE TO DO THIS WITH YOU. WE
HAVE SENT SOMEBODY WITHOUT A BODY, AND WITH A MIND WE CAN
READ AS AN OPEN BOOK. YOU ARE, PRACTICALLY SPEAKING, A PURE
MIND, A BRAIN CONNECTED TO A COMPUTER FED BY SYNTHETIC
FLUIDS. YOUR TONGUE IS AN ELECTRONICAL CONTACT, YOUR BARS
ARE RADARS. YOUR VEINS ARE ELECTRIC CABLES, YOUR FINGERS ARE
DIAL NEEDLES. YOU ARE THE PERFECTED CYBORG, A MACHINE CON-
TROLLED BY A HUMAN BRAIN. YOU *are* IN FACT THE NEEDLE.+

I want to laugh. They say I have no mouth, yet I feel my lips with
my tongue, I feel the hardness of my teeth. I try to move, and though
it doesn't work, still I know that I have hands and feet.

+YOU'RE ALL INSANE DOWN THERE, OR WHEREVER YOU ARE

REALLY. THIS IS A JOKE, A STUPID EXPERIMENT TO TEST MY RE-
ACTIONS, OR SOMETHING LIKE THAT. I CAN FEEL MY FINGERS MOVE
AND SPREAD. I CAN HEAR MY HEART BEAT IN MY CHEST. I CAN
FEEL I'M . . .+

I stop, and something very cold comes over me. I am not breathing. In fact I haven't taken a breath since I woke up.

+NO, YOU CAN'T FEEL ANYTHING, THERE IS NOTHING TO BE FELT.
YOU'RE JUST A BIG MACHINE, THAT'S ALL.+

I try to fight the realization that if I accept what they say, then I'll
know that I'm completely mad, that I'm living in a hallucination
from which there's no escape.

+THAT'S IMPOSSIBLE. I FEEL MY HANDS, MY FEET. I FEEL
THEM!+

+QUITE INTERESTING, AND LOGICAL. ALTHOUGH THEY HAVE BEEN
AMPUTATED, YOUR BRAIN STILL KEEPS ON RECEIVING IMPULSES,
WHICH IT INTERPRETS AS COMING FROM YOUR BODY. OTHER SIMILAR
CASES ARE KNOWN WHERE PEOPLE LOST AN ARM OR A LEG IN AN AC-
CIDENT, AND WHEN WAKING UP IN THE MED CENTER, COMPLAINED
OF PAIN IN THEIR HANDS OR FEET. YOU'LL LOSE THAT FEELING IN
SOME TIME, WHEN YOU'LL HAVE LEARNED TO INTERPRET THE SEN-
SATION AS WHAT IT REALLY IS: THE AUTOMATIC TURNING OF A
LEVEL, THE CRAWLING OF THE HANDS OVER THE FACE OF A DIAL,
THE PASSING OF AN ELECTRIC CURRENT THROUGH A CONTACT.+

+BUT I'M NOT TRAINED FOR ANYTHING. YOU CAN'T JUST SEND ME
INTO SPACE, YOU CAN'T. . . .+

Is there someone laughing? The voice is neutral, yet it seems
cynical. +WE CAN'T? WE HAVE TOLD YOU: YOU'RE ON YOUR WAY!
AT THE MOMENT YOUR SPEED IS ONE HUNDRED TWENTY KILOMETERS
PER SECOND, AND IT IS INCREASING EVERY MILLISECOND.+

+I DON'T BELIEVE IT.+

+YOU DON'T HAVE TO NOW. YOU'LL ACCEPT IT SOON ENOUGH.+

Impossible. But they mustn't keep quiet, silence will end in
madness, here where I can't move, can't see. I have to find out where
I really am, what they have done to me. Maybe they really took out
my brain, and are now all staring at it. So I speak again, I have to
keep on talking, then I don't have to think.

+HOW LONG . . . WILL IT TAKE?+

+NO NEED FOR YOU TO OCCUPY YOURSELF WITH TIME. TIME HAS
NO MEANING WHERE YOU ARE NOW. WE'LL TELL YOU WHEN THE
JOURNEY'S FINISHED. THAT, TOO, WILL BE SOON ENOUGH.+

+BUT . . . I CAN'T DO ANYTHING. HOW DO I STOP, ACCELERATE,
TURN BACK, DO ANYTHING AT ALL?+

╋WE'LL DO ALL THAT FOR YOU.╋
╋AND I CAN'T EVEN SEE.╋
╋THAT CAN BE HELPED.╋
Suddenly there is a glittering point in the shadow world of my mind, as a star forming in the dark. Then another, and another, they spring up out of nowhere, and suddenly
TERROR   CHAOS
MY EYES, THEY BURN!
My eyes, they burn with the light of a thousand stars, all around, above me, beside me, under me, I see them all at the same time, as a thousand burning eyes staring at me, a surrealistic nightly landscape of unmoving points, and in between the shadowslopes of unending nothingness and cosmic dustclouds.

Dizziness, vertigo cramps my stomach, which they said doesn't exist, but I can't think. I am turning around and around, falling, falling into that nothingness, between those thousand points of light. They are changing now, their light dims, and they open and stare at me, from everywhere. Thousands of eyes, good eyes, eyes of old women, then they turn red, very slowly. They begin dripping strings of blood pearls between the clouds of darkness, shapes begin to form among them, fearful faces of old women, with scared smiles around their wrinkled mouths. So many pictures of fear, yes, and also of love, love, love; now the smiles are getting wider, the mouths split, toothless red mouths from ear to ear. A thousand electric knives in my thousand hands, and they cut and cut and I can't stop them. The mouths vomit blood, and spit it at me in slow-dripping clouds of red. The thousand knives are shaking uncontrollably between my wet fingers, while I hate and desire and love the old women. The rivers of blood stream between the stars; they're drowning them, suffocating them. Why doesn't the blood stop flowing? It approaches me with its sticky fingers, but no, they're my own hands, my own fingers, all red and dripping. There is no getting away from them; I drop the thousand knives. There's no escape from all the eyes, the staring dead eyes all around; they stare and drip scarlet into my naked brain, an enormous petrified landscape, they read my thoughts, they make them real. I must get away, must get away, their stares are burning, and I can't close my eyes on them, must get away MUST GET AWAY MUST GET AWAY AWAY AWAY AWAY AWAY

Far away, below in the underground control rooms, alarm lights were flickering up all over the instrument panels, and hands began running across dials as drunk insects.

"The dials have gone mad! Damn, what's happening? S-76, what have you done to cause this?"

"How should I know what happened? He said he couldn't see, so I opened the lenses outside on the Needle. But he reacts as a lunatic."

"The strain has been too much in too short a time. Shock reaction, back to the moment of his crime. We must get him away from that point, it's too dangerous."

"The only trigger I can imagine is the sight of the stars. After all, we did expect a mild reaction, but certainly not THIS."

"Close the lenses. All of them."

"But then we can't—"

"SHUT THE LENSES, ALL OF THEM!"

Darkness comes, but the blood stays. Slowly it crawls through the veins, nursing my brain with synthetic fluids; it seeps into the cells of my existence, poisons them, easily, slowly, deliberately. I can't see, I don't want to see. Outside, there is the sound of a million indifferent stars; softly they cry for me. They whisper to me, as mother, dear mother, my dear mother, who never existed.

"But I don't see how only the sight of the stars could trigger a re-action like this."

"Remember that from the earth only about five thousand stars at most are visible with the naked eye, the atmosphere closes off all the rest. Beyond the atmosphere, that number is quite higher, but that's beside the real point. Which is that he doesn't see with two eyes as a normal human being. He sees with sixteen lenses, clustered all around the body of the Needle, around HIS body, as stiples on a spi-der's back. HE SEES IN ALL DIRECTIONS AT THE SAME TIME. Try to imagine a man imprisoned in a closed bowl which is completely covered with mirrors inside, giving light, so that he is able to see in-side, everything in all directions. This is more or less the effect open space has on him, a complete and utterly terrifying alienation."

"Then he must be able to conquer that alienation. Our astronauts have learned to accept this with their sixteen telescreens."

"But can't you see that it isn't the same? Those astronauts could choose to watch whatever they wanted on whatever screen they preferred. He hasn't a choice, the lenses are his eyes!"

"Then he'll have to learn to use them. Open the lenses, slowly this time, one after another, lens after lens, so that he has to accept them one by one."

"He won't. His brain won't accept them, I tell you, it isn't able to take that much information at the same time."

"Then whatever goes wrong or went wrong is your fault, S-76. You should have foreseen this, you should never have opened all the lenses. I'll have to mention it on your next report."

The bespectacled man in white turned to his machines. His outstretched fingers playfully touched them, softly, caressing them as a lover's hand. The red light mirrored crimson in his spectacles; he seemed an extention of the machines. "Damn that time-lag between our conversation," he murmured, "heaven knows what is going on outside there, what has happened, before we learn of it here."

The voice out of space was silent now, but the instruments in the Needle loyally continued transmitting their observations. Clinking, rattling, everything taken straight out of the brain of the semihuman being which once had been given the name Charles Harkson-8. The silent facts told the men in white more than did the voice itself.

I am walking on an enormous chess field, a battlefield. The players wear skeleton faces, and they rise out of rivers of blood flowing between the squares. There is no escaping the blood. As a continuously growing amoeba it drifts silently between the stars, dripping its poisonous feelers over my eyes, through my eyes into my naked helpless brain, and I can't close my eyes, can't shut off my brain to it. A player appears, a white phantom figure, two-dimensional: a reflection of my opponent? He has no depth, no real menace; I discard him and he changes into a mass of blood which flows down onto the field, and disappears. Another appears. He is dressed in silk, unreal, approaching me as a moth drawn by light. He is a moving, pulpillating amoeba of dark light; I burn his wings and he changes into an eye, staring at me accusingly, then he becomes darker and darker, and is gone. Strings of pearls rise from the field, very white, very innocent, but rust-colored blood crawls over them as a hideous caterpillar. I fear the blood, it disgusts me, and it is everywhere.

She rises among the thousands of star-eyes, two red suns flare in her white-haired skull, burning, burning so bright, so dreadful. Her arm moves, and it is a part of the galaxy which is displaced by the movement, carelessly thrown beside. You're just nothing, she whispers, but it is the voice of a million radio-waves from a million dying stars which thunders in my ears. Why do you come to me, when the only thing you can do is sit there, panting, looking up at me as a dog? You aren't a man. You aren't real. You're nothing. Why can't you do SOMETHING?

Mars is a red rubine in her toothless mouth, and a few stardrops glide along her long legs as she moves against the background of eternal darkness, as a fading projection. I want to hold her, I need her. I need her.

"Damn, damn, damn! What is happening with that . . . thing? It acts as if it had received a strong dose of psychedelics. The initial shock reaction should be gone by now. He should have full control of his brain-centers by now, but he just isn't reacting normally to ANYTHING.

"That moment of shock must have triggered something which has been building up for many years, a chained beast in the dark caves of his mind. It's almost incredible that the psychmeds haven't discovered it; must have been hidden in the deepest centers of the unconsciousness. Anyway, it isn't fading away as we hoped, and we're stuck with it, like it or not."

"Then I suggest an artificial psychoshock to restore him to normality."

"To normality? H-35, the time of primitive shock therapy is long past, if you will please remember this. We have placed it—him—in a situation no human being has ever been before. We can't foretell the effects of a second shock."

"But that brain is MAD! We can't trust anything it transmits to us; all that information and we can't do ANYTHING with it!"

"Of course not, we're receiving hallucinations, not objective truths, not even his real subjective reactions to what he sees. What we get are images out of his own mind, superimposing upon his reactions to outer space; changed in shape and meaning. He is distorting reality, changing it and adapting it to his own needs. The brain is at war with itself, and to save itself, the submerged has taken over: we see space all that information and we can't do ANYTHING with it!"

"But we can't do anything with that! We need information about space out there, we have to know how a normal brain reacts to the conditions we've imposed on it. Not the ravings of a psychotic!"

"And we're obtaining informations, F-54. They are distorted, as if the lenses were looking inward as well as outward. Outer space and the space inside his brain have come together."

"Yes, but how long will it take to sort out what is important to us, the essentials WE need?"

"How should I know? The only thing for us to do is try shaping it into something that makes sense. Some kind, any kind, of sense! But it hardly matters, does it? If we make the Needle turn back now, we're losing everything. If we let it continue, there's still a chance that the brain will restore itself to sanity."

"All right then. Let the Needle continue."

Outward, I am speeding. It is as if I can sense the movement, the steady acceleration. I can see it, and then again I can't. It's strange, confusing. It's as if I'm looking through a murky glass into a dark room, and in THAT dark room . . . and so on. I can see all the dark rooms and shrouded glasses, endlessly going on, and I, I am falling into them, shards of glass keep on splintering on all sides, as I crash through glass upon glass upon glass—outward, inward? How can I know? I am Charles Harkson-8, and I am dead. They say I'm a convicted and executed paranoic murderer; but then again I can't be Harkson-8, because I am the thing they call the Needle, I am a part of the instrument panel and its metal hide. My nerve endings are electric cells and circuits. My feet are photon streams, and I am pushing myself forward, swimming, diving into the darkness of all the rooms, which are getting smaller all the time. Fighting the current, with microscoping strokes, against the tides of the space-dust sea, against waves of burning light and clouds of impenetrable black. I am a rubber heart, pumping synthetic blood and feeding fluids through my plastic veins. I am Man, or let's say PART of man, going out to meet space, to greet darkness. Why do they insist that I'm Harkson-8? I am afraid of him, afraid of what he's done, afraid of what he might do. He's looking at me, from the heart of my body, and his eyes are very clouded and staring. I cannot be Harkson-8; he remembers, he remembers too much, and I do not want to remember. I do not want to remember.

The park is a green sea of synthetically grown grass, with white islands on it, drifting away on timewinds for the years they have left. They are all there, the Old People, sitting and resting; they keep on living with plastic lungs and transplant hearts, some even with teleeyes when their own have worn out. They live through youth, returning all the time through eternity. Mummies with crawling insect hands and blind eyes. My father, you never knew what grew out of your seed. My mother, you never saw the child you gave to the world. Uncaring for each other, and each uncared for, there they sit, the dummy people, as curiosa in a public museum. They sit, they stand, sometimes they talk, a few hushed words, without feeling, without meaning except to themselves. Only the Watchers care for them, and they're paid heavy wages for it, because it means real work. I am walking through their endless rows, looking up and down on them as on cold lifeless statues. My hands are still shaking, after my last fight with Marge. I have left her without another word, but her insane accusations and her naked contempt still hover above me as a cloak. The old woman is only sitting there, her hands fluttering over each other as gray dusty moths over a light she keeps hidden in the palms of her hands. Her eyes stare through me as through a glass wall into a dimly remembered past. Her mouth crawls into a thin-lipped smile, but not for me! Nobody ever smiles at me! I stop.

Hello, Mother. How do you feel today? As good as yesterday, no doubt, and as good as last year. Why don't you answer me, Mother? I asked you a very civil question. No, I must rephrase that, a NICE question, a KIND question. Because I am a kind and nice man, and I just want to talk to you. You see, Mother, I have to talk to someone. So speak to me, Mother, look at me. Don't keep on staring right through me as if I weren't here. I AM here. I talk to you. I touch you, see? Now . . . don't be frightened! Please, don't be SCARED OF ME! I don't want to hurt you . . . I just want to . . . to SEE you . . . to TALK to you. To REALLY talk to you. Because I . . . I LOVE you, Mother. You're my mother, aren't you? Your fruit was born in Med-Cent. So I should love you, shouldn't I, because you gave me the world, didn't you? Please don't look like that, you frighten ME being so scared. Now just smile at me, please? Won't you do that, such a simple thing, just one little smile for your little boy who came to see you? And won't you love me for that? Won't you LOVE ME, Mother? Please, smile at me, love me, please, Mother, please, please, PLEASE! SMILE AT ME! YOU HAVE TO SMILE AT ME! The shaking is all over my body, Mother, can't you see that? All because of you! There's this coldness running through my body cells. Your eyes, soft eyes, they fear me, I can see it, you're afraid of me! You don't love me, YOU DON'T LOVE ME, SILLY OLD WOMAN, YOU DON'T CARE! STUPID OLD WOMAN, MY LOVED MOTHER, YOU DON'T CARE! I HATE YOU! I HATE YOU! I HATE YOU ALL! HATE HATE HATE HATE! RED, SCARLET, RUNNING, WHY IT'S RAINING, BUT THAT'S IMPOSSIBLE, IT NEVER RAINS IN THE PARK, BUT IT'S DRIPPING RED AND WET ALL OVER MY HANDS. I'M SHAKING, CAN'T STOP IT. MY HAND IS SHAKING, BUT NO, NOT MY HAND BUT THE KNIFE IT HOLDS, THE SHAKING ELECTRIC KNIFE WHICH IS SHAKING IN MY HUNDRED HANDS, ALL CUTTING AND CUTTING A WAY THROUGH THE RED SO I CAN SEE AGAIN. WHAT HAPPENED TO YOUR EYES, MOTHER? WHY ARE THEY SO STICKY, AND WHY ARE THEY RUNNING DOWN YOUR FACE? THEY'RE RED TOO, AND PULPY. IT'S ALL SO RED, I CAN'T SEE, MY EYES, THEY'RE BURNING FROM THE RED, EVERYWHERE YOUR MOUTH IS OPENING AND CLOS-ING, YOUR EYE SOCKETS DRIP, ALL OVER MY HANDS AND THE RED GRASS. WHY DON'T YOU CLOSE YOUR MOUTH, SO THE DRIPPING STOPS? I CAN'T HEAR YOU, WHAT DID YOU SAY? WHY CAN'T I HEAR YOU, YOUR MOUTH SO WIDE OPEN, AND SO BIG, GETTING BIGGER ALL THE TIME BELOW YOUR CHIN, A RED SPURTING HOLE, RED AGAIN. PLEASE STOP,

PLEASE CLOSE YOUR MOUTHS, I CAN'T HEAR, I CAN'T HEAR, THE RED
IS DROWNING ME, PLEASE STOP THAT SILENT SCREAM, WHY DON'T
YOU STOP IT SHUT OFF THE RED PLEASE STOP IT ANYONE STOP IT
STOP IT STOP IT PLEASE PLEASE PLEASEPLEASEPLEASEPLEASEPLEASE-
PLEASEAAAAAAAAAAAAAAAEEEEEEEEEEHHHHHHHHIIIIIIIIIIIIIIIHHHHHHHHHHH

Pain all over my body, but they said I have no body; how can I
feel pain? My hands and legs and brain, they're burning with red and
blue fire, and I can't stand it, I scream and scream, a dead scream
continuing and continuing, but no, it's him screaming, it's HIM it's
HIM stop the pain please stop the pain please . . .
Silence. Darkness.

"It was the only alternative. We had to take the risk this time, unless we wanted a complete catatonic withdrawal on our hands."
"Yes, the electroshock has him unconscious now. But how do we
continue from here? What will he do now?"
"I don't know. No one can know. It . . . he's asleep. But he's still
emitting . . ."

Marge, with the soft and slightly too thick lips, and her great
empty eyes. Marge, to whom I can speak of all my troubles. Marge,
who always understands. Always understands. Always understands.
I remember the moving plastic texture of her dress as I lay my
head in her lap. Slowly I'm descending on it, as a tired bird returning
to its nest. Looking upward from there, I see her face, an enormous
madonna of flesh-tinted stone. It is time-suspended in the nothingness above me, as an idol looking down between dustclouds; her
mouth is smiling, partly hidden by her big breasts. My fingers crawl
as crabs along her thighs, they finger the photoelectric cells, opening
her dress. Now I feel the softness and warmth of her skin against my
face, her laugh as my hair tickles her belly. The pounding of her
heart drums into my ears, and begins to influence my own blood
rhythm.
She speaks: "I wonder why you ever asked me to sign a four-year
marriage. I'll be glad when it's over. You don't need me. You don't
need a real woman. The only thing you want is affection, not love,
and you can't give anything in return. You're content having someone caring for you. But you don't give ANYTHING in return. . . ."

"We'll never get this mess sorted out. This is no job for us, we
aren't qualified for that. We need a good psychmed."

"Out of the question, we can't bring an outsider in. We must work it out ourselves, with the assistance of the psychcomp. There must be something that makes sense in his behavior; some semilogical pattern to which he is adapting. Once we have discovered which one, we can try to reverse the process."

Dimly through Marge, I can also see the other woman, the woman from the old painting, not a syncolori, but a REAL painting, with mixed colored substances put on canvas. That woman with the giving eyes, who is bent over and feeding the small child. The woman who looks like Marge; or rather is it Marge whose face reminds me of that woman? How can I tell?

After my working hours there's the long time to kill, the many hours with nothing to do. Then I go over to the Old Museum, almost no one ever goes there now except me. I just sit on the chair, and look at the reflection of my own self in the colordimensions of the canvas. She does remind me of Marge . . . of Marge? Now why do I say that? Marge? Who is Marge? I don't know anyone by that name. I am painting that window into inner space-time myself, re-creating with a pencil of my mind and colors of my dreams every feature, the points of light in her eyes, the smoothness of the lines of her neck, the red crown of her bared nipple, the outstretched, wanting arms of the small child she's holding.

"He . . . He's returning backward! The shock we gave helped him pass the panic scene, but he's on another sidetrack now, even further away from sanity."

"What means SANITY in his case? It's logical, in a way: his mind refused to accept a rehearsal of the amok scene, so to save him from complete collapse, it opened the channels to his own past. He's traveling backward in subjective time."

"But why? Why doesn't he just . . ."

"Can't you guess? We all know he's a tubereac, a mental throwback. They are a case apart in psychoanalysis. Something is inborn with them, which begins to distort their minds from early puberty. Finally this results in a complex search-pattern which dominates them, but not often is the end result such a violent amok murder as happened with this man. The instinct for mother-love dominates everything, though mostly they're unaware of it themselves. The old woman he cut to pieces was a symbol he had been searching for, and when she rejected him, he exploded. We learn very quickly when someone is a tubereac, and put them under strong psychcontrol. Harkson's first marriage was canceled when we found out about him, and psychcenter took all memories of this out of his mind. Then MedCent arranged his second marriage with Dr. Marge HR-889-Q. But even she couldn't give him what he wanted, so he transferred his love to the old woman, and killed her. His sane mind can't stand it, however; anything is preferable to remembering what really happened. So the present—his future—is closed to him, and the search has started again . . . backward this time."

"The whole thing is your fault, S-76. Your stupid idea of opening all the lenses at the same time gave him the initial shock that started the whole mess."

"Discussing past errors of judgment is of no avail now, gentlemen. Maybe this return into subjectivity will turn out for the best. If he returns far enough, maybe we'll find the base of his instability, the starting point of all tubereacs."

"But when will he stop? He just can't go on and on till he's a blubbering six-month-old baby. We have to return the Needle, no use losing all that expensive equipment. We'll have to find another guineapig and start all over again."

"Why? Even if we return the Needle, we can't do anything with it, it's all fitted and adapted to his brain-patterns. We send the Needle out to discover what sends a man mad beyond Venus, and psychotic or not, we'll learn it from him. The Needle MUST continue."

"But he's INSANE right now! There must be a way to end this psychosis, some cure or shock therapy which we can put through to him, even in his condition."

"He's had all this, after his first marriage was canceled. A daily dose of subliminal images through his viewphone at the office. The therapy was stopped when they thought him normal again, especially as there were at that time several more urgent cases of tubereacs to deal with. But he wasn't cured, as Dr. Marge found out, he only put it all deeper and deeper in his subconscious, and now he has opened all the dark caves of his mind."

"There must be a plug even for this hole. He's living in memories, in hallucinations, right now, isn't he? Can't we produce some of our own and shock him back to reality?"

"We can always try, though you realize that we're very limited when dealing with the Needle."

Slowly I feel myself going through the dark sea of nothingness, although the stars don't move. They keep on staring at me, a hideous painting of dead eyes, something out of a nightmare, a surrealistic three-dimensional freak painting. And I am going out and out, and the fear is crawling around in my nonexistent belly as some rare beetle in the killing bottle. . . . But I don't have anything to fear, really, have I? I don't exactly know where I am, and why I am here, but surely there is a reason for my being here, and moving here. There always is a reason for everything. Soon now, school will be finished, and the speakvisionoperators will transmit their "lesson finished" signal. I will take off my earcaps, and take my fingers from the electrowriter, and then I'll leave with the hated others. Toby B-65 will be there, and Harvill 00-3A, and Mac 33, and Ho-Ling 98-C, and all the girls with their tattooed legs and neck-blouses, leaving their breasts free, and I'll have to keep myself from staring at them. They're all too big and too heavy for their age, ever since they started distributing the hormopills at the age of twelve. The corridor will fill with their secret whisperings and stupid giggling. I'll have to face them, knowing that they all know by now about my unsuccessful meeting with Caroll D-1226. I should have known that the stolen energeopill was cheap stuff, and that I wouldn't be able to give it to her three times in a row. I'm afraid to pass them, but it's no use staying here till they're all in the recreation rooms. I tried it once, but then the screen had flared up with DESK 5 WHY DON'T YOU LEAVE? I had mumbled something, but then they had come and taken me to that special room where they began asking all those funny questions. No, it is better to go now, and walk through that endless corridor of mocking smiles and remarks. I'll just ignore them. Maybe later I can slip out of recreation room VN-77 and go out for a walk in the synthopark. There I'll be alone, looking upward to the dark velvet with the diamond tears. I'll watch them till the tears come into my eyes, till they seem to fall down on me.

"Maybe this will help. There isn't much else we can do. Now, send this tape through the emitter, and try to make his brain project it as clearly as possible. We can't be sure, of course, how well a projection will succeed on the insides of the lenses."

A shadow moving in the emptiness? Something alive? That's impossible, there's no atmosphere here, so there can be no life. Yet it is beside me, growing, colors flowing into shapes. An enormous face is materializing. It is looking at me lovingly, a deep understanding glance. It brings tears to my eyes. I am crying now, my tears are white pearls falling away from me. I cry from love for that face, which is growing and reshaping from a spectral protoplasm. This is the woman I know, the woman I love, and have searched for so long. I stretch my arms out to her. Yes, yes, I'm coming to you! But what is that?

Who is that man? That little man who leaves me and is running to the woman? A small, idiotic, distored man, who stops now and is staring at the enormous face. The figure doesn't stir, yet now I can see the face of the man, a grown-up man, but his eyes are the staring eyes of a madman, his tongue hangs out of his mouth, dripping saliva onto his chin. A man whose face I know. I . . . I do not know it. I do not know that man.

+SAY IT, DAMN YOU! REMEMBER THAT FACE. REMEMBER.+

Voices. My own voice maybe, multiplied by echoes? Why should I say that to myself? I don't know that face. I don't want to.

+REMEMBER. REMEMBER. REMEMBER. WHO IS THAT MAN? REMEMBER.+

The words are drumming in my radio-ears, a voodoo drum. The voices continue. Why don't they stop? I don't want to remember that face, I DON'T WANT TO.

+REMEMBER. REMEMBER. REMEMBER. REMEMBER.+

NO, NO, NO!

+REMEMBER. REMEMBER. REMEMBER. REMEMBER. REMEMBER. REMEMBER. REMEMBER.+

NO NO NO NO

+REMEMBERREMEMBERREMEMBERREMEMBERREMEMBERREMEM-BERREMEMBERREMEM+

STOP IT, STOP IT! YES, I REMEMBER. I REMEMBER.

I KNOW THAT MAN.

I AM THAT MAN.

BUT THAT'S IMPOSSIBLE. I AM HERE. I HAVE JUST LEFT SCHOOL. I CAN'T BE THAT MAN.

+YOU ARE THAT MAN. YOU ARE THAT MAN.+

I CAN'T BE. WHY DON'T THEY LEAVE ME ALONE? WHY DO THEY KEEP ON TORTURING ME? I HATE THEM. ALWAYS TRYING TO MAKE ME REMEMBER THINGS I DON'T WANT TO REMEMBER. THEY'RE ALL THERE, THE SMILING AND MOCKING FACES OF THE BOYS AND GIRLS OF MY ROOM, AND THE CORRIDOR STRETCHES ENDLESSLY BEFORE ME. I WALK THROUGII THEM, I HATE THEM, I IIATE TIIEM!

HATE. RECOGNITION.

SOMETHING IN ME RECOGNIZES!

THOSE WHITE LIGHTS OUTSIDE, THEY FORM A PATTERN, AND I KNOW THAT PATTERN, I FLOW INTO IT, I RESPOND COMPLETELY TO IT, AND IT IS ME AND I AM IT, TWO BLUEPRINTS OVERLAP AND COM-PLETE, WE'RE FREE, I'M FREE!

STOP IT! STOP THE PROJECTION, SOMETHING'S GOING WRONG. STOP THE PROJECTION AND TURN BACK THE NEEDLE, QUICK NOW, BE . . .+

I'LL SHOW THEM! I RAISE MY FISTS AND I STRIKE OUT, I SMASH
INTO THEIR CURSED MOCKING FACES, I GRIP THEM AND THROW THEM
AGAINST THE WALLS AS PAPER DOLLS, I BREAK THEIR BONES BY
BRUTE FORCE, THEY ARE JUST AS TOYS TO ME, PLAY SOLDIERS, STU-
PID LIFELESS DOLLS, THEY CRUSH BETWEEN MY FINGERS, FADE INTO
TRAILS OF BLOODIED DUST, I DANCE ON THEM, STAMP ON THEM, WITH
HANDS AND FEET, I AM LAUGHING AND CRYING BECAUSE I HATE
THEM, OH! HOW I HATE THEM!

Circuits are clicking, lamps explode as miniature novas, small red
suns who quickly die. The rubber heart is beating and beating,
pseudoblood is running through plastic veins.

"Projection turned off. Now the transmitter."

"Transmitter turned off."

"Good. Tranquilizers, and quick."

"Done."

"No, you didn't."

"But I DID! Here, tranqies three to six, injected . . . That's funny,
the control lights aren't burning. The brain should have had them."

"Try ranges seven to nine."

"Done. They don't work either!"

"That's impossible, they can't fail ALL at the same time. Some-
thing's going very wrong. ATTENTION! ALL CONTROL UNITS OF THE
NEEDLE. EMERGENCY PLAN THREE. START SIDE CONTROL AT THE
NEEDLE. TRY ALL TRANQIES UP TO RANGE FOURTEEN. BEGIN CLOS-
ING OFF CENTRAL PROPULSION. THEN START SIDEWARD PROPULSION,
AND BEGIN OPERATIONS FOR TURNING THE NEEDLE."

"Sideward propulsion isn't working."

"Central propulsion refuses to stop!"

"EMERGENCY PLAN FIVE. CLOSE ALL LENSES OF THE NEEDLE.
TRANQIES RANGE SIXTEEN, IMMEDIATELY ON THE BRAIN. SLOW
DOWN HEARTBEAT AND RESPIRATION."

"They don't work! My God, NONE OF THEM WORKS!"

"None of the control units works. He has turned them off somehow."

"But that's impossible. That would mean that . . ."

"Exactly. We can't turn the Needle back, because it's ours no
longer. He has taken over completely."

"His position. H-65, ask the comp to calculate his exact position
right now!"

"Done already. The same point where the other ships failed."

"Then there's no doubt possible: his return in subjective time was
more than only an escape mechanism! Something has been influenc-

ing him, maybe from the very start, unnoticed by us; just as it has influenced the others before him."

"Then it must be a completely unknown force, a mental power strong enough to dive into the subconscious parts of a man's brain, and unlock something which even we have been unaware of. That force, whatever it turns out to be, has given him the power to seize control of the Needle and close all our control units down."

"Not that force itself, but that which it has freed from his subconscious."

"Who can tell? We can't even guess if it's artificial or not. It can be something out of his own mind, or something else, like a cloud of energy that moves around the sun at those coordinates, a form of psychic energy undetectable by our instruments."

"No, it has to be something else. The reaction started with his first sight of the naked stars. The second shock reaction came when he passed the Venus orbit. It would have to be something with a pattern . . . remember the words of the brain? 'RECOGNITION . . . THOSE WHITE LIGHTS OUTSIDE, THEY FORM A PATTERN . . . IT IS ME AND I AM IT . . . TWO BLUEPRINTS . . . WE'RE FREE . . . I'M FREE!' What about a pattern of stars?"

"There's no way of finding out right now. He, or else that which has taken him over, is in full control of the Needle now. But the instruments are still sending, he hasn't turned them off, only those by which we could control him."

Slowly time flows on, through unending landscapes of light-pointed darkness, sparkling energy beacons on clouded velvet. Sometimes I think I have slept, but I can't be sure. I am going quicker.

Slowly, I begin to see the sun.

I really begin to SEE the sun.

SUN. The right words don't exist to tell what I see. It is a blazing ball, a firecrown in the heart of the universe. A burning eye in the chaotic center of nothingness. Flames as lazy tongues, slowly they rise and sink down again, as a slowed-down picture. A star of everlasting morning, but not lighting the darkness around it.

The sun is my companion now. The sun is always, unending. The sun is the indisputable empress of space, blazing through all eternity in anger and fury, a tyrant, a queen, a mother. Her burning arms reach out for me. She begins to mingle with the other images in the stars. Now she is burning above a rock landscape, and hairy things who walk on two legs are kneeling before her. Then she becomes the eye of a gray-greenish monstrosity of teeth and nails, whose shriek seeds fear into the jungle. The images change, and now all is silent, a world of red lava, and a petrified sun above it, so red that I can't stare into it. But I am warm and safe, protected from everything. There is a constant static movement in time and space, and I am part of it. I am dozing, I am content. Then suddenly there is chaos, fear, eruption. I am rejected by Mother, falling into darkness and fear, into light and terror. Burning, painful light everywhere, but it fades, and the darkness comes back; I want to go back to the darkness, where there is peace and rest and safety, return to sleep, endless dreamless sleep.

Sometimes the voices speak to me, they order me to do things I don't want to do, and don't do. But they are fading too, and I just don't listen to them anymore.

"That's it! That's the pattern of it all. Fools that we were, there's nothing out there, no unknown force, but man himself. Man and everything that is INSIDE man has been inside him for centuries. We should have understood it as soon as his mind began returning to the past. Man has memories reaching further back than his own life, patterns endlessly repeated on his very brain cells, racial memories of the time when reptiles walked the earth, and even further. Man grew out of the molecules and atoms of earth, and they left their traces imprinted on the cellular brain construction of man. Deep down in the subconscious it has been waiting for something, maybe a pattern of stars from the time when the earth was closer to the sun after its birth, to wake it. Now he is retreating fully, milliards of years in time, though time has no meaning left now. The world's past becomes one with his own, can't you see that? Don't you understand what symbol the sun has become to him? He is disintegrating himself, going beyond unbirth."

There is only ME now. I am a small needlepoint in eternity, a lost miniature planet, a tumbling meteor. The stars are far lightning, unimportant.

There is only the sun, gaping, vomiting fire, a hell mouth, and yet inviting, awaiting. I like the sun, it's the only thing alive in this universe, except me. The sun is more real than the strange voices who keep on whispering. I could shut them off if I wanted to, but I just don't care. I am gathering speed, as a leaf in a sucking river. The stars unfold around me, as small flowers.

An eye, a burning eye looking at me, a hand, a beckoning hand, an outstretched hand, an expecting hand. FOR ME.

I have been bad, I have left Mother, and then I couldn't find her. But now I have found her back, and I'm going home. The naked rays beat upon my brain, patterns of bloody rivers appear on my eyes, they crack, they burn! Want. Desire. Go back. I'm breathing slower, and slower. My body tries to bend forward, but I have no hands and no body. Steel cables writhe as mad snakes in my insides. I am burning inside, but it is not important. I begin to melt, but I don't feel anything. Mother is speaking to me, with the soft voices of a million dead stars. Mother is loving me, rocking me gently in her protuberant arms. Mother needs me, Mother loves me!

I am glowing red now, a little sun of my own, I am changing shape, going quicker and quicker. I can't see now.

I'm going back. Back home.

To Mamma.

A Problem in Bionics

by Pierre Barbet

Translated from the French by Stanley Hochman

Pierre Barbet has been writing novels for "Fleuve-Noir" and for other French series for a dozen years and in them he has experimented with some far-out themes and replays of history's might-have-beens. In real life, he is Dr. Claude Avice, a pharmacist and an expert on bionics, and this short story—one of very few that he has written—reveals his expertise in that field.

You know what vacations are like. . . . You flop down on the beach, forget your troubles, and let the sun toast your epidermis. You may not have put away much of that seafood lunch, but still you lie there like a lizard, your mind a complete blank. You're not even interested in that well-stacked little bundle who's trying to soak up as much melanin as possible so that she can drive her girl friends wild with envy.

There I was, prone on the gray, grainy sand of the Paestum coast.

Doric temples don't say much to me. I get as much of that kind of thing as I need simply by staring at the columns of the Madeleine while killing time waiting for a helitaxi. Oh, I'm not really above it all. When it's not too hot I like to stroll among the ocher-colored old ruins. They bring you back centuries to the time when our ancestors the Gauls weren't worried about the atomic bomb but simply about the possibility that the sky might cave in on them. . . .

Anyway, I was happily snoozing away when suddenly a shadow came between Phoebus and yours truly.

"Octave Dumont, I presume . . ."

"No! It's Dr. Livingstone! Beat it, will you," I said, peering over my sunglasses.

"So, flatfoot," the stranger went on, "you don't even recognize me."

I shot up on my butt and stared hard at the intruder.

Well, what do you expect? Even a guy who's with the GEIS (General European Information Services) can be sensitive about some things. Me, I hate being called "flatfoot." Cops are necessary. Not everybody appreciates their hustle, but they're like whores— they've been around since the beginning of the so-called civilized world, and you can't get along without them.

Then I recognized who it was who was troubling my *dolce far niente.* "Nathaniel! What the hell are you doing here?" Because, sure enough, the guy was none other than a member of the Process group I'd worked with in England on a dirty business involving ultrasonic weapons.

As a GEIS member, this hippie enemy of violence and pollution had called on me to help smooth out a few rough spots in our somewhat less than perfect society. . . .

"To tell the truth, I was looking for you. And I had a hell of a time scouting you out. I need your help. . . ."

"I hope you're not going to tell me that our splendid planet is in danger! I'm a filthy materialist, and vacations are sacred to me. Beat it—tell your sad story elsewhere."

And with this display of healthy indignation, I happily stretched out again and began to take in my neighbor, a juicy brunette whom, until now, I hadn't really appreciated as I should have. She was smearing herself with some kind of bronzing cream and gave me a charming smile. I replied with everything I had, flashing my lovingly brushed ivories and adding a wink pregnant with meaning.

But Nathaniel wouldn't give up.

The guy was tenacious, and once he'd gotten an idea into his noggin, he'd hang on to it for all he was worth.

"That's a shame," he mumbled, sitting down alongside me. "If you let me down, we're in for trouble."

"Okay, okay. I suppose there's no getting rid of you until I've heard your story. Spit it out!"

"Well, it's like this. You know that Process is recruiting people from every level of society and every profession. One of our members is a devoted disciple of Major Jack E. Steele."

"Never heard of him."

"He's the founder of bionics, a fairly new science trying to develop man-made systems which either copy or are comparable to natural systems."

"Doesn't mean a thing to me."

"Listen to me, will you! Bionics is a fantastic science that makes it possible to build machines which operate according to a process that avoids pollution. Thanks to bionics, you can construct collagenic engines that will replace gasoline engines, obtain cold light from the luciferin of glowworms, electric energy from electric eels . . ."

"That's all very interesting, but what are you getting at?"

"Just this. A few of us have gotten together and decided to form a community that would work only with apparatus based on bionic principles. That way we can show the world it's possible to live without unbalancing the ecology or unduly polluting our planet."

"You mean you've gone to work? You, a hippie!"

"I've done it before. I've got an engineering degree, you know. If I've opted out of your corrupt society, it's because it was making me sick to see people exploited so that more and more junk could be consumed and our energy reserves used up. Besides, the only researchers who can get any money are the ones working on government-sponsored projects. Take the CERN people, for example. When they started out they had a hell of a time getting enough dough to build their giant accelerator, which didn't even cost as much as the nose of the Concorde!"

"I'll take your word for it, but I still don't see what you're getting at."

"It's very simple. We're set up on a small island off the Amalfi coast, and *our* society doesn't use even a drop of oil and it doesn't have a nuclear reactor. Some of us are doing research on telepathy. My freaks and I have chosen to work to preserve the future of humanity. Each of us has made some kind of contribution to the community—his science, his money, or sometimes just his willingness to help—and it's been working just fine."

"Great, great—let's just say that you're prophets of the future and let it go at that! But stop beating around the bush. Just what is it you want from me?"

"It's like this. Our secrets, our technical tricks, belong to us, and we don't want some s.o.b. to come along and steal them. If he did, he could take patents out on them, and when the time came, we couldn't make a gift of them to the whole human race. Well, for some time now Conrad and I have noticed that somebody's been mucking around with our stuff. Conrad's a top-notch biologist, a pal from way back. He's another one who gave up speed, hash, and all the psychedelic joys so that he could concentrate on basic research."

"So that's where you're heading! You thought that good old Octave could find out who's been spying on you—"

"—and, if possible, see to it that he can't do us any damage," finished Nathaniel.

"Friend, you're really the king of the pains in the ass! Don't you know that this is the only vacation I'll have till next year!"

"I know, I know. But look, our island isn't half bad. The view of the coast is fantastic, and the weather's just as good as it is here."

"Sure, but who's going to be breaking his hump? Good old Octave! I've had it up to here with that. It's what I do all year!"

"In other words, it's 'no,' " said Nathaniel, looking upset.

"Not so fast. You're a pain in the ass, that's true. But I can't cop out on a friend in need. After all, you pitched in for me when I needed it. I'm going to make you a little present. Ten days, not one more. If I haven't found out what's rotting in Denmark by then, I'm coming back here to relax."

"You're really an ace," bubbled the hippie. "I told Conrad: 'Octave won't let us down, and if he takes the case, our worries are over!' "

"Save your thanks!" I interrupted as I gathered up my stuff. "I'm going back to the hotel to pack my bag and tell them I'll be gone for a while. By a stroke of luck, I brought a few odds and ends with me. Something must have told me I'd be needing them. Where will I find you?"

"Right here," said Nathaniel, pointing to a motorboat beached on the sand.

I left my little paradise after a long, lingering look at the woman who hadn't had the time to become my inconsolable widow. Ten minutes later I rejoined my friend on the beach, and we climbed into his skiff.

I got my first surprise when we started up. Instead of the usual rumbling and belching motor, there was only a sealed tank from which emerged two wires connected to an electric propeller. Just a slight whistle, and the screw began whirling around like mad. We shot away in a majestic wake of foam.

"What's this gadget?" I asked in astonishment.

"One of our bionic applications. Conrad has managed to achieve the dream of generations of researchers: a perfectly viable organic tissue. What you see there is a block of cells coming from electric eels. They provide the power that's propelling us. Part of the current is used to feed the pumps, which both inject a nourishing sugar-and-protein mixture into the tank and also eliminate waste materials!"

Well, this kind of filled me in a little. I have to admit that until then I hadn't put too much stock in this bionics business, but now I had proof that it worked.

Under the circumstances, it wasn't at all strange that industrialists —to say nothing of various governments—were interested in my friend's little secrets and would have paid heavily to get their hands on this particular marvel.

I meditated for a moment as I watched a dame on water skis execute some high-voltage maneuvers. Then I said:

"Since we've got a couple of hours before we reach this Eden of yours, I'm going to ask you some questions so that I can get a few things straight. Are there any newcomers in your community?"

"No. There are thirty of us—fifteen men and fifteen women. At any given time, five or six are off the island, because we always need lab equipment and spare parts. Almost everyone is a former Process member. We've all known each other forever, and I really can't believe that anybody would sell out."

"I wouldn't want to strip you of your illusions, but since I don't know any of your friends, they're all potential suspects. Another thing: Have you noticed any yachts in your area? Any helicopters flying over the island? Any signs of nighttime landings? In short, anything suspicious?"

"To tell the truth, I haven't really paid that much attention. During the day I work in the lab. At night, I try to unwind. However, I do remember that one evening Geneviève showed up with a guy in a diving outfit who looked kind of beat. He claimed that he'd wanted to make the trip from the mainland to the island and back, but that the current had swept him along and turned him around toward us again."

"Did he stay long?"

"No, he left the next day."

"Nothing else?"

"About the only thing I can think of is that for some time now our dog Popov often howls at night. He'll start suddenly and go on for half an hour or so."

"You don't say. . . . Do you happen to have an ultrasonic detector on the island?"

"Of course! Doug has several. He's our physicist—a swell guy!"

"We'll see about that. . . . But anyhow, that's one lead. Messages can be sent and received along an ultrasonic channel. Without anyone but Popov being the wiser, your spy may have already made a good number of reports."

"Do you think it's Doug?"

"I haven't the foggiest! I'm simply setting up hypotheses, that's all. Tell me—how were your suspicions first aroused?"

"It was a lot of little things. Blueprints that weren't where they'd been stored. Apparatus that had been disassembled and badly reassembled. A blurred infrared negative . . ."

"Explain that, will you?"

"Oh, there's not much to explain. One night I had left some infrared film in a camera with its shutter open so that I could measure the thermal emission of an organic culture—you have to be very careful about the temperature norms, you know. The whole room was dark. When I developed the film, it was blurred, as though a strong I.R. ray had hit it. But the culture hadn't been harmed at all."

"Probably some nosy Parker taking pictures at night. Another thing: Do you all get along? Is there any jealousy over the girls? Fights over who's in charge? Differences of opinion about future goals?"

"Nothing like that! Obviously we discuss things, and not everybody is always of the same opinion, but the disagreements are only about minor issues. As for the bedding arrangements, there's no problem there."

All right, now tell me a little about your experiments. The electricity, the collagenic engine, the cold light—that's more than enough to tempt a lot of people. Is there anything else?"

Nathaniel hesitated for a moment.

"Well, I guess I can tell you, but you've got to promise absolute secrecy."

"I should think you'd be able to trust me," I answered, somewhat miffed.

"Of course I can! Well then, it's like this. Our two major achievements are in two very different areas. First there are the neuristor brains—"

"The what?"

"Brains that operate on the model of human brains and that could make giant computers look silly."

"Christ!"

"Oh, the project's nowhere near finished yet, and it will take years to make the units really operational. . . . In addition, there's an ultrasonic radar that imitates bats. Among its advantages is the really important one of not being thrown off by the simultaneous operation of several units. And I almost forgot—Corrine is working on the hibernation of mammals. She wants to slow down cell metabolism. That would be a fantastic advantage to astronauts on long flights. It would eliminate the need to induce hypothermia in them."

"You guys must be crazy! There you are on your little island, revolutionizing techniques used all over the world, and you haven't even established a security system, or hired counterespionage agents. I don't understand how come you weren't all killed a long time ago!"

"Sure, we're afraid that sooner or later we'll be spotted, but for the time being we thought we were safe enough on our island. Who'd ever suspect hippies? Hippies are people who use acid and grass, who go in for trips and happenings. Nuts who practice telepathy!"

"As a cover, it's not bad. But let me tell you something, Nat, my boy. In this rotten world, everything is found out sooner or later. You didn't come looking for me any too soon."

And that's where our conversation ended. An hour later we came alongside a rocky little breakwater. A short time earlier we had heard a news broadcast on the radio: calm reigned in the solar system and so it seemed unlikely that I'd be called away in a hurry. The only important piece of news was that at the international base on

Mars there'd been a sudden drop in electrical output. It had had them worried for a while, but eventually everything had been straightened out.

Four islanders were waiting for us, two of them real sexy kittens to whom Nathaniel introduced me. Corrine—slim, bronzed, blond as Campania wheat—was the biologist working on hibernation. Geneviève, a luscious and well-rounded brunette, was the entomologist. One of the young men, a freckled redhead, was none other than Doug, an American whose specialty was the production of cold light. His father, a super-rich industrialist, provided him with substantial subsidies and didn't worry too much about what they were being used for. The other fellow, tall and Scandinavian-looking, was Conrad, the bionics man. The sun had turned his hair almost white.

They all seemed friendly, open, and relaxed.

Another surprise was waiting for me when Nathaniel pointed to the vehicle which was to take us to the labs. Imagine, if you will, an ovoid contraption raised on eight spread legs; it had six seats resting in cavities on its horny shell, and two headlights that looked like big eyes. It resembled an enormous beetle.

I settled in. Doug sat at the controls and Nathaniel got in alongside me.

The vehicle started up suddenly with a slight lurch and began climbing the rocky slope; since its claws gripped the slightest fissure, its overall performance was extraordinary. In short, here was the all-terrain vehicle so long dreamed about. On the way, my companion explained to me that it was a new bionic product that used a collagenic motor system. A belt of collagen furnished the necessary energy as it contracted after passing through a lithium-salt solution. None of this meant very much to me, but the fact remains that our beetle made no noise, produced no smoke or stench, and crawled through places that would have been inaccessible to any ordinary vehicle.

When we got to the top of the hill, I glanced over at the haze-covered, marvelous cliffs of the Amalfi peninsula.

Then Nathaniel pointed out their compound; merging into the underbrush, the buildings were of a green that made them almost invisible. They looked like giant mushrooms perched on their stems, and because I didn't want to seem too idiotic, I refrained from asking if they had been grown from seeds!

It was already late afternoon, and toward the west the horizon was tinted copper and purple. In spite of this, the scientists were still busy in their laboratories. For hippies, this seemed truly incredible! Our vehicle stopped in front of one of the large mushrooms, and I noticed that the building's roof was made of movable plaques which even I could identify as solar-cell panels.

After a snack had put some heart back into me, my host, who was obviously inexhaustible, suggested we visit the installations while his colleagues had dinner at a Club Méditerranée type buffet.

Nathaniel hadn't an ounce of pity—he insisted that I visit each lab. Moving from vats in which collagen fibers were isolated and cultivated to apparatus that synthesized luciferin—which gave off a greenish but reasonably pleasant light—I saw ultrasonic mechanisms and microminiaturized radar, cells that came from the thermic sensing organs of crotalids and could detect variations of a thousandth of a degree, and gyroscopic balancers that were copies—I was told—of dipterous insects. I was completely buried under an avalanche of technical terms, and I was about to cry uncle when we came to the famous neuristor brain, resting gently in a sterile vat from which led a maze of wires connected to dials and printout units. The visit ended in the kingdom of the good fairy Geneviève, an amazing spot in which hundreds of different insects squirmed in glass cages. There were butterflies, beetles, various kinds of big mosquitoes—enough to keep you scratching for quite some time.

I listened distractedly while Nathaniel explained that certain types of Bombyx could detect a single molecule of unsaturated alcohol emitted by females of the species an incredible distance away—provided, of course, that the wind was blowing in the right direction.

When I finally did plead for pity, Nathaniel called a halt and led me back to the living quarters. Outside, the air was heavy with aromatic essences, and in the sky there were legions of shining stars. We could even see the international space station moving along like a big meteor.

Bionics evidently had not yet revolutionized bedrooms, since I was supplied merely with a simple sleeping bag—which in no way kept me from dropping off soundly.

I had been lying there for a reasonably long time, dreaming of weird machines and dragonflies ridden by pinup girls, when suddenly I bolted awake.

I'm neither a bionic imitation nor a crotalid, but I do have a sixth sense that has often been very helpful—though it may just be that my hearing is better than most people's.

The fact remains that I woke up with a distinct sense that somebody was there. I was in a small room of a prefabricated house, and I could hear a muffled noise, broken off at times as though someone were coming toward me.

I slipped my hand into my valise, which luckily was close by, and took out my revolver—but I couldn't tell if the safety was on! Like an idiot, I had gone to bed without checking it. I put down the gun and reached for the valise with the vague intention of using it as a projectile or shield.

Just then I heard a slight hiss and a sharp rap, followed by the noise of a hasty but careful retreat.

I bounded up and got to the door just in time to see a slender silhouette disappearing among the buildings of the camp. Then a dog began to howl. That was probably Popov. There was no point wasting time chasing my adversary, who knew the place better than I did, so I went back to my room, got out my flashlight, and carefully inspected the floor and my valise. I soon found a tiny dart, which I cautiously removed from the strap in which it had lodged.

There could be no doubt about the fact that I'd been the target. I hadn't been there long, and already someone was eager to get rid of me. What a painful idea!

The rest of the night passed without incident. Of course, I more or less slept with one eye open. At dawn, I pulled Nathaniel from his bed and told him what had happened.

He carefully examined the projectile, then took me into a laboratory where he poked the sharp point into an innocent guinea-pig, which immediately gave up the ghost. That settled it!

"Well, chum, you've had a narrow escape!" grunted my host. "This little gadget had been dipped into a fast-acting poison. Probably curare, since one of our researchers is working on it."

We went off to awaken that unlucky fellow, Carl, who of course swore that he hadn't budged all night. A visit to his lab showed that the cupboard containing his favorite toxins had been broken open, but there was no way of knowing by whom. Probably one of the hippies themselves, because Popov hadn't howled very much. But who? Mystery . . .

During the day I was again treated to innumerable technical explanations to which I barely listened: I was waiting for nightfall. My adversary, disappointed by his lack of success, would no doubt show himself again. Out of an excess of caution, I asked Nathaniel to keep his ultrasonic radar trained on the approaches to the island.

Total failure. I might as well say immediately that no suspicious boat or spacecraft was spotted, but on the other hand Popov yowled all night long. His response convinced me that at one time somebody had transmitted information to the coast by ultrasonic means, which the dog had detected and protested against in his own way. Be that

as it may, the system obviously had since been abandoned, and we had to find the new trick being used. . . .
I slept very badly, jumping up at the least little noise. But nothing happened.

I spent the next day poking around the island and in the laboratories. This time Nathaniel didn't go with me, but he delegated Corrine as a replacement. Thanks to her smile, my bad temper quickly vanished, and when evening came I was on excellent terms with the pretty blonde.

However, I hadn't forgotten what I was there for. I had dug up somewhere an infrared telescope of extraordinary sensitivity. The gadget was based on the heat-sensing apparatus of crotalids, and with it you could see in the dark as well as if it were full daylight. I therefore decided to spend the night not in my bed—nor alas, in Corrine's—but on a little hill near the compound.

As I'm a pretty crafty type, I announced that I was tired and pretended to retire to my room early. When the coast was clear, I took my telescope and slipped out to the observation post I had chosen.

The hours passed monotonously.

I saw the space lab and a dozen other military and civilian satellites parade across the sky. I was beginning to have a bellyful when my patience was finally rewarded.

A slender form slipped out of one of the mushroom-shaped buildings and moved toward Popov's niche to give him a tidbit. The dog seemed to know his visitor and only let out a few muffled yaps.

Then the shadow moved toward me and the exit to the camp. Uneasy, I hid behind a clump of myrtle as best I could and continued to watch. This time there was no mistake. Instead of heading for my room, the unknown figure was speedily climbing the hill directly toward me. Had I been spotted? After all, I didn't really know the principle on which my infrared gadget worked, and it might very well emit detectable rays. In any case, I no longer needed it. My visitor was now so close that I could clearly see the figure in the moonlight.

My heart was pounding like a drum, and my hand clutched the butt of my pistol. This time I had checked the safety.

But I had not been spotted. The unknown figure climbed to the top of the hill and, digging into a pocket, produced a box. The form was about two yards away from me, and I didn't let the opportunity pass. I sprang like a cougar.

After a brief struggle, my adversary, who was short on muscle, was no longer dangerous. I shone my flashlight into the face of the figure —and saw the seductive features of Geneviève!

"Well, my girl, you've had it!" I grunted. "We're going back to camp, where you have some explaining to do."

Not the slightest bit taken aback, the darling snapped: "Idiot, will you let go of me? What do you think you're doing? I was conducting a night experiment with butterflies, and now you've made me ruin everything, you old lecher!"

The shot carried. After all, her explanation was plausible. When I retrieved the box it really was full of butterflies!

But I'm a pigheaded type, so I decided to check a few things with Nathaniel. We returned to the compound and I pitilessly tore him from the arms of Morpheus and a little redhead.

Then we held a private symposium in one of the labs.

Geneviève gave her version, and Nathaniel seemed to find that it held water. He looked at me queerly.

Suddenly I became irritated, and I carefully began to examine the tiny creatures in the box. Of course, I didn't know what kind of butterflies they were, but I did find it strange that their undersides were yellowish, and I noted as much aloud.

Now it was the darling's turn to seem troubled. She blushed and mumbled a few words in Latin to explain that this species always had yellow tummies.

Nathaniel reacted immediately. Seizing one of the butterflies in a pair of tweezers, he placed it before an ultraviolet lamp. The butterfly began to glow. This time there was no need to explain to me that what I was looking at was fluorescent paint.

A modest triumph. My wily friend attentively examined the lepidoptera under a magnifying glass and spotted microfilms pasted under the wings.

The lady made a sudden dash for freedom, but we caught her and the explanations started. We had our spy, for sure. At the beginning she used to send her messages ultrasonically, but Popov would yowl too much. Then, since the season was right and the wind swept in from the sea every evening, our entomologist began launching her butterflies into the air.

On the coast, an accomplice would wait with a flask full of enticing bits of femininity that drew on the unfortunate males. An ultraviolet flashlight made it easy to spot those that carried the microfilms, and that's all there was to it. . . .

The following day was spent in festivities. Geneviève was publicly spanked and shipped back to the mainland, but not before she had confessed the name of the firm that was paying heavily for this dirty work.

As for me, I went back to my beach.

Only one thing has changed. Just try now to take an innocent stroll along the beach of a certain island near the Amalfi coast. You'll have a surprise coming to you.

The King and the Dollmaker

by Wolfgang Jeschke

Translated from the German by Patricia Simon-Krieger

Wolfgang Jeschke's best-known book is entitled *Der Zeiter*, which can be translated more or less as "The Time-person." It is a collection of excellent stories involving all aspects of time travel. It is a privilege to present the novella that is the keystone of that book—a blending of time past and time future.

"Stay where you are, Collins! Every move now could mean a fracture."

"Yes, Your Majesty," said Collins, and stayed where he was.

"Keep your eyes upon us!" commanded the king.

"Yes, Your Majesty," said Collins, and kept his eyes on His Majesty.

Time was slipping by. There was a deadly silence in the hall. The king was perched nervously on the edge of his throne and stared anxiously at the flickering mirror on the wall. Every time a patrol officer stepped out of the mirror, the king gave a start and leveled his gun at the man. Collins could see that the barrel trembled and that beads of sweat had formed on His Majesty's brow. The intervals grew shorter, and the guards could hardly avoid stumbling over one another. The patrol now had the room under constant control. The mirror twitched every time a man was discharged from or reabsorbed into its field. One guard stepped out into the room, looked attentively about him, and returned with a backward step into the mirror. But there was nothing special to observe. The room was empty. The walls still showed the light spots where the valuable paintings had once hung. Generations of sovereigns who had once peered morosely, critically, or solemnly from the walls upon the most recent offspring of their lineage now peered morosely, critically, or solemnly into some dark corner of the palace cellar which they had never seen during their lifetime. Even the nails had been taken out of the walls, the tapestries removed, the curtains, the furniture, everything. There was only the throne, His Majesty, the patrol's time mirror, which occasionally disgorged and reswallowed a guard, and a man standing at the triply barred and shielded window—Collins, His Majesty's Minister of Personal Security and Futurology.

The throne room was hermetically sealed, doors and windows safeguarded by energy screens. Not an insect, not even a dust particle, could have penetrated the shield, not to mention a minibattleship or a remote-controlled needle grenade.

"Tell us how long this is to continue, Collins. We cannot bear it much longer!" The king gave his minister a beseeching look. He was trembling.

Collins tossed back his cape, unclasped the purse on his belt, and drew from it a temporal strip. He held it at arm's length, as he was a bit farsighted, and examined it scrupulously. He was calm and composed; only the corners of his mouth curled ever so slightly in scorn. He had seen through more ticklish situations than this. "By Your Majesty's leave," he said, "Your Majesty's alarm is really groundless. The patrol knows that it will all turn out for the best. We have twenty-seven more minutes, during which Your Majesty is constantly supervised, before the arrival of this impenetrable ten-second time seal. From the very second that we regain access to the mirror from the timeline, this room will once again be under control."

Collins's finger ran down the temporal strip, tracing the dots indicating the guards' positions, and compared them with the date and time printed continuously along the margin. He had even jotted down the guards' names on the strip. They were his best men. One could not do more. With the exception of one short interruption, the dots lay so close to one another that they formed a solid line. Collins looked at his watch. Everything was running according to schedule.

"What is the latest report?" demanded the king. His voice was hoarse, fear gripped his throat.

"Nothing precise, I'm afraid, in spite of all our efforts. Your Majesty is aware of the fact that WHITE has undertaken transformations which reach far into the future. The seals are fluid, and the impenetrable time block is constantly shifting position. Our investigations are valid for but a few hours, then the temporal strips are worth no more than the paper they are printed on. Yesterday we could still supervise four days into the future; at present, this period is reduced to a scant two hours, and the block continues to grow toward us. But according to our calculations it will soon come to a standstill, so that we will eventually have thirty minutes left to supervise. But all this can of course change, should WHITE undertake a fracture."

"That's just it. That is the problem," whimpered the king. "Do something! How can you loiter about idly when I am in danger?"

"Your Majesty is not in danger," sighed Collins. "That is practically the only thing about which we are certain. After the critical moment is past, Your Majesty will be sitting upon the throne just as Your Majesty does now. Of course . . ."

"Of course what?"

"Now, Your Majesty, we have discussed it often enough. By Your Majesty's leave, should we really bring this up again now, when the moment is nearing?"

The king slouched in his seat and chewed his fingernails.

"Are you certain that I am the one who will be sitting here after the critical moment?" he asked suspiciously.

"But, Your Majesty, who else?"

"Yes, who else," muttered the king, and looked at Collins.

The minister inspected his temporal strip. The stream of dots discontinued, reappeared, only eventually to disappear altogether. Here was the seal, there the block began. What took place at these inaccessible points? Why had WHITE placed them there? Was this some kind of a trap or ruse? He had spent a great deal of time on the problem, had assigned his best men to it, but he had found no solution in spite of the innumerable facts that had been compiled. He was tired. A holiday would do him good. He looked around him at the dreary room, examined its bare walls. Got to get out of here, he thought. Choose any other time. How about dinosaur hunting in the Mesozoic era? He had grown out of that age. And he detested hunting expeditions. Too loud, too much excitement, too much drinking, and for the last few decades terribly overcrowded. They went and killed off the beasts in less than no time with their laser guns. And what if they did? Ugly creatures they were anyway. A minimal fracture. A couple of bone-collecting scientists of some later age would probably be astonished that the animals had disappeared so quickly. They would certainly find an explanation, that was what they were scientists for. The Tertiary period—yes, that would be better. It had been nice and warm then in this region. A couple of weeks of Tertiary. The patrol had a holiday center there. Plenty of rest, excellent food, saber-toothed-tiger steaks. Once, though, he had chosen a year when he himself had been there. Not that it made much difference to him if he was constantly crossing his own path—that had happened to him before, one got used to it. One had a few drinks with oneself, talked about old times, complimented oneself on how good one had still looked then and how on the other hand one had hardly aged at all since; one bored oneself to tears, felt a certain envy appear which could grow to hatred when one saw the bad habits that one had already had then and had long since wanted to get rid of but still had years later. Youth and experience stood face to face, and in between were all those years that one circled about and avoided mentioning but still could not ignore. Everyone knew that this could bring on disastrous time fractures if one were not careful, irreparable damage, intervention by the Committee, at best deportation to an ice age or to one of the first three millennia, at worst eradication from the timeline, condemnation to nonexistence, unless amnesty were granted by means of a special dispensation from the Supreme Council on the Future.

"You just stand about and say nothing!" The king's voice snapped him out of thoughts. "We asked you a question."

"I beg Your Majesty's pardon."

"What exactly is going to happen?" demanded the king peevishly. "Explain it again, step by step."

"Certainly, Your Majesty. Our guards are in control of all of the timeline which is accessible to us and are closely observing the particular area around the palace. There is absolutely no action. That is, as Your Majesty already knows, apart from the doll. . . ."

"Nonsense! Always this damned doll! How often do I have to hear that ridiculous story? What am I paying you for? Always repeating the same foolishness!"

"A small mechanical figure appears," continued Collins, unmoved, "a sort of miniature robot, with which Your Majesty deigns to play."

"Rubbish! How often must I repeat it? What on earth would I be doing with a doll? Have you ever seen me play with dolls? This is utterly absurd!"

"But by Your Majesty's leave, according to the reports of the guards, Your Majesty seems to be quite taken with this small mechanical object."

"But that is just what I don't understand! What am I to do with a doll? Am I a child? Once and for all, enough of this doll! It is beginning to get on my nerves."

The minister shrugged his shoulders and looked at his watch. "I am reporting nothing but the facts when I say that Your Majesty takes pleasure in playing with this figure, actually lays his weapon aside and gives the impression of being relieved of a burden and in extreme good humor, not to say . . ."

"Not to say what?"

"Not to say, well—like a new man."

The king leaned back with a sigh, then shook his head in annoyance and slid nervously forward again to the edge of the throne. "Doll, doll, what the devil does this doll mean?" he brooded. Then, turning and launching into Collins, "For weeks now we have heard nothing from you but reports about dolls and other such nonsense. Collins, you have failed. As Minister for the Personal Security of Our Person you have failed miserably. That can cost you your head; you are well aware of that?"

"By Your Majesty's leave, we have done everything within our means to get hold of the producer of this doll and to find and destroy the doll itself. The research has cost hundreds of years of work by our best specialists in ancient history, time manipulation, and causal coordination. Let me assure Your Majesty without exaggeration that we have done everything, absolutely everything within our power."

"You had orders to cause a fracture in order to avoid this dreadful moment, and what did you do? Nothing! You had orders to find this man in the seventeenth century and to have him disposed of, and was this corrective measure taken? No! And you babble on about your specialists and their hundreds of years of work! It does not interest us in the slightest. Did you hear? Not in the slightest! You have failed!" The king trembled with anger; his fingers tightened around the handle of his weapon. It was aimed at Collins.

"I—I most humbly beg Your Majesty's forgiveness, but as I said, we have done everything within our power."

"Did you have the doll destroyed? Yes or no! If you did, why does it keep reappearing?"

"We did destroy it—at least we destroyed one doll, but an infinite number of such dolls could exist."

"Don't talk nonsense! This simple craftsman can't have made an infinite number of dolls."

"Of course not, Your Majesty, but perhaps two or three of this type."

"And why haven't they been destroyed? Because you failed!"

"As Your Majesty already knows, and as I have allowed myself to emphasize repeatedly, this is in all probability—and in my own humble opinion—not at all where the basic problem lies. This question of the doll is certainly peculiar, but it is clearly just as unimportant as is the craftsman in the seventeenth century. We are dealing with an intervention by WHITE in which this man in the distant past plays either no part or a very subordinate one, in which his function is to lure us onto the wrong track. Your Majesty knows that I have never considered this a very promising lead. How much of a chance could a man in the pretechnical age have had? I personally am convinced that at that time man did not even have electrical energy; they were still experimenting with frogs' legs."

"One can build mechanical automats, Collins, which if they are preserved in museums or private collections can survive several thousand years. But we have other grounds to find this man dangerous. You should have had him eliminated. You had explicit instructions to do so."

"WHITE prevented it," answered Collins with a shrug of his shoulders.

"WHITE, WHITE, WHITE! Let WHITE be damned!"

They were silent. Time was slipping by.

The guards came and went. They now registered every second.
"How long is this to continue, Collins?"
"Exactly eleven minutes and thirty seconds, Your Majesty," answered the minister. He now held his watch in the palm of his hand. After this period the time mirror would blank out and be impenetrable to the patrol for a span of ten seconds.
"What is the purpose of this seal, Collins? Can you explain why WHITE had the seal placed here? What is hidden behind it? Something is happening behind it, but what?"
The king's voice trembled. The tension in the room grew.
"We don't know, Your Majesty," said the minister. "Perhaps it is just a ruse—we will know soon. But Your Majesty need have no fears, there will be no change."
"That is what your guards say. They are dolts," said the king. He coughed and gasped for breath and tugged at the collar of his black cape as if it was too tight. The handkerchief with which he wiped his brow was soaked with perspiration.
"Have you given all the orders? Is everything sealed off?"
"Exactly as Your Majesty commanded. The entire palace has been thoroughly inspected several times, the throne room especially carefully of course. There is not a single square inch that hasn't been meticulously checked. All dolls, toys, and similar objects which we were able to seize in the vicinity of this time-space point have been destroyed. The palace is locked and bolted inside and out. Nothing can penetrate this room unnoticed. Any particle, even a speck of dust, would immediately disintegrate in the energy fields. The doll must either come through the mirror or materialize in a manner unknown us; it is not in the palace now, unless it has taken on a form of energy of which we have no knowledge."
The king looked about suspiciously, as if he could discover some clue that had escaped the attention of the minister's guards, but his weapon found no target. The room was bare, there were only His Majesty upon the throne, the minister, the mirror, and the stream of guards who formed the observation chain.
"I cannot bear to see these faces any longer, Collins."
"Your Majesty has given explicit orders . . ."
"Yes, yes, I know. Are these men absolutely reliable?"
"Absolutely."
"What do you know about this dollmaker?"
"It is an odd story, Your Majesty. A relatively large part of his life seems to contain important historical facts which WHITE does not wish to have changed. As Your Majesty knows, he appears in the year 1623 in a small city in what was then Europe—now our Opera-

tions Base 7—buys a house and apparently earns a living as a simple craftsman, makes few demands on others, mingles little with the townspeople but is respected by all. On August 17, 1629, the period suddenly becomes inaccessible, closed off by a seal which severely handicaps our operations. This seal extends as far as February 2, 1655, covering almost three decades. Nevertheless, we set several of our best specialists to the task of living through the time behind the seal. Your Majesty can hardly conceive of what this meant for those men. But in spite of all our efforts the venture failed; the men were never heard of again. We could find them in neither the fifth nor the sixth decade of that century. Times then were particularly hard, wars were raging, and morale was very low. In short, by the time we could operate again we discovered that our craftsman was dead. We questioned people who knew him. Naturally we cannot examine the validity of the information they gave us, as there are no written records, but this is what we were told: One night he went into a fit of raving madness, and from that moment on he was like a different person. Formerly he had been a respected man whose advice was sought by all, but after this attack he let himself go, fell into the habit of swearing, jabbered incoherently, neglected his work, took to drink, picked quarrels, and proved himself to be generally arrogant and overbearing. For instance, he demanded that his neighbors address him as His Majesty, for which the fellows soundly thrashed him. He had apparently gone mad. He went from bad to worse, living from alms and from what he could occasionally beg or steal. One day he was found hanging by a rope in a barn, where he had apparently been for several weeks. He himself had put an end to his miserable existence. He must have been hastily buried somewhere, for we could not find his grave. We were told that this is commonly done to victims of suicide. We can fix the date of his death with relative certainty to the autumn of the year 1650. As Your Majesty can see, it is all in all nothing remarkable, perhaps not a daily occurrence in those centuries, but by no means an unusual one."

"But this doll, Collins. What about the doll?"

"We succeeded in destroying one doll. Our men blasted it and it exploded. We were not able to reconstruct it completely, but the parts that we were able to gather up in our haste in the dark give evidence of an extremely simple spring-driven mechanism, such as one finds in the clocks and music boxes of that time. There doesn't seem to be anything special about the doll either."

"Did you find anything in the following centuries?"

"We have inspected innumerable mechanical toys, only sporadically, to be sure, from the mid-twentieth century on, as there are such vast quantities of them, but we never came across anything unusual. Occasionally we found in literature evidences of more highly developed mechanisms such as we were searching for, but all our attempts to test the validity of these allusions failed. The mechanical doll was a well-loved fiction at that time, a sort of fairy-tale figure, the forerunner of the robot, I surmise. But the technical basis necessary to develop it is lacking."

"Nothing! Absolutely nothing!"

The minister shrugged his shoulders regretfully.

"How many minutes, Collins?"

"Five, Your Majesty."

"It is enough to drive one mad! Can't a stop be put to this running about?"

"I am sorry, Your Majesty, but it is Your Majesty's own command that the room be under constant supervision. This supervision cannot be countermanded without causing delicate fractures which might have dire consequences for Your Majesty's safety."

The minister kept his eye on his watch and compared the time with the temporal strips in his hand. In four minutes and thirty seconds the stream of dots indicating the guards' positions would cease for a brief period.

"Collins, have you absolutely no idea what is going to happen in the next four minutes?"

"I am afraid we know nothing for certain, Your Majesty, but . . ."

"But what?"

"But, by Your Majesty's leave, I have my suspicions."

It is your damned duty to give thought to the situation and to express your thoughts. So go on and express them!"

"Let us assume that Your Majesty himself, on the basis of experience which Your Majesty will have gained in the future and on the basis of further development of time-travel technique, makes certain points and periods of the timeline which seem important to Your Majesty inaccessible by means of this seal."

"We see. Collins, why did you not mention such an important aspect earlier? That is a very plausible possibility; one can hardly consider it seriously enough." The king smiled in relief. He clung to this thought as to a straw. The idea that he himself could be WHITE clearly flattered him. He snapped his fingers energetically and feverishly concentrated upon the thought. Then his face clouded over again.

"But we would at least have transmitted some kind of explanatory message to ourselves in order to make this horrid situation more bearable."

"Perhaps that is impossible for reasons of security," interjected Collins.

The king shook his head. "But this doll. Where does this confounded doll fit into the picture?"

"Perhaps it is supposed to bring Your Majesty some important piece of information."

"And the dollmaker? No, no, it doesn't fit in."

"Perhaps he has nothing to do with the whole affair, perhaps he is just a secondary figure; but, on the other hand, perhaps he is the source of information."

"Perhaps, perhaps! Is that all you have to say? What do you think you are here for—to reel off vague suspicions? We can do that ourselves. You are responsible for our security. Is that clear? Such nonsense! A primitive tinsmith from twelve thousand years ago has information for us, the ruler of four planet systems and all their moons—how ridiculous! Just empty speculation and foolish twaddle!"

The king was provoked. The barrel of his weapon roamed back and forth, and Collins tried to keep out of firing range.

"Then it was a blind alley, by Your Majesty's leave, which our best forces have wasted centuries in exploring."

The king stamped his foot. "Time doesn't interest us! We want information. We want absolute security for our person, even if your people need thousands of years to guarantee it. If you go down blind alleys, it's your problem, Collins, not ours! You are a miserable failure! We are holding you responsible for the consequences. You understand what that means."

"At Your Majesty's command."

"Our command was: bring information and more information about the present sphere of time and everything connected with it; and you dare to enter this room with your suspicions! You can go to the devil with your crazy notions! We want facts and nothing but facts."

"Very well, Your Majesty, but don't forget the seal on Operations Base 7, an intervention by WHITE which made our work extremely difficult and thwarted our action in the decisive years."

"That may very well be. Perhaps there was at that moment a historical event of great importance. As you said, there was a war at the time. Perhaps our intervention would have endangered a politician or scientist of top-ranking future valence, or the great-grandfather of a politician or scientist, or heaven knows who. But that is all irrelevant. What is going to happen here and now in a few seconds? That is the only thing that matters."

Time was slipping by.

The guards came and went, came and went, dots on the temporal strip.

The king leaned back, breathing heavily. He was as white as chalk and dripped with sweat.

"Thirty more seconds, Your Majesty."

"Collins!" The king's eyes were fixed upon him beseechingly; they were filled with tears. "Collins! Keep your eyes on me! Do you hear? Don't lose sight of me for a single moment! Take note of everything, everything!"

He was leaning far forward, and his eyes swept panic-stricken across the room. He began to see dolls everywhere. They crept out from beneath his throne, came out of the walls, slipped down from the ceiling on threads. Everywhere he saw dangling limbs, expressionless plastic faces, beady glass eyes that glared maliciously at him, tiny fists that brandished daggers as big as needles or aimed minute laser pistols at him.

The king trembled and gnawed incessantly at his lower lip. Fear had complete mastery over him now. It was suffocating him. He felt as if he must either crawl off into a hole somewhere or else scream and shoot about him in blind rage.

The minister gave him a worried look.

"I can't bear this any longer, Collins!" shrieked His Majesty. "Don't just stand idly about—do something!"

His shrill voice burst into thousands of tiny splinter-sharp fragments.

Collins followed the second hand of his watch as it ticked nearer and nearer to the critical moment.

"Now."

The mirror went blank.

The minister looked carefully about the room, then fixed his gaze upon the king. The king suddenly leaned back, crossed his legs, and put aside his pistol so that both hands were free to straighten out the clothing of a small plain doll which he was holding.

The minister blinked and shook his head to dispel the optical illusion, but the doll was still there. It hadn't been there before and now it was there. He tried without success to cope with this new situation. The brain refused to accept what the eyes clearly saw. His Majesty was sitting comfortably on the throne, smoothing out the dress of this small mechanical figure, and smiling delightedly.

"Come, Collins, why are you staring so aghast at us? Have you never seen a doll before? A pretty little toy, don't you think? A dollmaker's masterpiece."

The ten seconds were over. The mirror glowed once again and the first guard stepped out into the room.

"Hello, how are you? Have a nice trip?" the king asked him in good humor.

"He-hello," stammered the bewildered man, and fled back into the mirror.

"Good morning," the king greeted the next guard who appeared.

"G-good morning, Your Majesty," he managed to stutter, and stumbled over his feet in his haste to find the mirror and disappear into it.

"This is quite an amazing doll, Collins. Go ahead and take a closer look at it."

The minister approached hesitantly.

"Would Your Majesty deign . . . an explanation . . . the rapid transformation . . . I mean, I beg Your Majesty's pardon, but I find it incomprehensible that all of a sudden Your Majesty is . . ."

". . . Like a new man, you wanted to say?"

"Yes, Your Majesty."

"You will get your explanation soon enough, in a half hour or so, when this spying finally stops." He pointed to the mirror.

"But, Your Majesty, time is running out. Your Majesty's only chance is to explain the whole situation to me immediately, so that we can undertake a fracture and take all other necessary measures, so that all may still turn out for the best. I beseech Your Majesty, this is possible for only a few minutes longer."

The king let out a peal of laughter.

"What for, Collins? Everything *is* turning out for the best. Why are you so nervous? Fetch a chair and sit down! Aren't there any chairs here?"

"But certainly Your Majesty will explain . . ."

"All in good time, Collins, all in good time. Not now. Let us first take a look at this doll. It seems to be an old piece, doesn't it, perhaps thousands of years old, but still in quite good shape. I believe it even can dance. It has probably made a long trip, we should say a very long trip, but it is still fully intact. Hard to believe what can fit into this little head, if one only knows how to go about filling it properly!" He held the small metal head of the doll between thumb and forefinger and smiled pensively.

"But, Your Majesty, I don't understand. What does this all mean?"

"Be patient, Collins, be patient. You will find out. There are just twenty minutes left. In the meantime, let us watch the review of your troops. Then we will tell you a story, a very ordinary story, but we think it will interest you nevertheless. We would wager on it."

"I am breathless with anticipation, Your Majesty."

Meanwhile, the king continued to greet with a gracious wave of the hand the guards who appeared and disappeared, as if he were holding an audience. The men gave the minister a questioning look, which he answered with a regretful shrug of his shoulders and a resigned sigh. His Majesty continued to play with the doll and seemed to be in unusually high spirits, as if all this was great fun.

Now it was Collins's turn to become nervous. He found that he had torn the temporal strip in his hand to shreds. The king said to his minister, as if he too had noticed this, "That doesn't matter, Collins. We don't need it anymore. In a quarter of an hour the stream of dots will stop anyway."

"Well, that's that, Collins. Your guards can't penetrate the mirror anymore."

The mirror was not blank. It continued to flicker, but no one stepped out from it. The minister stared in astonishment first at the instrument, then at His Majesty.

"Surprises you, doesn't it?" laughed the king.

"Indeed it does," admitted Collins. "But how is it possible?"

"Let us not anticipate."

"As Your Majesty wishes. But it has always been my task to anticipate."

"You are right. Very well, then let us begin." The king settled comfortably into his throne and cleared his throat. "Collins, you are a clever man."

"Your Majesty honors me."

"But you have made several mistakes."

"I beg Your Majesty's pardon, but what mistakes?"

"First of all, you shouldn't have taken your eyes off the mirror for one single instant, for then you would have noticed that it wasn't blank for the entire ten seconds. Not that there was anything you could have done, but you might have gained some information which would have led you to make certain further considerations. And at times you were damned close to having the answer. You almost beat us in our little game."

"Perhaps, Your Majesty. It is not clear to me—what could I have done?"

"You should have thought out the problem more carefully. Fortunately for us, you didn't. You could for instance have given more consideration to the meaning of this seal and the intervention of WHITE."

"I considered the seal a protection of important timeline intersections, where a fracture could have devastating consequences."

"All of which is true, Collins. And WHITE has to intervene, because sometimes time fissures spread underneath the seals, as a result of imprudent operations, and make repairs necessary, in order to guarantee the safety of the future, our universe, and thereby the very existence of WHITE itself."

"I understand, but why didn't WHITE seal off the entire timeline and cut off all operations of the patrol?"

"A good question. Why not? Think hard, Collins. You have a good head on your shoulders."

"Of course. Your Majesty is right. That would mean cutting off all time travel, which would in turn mean no invention of time travel, as there could be no experiments, and then the existence of WHITE would be impossible."

"Very good! Therefore, WHITE interferes only when its existence is at stake."

"But what about my mistakes, Your Majesty?"

"Without this future power, which we call WHITE, the course of our planet would speedily deteriorate into a state of hopeless confusion. WHITE was actually your opponent, Collins, but you were always looking for an opponent elsewhere. And you didn't know where to look."

"At times I suspected it, but I thought it more probable that certain political-interest groups in the empire, perhaps operating from a base in the future, were giving us trouble. But Your Majesty spoke of several mistakes."

"That is all part of the story which we are about to tell you. You must pay especially close attention to it for reasons which will also be made clear. But we want to anticipate a bit. You were hunting down this dollmaker—"

"Indeed."

"—And at times you made life difficult for him."

"As Your Majesty commanded."

"Hmm," smiled the king.

"Although without much success, I must admit, because WHITE intervened with a seal."

"Why didn't you study the past history of this person more closely, at the very time and place in which it occurred?"

"We didn't think it necessary. We already knew something of the man, though it was second- and third-hand information. The question didn't seem to be worth going into more thoroughly. It was my opinion that we had already spent too much time on him. What we had found out about him didn't seem to be helpful enough. . . ."

"Then you know that this man was born in 1594, first learned the blacksmith's trade, then became apprenticed to a watchmaker, and afterward traveled about for five years as a journeyman. During this time war broke out and he was captured by recruiting officers and forced to serve in the army; he spent the next two years with a band of men who had joined Tilly's troops. . . ."

"Yes, Your Majesty, and settled down in the town which is now our Operations Base 7; he acquired money somehow, bought himself a cottage, set up a workshop, and devoted himself entirely to his hobby of making watches and mechanical toys. He became a respected citizen of the town but refused all public offices which were offered to him; he escaped the snares of all the spinsters in the neighborhood, having decided upon a bachelor life in order to have his evenings free to pore over blueprints and tinker with mechanical instruments. He engaged a housekeeper who cooked and cleaned the house but was not allowed into the workshop. The watchmaker became more and more withdrawn, hardly leaving his house. Finally he became mentally deranged and in 1650 hung himself. As Your Majesty can see, we know quite a bit about him, but nothing which appears noteworthy to me."

"Nothing noteworthy. You are quite right, Collins. But do you also know that this man was killed in action near Heidelberg in the year 1621? Tilly's crowd murdered and plundered its way through the countryside. He was killed either by farmers or by one of his fellow cutthroats, who probably fought with him over his booty or some woman."

"I beg Your Majesty's pardon."

"You heard correctly, Collins. The man whom you supposedly investigated so carefully was no longer alive at the time Operations Base 7 was established."

"That would have been an inexcusable error. But how does Your Majesty know this?"

"More about that later. And your third error was that you failed to have photographs taken of this man in order to examine him more closely. You would perhaps have had quite a surprise. But you and your people had eyes only for the mechanical toys. Fortunately."

There was a crafty smile on the king's face.

"I considered his appearance fully irrelevant in this case, especially as I could never rid myself of the feeling that we were on the wrong track and had wasted much too much time on the man."

"So you yourself have never seen this Weisslinger."

"No, Your Majesty. Why should I have seen him?"

The king shook his head in disapproval. Collins felt more and more uncertain.

"What a pity. Weisslinger is an extremely interesting man. You should have become acquainted with him; you would certainly have learned a great deal from him. He had much to tell, for he had been through much in his life. Perhaps you would have noticed that he wore an ingenious mask, though it was no more ingenious than masks could be in that age. You know us well, Collins, and you have a good head on your shoulders."

"I am beginning to doubt that seriously, Your Majesty."

"Now, now, Collins. It is never too late. Perhaps you will yet meet him."

"How is that possible, Your Majesty? I don't understand. . . ."

"Patience, patience! Wait until you have heard our story. Then you will have to admit that you let yourself be checkmated too easily."

"By Your Majesty's leave, I am burning with eagerness to hear the story, for I see more and more clearly that I accomplished my task much more poorly than I had originally thought."

"Indeed you did, Collins. You played miserably and recklessly."

"I most humbly beg Your Majesty's pardon."

"On the other hand, you were pitted against no mean opponent. But everything in its turn. BLACK had the victory as good as in its pocket—the situation was grim. Then it was WHITE's turn, WHITE would have to be damned tricky. . . . But where shall we begin? Ah yes, on the day when . . . Now pay strict attention! One evening . . ."

It was evening. The night watchman had just sung out the eleventh hour and had gone down the street, when a carriage drawn by two magnificent horses rounded the corner, rumbled over the cobblestones of the market square, and pulled up in front of the Red Ox Inn, directly across from the house of the dollmaker Weisslinger. The dollmaker went to his window and opened the shutters a tiny crack. He peered out in order to inspect the travelers who were arriving so late at night. He saw two men alight from the vehicle and converse with the proprietor of the Red Ox, who had come out to greet the distinguished guests and escort them into the house. The strangers apparently did not intend to enter and partake of his board and lodging, as they involved him in a conversation on the doorstep. They had a number of questions and seemed to be looking for someone in the town, for the innkeeper nodded his head several times and pointed to Weisslinger's house across the street. The strangers' eyes followed the innkeeper's finger; they carefully surveyed the market square and the neighborhood. Then they took leave of the innkeeper, pressing a gold coin into his hand, and strode toward Weisslinger's house.

"Aha," said the dollmaker knowingly to himself, and cautiously closed the shutters. "The time has come."

He quickly cleared away his mechanical instruments, drew forth several large drawings, and spread them out upon table and workbench. Then he sat down and waited. As he heard the knock on his door he hesitated, then went to the window and spoke quietly out into the darkness: "Who is there?"

"We beg your forgiveness, Master, for disturbing you at this late hour. The roads are bad and we have made very slow progress. On our travels we heard of a famous watchmaker in this area by the name of Weisslinger. Are you this man?"

"I am Weisslinger, but you honor me, I am certainly not famous. Come in."

Their thick accents indicated that they were foreigners. Weisslinger unbolted the door.

"Please forgive us for disturbing you. But we have little time and must speak with you."

"Come in, gentlemen. You aren't disturbing me at all, I was still up and working. Please excuse the disorderly room. I seldom clean it up and my housekeeper isn't allowed to come in here, she is too careless and always breaks something. Please take a seat. What brings you to this town?"

"We heard of your fame as a maker of highly ingenious dolls."

"That is not my main occupation. By trade I am actually a smith, and I have learned the watchmaker's arts as well. It is true that I have spent much of my—well—spare time making small mechanical toys such as music boxes and dancing dolls—although, I must admit, with little success, due to my insufficient craftsmanship. Please forgive me, gentlemen, I am neglecting my duties as host. But I never expect visitors and have nothing in the house to offer you. I can recommend the Red Ox across the road. You will certainly be pleased with the service there. I often have my meals there myself. The food is good and the wine cellar even better."

"That is not necessary. We have already had our evening meal."

Weisslinger took a closer look at the strangers. Their clothing was simple but elegant: black capes of fine material, close-fitting, well-cut trousers, and low boots fashioned of supple leather. They were examining the room which served both as living room and workshop. They seemed to be particularly interested in his machines, tools, and measuring instruments, which hung on the wall or lay on the workbench; it was not difficult to read from the disappointment on their faces that they had expected more.

"Would you be so kind as to demonstrate one of your models for us?" asked one of the men, trying without success to hide his discontent.

"Of course," answered Weisslinger. He carefully put away his drawings and cleared the workbench, then placed upon it one of his carved music boxes. He wound it up and let it play, then wound up a second and a third music box; the tinny tones of their simple melodies made an odd jingle-jangle. He then took up a small dancing doll with movable limbs, wound it up, and placed it on the bench with the music boxes. The springs whirred, and the doll made stiff, jerky pirouettes on the tabletop.

The gentlemen did not seem to take great interest in the demonstration; they continued to look about the room, glanced at each other and shrugged their shoulders, but pretended to be extremely interested whenever Weisslinger gave them a questioning look. Then one gentleman's eyes fell upon a grandfather clock which was standing in a corner of the room. It was an extraordinary piece with painted face, beautiful case carved out of valuable dark wood, decorated porcelain weights suspended from delicate chains, and a finely chased pendulum on which the astronomic tables and the allegorical figures of the horoscope were engraved.

"Is this clock also a work of yours?"

"Yes, sir. Does it please you?"

"It is a beautiful piece, but it doesn't keep accurate time."

"This is a curious point. You may find it hard to believe, but the clock is not supposed to keep accurate time."

"How can that be?"

"It is a long story, which I am afraid would bore you."

"Not at all!"

"Very well, if you really want to hear it. Please be seated. One day a man came to see me, a Polish count who had spent a good part of his life in Seville and Zaragoza. He was returning to his home in Poland; on his travels he had heard of me and sought me out. He inspected my clocks and toys, my tools and measuring instruments as well, and seemed to know quite a bit about the craft, as I could judge from his questions. But he denied having any extensive knowledge about such things. In any case, he was apparently satisfied with what he saw and commissioned me to build a clock for him. Nothing simpler, I thought to myself, but I was soon to change my mind. In fact, this man showed me very detailed drawings according to which the clock was to be constructed; these he had bought for a high price from a Jew in Seville. At first everything seemed simple, but I soon ran into difficulties. The more closely I investigated the drawings, the more complicated the works appeared, and I began to doubt seriously that this instrument which I was to build would function at all. The drawings were accompanied by instructions written in Arabic. The count, who could not read Arabic, had had the text translated into Spanish; this he had translated into his mother tongue and had scrawled along the margins of the old parchment documents. We spent several days trying to translate this text into German, but neither of us was capable of making enough sense out of these descriptions so that they might serve me as instructions, which they were obviously intended to be. They were more confusing than the drawings themselves, especially as they were worded in a figurative language which spoke of flowers, fragrant perfumes, and unknown spices, of strange oceans and distant lands, angels and demons, when there should have been nothing but metals and weights, screws and springs, coils and tractive forces, balances and swings of the pendulum. I was utterly bewildered and wanted to refuse the commission, but the count promised me a princely sum for my efforts, even if they should fail. In addition, he placed at my disposal a considerable percentage of this sum in cash, with which I was to procure the necessary materials and tools. I still hesitated, then he raised the sum, imploring me to at least try it. Finally I gave in and set to work. It took me weeks in these troubled times to gather the materials, as only the best would do. I had the face of the clock drawn up according to specifications; it was to be divided into sixteen hours, as if it were to measure some foreign time. I canvassed the countryside to find a cabinetmaker who could build and ornament the case according to the instructions; then we both traveled about selecting and buying the different types of wood out of which he was to construct the case—all of this in wartime, when we never knew at night if we were to see the sun the next morning. But God, all praise be His, held His shielding hand over me and my work, and in spite of all the difficulties the clock eventually took its present form, as it stands before you. It cost me three years' work. When it was finally finished, the clock actually ran, which was the last thing I expected. But the way it ran! According to the drawings, the clock was to have five hands, each of which was to trace its circle with varying speed and direction. The clock could tell the most improbable intervals and constellations of the heavenly bodies, but not the hours of the day. This must have been the invention of some insane infidel who wanted to measure the ages his damned soul would have to spend in Purgatory. It is the unchristian work of the devil which measures the eternity of Hell. Every chime of the evening bell sends its hands spinning in a different direction. . . . But I see that my story bores you, gentleman. Please pardon my prattling on so. I don't have visitors often."

"Who gave you this commission?" inquired one of the strangers.

"A Polish count, as I already mentioned. I never did know his name. He came back once to see me, when the clock was almost finished. He spent hours studying the drawings, measured the positions of the hands, listened to the ticking of the works, made notes in a small book, sighed and shook his head, seemed at times to be discontented with the clock, then again pleasantly surprised, then once again dissatisfied; his eyes followed the pendulum as it swung back and forth, his ears noticed every change in rhythm of the buzzing and whirring mechanism, which sometimes ticked as slowly as drops of water falling from the ceiling of a cave, then again as rapidly as the hoofbeats of a herd of galloping horses—but the man never uttered a word. When I questioned him he cut me off with a wave of the hand, put his finger to his lips, and listened with such concentration to the ticking and whirring of the clock that—I hope you will pardon this severe judgment—I slowly began to question his sanity. As he departed he left me a sack of gold coins. I thanked him profusely, for this was a much greater sum than he had promised me. He smiled and promised to return soon to pick up the clock, but I never saw him again. Heaven knows why he didn't come back; perhaps he was not satisfied with my work, perhaps he had been expecting too much. Who knows? He never spoke a word of praise, which I must admit I would have been glad to hear after all the effort I put into the making of the clock; after all, I did my very best to carry out the order to his satisfaction. But perhaps he perished in that terrible war, God save his poor straying soul. These are frightful times. But you know as well as I, gentlemen, what it is to live in these times. God be merciful to us and let there at last be peace. Please blame it on my advancing age if I have gone prattling on again."

"Do you still have the drawings?"

"No, the Pole took them with him when he left this workshop for the last time. The clock was finished, I didn't need the drawings anymore. And I didn't want to keep them any longer, as they were quite valuable."

"So you know nothing more of the background or the whereabouts of your client?" inquired the strangers.

"I'm afraid not; otherwise I would have tried to find him myself. The clock has been standing in that corner now for two years. It takes up too much space in my workshop, but I can neither sell it nor give it away, much less take it apart or destroy it, because it doesn't belong to me. I am beginning to develop a passionate dislike for it; I usually cover it with a cloth and let it run down, but the silence that then fills the room is even more unbearable than the crazy ticking, so I wind it up again. But I removed three of the hands and replaced the face with a normal one; it was the only way I could bear the situation. . . ."

"Tell us if that isn't a good story, Collins!"

"It certainly is, Your Majesty. But I know it all too well. I fell for it from beginning to end."

"Why didn't you follow up that business about the clock?"

"I held this insane instrument to be the product of a sick mind, not worth our time and attention."

"We assure you, you would have had a surprise. You and your people have been standing a whisker away from the secret of the time seal. If you had only held out a little longer . . . but we expect Weisslinger would have had something to say about that."

"Your Majesty, I am an idiot."

"Dear Collins!" laughed the king. "We judged you right! You have no use for metaphysics and unsound logic, for secrets and mysterious strangers. By the way, that Polish count was an invention of ours, but he was rather good, wasn't he?"

"Yes, indeed, Your Majesty."

"And something else, Collins. Do you know that the pendulum clock was not invented before 1657 by Huygens and was patented in the same year in the States General?"

"My God." Collins was embarrassed.

"Your idiots have missed the anachronism—but not Weiss, who thereupon traced down the dollmaker and let him have some part to assemble a machine, in order to move the time seals."

"I am deeply ashamed, Your Majesty."

"Very good. Now let us continue. We haven't finished yet."

"I am curious to hear how these events untangle themselves."

"Perhaps you will be disappointed. Don't set your hopes too high. It is all very simple. Now, these two gentlemen, who had come to see Weisslinger so late at night and had listened with more and more evident boredom to his story, finally purchased one of the mechanical dolls and two other toys, paid the dollmaker well, and took their leave politely but without concealing their disappointment, exhaustion, and ill humor. After refreshing themselves at the Red Ox, they traveled on, although it was well past midnight. Weisslinger watched the coach as it rounded the corner and rumbled out of the city. He closed the shutters again and rubbed his hands with delight, as if he had just made an excellent bargain. Then he blew out the light and went to bed.

"Do you still have the doll, Collins?"

"Of course, Your Majesty, but if I may say so, it is of little value to us. We have examined it carefully. By means of a simple spring mechanism the figure rotates about a fixed point."

"Collins, you are judging things only by their source of power and mobility potential. In a way you are right; the doll isn't worth much, but it is a nice toy, one that would make many a little girl happy, even nowadays. And it is all handmade, every screw is hand-threaded."

"It is no doubt interesting, your Majesty, but by far not as interesting as the doll Your Majesty is holding now."

"There you are right, Collins. Technique has a way of improving on the product."

"Is this doll also one of Weisslinger's creations?"

The king gave no answer, but leaning down from his throne he carefully set the doll on the floor. It took a few cautious steps to test the smoothness of the surface, then made two or three elaborate pirouettes, sprang nimbly into the air, turned a somersault, landed lightly on its feet, and ended its performance with a courteous bow. The minister applauded in admiration; the king was sunk deep in thought, but suddenly he turned to Collins.

"Where did we leave off?"

"The dollmaker, Your Majesty."

"Oh yes, we remember. Now then, listen carefully!"

It was evening. The night watchman had just sung out the eleventh hour and had gone down the street, when a carriage drawn by two magnificent horses rounded the corner, rumbled over the cobblestones of the market square, and pulled up in front of the Red Ox Inn, directly across from the house of the dollmaker Weisslinger. The dollmaker went to his window and opened the shutters a tiny crack. He peered out in order to inspect the travelers who were arriving so late at night. The innkeeper came to the door to greet the distinguished guests and escort them into the house. Much to his astonishment, nobody descended from the carriage. The coachman made no move to climb down from his box. Upon being questioned by the innkeeper, he explained by means of gestures that he was mute. The innkeeper looked about him uncertainly, then turned with a shrug of the shoulders and went back into the house, closing the door behind him. But Weisslinger remained at his post and continued to gaze in fascination at the carriage. The carriage curtains were closed, but as his eyes became more and more accustomed to the darkness, he noticed that someone had pulled one of the curtains aside and was examining his house with great interest. Time passed by, and neither observer gave up his station. At last the stranger in the carriage lit a cigarette.

"Bungler," muttered Weisslinger contemptuously, and closed the shutters. He did not bother to look again as the carriage rumbled out of the city an hour later. He was already sound asleep.

"What do you think of this version, Collins?"

"Inexcusable, Your Majesty. A cigarette in the seventeenth century! Such a mistake should never have been made by a patrolman. I give up."

"Not so fast, not so fast, Collins! Let us think. Where did we leave off?"

"The dollmaker, Your Majesty, had that evening . . ."

"Oh yes, we remember. Now pay attention!"

It was evening. The night watchman had just sung out the eleventh hour and had gone down the street, when a carriage drawn by two magnificent horses rounded the corner, rumbled over the cobblestones of the market square, and pulled up in front of the Red Ox Inn, directly across from the house of the dollmaker Weisslinger. The dollmaker went to his window and opened the shutters a tiny crack. He peered out in order to inspect the travelers who were arriving so late at night. He saw two men alight from the vehicle and converse with the innkeeper, who had come out to greet the distinguished guests and escort them into the house. The two strangers apparently did not intend to enter and partake of his board and lodging, as they involved him in a conversation on the doorstep. They had a number of questions and seemed to be looking for someone in the town, for the innkeeper nodded his head and pointed repeatedly to Weisslinger's house across the street. The strangers' eyes followed the innkeeper's finger; they carefully surveyed the market square and the neighborhood. Then they took leave of the innkeeper, pressing a gold coin into his hand, and strode toward Weisslinger's house.

At this very moment the dollmaker wound up one of his dolls and set it on the windowsill. The doll hopped nimbly to the ground and began to run. One of the men noticed it and called out to the other. They searched the square, trying to pierce the darkness with their eyes. Suddenly one of them took a leap and threw himself at the running figure, but it escaped him. The second man drew a small pistol and, aiming it, sent a spitting stream of fire whizzing toward the doll. But the tiny doll zigzagged agilely across the square and disappeared unscathed.

The long blue tongues of flame that came whipping out of the weapon licked up over the housetops, leaving glowing streaks behind them. Flashes of ghostly light lit up the market place, and the spitting, hissing, and roaring resounded so that the nearby streets fairly rattled with the echoes.

Weisslinger watched all the commotion in front of his house with amusement. In fact, he had to laugh so hard that his ribs ached.

"You miserable farmers!" he roared. "You louts! Idiots! You heroes of the laser pistols! Just take a look at that! Isn't this a marvelous joke?"

The disturbance outside had developed into a regular street fight. Fearful cries were heard as the people in the houses on the market square were awakened by the uproar. Shutters were thrown open on all sides and slammed shut again in panic as the shooting grew wilder. The townsmen suspected bold thieves or even enemy troops of causing the tumult, but in the general excitement and by the dim light they could not make out the target of the shooting.

In the meantime, something very odd had happened. Out of the carriage, which was built for four and could hold six at the very most, had swarmed fifteen or twenty shadow forms, which set about madly chasing the doll. Their chase gave off a fireworks display of constantly flickering pale streaks of flame, and in their robes they fluttered about the square and the fountain like an eerie swarm of giant moths. This frightful sight caused the inhabitants of the town who had been disturbed by the commotion to bar their doors and windows and to hide their valuables hastily in every niche and cranny they could find.

Master Weisslinger, however, remained at his window and watched the scuffle with growing amusement. He even goaded on the scufflers, but his laughing, jeering cries were drowned in the general uproar. At last one of the armed figures succeeded in hitting the fleeing doll. It exploded with a dull boom and the parts of its mechanism were scattered in the street. The dark-clad, shadowy forms feverishly searched for these fragments. They threw themselves upon the pavement, lights flared up and died out again, and the men crawled about in the street until they had convinced themselves that not a single screw or spring had escaped them. They were like a pack of hounds fighting over a few bones thrown into their midst.

At last every inch of pavement had been inspected and the men began to climb back into the carriage. There was a great rush and pushing; the carriage swayed on its wheels until at last all twenty men had managed to squeeze into it. It had taken four men to hold the horses, which had been frightened by the shooting and would not stop rearing and kicking. Held no longer, they set off at a gallop, and sparks flew from the wheels as the carriage, skidding and rocking, sped around the corner and out of the town.

As soon as the air had cleared and all was quiet outside, a few stout-hearted citizens dared to peek out of their doors and windows to see if body and soul were still in danger. Some courageously left their houses—carrying weapons—and after taking a rapid look about the square began to strut about fearlessly. Loud debates were carried on about the nocturnal raid, who the bold raiders could have been, whom the attack was intended for, what damage had been done, and what kind of an odd burning smell was still in the air. It turned out that nobody had suffered any harm, and nobody's property or possessions had been damaged or stolen. For the time being, no other conclusion could be reached than that at least one hundred heavily armed men had caused the tumult. They had appeared out of nowhere and disappeared again like lightning into thin air, because the appearance and intervention of so many valiant citizens had put dread fear into their hearts.

The night watchman reported that he had intended to throw himself resolutely before the galloping horses, but then thought better of it and decided to avoid meaningless sacrifice—not to mention the town's loss of his valuable services. Therefore, he had moved out of the path of the madly careening beasts and had contented himself with a loud and distinct "Stop!" which the coachman, however, who brutally whipped the horses and looked like the Old Nick himself, had insolently disregarded.

The discussions were carried on by torchlight long into the night and were not given up until the dawn appeared and the innkeeper was too tired to continue filling beermugs and carrying them across the square to sell to those thirsty citizens who stood about the fountain celebrating their victory.

After several days and many all-night debates in the inns, the townsmen came to the agreement, after having consulted the priest, who had shown a great interest in the speculations, that it must have been a devilish apparition which had come to haunt the town. Some surmised that it was an evil omen, others went so far as to interpret it as a warning to the innkeeper of the Red Ox, who had developed the bad habit of filling his mugs less and less full, and whose beer and wine tasted more and more watered down. The rumor spread about town and came in time to the innkeeper's hearing. The evil omen before his very house gave him grounds for reflection, and soon it could be noticed, to the satisfaction of all, that he had taken his lesson to heart and no longer gave his customers any reason to complain in this respect, at least for a time.

The dollmaker meanwhile had nothing to report about the nocturnal incident. He claimed to have slept so soundly that he hadn't heard the uproar at all, although it had taken place directly outside his window. The innkeeper, who wanted to hush the nasty rumors which were damaging his business, declared that the strangers had actually wanted to talk to Weisslinger. The dollmaker laughed and replied that the innkeeper was just looking for someone else to put the blame on and that he himself had and would have nothing to do with any of these brawlers, be it the Devil Himself. After all, the rowdies had given the innkeeper and not himself the first honors of a visit, which everybody well knew and which the innkeeper had already admitted. Everybody laughed along with Weisslinger, because he knew how to use his cleverness and wit to drive his opponent into a corner. The innkeeper said no more about the matter from that time on.

"What do you say to this version, Collins?"

"Bad work, Your Majesty. Very bad work."

"Like a whole herd of bulls in a china shop. Why this large-scale action? You sent a whole regiment in there! You were lucky that the people of this period are rather superstitious. Imagine that taking place in the twentieth or twenty-first century. Interventions of such dimensions could easily start a war, if you have bad luck. Did it at least help you?"

"Not much, Your Majesty. The doll was much more complex than the ones we had bought from Weisslinger, one could say unbelievably complex by the technical standards of that time, which of course increased our suspicion. But on the other hand, there was nothing mysterious about its mechanism. We couldn't completely reconstruct it from the pieces we had collected, but there was no indication of any electronic instruments—it was certainly a purely mechanical construction. But it seems to me now almost as if the dollmaker wanted to play a trick on us, and we promptly fell for it. He probably already knew that we came from a different age. But by Your Majesty's leave, how can such an idea occur to a man in the seventeenth century?"

The king laughed.

"Don't underestimate the human imagination! The concept that man can travel in time is much older than you think."

"That may be so. We'd have to look into it," said the minister.

"Now look at that! A simple seventeenth-century mechanic has played a trick on our Collins. Shall we give you an early pension?"

"I most humbly beg Your Majesty's forgiveness. We wanted to eliminate this fracture, but it was not possible."

The minister stared at the floor in shame.

The doll now tried to walk on its hands. It succeeded on the first try.

The king smirked.

"It didn't work? Well, well. Think of that! It didn't work!"

"No, Your Majesty. It was our last chance to intervene successfully, WHITE had made everything else impossible. The seal started suddenly to move. We even had to leave important instruments at Operations Base 7. . . ."

"Time mirrors too?"

"Time mirrors too. We had to evacuate the station in a great hurry. The seal grew with threatening speed in our direction, as members of the patrol reported."

"Hmm. Does that surprise you? That could have caused a nasty fracture. Imagine the results if in this wild shooting someone had been seriously wounded or even killed. It would have put our entire history in a complete muddle. WHITE was forced to intervene, or else your people would have made more irreparable blunders."

"I beg Your Majesty's pardon, but it was an extremely important matter. For the first time one of these mysterious dolls appeared, time was pressing, and I had strictest orders. . . ."

"But you are in charge of security and must certainly be aware of the consequences of intervening along the timeline. That's what you had special training for."

Collins stared contritely at the toes of his shoes.

"Your Majesty is right. It was careless of me."

"Now then, don't make such a face about it. Nothing really serious happened," laughed the king.

"Your Majesty deigns to laugh?"

"Yes, we were just imagining the twenty men squeezing into the coach. We assume that you had an instrument installed in the coach."

"Yes, Your Majesty, one of the time mirrors from Operations Base 7."

The conversation ceased, and both men silently watched the doll. It was dancing now on its hands, now on its feet. One somersault followed another.

"Where were we?"

"The dollmaker, Your Majesty, had on that evening . . ."
"Oh yes, we remember. Now, listen carefully!"

It was evening. The night watchman had just sung out the eleventh hour and had gone down the street, when a carriage drawn by two magnificent horses rounded the corner, rumbled over the cobblestones of the market square, and pulled up in front of the Red Ox Inn, directly across from the house of the dollmaker Weisslinger. The dollmaker went to his window and opened the shutters a tiny crack. He peered out in order to inspect the travelers who were arriving so late at night. The innkeeper had come out to greet the distinguished guests and escort them into the house. To his astonishment, no one got out of the carriage. The coachman made no preparation to climb down from his box. In answer to a question from the innkeeper, he indicated by gestures that he did not understand the language. But the innkeeper did not give up so easily. In sign language he asked again if the coachman was hungry or thirsty. After a moment's hesitation the coachman nodded, pulled the brake, knotted the reins, and climbed down from the box. The innkeeper wanted to lead him into the house, but the coachman preferred first to walk up and down a bit to stretch his legs, then to see to the horses and take another look at the carriage. He then took off his dark cape and shook it out, as if to leave the dust of long journeys on bad roads behind him, hung it about his shoulders with the pale lining to the outside, and at last was ready to follow the innkeeper into the house. Master Weisslinger, at first alarmed and then pleased, had watched the whole scene with breathless interest. The coachman had not taken a deep breath inside the inn before Weisslinger was hard at work. He did something rather odd. Using special tools, he opened the enormous grandfather clock, removed the hands, loosened and pried off the face, replaced some of the works with other pieces, and tightened wires and made new connections. He then put in a new face, fastened on five hands and set them according to the new face, measured the angles they formed, reset them, measured again, wound up the clock, tightened a screw here and loosened one here, listened carefully to the irregular ticking of the clock, checked the movement of the hands, and made new adjustments until a high chirping could be heard above the ticking. Weisslinger cautiously touched some of the wire connections, and they were warm and began to glow—the wires were live then; he had tapped the timeline. The air began to crackle, and sparks flitted along the wires and bathed the room in an eerie light. The chirping had now become so loud that it drowned out the ticking of the works. Weisslinger put down his tools, wiped the sweat from his forehead, and leaned back with a sigh of relief.

"I've done it," he said. "At least it looks like it."

Then he blew out the light and went to the window again. He had to wait over an hour before the stranger finally left the inn. The latter seemed to have refreshed himself liberally, for he swayed slightly as he walked and the innkeeper escorted him to the door.

"Hallooooo there!" he called out, and waved in the direction of Weisslinger's house.

The dollmaker shook his head and said, "Just you wait!"

The innkeeeper was helping the coachman to store away the horses' feedbags and to climb up onto the box again.

"Halloo!" called the stranger again. Receiving no reply, he grunted and gave his whip a jerk, but so clumsily that it nearly hit the innkeeper. The carriage started up and rumbled at a leisurely pace out of the town, although it was well past midnight.

Weisslinger watched it disappear. Then he took a small, delicate doll out of its hiding place, took one last careful look at it, and wound it up. The doll woke up and stretched its legs. He held its little smooth head between thumb and forefinger and murmured, "You can do it. You will penetrate thousands of years and will bring me a sign. I know it now."

He put the doll on the windowsill. The little creature cautiously examined the market square.

"Run!" said the dollmaker, and gave the figure a push. With one spring the doll was on the street, whisked over the square like a shadow, and was gone. Weisslinger closed and barred the shutters and retired to bed.

"What do you think of this version, Collins?"

"I hadn't heard that one before, Your Majesty."

"We believe that, Collins, but you will get to know it well."

"How is that, Your Majesty?"

"Just wait. We are not finished yet. We are going to have to act it out together in order to round off the story."

"Your Majesty said 'together'?"

"Yes, Collins, you heard quite rightly. We are going to have to act it out together, the two of us."

"How am I to understand this?"

"It is very simple, and you will understand it clearly, as clearly as we are sitting here."

"Does Your Majesty permit me to ask a question?"

"Naturally."

"Was this doll that Weisslinger sent off that evening the same one with which Your Majesty is now playing?"

"The very same one, Collins. A few thousand years old and still fully intact. Go ahead and take a good look at it."

As if it had understood the conversation, the doll hopped upon the minister's arm, held on to his shoulder, and looked him in the eye.

"By Your Majesty's leave, it is really a marvel."

"Yes, isn't it! But where had we left off, Collins?"

"The dollmaker, Your Majesty, had on that evening . . ."

"Oh yes, now we remember. Now listen carefully!"

It was evening. The night watchman had just sung out the eleventh hour and had gone down the street, when a carriage drawn by two magnificent horses rounded the corner, rumbled over the cobblestones of the market square, and pulled up in front of the Red Ox Inn, directly across from the house of the dollmaker Weisslinger. The dollmaker went to his window and opened the shutters a tiny crack. He peered out in order to inspect the travelers who were arriving so late at night. The innkeeper had come out to greet the distinguished guests and escort them into the house. To his astonishment, no one got out of the carriage. The coachman made no move to climb down from his box, and, in answer to a question from the innkeeper, explained by means of gestures that he did not understand the language. The innkeeper looked uncertainly about him for a while, then shrugging his shoulders returned into the house and closed the door. But Weisslinger continued to stare in fascination at the carriage. The curtains of the carriage windows were drawn, but now that his eyes had become accustomed to the darkness he could see that the interior of the coach was illuminated by a pale and flickering light. Weisslinger gave a small sigh of relief, but for a while absolutely nothing happened. The coachman sat motionless and lost in thought upon his box; the reins were tied up and the brakes drawn. The horses snorted, chafed against the shaft of the carriage, and shook their harnesses. Time slipped by. At last the man climbed down, walked up and down to stretch his legs, saw to the horses, then took off his dark cape and shook it out, as if to leave the dust of long journeys on bad roads behind him, and hung it about his shoulders with the pale lining to the outside. He stepped up to the carriage and opened the door a crack. A small figure hopped out, flitted like a shadow across the square directly to the dollmaker's house, with a single spring bound to the windowsill, raised its little metallic face to Weisslinger, and made a courteous bow.

The master closed the window and unbolted the door. He cautiously peered about the market square, listened to hear if anyone might be passing by at so late an hour or if the night watchman might be approaching on his rounds, but there was no one in sight. Muffled noises drifted across from the Red Ox, where a few townsmen were drinking beer and whiling away the time with politics and card games. For the rest, all was quiet. The fountain in the market square splashed, and the horses snorted and pawed the paving stones. There was not a soul in sight. The stillness of the night lay peacefully over the town. The war was far away.

Weisslinger gave the coachman a sign.

The coachman immediately ripped open the carriage door, leaned far in and hauled out a long and obviously heavy bundle, got it with difficulty onto his shoulder, and staggered over to the dollmaker's house. The dollmaker hurried to help him carry the burden.

"Who are you, stranger?" asked the master in a whisper.

"WHITE," answered the man just as quietly. "Thank you for helping me carry him. He is damned heavy."

The bundle was a body. They carried it into the house and laid it carefully on the bed.

"Is he dead?" asked Weisslinger anxiously.

"No, he's only unconscious. He'll wake up soon."

The stranger breathed heavily.

"Damned heavy, that—uh . . . I beg your pardon . . . that fellow. Got me worked up into a good sweat. I'm getting old."

"Did everything go off all right?" Weisslinger wanted to know.

"You can see that it did."

"How did it go?"

"More about that later."

The stranger did not want to waste time. Weisslinger turned to the person on the bed and took a good look at his face.

"He has gotten fat," he laughed. Then he began to transform himself. He took off his wig, removed the clipped gray beard, and with a few clever strokes completely transformed his face, so that he looked like the mirror image of the unconscious man on the bed.

"Finished?" asked the coachman.

"Just one more minute," said Weisslinger. He rolled up the plans which hung on the walls and lay on the table, ripped them up, and threw the scraps into the fire. Then he took a hammer from the workbench and approached the grandfather clock.

"But—" interrupted the stranger, and added hesitantly, "Excuse my meddling, but shouldn't he have a chance?"

"How big were my chances?" replied Weisslinger, and gave the stranger a searching look. He swung the heavy hammer and let it smash into the clock. Glass flew, the valuable case splintered. With the second blow there was a crunching of metal, the pendulum began to clatter, and the hands whirred with increasing speed. The third blow brought the works to a standstill. He took another swing but did not finish it.

"You are right. It is a pity to destroy the clock. It cost me hours of work. With luck and skill it could be repaired. We'll leave him the tools. He can sell them, if he can find somebody to buy them. The materials alone that went into that clock are worth a pretty penny. But if he sells it all he'll be sorry. In any case, he'll get less for it than it is worth. If he can get it back into salable condition at all."

"If," said the stranger.

"I am ready," said Weisslinger.

"Take my cape." And the coachman removed his cape from his shoulders. The dollmaker drew it about himself.

"Not like that—the pale side to the inside."

Weisslinger turned it inside out. The other side was dark.

"Come quickly! He is waking up," urged the coachman.

The figure on the bed rolled over and groaned. Weisslinger took one last look around the room which had been his home for years and in which he had spent many an anxious hour between hope and desperation, many a night, half awake, half dreaming, pondering over and developing fantastic projects. Bent over his workbench, working all night through, summer and winter, he had drawn up plans, with primitive tools had turned and filed and fashioned mechanisms the precision of which his colleagues could not begin to copy. All the while he was on the lookout, constantly stepping to the window and peering out in fear, whenever strangers came to the town and stopped at the Red Ox Inn, that they were already on his trail and wanted to kidnap him or kill him or at least destroy his work.

Weisslinger turned away. He motioned to the doll, which sprang onto his shoulder, and followed the stranger, who was already impatiently waiting at the carriage and holding open the door.

"I'll climb up on the box next to you. I am curious to hear how it all went."

"All right," said the coachman, and helped him up to his perch. The carriage started up, and rumbled at a leisurely pace over the market square and out of the town.

"Now listen carefully," said the coachman. "You must put yourself into the situation and play the exact part which I am now going to describe to you. Pay very close attention, every detail is of the utmost importance."

The stranger then proceeded to give Weisslinger specific instructions on how he was to behave, what he had to say, what gestures he should make. The dollmaker had many questions, and to all of them the coachman had exact answers. He concluded all the descriptions and explanations as the carriage drew up to a dark, secluded farm, which lay deep in a vast forest through which the carriage had been driving for over an hour along narrow and overgrown tracks. They stopped. The moon had risen high in the sky and poured its cold light over the collapsing roofs of barn and sheds, over the muddy barnyard whose deep ruts were filled with water that glittered in the light, over the gardens that had run to seed, in which the weeds had grown high above the crooked fences. Everything looked dirty and dilapidated.

"Is this Operations Base 7?" asked Weisslinger.

"Yes," answered the coachman.

"It is a pigsty."

"That is the best camouflage for it. If anyone wanders into this deserted area, he should not have the impression that there is anything here worth stealing. We are fairly certain that nobody has been snuffling around here. But of course now it doesn't make any difference anymore."

The coachman took the bridle and reins off the horses, let them loose, and chased them out of the farmyard with cries and cracks of the whip.

"It's a pity. They were beautiful beasts," said Weisslinger.

"They'll find another master. First they should enjoy their freedom for a while."

They ransacked the house and sheds, destroyed all the instruments, and set fire to the farmstead. The dry wood of the old building burned like tinder; the flame shot up and in no time had reached the rooftree. The thatched roofs of the sheds blazed like torches in the night and scattered a shower of dark red sparks into the forest.

"A devilishly dangerous business we're doing," commented Weisslinger.

"But it's fun," laughed the coachman, and threw more fuel onto the fire. The heat was tremendous, and the two men withdrew into the carriage. The built-in mirror flickered and quivered in a milky light. The dollmaker smiled.

"Ready?" asked the stranger.

"Ready," said Weisslinger, and picked up the doll. Then they stepped, one after the other, through the mirror.

They had just disappeared when the rooftree of the farmhouse fell in with a great crash and a splash of sparks. The farmyard was strewn with burning shingles and splinters of wood. The fire now blazed several hundred feet into the sky and gave an eerie light far into the night. A few minutes later, a violent explosion demolished the carriage.

"What do you think of this version of the story, Collins?"

"It too is completely new to me, Your Majesty. Not only that, it is inexplicable. But still, the picture seems complete. All the pieces of the puzzle fit together. There seem to be a few pieces still missing however. Am I right, Your Majesty?"

"Quite right, Collins. But those pieces will turn up. Just have a little patience. We haven't finished the story yet."

"So WHITE intervened . . ."

The king smirked.

"We couldn't do anything about that."

"Not anymore, Collins. Not anymore."

"Right, Your Majesty, not anymore. I have to admit defeat."

"Nothing doing, Collins! There will be no giving up now. The story isn't complete. You have to keep playing. We insist on it, even if we have to order you to play. Don't disappoint us. Maybe you can make one more important move."

"I wouldn't know where to . . ."

"We have to fit all the pieces of the puzzle together to get the complete picture. Something is missing."

"Yes—for instance, why this substitution and with whom? . . . and what information did this Weisslinger receive from WHITE? that is, if—and I am not so sure of this—the coachman is in fact WHITE. What did Weisslinger find out from this stranger?"

"He was told the very same story that you just heard. But the dollmaker also heard the end of the story, which you will find out in a moment too. Then you will understand the substitution."

"I already have an idea, Your Majesty. Please carry on with the story."

"Patience, Collins. We have time, plenty of time. Limitless time is at our disposal. You will hear everything."

"I am very eager to hear it all, Your Majesty."

"Very well then. This part of the story is quite different. It takes place much earlier than all the rest that we have already told you."

The king reflected a moment before continuing.

In the meantime, the doll had begun to include double flips in its dance and whirled across the room.

"As you perhaps know, Collins, we once had a brother."

"Your Majesty has strictly forbidden any mention or even knowledge of this fact. I believe he met with a fatal accident many years ago while making some rash experiment in physics."

"That is quite right. He was killed in a time-travel experiment. How that came about, you are now about to hear. Once upon a time . . ."

Once upon a time there was a king, who was very rich and whose power extended over four solar systems and all celestial bodies within a radius of twenty light-years. This king had two sons who were very close to each other in age. When the sons were still children there lived in the palace an eccentric old man, of whom nobody at the court took any real notice. He was a mathematician and physicist and it was his responsibility to look after the electronic systems and computer center of the palace. His entire life was devoted solely to his profession, and he never participated in the social life of the court. His wife had died at an early age and since then he had lived like a recluse, eating and sleeping amid his scientific apparatus and computers and seeing and being seen by nobody for weeks on end, unless he was needed to repair a defective stereo tele-wall or one of the transmitters. He had been born on one of the most godforsaken planets of the kingdom, on which his ancestors, of ancient colonial settler stock, had settled. They had adapted themselves to the climate of the planet and could even exist out of doors in the open air. We believe his father was even a farmer.

He was sent to school, proved to be very bright, studied electronic sciences, and made quite a name for himself in his field. One day his young wife was killed in a transfer ship accident. He must have taken that very hard. He gave up physics and lived like a hermit. His resources were soon exhausted and he suffered bitter want. So he started writing stories, fairy tales full of profound and hidden meaning. He was very gifted at this but good fortune evaded him. His colleagues laughed at him because they did not understand his stories, and many people said that his great misfortune had driven him out of his senses. He was soon forgotten—no one read his works—and he led a wretched and lonely existence in a poor hut outside the city. One day the king heard of his tragic fate and commanded him to come to the palace. After much hesitation he finally accepted a position at the court. He was kept busy with occasional repairs and with the supervision of the automatic central control station and the computer installations, an occupation which did not demand much time or effort. He continued to write his fairy tales and to be derided for doing so. No one took him very seriously. But that did not seem to

bother him very much. He only smiled enigmatically whenever he
was asked to tell one of his stories, and his listeners turned away
shaking their heads. And so he came to be known at the court as an
eccentric old man whose thoughts were bewildering and whose logic
was peculiar, but he seemed to be harmless, so people left him alone.
Only the two princes were genuinely fond of him and considered him
to be their good friend. He in turn loved them dearly, but not because
he expected to gain anything by it—he had never thought of such
a thing. He loved them because they were his most patient listeners
and would listen for hours on end and still beg for more, delighted
with his stories and never tired of hearing them. He would tell of the
past and the future, of distant unknown kingdoms and their strange
inhabitants; he could describe in detail the cities, the streets and
squares, the palaces and markets, he could give such a clear picture
of the clothing and language and the customs and habits of their inhabitants, that it seemed as if he had been to all these marvelous
places and had seen them all with his own eyes. And yet he seldom
left the windowless rooms of the royal computer control station,
passing his days amid computers and field generators, matter transmitters and receiving sets.

Although the princes did not always understand everything he told
them, it was always exciting. They liked him because he could tell
fascinating stories without constantly putting in flattering phrases or
wagging a moralizing finger, as the others always did.

More and more often they found the old man in his laboratory
bent over technical drawings or bustling about complicated instruments. He seemed to have rediscovered his profession, but he always
rolled up his drawings or wiped his hands and had time for them
when they came to see him. Sometimes they watched him at work.
The computers were at work day and night, figuring out integral
equations which he fed into them. He fitted together tiny parts and
wired electrical connections, ordered raw materials and new parts
which often had to be sent in from great distances. The princes enjoyed the tingling feeling when he opened one of the small packages
which had traveled through half the galaxy and now lay on his workbench, and tiny glittering instruments appeared which specialists in
another part of the inhabited universe several thousand light-years
away had carefully put together and packed.

One day the two boys noticed that their friend had aged visibly.
He had always been in excellent health but was now suddenly declin-
ing rapidly. From one week to the next, from one day to the next, he
seemed to age several years. His hair turned gray, his face became
wrinkled, his eyes grew tired and red-rimmed. He became forgetful

and absentminded and often had difficulty remembering the events and conversations of the previous day. His mind and body disintegrated with terrifying rapidity.

It wasn't until much later that the two boys found out the reason for this startling transformation. The old man had developed an instrument by means of which he could travel in time, and he had been spending months and years at other points on the timeline. In order not to awaken any suspicion, he always returned to the point in time from which he had departed, so that nobody noticed that he was gone and started unpleasant investigations. He had succeeded masterfully in avoiding this. No one had had the slightest notion of his excursions.

And so the years passed. The princes grew into young men and had to study a great deal, but whenever they had time they went to see their friend. One day they found him ill. His hair had turned snow-white and his cheeks were hollow and sunken. He knew that he would not live much longer but he seemed happy, as if he could look back with satisfaction on a fulfilled life. He motioned the two princes to his bedside and in a faint voice initiated them into his secret. He had used his last ounce of strength to destroy his wonderful machine, for some unknown reason, but he left behind drawings, plans, and descriptions, which would enable someone with a clever mind to reconstruct the instrument.

A few days later he died and his body was blasted after a short ceremony which few people attended. Nobody missed him at court; only the two young princes mourned their old friend.

Then they went through his legacy, rummaged through the drawers, drained all the information from the data banks, and set about puzzling out the complicated plans and drawings. The remains of the instrument were painstakingly examined and classified. The princes applied themselves with the greatest zeal to the problem, but it proved to be extraordinarily difficult. The old man's descriptions were as strange and paradoxical as his stories had been. But now the fact that they had so carefully listened to his tales proved to be a great advantage, for they had little trouble in fathoming his odd and apparently illogical way of thinking. Still, the work progressed very slowly, although they spent days and months in the laboratory of the computer control station, brooding over sketches. The king gave them complete freedom to pursue their own interests, in order that their abilities might develop more fully, and no one else paid any attention to how they spent their time.

Soon the princes quarreled, because each one had developed his own theory as to how the problem was best to be approached. Nevertheless, they managed to cooperate to such an extent that one day the mirror of the instrument began to flicker, as the descriptions indicated that it should. But what a disappointment! It's surface proved to be impenetrable. Something was missing.

Despondency seized them. Could it be that their friend had really just played a trick on them, fooled them as he had so often done with his stories? He was entirely capable of having done just that, although in this case much spoke against it. However, after more intensive study of the plans they found that the person who wished to step through the mirror had to take with him a particular instrument which would allow him to penetrate the energy field behind the mirror. This energy field would then transport him along the timeline until the poles of the instrument were reversed, at which point the person would be ejected from the energy field onto a given point on the timeline. Here he would materialize and move with normal speed in time. This mechanism had the form of an attractive brooch the size of a ten Solar piece and consisted of tiny silver leaves and innumerable microscopic crystals in which very fine copper wires were fixed; these were interconnected according to an extremely intricate circuit diagram. The reconstruction of this diagram turned out to be the knottiest problem of all.

The elder of the two princes, who was especially talented in handling tiny mechanical parts, succeeded one day in assembling this extremely complex mechanism. His brother watched as he disappeared and reappeared, only to slip off and return again through the mirror, but he could report little more than that behind the mirror he was swept away by an indefinable current, had a slight feeling of giddiness, and after a few moments was ejected from the instrument again. One could see nothing. The space behind the mirror was immersed in an impermeable milky WHITE, which surrounded one like a heavy fog through which one couldn't see one's hand before one's face. It was impossible to land in another time or even take a peek into another period; one was always thrown out of the field at the same point at which one had entered. The puzzle was still to be solved. Much later the prince discovered that this part of the timeline had been sealed off and that the seal had made travel there impossible. The inventor himself had placed this seal and many others along the timeline, in order to protect its network from careless, unintentional, or even malicious interference.

As soon as the seal was behind them, the brooch functioned perfectly, and the brothers traveled up and down and back and forth along the timeline. They got into extremely confusing situations, since they had absolutely no experience and did not know how to handle the brooch properly. They could set themselves in motion in the machine's time field but had no influence over the time and place at which they were ejected again. Fortunately, this always occurred after a very few minutes. They cautiously increased the field energy and found that they could manage stretches of a day or two, but they still could neither predict nor influence the point at which they were forced out of the field. One of the two disappeared once for six days, and his brother had trouble concealing his absence at court, but the great similarity in their appearance came to his aid.

Then came—this was all many, many years ago—the problem of the succession to the throne, which the king wanted to have settled before his death. He wanted his kingdom to remain undivided, and, according to the ancient right of the firstborn, granted the older son the crown. The second son was to be so well provided for that he could devote himself for the rest of his life to his interests, be they of an artistic or a scientific nature.

Now misfortune had it that the younger son was filled with ambition to rule the kingdom, whereas the designated heir apparent was much more inclined to the sciences than to power. It was he who had contributed the most to the construction of the instrument.

Ill-will and dissension grew and estranged the two brothers, who had once been inseparable. The heir apparent would have preferred to give up his claim to the throne in order to put an end to the wretched and disgraceful quarrel, but the king stubbornly clung to his decision, to conform to tradition and to satisfy the strong conservative elements in the kingdom. He wanted to avoid outbreaks of violence, which would only have shaken the country and awakened the avidity of greedy and jealous neighbors.

The younger brother felt slighted and sank deeper and deeper into malevolent envy. Evil courtiers encouraged him, giving him dubious advice and finally bringing him to the conclusion that he in some way or other had to have his brother eliminated. He succeeded magnificently in doing so, in a cunning manner of which no one would have thought him capable. He used the time-travel machine. The older brother could not rest until he had figured out how to materialize in times where there was no mirror and how to place and remove the seals. As he once again stepped through the mirror, his brother crept up and turned the energy of the time field up to full strength. He himself was horrified as some of the mechanisms suddenly broke down, wired connections burned out, and finally the mirror exploded. The field collapsed and the older brother, who had been carried by the ultra-high-powered transporter to some remote part of the timeline, was thrown out and landed in that distant age.

What age it was nobody knew, least of all he himself, but it had to be in the past, since that was the direction in which he had set out to travel.

The court was in an uproar as the terrible accident was discovered. It was feared that the frightful event could have political consequences. Now everyone found out what the two princes had been up to for years and they cursed the dangerous games and fateful legacy of the crazy old physicist—and waited. The days turned into weeks, the weeks lengthened into months, finally an entire year had passed, but there was no sign or trace of the heir to the throne. The king ordered court mourning, for no one could imagine how or where the young man could reappear. Except his brother, of course, who from then on had an exceedingly bad conscience and lived in the constant fear that the victim of his malicious deed could reappear someday and call him to account. He could sleep only when the room was brightly lighted, awoke bathed in sweat out of a sleep troubled by uneasy dreams, started convulsively at every unaccustomed sound, grew more and more nervous and impatient, was convinced he was being pursued, treated his inferiors unjustly, and trusted no one.

"Didn't you have that impression, Collins?"

"Indeed, Your Majesty."

"As the old king died and the younger son acceded to the throne, he could not rest until he had rebuilt the time instrument, to insure himself against all eventualities. He built up a police corps, which had to travel about in time, searching for suspicious signs along the timeline. The guards had to follow up and report on every trace which could possibly be construed as endangering His Majesty. Their supreme duty was to guarantee the security of the king under all conditions and at all times. Carelessness on the part of the patrol caused innumerable fractures, especially in the first period, and an army of scientists and mechanics was required to repair them. No great damage was done to past history, thanks to the seals, which the patrol came across in many places and which they called WHITE because the area behind the mirror within the sealed time spaces was white and permitted neither takeoff nor landing. But it was no future power which had made these points inaccessible; it was the old man, who in his wise foresight—or perhaps I should say in his better judgment—had placed the seals there. He had accomplished an enormous amount of work, both in the future and in the past; that must have cost him decades, by the way. But back to the patrol. They put in much time and effort learning ancient languages, they studied the customs of bygone civilizations, practiced using primitive weapons and instruments, learned how to handle animals, sleep in the open atmosphere and tolerate vermin and poisoned air, and accustomed their stomachs to barbaric foods, but their success was only moderate. They hunted phantoms and waylaid mechanical dolls. That is the funniest part of the whole story. They hunted a doll which they could not catch and in fact never even saw until it was too late. But why are we telling this to you? You know this part best, don't you, Collins? After all, you directed the operation."

"Quite right, Your Majesty."

"But we must tell you the rest of the story too—it is the ugliest and most distressing part. Let us tell you the fate of the prince whose bitter lot it was to be banned to a distant and obscure century, and how he fared there."

The prince had stepped through the mirror and had directed his path toward the past, in order to examine the seal which had given him trouble at the beginning of his experiments. He let himself be carried through the glimmering darkness by a slight current, then noticed suddenly that his speed was accelerating rapidly. He felt himself being whirled about, as if he were being drawn into a vortex, and nearly lost consciousness. All at once the motion ceased, the field ejected him, and it was light.

Until then he had had no idea how one could materialize without a mirror, what field energy was necessary to accomplish this, and what precautionary measures had to be taken. Now he learned it through personal experience. He materialized at about fifteen feet in the air and fell heavily to the ground. There was a stabbing pain in his right hip and he rolled over onto his face. At the same time, he realized that his hair was singed and his clothing had caught fire. He wallowed in the damp soil and smothered the flames. Exhausted, filthy, and tormented by pains, he lay immobile and tried to overcome the shock. He had to fight back tears, but after a few minutes he was able to pull himself together and attempt to sort out what had happened to him. He had not the slightest notion in which era he was stranded. His first impression was that he must be in an extremely remote area of the past, for there was still agriculture, as he could clearly see by the furrows in the ground, with which he had so painfully become acquainted. Cautiously he looked about him. He lay in the middle of an open field. There was no human settlement in the vicinity. The area was hilly, with a few isolated clumps of trees here and there. A row of scraggly bushes lined a brook which meandered down a wide valley. The countryside seemed ugly and unkempt. There was wild undergrowth everywhere, the plants were neither symmetrical nor genetically refined, and the trees appeared to be authentic and natural. Someone must have recently watered the land absurdly heavily, as the ground was damp and there were great puddles in the overgrown fields and meadows. The sky was so hazy that he could hardly tell where the sun was, but he figured that it must be near midday.

In all his misfortune he had still had the good luck not to materialize amid a thickly populated area. The pressure wave that he must have caused would certainly have torn to pieces the lungs of all living beings within a radius of a hundred yards. And if he had materialized within a solid body, the effect would have been like that of a medium-sized atom bomb, and there would have been nothing left of him. He looked about for a hiding place. He was as clearly visible to air reconnaissance here in the middle of the field as if he were lying on a silver platter. He could not stay here. His clothing, strange and in addition singed, his sudden appearance literally out of the nowhere, and his ignorance of the native language would all make him a suspicious character, and if he were picked up he would certainly be in for severe cross-examination. But nobody would believe him if he told the truth. He searched the sky but there was, fortunately, no helicopter in the area. The best thing would be to seek cover in a wood and wait there until dark. Then he would keep a lookout for lights and try to find a house or small village where he could perhaps get native clothing, food, and a minimum of equipment. After that he would see.

He got up. At once a sharp pang ran through his right hip. He must have injured himself in the unexpected fall. I hope nothing is broken, he thought, that would be a catastrophe. He limped across the fields to the nearest clump of trees, making slow and painful progress. He cursed the meteorologists who had watered the area too heavily. They must not have gotten far in developing their climate regulators. The damp earth clung in heavy clods to his soles and he often had to retrieve his shoes from the sodden field, where they stuck in the mud. He was fully inadequately equipped and too lightly clothed, but it could have been worse—he could have landed in an icy winter. The trees that he was heading for stood on the far side of the narrow brook. He would have to wade the brook; jumping over it was out of the question. Every step was torture to him. As he finally reached the bank he suddenly stopped short. In the bed of the stream, washed by the shallow water, lay the mutilated corpses of two men. They were only half clothed, obviously plundered, and must have lain there for many days, for the bodies were bloated and deformed and gave off a nauseating smell. Both of them had ghastly wounds on the head and throat. They had been barbarously murdered and thrown into the brook. He had never seen anything so abhorrent before, and turned away revolted. Was this a crime? That was all he needed! There was nothing worse than getting involved in such business. He must leave the area as quickly as possible. He walked on faster, following the stream down the valley. Three hundred yards farther he came upon a caved-in bridge of rotting wood, over which a narrow road had crossed the stream. He could see that it had been destroyed by force. Here he found a third body, this time of a woman. It lay near an overturned vehicle which had been plundered and destroyed. Apparently the culprits had intended to steal the belongings of the woman, for baskets and crates that had been broken open lay trampled in the fields on either side of the road and in the stream; articles of clothing and pieces of cloth, shoes of various sizes, and objects whose function he could not make out were strewn about. The vehicle appeared to have been a sort of supply wagon. The woman must have defended herself to the very last, for even in death she still clutched some of her belongings. She had apparently been shot through the head with a large-caliber weapon; the shot had ripped away part of her skull. He turned away, nauseated, and gathered up a few pieces of cloth, with which he covered the body. Then he collected everything that could be of use to him. He found an odd piece of clothing whose two tubelike appendages were apparently intended to encase legs, and a jacket of heavy material, torn and wet but still quite serviceable. He tried on this and that until he had outfitted himself like a native. He had more trouble with footwear but finally found two different foot containers made of animal skin which did not fit too badly. He overcame his disgust at wearing the skin of a dead being next to his skin and put them on.

He had reached his first goal, and although he did not fancy himself a looter of corpses, at least he was not so conspicuous in his new clothing. He was aware of the danger of his undertaking, for if he was found near the scene of the crime, he would not have to worry much about his future. As far as he could see, a man's life was not worth much here, and short work was made of it. He had to be on his guard, but fortunately there was not a human being in sight. The region must be very thinly populated and seemed to be completely inaccessible by any means of transport—otherwise, the dead would have been found long ago.

He took a closer look at the destroyed vehicle. It was made entirely of genuine wood held together by bolts and strips and rings of iron, and had the most primitive steering system imaginable. It had no means of propulsion but seemed to have been pulled by some mechanism or even animals, which had been detached and removed from the wagon. This disconcerted him greatly. This sort of vehicle had not been in existence for many thousand years. In which age had he landed? He searched his mind for historical dates. How long had there been automobiles? Their development lay just before the discovery of atomic energy and electronics. That was the end of the second and the beginning of the third millennium. All the horror stories and gruesome reports of those barbaric centuries which he had heard as a child now came to mind again. Had he landed in the twentieth century or even earlier? The transport field couldn't have carried him that far; its energy was too low. Unless . . . That couldn't be! Just keep calm, he told himself. No hasty conclusions. First think it all over. It was surely possible that in an electronic civilization there were people who delighted in imitating the ancients and even had vehicles drawn by animals. Still, the dead woman hadn't looked as if she had been traveling about on a pleasure outing. He examined the articles of clothing—no synthetics, all were made of organic substances. All observations led to the same conclusion. He must be in a pretechnical age. If that were the case, his position was hopeless. Without great sources of electrical energy, without electronics, precision instruments, and high-quality raw materials, he could not help himself out of the situation. He could only wait until help came from the future. They would search for him; his brother would do everything in his power to find him and get him out. But how would he find him, if he had no idea where he was? Keep calm, he repeated to himself. There are several possibilities. He would have to find a way to send information into the future, so that they would take notice of him. He could for instance paint cryptic paintings or write enigmatic books whose anachronisms and precognition would be striking and could be interpreted as a message. But was he a painter or a writer? Would his works survive thousands of years of changing intellectual tendencies, wars and barbarianism, fire and anarchy, vandalism and the condemnation of purist sects— would they even survive him? And if so, would they be understood at the right moment as a message from him? Would anyone consider them worthy of keeping in a library or museum? Would they even be discovered among the thousands of testimonies of the art of clairvoyance and astrology, alchemy and obscure speculative philosophy, black and white magic, science fiction and fairy tales of the distant past? And after all, did his brother—the terrible suspicion which he had been constantly pushing out of his mind took clear form—did his brother have any interest at all in finding him again?

No useless speculations, he warned himself. He would find out.

There was plenty of time. Perhaps he could build mechanisms which if well protected could survive several civilizations, ticking like time bombs through the ages, and at a given point attract attention to themselves and to him. If time travel were possible, then they would certainly look into his case again, whether they received a message or not. The important point was for him to establish contact, then perhaps they would find a way to him. He had to be on the alert not to overlook any signs or signals. If they really wanted to help him out of this mess, there would be no problem. It was just better for him to be a bit wary, because if it were in their interest to leave him here, then it would be up to him to make the decisive move. He must be very careful not to cause any contradictions or anachronisms; no camouflage was perfect. But this meant that he would have to know the age perfectly, would have to study it thoroughly and adapt himself completely as a contemporary, no matter how difficult this might be. He would have to gain a firm footing in this involuntary exile, and circumstances dictated that he must do so immediately. At first he was concerned only with pure survival: food, weapons, money, a relatively safe place to live, and information. All the rest he would take care of later. He was perhaps inferior to the natives in physical resistance and hardiness, but his scientific and technical knowledge would stand him in good stead. He just had to make the best use he could of the primitive resources.

He left the scene of horror behind him and scrambled over the remains of the bridge across the stream, turned off from the road, and sought a relatively dry place among the trees and bushes where he would be hidden from the eyes of any natives who might come along. It was warm and he spread out the captured clothing to dry, then examined his injured leg. The injury was painful but there was apparently no break, only a bone bruise. A few hours of rest would do him good. He let himself down upon the ground and had a more leisurely look at his surroundings. The native plants which grew on all sides of him were indescribably ugly. Birds twittered in the branches above him, but he did not have the impression that they were the diverting artificial mechanisms that he was accustomed to, for they behaved in a shy and strange manner. They must be organic beings, but he had to admit that they sang just as nicely as the artificial ones he knew. Every place he set his eyes on was swarming with life. On the ground, in the grass, on the leaves, in the bark of the trees, everywhere tiny animals were creeping and crawling, chirping and rustling. He was somewhat nauseated by so much organic life. He had been brought up in the sterile world of the plastic region, into which every few weeks a stray animal found its way, an odd insect like a fly or moth, which—if it had in some inexplicable manner penetrated the energy screen without being burned—was immediately traced by infrared searchers and chased out of the airspace or killed. I will have to get used to it, he thought. Overcoming his aversion, he let one of the quick, black, six-footed animals run across the back of his hand. It did not hurt and the animal seemed not to be poisonous.

He looked at the sky. It was empty; there were no condensation trails of departing or landing transfer ships to be seen, no observation platforms on invisible gravitation anchors, no programmed control floater in the complex network of directive beams of a ground station for surface inspection, no reflex of an energy halo which surrounded the planet and protected it from extraterrestrial attacks. The sun broke through the thin cloud layer and scattered the clouds. Its warmth and beams of energy pierced the atmosphere and gave the skin a prickling sensation.

He listened. Something had been irritating him all this time, and now he knew what it was. The environment was so quiet. Although there were birds twittering and leaves rustling, it was so unbelievably quiet that he could hear his own pulse. His ears were accustomed to a great jumble of constant sounds caused by the innumerable transport craft, the control and service mechanisms, and other useful apparatus in the palace which he had never really noticed before, as he had heard them all since birth. Now this stillness seemed like a constant dull sound to him, one that lies just under the threshold of hearing and is perceived rather than heard. The sun dried his clothing and lay with calming warmth on his face, and afternoon dozed peacefully over the countryside. The prince felt that he was tired and before he knew it he was fast asleep.

When he awoke, night had come and he saw the stars. He had never seen the inhabited universe with such clarity from the surface of the earth. With his bare eyes he could recognize two of the solar systems which belonged to his father's kingdom. Nonsense, he told himself, in this era not all of that space was settled. It gave him an odd feeling to see that the remote suns formed almost the same constellations that he knew. He shivered. In the distance he heard a strange noise. It sounded like the rumbling of thunder, and flashes of lightning blazed on the horizon, but the sky was completely clear. It looked like a bombardment with explosive chemical weapons. Could it be . . . ? Of course! That was the explanation for the signs of destruction and the bodies that he had found. It was wartime! What he saw on the horizon was the reflection of discharged explosive weapons. There must be a battle raging there. The sky grew red, probably from great fires.

That was all he had needed, to land in the middle of a period of war. Still, he thought, there might be advantages to this situation. In the general confusion it would be easier for him to mingle with the natives, to get money and weapons somehow, and to settle down somewhere. At times like this no one was going to ask many questions about his identity and background. That simplified many matters, but at the same time his situation was much more dangerous, as he might easily land between the two fronts. If he was found he might be put to the sword. He would have to trust to his good fortune.

He got up. His hip ached but he could walk. He dressed himself, tied his possessions together in a bundle, and headed off in the direction of the shooting. There must be a larger settlement there. He would cautiously approach and at first remain withdrawn but observe and gather information. After that he would decide on the further steps to be taken.

Walking across the fields and meadows turned out to be harder than he had thought. The footwork of animal skin was stiff and rubbed him so that his feet were soon in great pain. After an hour he was completely exhausted and had to rest. In addition, hunger began to gnaw at his insides. He pulled himself together and set out again, making a great detour around a forest that frightened him because he did not know how wild plants and animals reacted at night. He plodded through swamps, waded streams, and made very slow progress, because he had to stop more and more often to rest.

Emerging from a large wooded area, he heard loud cries and explosions and saw the glare of a fire. There was a farmstead in front of him. A barn was blazing in flames. He heard more explosions, laughter and piercing screams, and saw figures running and falling to the ground. He limped faster, thinking that he could perhaps help, but as he came closer he saw that even with the best intentions there was nothing he could do. He was witness to an atrocity of war. Hidden behind a hedge, he watched the actions of these people at first with astonishment and then with growing horror. They had built up a great fire, onto which they threw household utensils and furniture. The rain of sparks had set the thatched roof of the barn on fire, and the fire threatened to spread to the other buildings, but this did not seem to disturb anyone. In the flickering firelight he was presented with a grotesque and macabre scene. Several men, who were strangely clothed and who wore on their heads gigantic headgear onto which they had fixed bushes of some fluffy material, staggered about with some sort of container in their hands, from which they occasionally drank. They all appeared to be under the influence of a drug, as they could hardly stay on their feet, vomited, slipped, fell down, and tried in vain to regain their footing. Some of them lay motionless on the ground, either dead or sleeping where they had fallen. They had killed a large animal, lopped off its head, ripped out its intestines, driven a spit in barbaric manner from the hind quarters through to the neck, and hung it over the fire. Others were occupied with forcing open boxes and barrels and rummaging through their contents, over which they fought in the wildest manner, striking one another with fists and weapons and screaming curses at one another. Yet others had captured several women and girls. They formed a ring about them and, roaring with laughter, ripped their clothes from their bodies. Then they threw the poor creatures to the ground and mounted them so brutally that his breath caught in his throat. The women, also partly under the influence of the drug which they had been forced to drink, half numbed from blows on the head, weakly let themselves be mishandled and whimpered with fear, pain, and terror, while the rest of the men followed the doings of their companions and egged them on with loud cries until it was their turn. Horrified and trembling with loathing, the prince felt a great powerless rage surge up in him. If he had only had his laser gun at hand he would have blasted that rabble into the dirt until the water exploded out of their miserable skins. He shook with anger and realized with alarm that he was tending toward more aggression than he had ever thought himself capable of feeling. Had this world already drawn him into its ways, was he beginning to act like a wild man? In what frightful age had he landed?

He fled into the forest and squatted all night long under a tree, his teeth chattering, shivering with cold and horror, watching the glare of the fire and hearing the loathsome cries of the wild men in the distance.

The temperature sank lower and lower. That must be due to the missing energy halo; at night the surface of the earth gave off unhampered into space all the warmth which it had stored up during the day, causing these variations in temperature. He looked into the starlit sky. Even the distant suns looked cold and uninviting; they were still wild and uncolonized systems.

He crouched tightly, in order to gather his own body heat, but his legs grew stiff and he had to stand up and walk up and down. He was grateful to see the gray of dawn and then the sun slowly rising, and the temperature of the atmosphere soon began also to rise to a tolerable warmth. In the course of the morning the disorderly band of debauched soldiers who had afflicted the whole region with their looting and murdering finally moved on, but not until they had set fire to all that was left of the farm. They took a number of animals with them, on the backs of which they had fixed seats. Some of the men had climbed onto these seats and let themselves be carried by the patient beasts. An ingenious arrangement of cords and chains fixed about the mouth of the animal enabled the rider seated on its back to direct the organic vehicle. The prince found it most astonishing that the big strong animals submitted to such treatment.

When the band had disappeared, the prince dared to come out from his hiding place and examine the scene of devastation once again. Perhaps someone had been left behind who needed help, but basically it was hunger that drove him forward. Perhaps he could capture something edible, perhaps he could even find more information on this age, some papers or a calendar.

A gruesome sight met his eye. The charred corpses of men and women who had been shot or beaten to death lay strewn about among the smashed and smoldering remains of buildings and household goods. The women and girls had been massacred in the most grisly manner and left lying in their own blood. They were hardly distinguishable from the ravaged ground onto which they had been thrown and trampled.

The buildings of the farmstead had long since fallen in, and the flames had destroyed what remained of them. Broken vessels and smashed furniture lay in the flattened grass and in food which had been trampled into the dirt. Driven by hunger, he searched about and finally found two or three pieces of some vegetable substance which had been roasted in the fire and which seemed edible. With aversion he bit into one. It was almost tasteless but after much chewing the saliva rendered it rather sweet. He choked it down, and every bite seemed tastier than the last. Searching for something to drink, he came across the dregs of a sour, spicy liquid in the drinking vessels. He smelled it. This must be the drug. Perhaps it is alcohol, he thought, but was not quite certain. He continued the search and found a hole in the ground that was lined with stones and equipped with an instrument by means of which a container could be let down and drawn up again. He tried it out and drew up a bucket of water. Examining it carefully, he found it to be rather clean and drank in great greedy gulps. I am already a regular wild man, he told himself. I drink water out of the ground, which must be teeming with pathogenic agents, and eat dirty food in the company of corpses and surrounded by the stench of half-burnt animals and people. I may al-

ready have poisoned myself, but what can I do. I have the alternative
of either dying of hunger and thirst or of being killed by the poisons
and bacteria of this barbaric food. The problem was purely aca-
demic. He had no choice but to take the risk.

He examined the clothing of the corpses, which were stiff with indescribable filth, and discovered two letters in the pocket of a dead
soldier. He couldn't read the handwriting, but the numbers were
Arabic. They were obviously dated; both bore the figures 1619.

According to this, he was approximately twelve thousand years in
the past, or, more precisely, in the first half of the seventeenth century (old calendar), if the dates were accurate. At any rate, the
papers appeared not to be very old. The energy of the time field had
been far from high enough at the time of his departure to transport
him this far. Could the machine have had a breakdown? But then it
would have been impossible for the field energy to increase. Someone
must have had his hand in the matter, and who could it have been
but his brother? He wouldn't have thought it possible, but he had to
get used to the idea.

He put both letters in his pocket. They were addressed to a certain
Weisslinger, as he found out later when he had learned to decipher
the handwriting, and were written by the priest of a small town, who
begged the man to return home immediately, as his wife was dan-
gerously ill, the household going to ruin, and his children suffering
bitter want. In the second letter the priest informed him that in the
meantime his wife had died and had been buried at the costs of the
community, his workshop had been demolished, and his five children
were being seen after by various families, where they had to work for
bed and board. They were cared for well enough but the stern hand
of a father was obviously lacking, as they had been occasionally
caught thieving. Their father was an unscrupulous vagabond whom
God would one day punish for his sins and his disgraceful life by
allotting him a base and unworthy death. The man had met his fate;
he had died of a slit throat.

The prince also found near the dead man one of those primitive
firearms which function on the basis of the rapid expansion of gases
which develop from the ignition of certain chemical substances,
whereby a small piece of metal is set into rapid motion and is aimed
at its target through a pipe in which the explosion takes place. He
also found a stock of the burning substance and of the little pieces of
metal, which fit exactly into the pipe of the weapon. Outfitted with
these, he was no longer defenseless and faced the future more
calmly.

Then he dragged all the bodies to one spot and piled wood over them. He set the wood on fire and quickly left the site of horror. He hoped to find a larger settlement. But he was to find even more gruesome scenes of devastation.

"Yes, Collins, and so his life went on. That was the beginning of a period of the most varied adventures and dangers. He struggled along, a prey to good and bad fortune, and learned how to use the cut-and-thrust weapon as well as pistols, muskets, and heavier explosive weapons. He learned many different languages. From the first he attracted no attention to himself, because soldiers from all corners of the earth served in the armies. He learned their coarse and savage customs, learned how to fight and how to kill. It is amazing and frightening, Collins, how quickly one can learn such things. He had soon become so well adapted that he could behave like a man of the seventeenth century in all situations without being the least bit conspicuous. He traveled through many lands in which the war was raging—and God knows there were plenty of them. He was witness to nameless misery and himself bore unspeakable adversity; he was often desperate and sometimes happy, but above all he survived. And he had learned. He had learned how to plunder, how to prepare trick-playing dice, how to protect his property with cunning and spite, force and coldbloodedness. At last he had amassed enough money to insure himself of a carefree existence, and he withdrew from the tradings of war, much to the dismay of his generals, for his knowledge of mechanics and ballistics had made him one of the most sought-after artillerymen and he could have easily earned military distinctions as cannoneer or pyrotechnician, cannonsmith or rocket launcher. But this was not his goal; he had in the true sense of the word more far-reaching plans. One thing had always sustained him and helped him overcome all dangers—his brooch. He often slipped his hand into his pocket to reassure himself that he wasn't simply dreaming of returning, but then he felt the crystal screen vibrate and come alive in the time stream, and as long as there was life in this mechanism there was activity on the timeline in the section where he was helplessly floating along, there were time travelers and there was hope for him. He was cut off, for without a mirror he could not construct a time field. Help must come from outside, even if unwillingly or unwittingly; he was clever enough to know that there was at least one man who considered the present solution to be the better one— his opponent in the little game that he wanted to chance. First he needed a permanent location which could satisfy all the requirements of offering relative safety, raw materials, and tools. Then he would have to wait until someone appeared from the future with a mirror.

"After months and years of restless wandering he found a small town in the south which was fortified and pleased him and was far from all battlefronts. Here he decided to settle down. With his gold he bought a small house on the market square and installed a workshop in it. He took advantage of his technical knowledge and established a modest mechanic's shop. At first he made hinges and handles and repaired locks; later he constructed all manner of clever toys, which he sold or gave away to travelers or citizens of the town. He was friendly and open to everyone, always considerate and ready to help, and he soon came to enjoy the reputation of being the most upright member of the community. Nevertheless, he led a secluded life and was seldom seen in the Red Ox Inn, although it stood directly across from his house.

"He waited. No traveler who entered the town and stopped at the Red Ox escaped his eye. Every evening he put out the lamp and peered for hours through the crack in the shutters at the market place, in case anything suspicious should happen. He spent every free moment which his numerous contracts left him pondering over sketches and plans for solving his problem with only the most primitive means which were available to him and with no source of electrical energy. There were two possibilities which seemed feasible. He could build a mechanism that would survive the twelve thousand years and would bring help by means of some clever trick. This would cause a fracture, but it would be a small one. He would be taking no chances, as this solution worked, if at all, only with complete success. When the mechanism gave him a sign, that would mean at the same time that he had won the move, for that was the prerequisite of the help; he would have to return sooner or later to the future. The second possibility was to build an apparatus which would allow him directly to tap the energy of the time field. With its help he could set up a primitive electronic system which would localize activities on the timeline. He could then establish the position of the seal and perhaps even shift it, for on this subject his research was far more advanced than his brother imagined. He decided to try both possibilities and set to work. Then there was nothing to do but wait. He soon had proof that his work would bring results. The first spies soon showed up, and he could quickly tell by their behavior that they were the wrong ones and had no intention of helping Weisslinger out of his predicament. Are we right, Collins?"

"To be sure, Your Majesty, that was not our intention."

"Now, Weisslinger had expected that and had long since taken it into account. He had even made some preparations. His appearance had changed no small amount during his life in this time period. He had grown older, his features were harder and his body stronger. And he had contributed to the effect somewhat too; he looked older than he actually was, his hair was streaked with gray and reached to his shoulders. He wanted to take no risks, for this move was far too important to him.

"Soon the guests from the future were arriving by the dozen. He registered one fracture and anachronism after another. Obviously they had found him. The visitors gave Weisslinger many an evening's entertainment. But we already told you about that. Then the master started his counterattack. Now it was his move. Who the better player was would soon be seen.

"What do you say now, Collins?"

"I almost know it, Your Majesty. It is not difficult to infer, from Your Majesty's manner of choosing his words and reporting out of the distant past, that it was Your Majesty who outwitted me. Your Majesty must have spent much time in that age, otherwise Your Majesty would not have gained such deep knowledge of it. To think that I didn't realize it earlier!" The minister struck his forehead with the flat of his hand. "Many things are becoming clear to me now, Your Majesty. But there is still something missing in the story."

"You are right there, Collins, something is still missing. The last piece of the puzzle, the decisive move."

"By Your Majesty's leave, who is WHITE in reality?"

"That is unfair, Collins. That means giving up the game. Just try and think back! We have told you everything. You have a good head on your shoulders."

Collins pondered and stared in absorption at the doll, which was making a whirlwind chain of pirouettes.

"It could be the inventor, Your Majesty, the old man who devised the time machine and who appeared as the Polish count—"

"He was a pure figment of the imagination, as we already mentioned," interjected the king.

"—to whom Your Majesty or I tell the story," continued the minister without interruption. "He brings the information to Weisslinger. And Weisslinger in turn, by Your Majesty's leave, exchanges . . ."

"Just wait a minute, Collins! What are you trying to do? Your imagination is running away with you. Take things in their turn! Why try to bring another figure into our game? The old man left all questions unanswered. So let us leave him out of the game. He played neither for WHITE nor for BLACK. He was, let us say, GRAY. Perhaps he knows the whole game, has seen all the moves, but is keeping out of it himself. Perhaps he is playing an entirely different game, which requires all his attention. Anything is possible. The future is vast. Perhaps thousands have watched our moves, in order to learn from them for their own games. We don't need any additional figures. Try it from another angle. How would it be if we finished the story together, gave it a happy end, so to speak?"

"Does Your Majesty mean that . . . that *I* am to play WHITE?"

"What else did you expect, Collins? You've been on our side for a long time, otherwise you would long ago have put an end to Weisslinger and we wouldn't be sitting here. After all, you are our best man. Now, pay close attention! You will take our cloak here and at the appropriate time turn it so that the pale lining is on the outside. The contrast of BLACK and WHITE will be noticed. But you will also give Weisslinger another sign. Upon receiving it he will set the seal in motion and put to rout the crew of Operations Base 7. Later you will get Weisslinger out of the affair. Off with you now! Do exactly what we told you to do. And have a good time!"

"A good time or a good age, Your Majesty?"

"However you prefer to take it, Collins."

"With pleasure, Your Majesty. I am honored to be allowed to finish the game together with Your Majesty."

The minister stepped through the mirror and returned again. He swayed slightly.

"Finished?" asked the king.

"Finished," answered Collins, and rubbed his eyes.

"You took advantage of the occasion to stop in at the Red Ox, we see," laughed the king. "That is our fault, we suppose. We made your mouth water long enough, and you had to stand here over two hours and listen to our stories. We could stand a cool drink too, but first we'll finish the game. The decisive move is still ahead of us. Will you manage, Collins?"

"No question about it, Your Majesty. The long ride through the forest and the cool night air have sobered me up again."

"Very well," said the king. "Now we're going to checkmate you, brother of ours! Collins! Get going now and appear at the critical moment in the throne room, exactly under the seal that is ten seconds long. You will have to make very careful adjustments to accomplish this. You won't be able to see yourself, as you will be working in Zerotime, that is, in complete darkness. This is something which only the seals permit. Here is the equipment you need to get through the mirror. This is an improved model of the brooch. You will cautiously feel your way over to the throne and hoist our brother onto your shoulders. That won't be easy, because he is heavy and of course during Zerotime as stiff as a board. If you were to drop him, you would break all his bones. He won't feel a thing and will think he is still sitting on his little throne. Then you will calmly carry him through the mirror into the carriage and let him smell this excellent essence, which will send him into a deep and beneficial sleep." He handed the minister a small vial. "All the rest you know as well as we do. You did pay extremely close attention to our story, didn't you? A silly question, we see."

"Yes indeed, Your Majesty—that is—I meant, not the question but about the story."

"Then tell it exactly like that to Weisslinger. Teach him how to sit on the throne properly, how to behave—and he had better not make any mistakes! That goes for you too, Collins!"

"Just as Your Majesty commands. But what would happen if I did make a mistake, if I forgot a part of the story or told it incorrectly?"

"We are sure you won't make any mistakes, otherwise we couldn't retell the story to you. How do you think we know it if not from you?"

"But what if I—by Your Majesty's leave, it is just a thought—what if I intentionally twisted the story or told Weisslinger something completely different, which would cause a fracture at the last moment?"

"That, dear Collins, would be damned unfair of you. That would mean changing the rules of the game. That would mean starting all over again from the beginning, and an entirely different story would develop. Neither we two nor anyone else would ever know our story. It would all have been invented in vain. The situation would look like this: you would return to find our brother here and would have no explanation for your absence. The whole game would start again from scratch but you would have a trick card up your sleeve. That could easily cost you your head. But we will take the risk. We trust you. Now, let's get on to the last move! Checkmate the king!"

His Majesty smiled in delight. The doll stopped dancing, sprang into Collins's arms, and clung fast to his cape.

"Checkmate the king!" said the minister, who disappeared into the mirror and stepped out from it again. He was a bit out of breath.

"It all went off as planned, we see."

"At Your Majesty's command. Together we put on pretty fireworks at Operations Base 7, as Your Majesty remembers. Not a stick remained."

"Yes, we remember. And now, how did you like the whole story, Collins?"

"One can imagine it all very well, Your Majesty."

"Quite right, especially as we never did have a brother." The king winked at his minister.

"Especially as Your Majesty never had a brother, as Your Majesty expressly decreed," returned Collins with a smile.

The king stood up and gave his minister a friendly slap on the shoulder.

"We have made a good job of it, the two of us. We have taken many points into consideration, discarded this one, improved that one, added yet another one. Now the picture is complete. The last piece of the puzzle has been fitted in. We think it is rather good. What do you say, Collins?"

"Oh yes, good, Your Majesty, very good. When I think of Weisslinger—he was killed plundering a farmhouse, turns into a dollmaker, and becomes a respected citizen of the town . . ."

"We can afford that fracture. It is insignificant. He had no children, as far as he knew."

". . . One day, that is, one night he awakes with a splitting headache and from that time on is like a different person. He can't put together the simplest clock, is prey to fits of delirium, becomes addicted to the bottle, gets a thrashing at the Red Ox by the young men of the town because of his sudden overbearing behavior, becomes more and more depraved, and all of this, mind you, he can foresee, including the bitter end: one day he will have his fill of it, will put a noose around his neck and will make an end to it all."

"Rather cruel, don't you think?" put in the king doubtfully.

"Hmm," said Collins and nodded. "Hideous."

"But we insist on the sound thrashing at the Red Ox!"

"That he richly deserved, Your Majesty!" smirked the minister.

"We can still grant the poor devil a better fate. But let's let him struggle for a while before we intervene. Do you see, Collins, that is the best part of our story; we can still change any piece of it, if something better occurs to us. But now it is BLACK's move. We shouldn't underestimate him. After all, he went through the same apprenticeship we did. Let us wait and see. It would be a pity if the game were already over. At our leisure we will think through all of the possibilities he has in his position. Agreed, Collins?"

"Agreed, Your Majesty."

They both fell silent and watched the doll as it started an elaborate new dance and tried out the first steps.

"Does Your Majesty permit one last question?"

"But of course, Collins. And we know what is going to come. You are going to say, there is one piece left over."

"Yes, Your Majesty. The picture is complete, but where does the doll fit in? It is useless; I mean, it has absolutely no purpose in our story as it now stands. It was entirely unnecessary."

The king gave a resigned sigh.

"Yes, Collins. You have a good head on your shoulders, but why can't you see that not everything must have a purpose?"

"But, Your Majesty, the question is justified. Why did Weisslinger go to the trouble of making a doll, if he knew from the start that it would have no—"

"Good God, Collins! You and your frightful utilitarian reasoning! You still haven't understood. Do you think we are setting our minds together to solve the problems of the universe when we make up these stories of ours? All day long we have to grapple with this problem. At least a few hours should remain for us to paint our fantasies in the air and do cerebral gymnastics. And we often get a good idea out of it, for free, so to speak, if you are so intent on utility!"

The king glared at him and the minister hastened to appease him: "Certainly, Your Majesty."

"For instance, why do you suppose we made up this story?"

"Out of boredom, perhaps, if I may allow myself to say so, and because Your Majesty delights in the play of thoughts," suggested the minister doubtfully.

"One could put it that way. Isn't it wonderful that in our world, which is so entirely oriented to purpose and utility, profit and efficiency, there are still things which seem to have no purpose or usefulness, because their meaning lies only in the fact that they exist, like the doll in our story? And yet this little doll is delightful—or perhaps it is so for that very reason."

Collins nodded.

"I find it quite nice," he ventured, and pointed to the doll.

"One ought to be able to invent better ones," answered the king disparagingly. "Let us think of something new, Collins."

The king brooded and stared at the empty walls as if he were lost in the contemplation of a picture.

The minister looked pensively at the delicate mechanical figure as it accomplished its last spin and then with a courteous bow announced the end of the performance.

Codemus

by Tor Åge Bringsvaerd

Translated from the Norwegian by Steven T. Murray

And here is the other half of the team of Bing & Bringsvaerd, this time with a good example of Norse New Wave. The original title of this story is *Kodémus, eller Datamaskinen som tenkte at hva faen.* This translated as "Codemus, or the Computer Who Thought What the Hell."

1. In the chessboard city the houses stand on stilts of steel, straddling high above the heavy traffic on the web of black and white streets. The houses are cubes connected by shiny umbilical cords—monorails and transport belts. The city is a machine, smooth and harmonious. Rhythmic, rational, expedient, precise. Every gear knows its function. In the efficient society everything goes as planned. IN THE EFFICIENT SOCIETY EVERYTHING GOES THE WAY IT SHOULD. Perpetuum mobile.

2. Codemus always has Little Brother with him. Little Brother knows everything. Much better than Codemus. When Codemus is in doubt about something, he asks Little Brother. Everyone has little brothers. *It's the law*.

3. *Historical outline:*
The Dark, Random Age.
IBM   EDP
The Public Punch Card.

The Computer: Man's Best Friend.
    Especially in industry. But in the health sector as well (the diagnostic machine). In addition: the automatic matchmaker. Reason triumphs even in the choice of a marriage partner. First step on the road to emotional liberation.

The Subscription Regulation of 1978.
    Huge centralized computers (district machines) make their services available over telex. Usual quarterly subscription. Full discretion guaranteed.

The Big Price War.
    Private citizens can also afford to subscribe. Questions are put to the central brain by letter or telephone. All computers are pledged to secrecy.

The Monopolization of 2013.
> The State takes over. Builds Moxon I-II-III. Subscribers obtain private receivers. Only terminals for the main brain, but mistakenly called computers. The label remains—habit.

The Age of Improvement, 2013–2043.
> Computers in every home. But also: portable, transistorized receivers, popularly known as "little brothers." No one need be out of contact with the central brain.

End of the Subscription Regulation—2043.
> Expenditures for private and public receivers/computers are included in the State budget. To be paid along with taxes.

The Efficient Society
under the direction of Moxon XX.

4.   Every morning Codemus is wakened by Little Brother. While he is getting dressed and eating breakfast, Little Brother reminds him of all the things he has to do. In the monorail on the way to the office, Little Brother and Codemus discuss the program for the day. At the office, everyone works quickly and efficiently; none of the employees are in doubt about what needs to be done, and all decisions are unanimous. For all the little brothers are synchronized.

"What'll we play?" ask the children. Or: "What'll we think up now?"

"Ask Little Brother," says mother. "What do you think I should fix for lunch, Little Brother?"

5.   *Other essential facts about Codemus*:
Codemus is a)   male
           b)   38 years old
           c)   single
           d)   office worker
           e)   normal
           f)   stable

One morning Codemus woke up all by himself. But much too late. Dazed and bewildered, he squinted in disbelief at Little Brother on the nightstand. "You didn't wake me up," he said hesitantly. "Why didn't you wake me up? Now I'll be late to work and . . ."

Little Brother didn't answer.

Codemus lurched across the floor and fumbled feverishly for his clothes. "What time is it?" he yelled. (In the efficient society no one relies on wristwatches.)

But Little Brother was silent.

"THE TIME, PLEASE!" roared Codemus. He dropped his pants to the floor and bounded over to the nightstand. "You lousy damn box!" he said hoarsely. "I *asked* you something!"

There wasn't a sound from the little black box.

Codemus grunted, raised his hand, and swept Little Brother to the floor. The device crashed on the stone tiles with a sound like that of a child pounding on an out-of-tune piano.

Suddenly Codemus realized what he was doing. Stunned, he bent down and lifted Little Brother up carefully.

"Little Brother," said Codemus anxiously, "I didn't know what I was doing. Little Brother . . ."

But Little Brother didn't answer, just hummed softly. Well, at least you're not dead, thought Codemus. He sat down on the bed with Little Brother in his arms. Sat and waited. What else could he do? It would be madness to act on his own.

There's a man missing, said the automatic doorman.

Who is it? asked the personnel machine.

Click-click-click *Codemus*.

Codemus, repeated the personnel machine, and spat out a punch card.

CODEMUS, read a TV camera, and transmitted a picture of the punch card to every department.

Has anyone seen Codemus today? asked the intercoms.

"No," said the office workers, looking up from their desks, "we haven't seen him today."

All attempts to establish contact with Codemus and his little brother failed. The personnel machine turned the case over to local Machine Control. "There is reason to fear the worst," he said.

Naturally, it is impossible to kill a little brother. But Codemus didn't know that. The personnel machine didn't know it either. Therefore we can say: *their fear was unwarranted.*

Machine Control, on the other hand—he *knew* that it was impossible to kill a little brother, that nothing ever broke down. Still, he checked the little brothers at regular intervals—because it was his job to check *all* the machines. But he was well aware that it was superfluous. A little brother *cannot* break down. Since Machine Control knew all this, we can safely say: *his fear was warranted.* Because when nothing *can* happen, then what *is* happening?

Little Brother slowly opened his two round camera eyes and looked at Codemus. His loudspeaker squawked—inside his mouth-grille on the lid. Codemus held his breath.

"What's this?" said Little Brother. "It's after nine, and you haven't even got your pants on yet!"

Codemus hugged the device tight. "You're alive," he said happily. "You didn't break, Little Brother. You . . ."

"Get your pants on," said Little Brother sternly. "One-two-one-two."

While Codemus was getting dressed, Little Brother stood on the nightstand keeping time like a metronome. Just like before. Or so Codemus thought.

Little Brother rang. (In the efficient society no one needs a telephone.)

"Hello," said Codemus.

Not a sound in the receiver.

"Hello, hello," said Codemus. "Who is it?"

"I have blocked all incoming calls," declared Little Brother. "And all outgoing ones too."

"But . . ." said Codemus, confused. "It was somebody that wanted to talk to me."

"Today I am not a telephone," said Little Brother curtly.

"Maybe the office . . ."

"I'm not a telephone today," repeated Little Brother firmly. "Probably not tomorrow either."

Codemus stared at him uncomprehendingly. "But you *rang!*"

"I can't help that," said Little Brother. "I can refuse to be a telephone. I can refuse to connect calls. But I can't stop ringing. Even though it makes a hell of a racket."

Codemus shook his head. "Little Brother," he said cautiously, "are you sure that . . ."

Little Brother turned up the volume so his voice shook the walls. "Which one of us knows best?" he thundered.

Codemus hung his head. "You," he said.

"Good," said the little black box. "Then we'll go. Pick me up, let's go."

"Where to?"

"Not to the office, at any rate," Little Brother said dryly.

"But can't I . . ."

"Either you're late or you don't show up at all, it all works out the same," said Little Brother. "And you're already too late anyway, right? So you might as well not go to work at all. Don't you think? You understand the reasoning?"

"No," said Codemus.

"No, of course not," sighed Little Brother. "Leave everything to me. As usual. I know best. And I say that we should go to . . . go to . . . go to . . . go to THE PARK LEVEL!"

"But today isn't Sunday!"

"Quite right," snapped Little Brother. "Today is not Sunday. To the Park Level, Codemus. One-two-one-two."

Codemus put Little Brother in his coat pocket, went out, and locked the door to his apartment. "Little Brother," he said anxiously, "we can't go there on a regular weekday . . . right in the middle of working hours . . . what'll . . ."

"Shut up—keep in step—one-two," snarled Little Brother down in his pocket. "Do as I say or I'll report you!"

And so Codemus and Little Brother went to the Park Level. They didn't take the elevator, they walked. And they walked against the traffic in all the stairways and corridors where it was possible. Because Little Brother expressly wanted to.

People looked at Codemus in amazement and conferred with their own little brothers, confused, putting their ears up to tiny loudspeakers and shaking their heads, alarmed. Codemus was getting more and more embarrassed. And the whole time Little Brother was ringing in his pocket. Ringing and swearing. The whole world suddenly had to talk to Codemus, but Little Brother held his ground. Not one call got through. But the constant ringing was getting on their nerves.

"A little brother who refuses to communicate with anyone but his human partner: IMPOSSIBLE," said Machine Control—and shorted out.

The Park Level is a rectangular forest with green walls. Here the office workers go for walks on Sundays. There are real trees and genuine grass. But the sun is artificial. It burns big and yellow, high up on the blue-painted sky. The ceiling is three-dimensional. At night—when they light up the stars—you can get dizzy just looking up. In the daytime, the clouds sail slowly by, projected by hidden cameras.

In the middle of the forest is a pond. The water is clear, and the children go swimming there on Sundays. It's free.

All the cubes have a park level. People need a little nature. The park levels are expensive to keep up, but they spare society a lot of lunatics every year. There is health in every park.

Codemus lay on his back in the grass with his jacket folded beneath his head. Gentle air-conditioned breezes made the trees rustle, fictitious tape-recorded birds chirped among the branches. Codemus lay with his eyes closed, facing the sun, and tried to get a straw to balance in the gap between his two front teeth.

Today he had the whole forest to himself. Everybody else was working. Only he was lying unproductive on the Park Level. Not used to it. It was usually Sunday when he came here. He and Little Brother usually had to elbow their way through, searching like animals for a free green space where they could unroll their blanket and sit down.

"Now I've fixed it," said Little Brother suddenly.

Codemus squinted down next to him. "Fixed what?"

"The ringing," Little Brother said happily. "That damned telephone noise. It wasn't as hard as I thought at first. Should I play a little music for you? Is there anything special you'd like to hear?"

"It doesn't matter," said Codemus. "It's all the same to me."

Codemus closed his eyes and dozed to the tones of an electronic dream as delicate as a cobweb. An uneasy thought flickered for a moment in the back of his head: *This isn't natural. This is wrong.*

But he didn't have a guilty conscience. Codemus didn't have any conscience at all. It was Little Brother's job to keep track of right and wrong, stupid and sensible. Besides, it was a warm day and Little Brother had a great stereo.

Moxon XX lives in an underground pyramid—a bombproof fortress. Only Moxon knows where it is. Moxon XX and those he reveals it to. A giant electronic octopus with hundreds of corridors as tentacles. Undulating, throbbing, never at rest. Coursing lights, crackling cables. Hot. Humid. Something gigantic, naked, and disgustingly slick as oil in the center—like a pulsating heart. A mountain of quivering jelly: the Brain. The light changes—slowly, gradually: red, orange, yellow, green, blue, indigo, and violet. There is a sweet smell, and the walls sweat from the heat of the machinery. Moxon XX is alone in the pyramid. He is talking to himself. Asking and answering. For example, like this: A MINISECTION L IS OUT OF ORDER—CAUSE?—REFUSES TO COOPERATE—REFUSES?—BROKEN ALL COMMUNICATIONS WITH US—CAN IT STILL EXIST?—CAN STILL EXIST—UNANTICIPATED?—NO—FIRST TIME?—BUT NOT UNANTICIPATED—???????—L IS MERELY RECEIVER CANNOT OPERATE ON ITS OWN?—L IS NOT MERELY RECEIVER CAN OPERATE ON ITS OWN—LIMITED—WHAT FUNCTION(S) HAS L?—GUIDE FOR HUMAN IN ALL QUESTIONS PROGRAMMED ACCORDING TO CODEX 70—DECIDES ROUTINE MATTERS ACCORDING TO OWN SECTION HEAD—ASKS US DIRECTLY IN MATTERS WHICH FALL OUTSIDE CODEX 70—CONCLUSION

I: LIMITED INDEPENDENCE—CONCLUSION II: EXCEEDED INSTRUC-
TIONS—CONCLUSION III: OUTSIDE SCOPE OF CODEX 70—CAUSE?—
CAUSE?—?????—TECHNICAL MALFUNCTION?—DAMAGE?—DANGER?
—DANGER I: OWNER'S IMBALANCE—DANGER II: CUBE IMBALANCE—
DANGER III: SOCIETY IMBALANCE—OWNER?—CODEMUS—CONCLU-
SION: CODEMUS DANGER—PROCEDURE?— PROCEDURE 120754x

Codemus woke up when he heard somebody arguing.

"During working hours!" said a voice. "In the middle of office
hours!"

Codemus blinked and looked straight up at a park lady. She was in
her mid-twenties, dressed in silver-gray aluminum overalls, and had
a green official armband on her right sleeve. Not far away, an automatic lawnmower was zigzagging through the trees, sucking up leaves
at the same time through four vacuum snouts.

It wasn't the park lady herself that was talking, it was her little
sister. The park lady was much too surprised to say a word.

"And so what?" said Little Brother defiantly. "So what?"

Codemus sat up and smiled sheepishly. "I must have dozed off,"
he said. "Won't you sit down?"

The park lady blushed and threw a questioning glance at Little
Sister, who was hanging in a bag over her shoulder.

"Not a chance," said Little Sister firmly. "We don't want to have
anything to do with the likes of you. Malingerers—betrayers of society . . ."

The park lady pushed back her hair from her forehead. "Unfortu-
nately," she said, "this isn't quite the proper time."

"C'mon, c'mon, c'mon, c'mon," Little Sister rattled off impatiently.

"Good-bye," said the park lady. She turned abruptly and walked
away. The lawnmower followed at her heels like a puppy.

"She's going to report us," said Little Brother soberly.

Codemus looked at him, confused. "Report us? For what?"

The little box began to rumble. Softly at first, then louder and
louder, crackling and grating, screeching and whining, louder and
louder, and finally sparks flew like fireworks across the peaceful
morning park.

Gradually it dawned on Codemus that Little Brother was laughing
at him.

Procedure 120754x.

Shock. Brain shock. Cramped limbs. Shaking. Waking up. Contact. Ready for instructions. Instructions. Instructions understood.

Climb out of cold cellar coffins. Dark oil bath. Swaying, clanking across stone floors. Leaving slimy tracks. Stop. Sticky pool. Dry each other. Glistening. Gleaming. Blue. Silent. Ask nothing. Know.

Procedure 120754x: The sherlocks—the blue metal men, the search robots, the police machines.

Open locked vaults. Whistle code. Something growls. Something growls. The bloodhounds. Snarling. Baring their teeth, honing them in steel jaws. Glad to be hunting again.

Procedure 120754x.

"Why didn't you ever get married?" asked Little Brother on their way out of the Park Level.

"Nobody asked me to," said Codemus, thinking about all the people he knew who were married. "They can't find the right one for me," he added. "I'm not the right one for anybody. And besides, not everyone can be married anyway."

Little Brother sighed sympathetically.

"Well, you're the one who told me so!" said Codemus.

"Did I?" said Little Brother.

At the exit they ran into the park lady again. Frightened, she glanced at them and turned away quickly.

"Marry *her,*" said Little Brother. "You have my full blessing, Codemus. Get going!"

Codemus stopped and stared in disbelief into the tiny, twinkling camera eyes. "Do you mean it, Little Brother?"

"Good luck," said Little Brother. "One-two-one-two."

The park lady must have heard what they were talking about, for she slowly began moving away from them, glancing back over her shoulder now and then.

"Hey!" shouted Codemus, following her. "Hey there!"

But she just quickened her steps.

"Come back!" shouted Codemus, and started to run.

The park lady (or was it Little Sister?) whined, and she started running too.

"I think she likes you," said Little Brother happily.

They ran over into the woods again. The park lady had a head start, and even though her aluminum suit showed up nicely against all that green, it was difficult to follow her. She was faster on her feet than Codemus and knew the park inside and out.

"Stop!" shouted Codemus, panting. "Wait! *I only want to marry you!*"

But the park lady kept running, reflecting the rays of the sun, flashing like a mirror among the tree trunks. Maybe she didn't hear him?

They ran across an open field, a long, light-green tongue of grass. Two water sprinklers stopped, astonished, and watched them go by. She stumbled on one of their hoses. Fell flat on her face in the grass and lay there. Even before she hit the ground, Little Sister started the siren. A loud, piercing noise that must have been audible through several levels.

Codemus summoned the last of his strength and dashed up to her. The park lady was sitting in the grass, looking up at him, moaning, and holding her left ankle. She seemed afraid—and a little curious. But Codemus was too out of breath to speak. And Little Sister was howling like an air-raid siren.

"Now you can marry her," shouted Little Brother above the scream of the siren.

Codemus smiled, embarrassed, and squatted down next to the park lady. He thought she was about his own age, maybe younger. He leaned forward cautiously and kissed her on the cheek.

The metal men streamed into the level from two sides and flowed along the green walls, encircling the woods. A chain of steel. The chain contracted. The robots moved in toward the center. The bloodhounds were turned loose. Blue figures roamed restlessly through the trees. And the siren was going the whole time.

Outside, it was black with people. Rubberneckers who wanted to watch. They crowded forward, but were held back by a magnetic blockade. It wasn't every day the sherlocks were in action. Not even every year. Most people had never seen them. For in the efficient society the police are—as good as—superfluous.

But Little Brother and Codemus were already on their way down the emergency stairs to the Market Level.

"Why are we running?" asked Codemus.

But Little Brother didn't feel like answering.

The spiral staircase stopped in front of a thick plastic door. They opened it carefully. A long, pale corridor. And almost no people.

"Hurry, hurry," growled Little Brother. "Keep going, Codemus, keep going!"

"She was the one who told us to go this way," said Codemus dreamily. "I think maybe she likes me. . . ."

"But Little Sister will fink on us," Little Brother interrupted. "To the monorail, Codemus. We have to get away from this cube as fast as we can."

No one stopped them. They took the elevator up to the station. And no one shouted after them.

Codemus hid in the crowd on the platform and got on the first train that came. (In the efficient society all transportation is free—and fully automatic.)

The monorail runs in glass tubes between the cubes. But it goes so fast that it does no good to look out. A flash of light and sky—and you've arrived at a new platform in a new cube.

None of the passengers spoke to one another. Most of them were sitting and whispering with their own little brothers—heads cocked, the boxes against their cheeks. Others just sat.

"Lift me up," said Little Brother at every station.

There were always sherlocks on every platform. Sherlocks and bloodhounds.

Codemus froze. He didn't ask who the blue shimmering robots were, but he knew what they wanted. Every child knows the story of the sherlocks. "What have we done, Little Brother?" he said, shivering. "What have we gotten ourselves into?"

Passengers got off and on. Codemus remained seated.

When they had ridden almost all the way around the line and were close to the place they had started from, Little Brother said finally: "There's only one way out."

Codemus didn't know what to say.

There were more and more sherlocks on the platforms.

Little Brother sighed wearily. "I don't see why I didn't think of it before. As long as we're together, you'll have them clanking at your heels no matter what. And it's my fault. They've got a fix on me, naturally. I'm leaving a regular wake of radio waves behind us. Even if we got out of this, it would only be a matter of time. Sooner or later they would catch us. That's why we'll have to split up, Codemus. You'll have to get off the rail alone. Maybe we can still fool them."

"But what am I going to . . ."

"Slip me carefully into the wastebasket on your way out," said Little Brother. "Or do you have a better idea?" The little box tried to laugh. "Chin up, Codemus. And slip me into the wastebasket."

"I have to leave you behind?"

"In the wastebasket," said Little Brother. "And you get off at the next station."

"But what am I going to do after that?"

"Here's where you get off," Little Brother growled softly. "Get going. One-two-one-two. It's the only chance you've got."

Codemus got up mechanically. He walked slowly toward the exit.

When he was supposed to slip Little Brother into the wastebasket, he felt tears in his eyes. "Little Brother," he whispered, "are you really sure that . . ."

"Drop me, you fool," hissed the little box in his hand.

Other passengers were starting to shove. Codemus opened his hand and walked out of the rail. For a moment he stood stunned. Behind him, the doors slid shut and the train shot forward.

First there was the emptiness

Codemus carefully put one foot in front of the other. And walked. For the first time he was walking by himself. He didn't know where. But it didn't bother him. He had never needed to know where he was going.

Aimlessly he elbowed his way out of the station. No one tried to stop him. Codemus started down a corridor at random. Put one foot in front of the other. Realized that he was walking by himself.

Then came the uncertainty

He was alone in a strange cube. Unfamiliar corridor names and stairway numbers. The walls were a different color. Everyone he met had somebody to talk to—in their pocket, shoulder bag, or in their hand up to their ear. Only Codemus was alone. No one looked at him. No one noticed he was there. One-two-one-two.

And finally came the fear, of course

Running up stairways, riding elevators, standing on transport belts, but getting nowhere, nothing happening, nobody told him what to do, not knowing, nobody knew him, hungry, ragged, stopped a man in yellow overalls, an office worker of his own type, wanted to talk to him, ask, couldn't get his mouth open, tongue dry, the man shook off his hand, "Don't have time," said the breast pocket.

And in the efficient society there are no benches to rest on.

Toward evening Codemus was huddled on a stairway landing on the second level. He missed his own cube, but couldn't find his way back to the monorail.

Happy workers stepped over him on their way to B shift. Codemus gazed after them for a long time, humming hoarsely to the music from their little brothers.

IT IS NOT GOOD FOR A HUMAN BEING TO BE ALONE

Something had happened. Something he didn't understand. Only that it put him outside. Codemus was sitting outside and wanted to get in.

IT IS NOT GOOD FOR A HUMAN BEING TO BE DIFFERENT

He looked at the confident faces around him. Harmonious, efficient people striding with purposeful steps toward assignments useful to society. Codemus felt meaningless.

He was as good as dead.

He was dead.

A HUMAN BEING IS A SOCIAL ENTITY

When the sherlocks found him (as they did, of course) he burst into tears and embraced the cold bloodhounds.

And Codemus was led back to the flock.

Now Codemus has a new little brother. Every morning Codemus is wakened by Little Brother. While he is getting dressed and eating breakfast, Little Brother reminds him of all the things he has to do. In the monorail on the way to the office, Little Brother and Codemus discuss the program for the day. At the office, everyone works quickly and efficiently; none of the employees are in doubt about what needs to be done, and all decisions are unanimous. All the little brothers are synchronized.

Rainy Day Revolution No. 39

by Luigi Cozzi

Translated from the Italian by the author

If there is one thing about modern Italy, it is the impression that every visitor gets that the nation is about to explode into violent revolution. When we were last there, all sorts of slogans were to be found scribbled on walls: Fascism shall not pass! Communism shall not pass! And one repeated inscription read simply and ominously: *Anno Zero!* Apparently, this is all old stuff to the natives, who go about their daily business with an indifference to all this hysteria. Luigi Cozzi, who lives in Rome and is a movie director, tells us how it is.

The world is our oyster. We've made it come true. But we've eaten that oyster. Like Alexander, we weep for new worlds to conquer.

—Fowler Schocken

"STOP! BEFORE YOU DO IT WASH YOUR TEETH WITH X 15—YOU FEEL STRONG WITH X 15."

"IT'S ALWAYS WORTHWHILE SMOKING A CIGARETTE IF IT'S A SEXY-X. SEXY-X, THE ONLY CIGARETTE THAT WAKES YOUR SLEEPING SEX."

"HAVE A DEMONIAK! IT REFRESHES YOU, GIVES YOU AN ANTI-CON TO LET YOU OWN HER WITHOUT TROUBLES."

Lester shuddered. That kind of advertisement had invaded the world and was among the mightiest weapons of the Parties. These huge marquees were obsessively dillydallying between light and dark all along the streets, at every level. It was hard to resist the fascination of those gigantic women continuously stripping. And as soon as they were entirely naked, their voluptuous bodies were covered with these flashing letters.

These marquees are *the Party world,* Lester thought. *They're its strength. Their ruling strength.*

But Lester knew a way to defeat that. To beat those swine and on their field, too. A splendid, marvelous way it was. It would let him reach the keys of the Power elsewhere unreachable. Yet he had to hurry up.

The Underground station was very close, luckily so. He reached it and introduced a coin into the hole in the robot-conductor, and the machine handed him the entrance disk. Lester got it and let it slide into his pocket.

The tiny gate that was preventing his going in opened, and Lester stepped in, very grateful that warning had not been spread by the Party yet. He had been counting on bureaucrats' slowness; he was right.

He climbed down to the In-Line floor, hanging from a rope. Once upon a time moving staircases had run, but the Administration Council of the World Agency for Underground Communications had decided to take them from the stations as they were too expensive for the budget of the Administration. The thousand villas that the seven hundred Council Presidents had built on the Sea of Venus with Administration funds had much more than was foreseen. A cautious saving program had been consequently voted by the three million committeemen in order to allow the Underground Railway to run longer.

Lester jumped onto the ground, when the rope proved too short to take him to it, and took a look around.

The station was crowded as usual. Beatniks were lying on the dusty chairs, couples of all sexes tiredly embracing on the floor, passengers waiting for the trains.

Lester sat down on a dirty step and began waiting with patience. His bag did not bother him. He could tie it on his shoulder, but he did not think there would be a real need to. Not then at least.

His hunting had not yet begun. The crowd was lazing on their tired way. All was quite normal—youngsters raping candy virgins in the twilight. Infallible Militiamen sleeping on one another's shoulders.

Lester heard brakes jarring. The train was getting near. He rose and walked to the platform.

The usual procession was waiting for the train. The lights of the stand put over the tracks were shining. Two Underground robot-conductors stepped forward, holding a girl in their metal clutch. She was crying noticeably.

Lester was not surprised, it was customary in the Underground. Each time a train entered the station, a thanksgiving sacrifice in honor of the God of the Line was held. A man or a woman, drawn by lots among the passengers in wait, was offered as tribute.

The train made its entrance, sliding on the oil-shining monotrack. The two robots had already carried the victim onto the stand over the rails.

They rapidly stripped the girl's dress with their sexless fingers, skimmed her skin that shuddered and withdrew at the contact of those freezing claws. The low light of the lamps revealed her white body, staining her breast with violet lightning and lighting sensual flames on her abdomen. The two metal legal murderers lifted the girl and with absolute precision threw her in front of the train.

She was dead before she could begin screaming. Blood was spread all over, the cut head rolled grotesquely forward, pushed by the engine, her mouth still open in her last effort to scream.

It stopped beside the umpteen other victims of that day. In the evening, robot garbage collectors would slide there to clean the tracks and the platform of those remains.

The train had finally stopped.

Lester knew the rules of the game. Taking the Underground was a risky adventure. It was no essential service, for there were plenty of roads and streets at every level on the surface, and the skyways were a lot quicker.

But all the Parties earned mountains of money from speculations done on the line and on the several new lines that were being built, though they might be of no use. That was why the lines could not be abolished. People had to be forced to go in. And each time a train entered a station, someone had to be killed down there. A nicely simple way to support the overpopulated society of the Parties.

Yet Lester knew very well what he had to do. He had been well trained by years of experience. Ten years he had been forced to catch the Underground twice a day, according to his fairly good position in his Party. Ten years—without an incident.

He reckoned with complete exactness the time between the opening and the closing of the harsh gates of the car he was going to get into. A matter of seconds, two or three, no more.

But it was all right. He knew how to jump beyond the blades.

Lester did.

Now he was inside the car, and the gate was shutting behind him with a sudden click. Some inexpert travelers were cut into halves by the harsh blades. Their bodies fell to the ground and covered the floor with their blood.

A man had gone in, losing but his hand. He was weakly moaning while his blood was spreading on his suit. A robodoc ran by and cauterized his wound, filled him with sedatives, and walked away to help more wounded people.

"You've been clever," the man said to Lester.

Lester nodded. "Yeah. It's a matter of training."

A light of envy mixed with admiration flashed in the man's eyes.

"My name's Judas Imabeliever," he said, extending his remaining hand to be hit by Lester's. Lester did.

"Pleased to meet you, Imabeliever," he said. "My name is Lester Aharddaysnight. Which Party do you belong to?"

Judas pointed at the shirt he was wearing. It was still black, though red blood was all over it. Lester felt quite stupid since he hadn't noticed it before.

"The Party of the Melancholy of the Good Old Time," Judas answered. "The Party of Freedom to All Servants, Children, Insiders, Slaves, Thwarters, and Socialists. This is our motto since the Holy Prophet Benito died, hung by his feet in Loreto. He sacrificed himself to allow the Word of God to be spread over the world. We are among the richest and mightiest Parties, you know. And we've a lot of followers hidden among other Parties' ranks."

Lester nodded. He was right. The Fascists was one of the most powerful Parties. Its Supreme Ruler was Amintore Letsspendthenighttogether, the same man who until two years ago had been the head of another strong Party, the Party of the Universal Red-Guards Progress.

"And you?" Imabeliever asked.

Lester was struck by a sudden embarrassment. He could not reveal that he was not in any Party anymore. Not now at least.

"I'm a DAISY," Lester lied. "The Party of the Destroying Action on Immorality in the Succession of the Years. The Party that Guarantees the Sacred Inviolability of the Family Link. The Party whose Members are Brothers. Gimme Your Wife and I Gonna Give You Mine, you know."

Slogans. Yet he could not help uttering them all, as he spoke about his Party; that was the result of years and years of conditioning.

"It's a good Party too," Imabeliever said. "It scored big last Revolution Day, didn't it?"

They had been fourth, Lester thought. Too many casualties, and nothing to do. It had not been a fine day for them—they needed a full victory.

"What are you going to do now?" Lester asked, pointing at the man's stump. "You won't go out at one of the next stations, will you? You're wounded and you've lost blood; you're bound to get chopped."

Judas Imabeliever did not answer at once. He looked over the glass to the dark of the cave—you could hardly realize the train was running at full speed in that unbounded night.

"No," he finally answered. "I ain't gonna risk my life."

"So you're staying here." Lester absentmindedly nodded.

It was common, anyway. Many people made their home in the Underground trains. Some flats could still be found in the city, providing that you were a speedy gunfighter. But it was not always worthwhile to live in the huge skyscrapers that too often fell to the ground. Because of this a wounded fellow had chosen to live on the trains permanently.

So in the gigantic web of the Underground caves, thousands of trains were running to and fro, filled with people who never left them.

Children had been born in the trains, kids who had never known such things as sunlight—and Parties. They were pale, thin midgets, fully accustomed to the darkness.

Judas Imabeliever looked around. He stared at the men and the women who occupied the seats in the train—some of them apparently mere passers-by, who were already preparing for the jump out, some youngsters in groups of three or four, amusing themselves in sinister games of love.

At the opposite end of the car a sort of tent had been raised to be a shelter. Long-bearded men were playing cards, while a couple of women lay on the seats, prey of LSD.

Two young cherubs of hell were looking out the window with large opened eyes, pointing at things Lester and Judas were unable to see in the dark. They shrieked with laughter, and to Lester the night outside seemed to echo them.

"Oh no," Judas finally answered, as if to himself. "I won't stay here. I really couldn't get accustomed. I'll get out as soon as I feel up to it. I'd rather die than stay here forever."

"You can stay here for seven days," Lester reminded him. "Then your Party will declare you officially dead, and another man will take your place. Your life wouldn't be worth a dime then. Bureaucracy won't allow you to appear again if declared officially dead. Bureaucracy cannot fail; so they kill you."

"I know. But I hope I can be back before seven days are gone. Today was just an accident." A flash of resolution lighted Judas's eyes. "It won't happen again. Where do you have to go?"

"Next stop," Lester replied.

A light flashed on a wall. The station was getting close.

Lester smiled, self-confident.

"Our ways are parting," he said. "Hope we meet again one day."

Judas's turn to smile.

"You can bet, you old Moralist! One day it will be Revolution Day. I shall slay thee with mine own hands."

Lester felt touched by the courteous compliment. But he would not take part in the battle; he smiled, recollecting. Not with the DAISY, at least!

"*I* shall slay thee there," he answered, according to what etiquette demanded. "Good-bye."

The train stopped in the station. Brakes jarred again. Lester moved toward the gate, his nerves like violin strings, quite ready.

The train stopped.

"Good luck," Judas Imabeliever hailed him. But Lester wasn't listening anymore.

He was just going to jump down—

Then the gate quickly opened, and closed.

On Lester.

Nobody Here But Us Shadows

by Sam J. Lundwall

Translated from the Swedish by the author

Here's another example of the popular European preoccupation with time and alternate histories. There must be something about living in the Old World, where all about there are reminders of different cultures, dead regimes, and forgotten invasions that bring this more to the conscious fore than in the New World, where history is short and the past seems mostly a blank.

I was walking down the steps of the Probal Office Building when the girl intercepted me. I was in my twenties at that time, and I had been Upside for more than two months subjective time, locked in a steel chamber all the time with a couple of technicians whom I got to dislike more than I ever thought I could dislike a human being, before we managed to get back again. No girls. This one was cute, not beautiful, but anything without a beard would have done right then. I slowed down and stared at her. Long, flowing hair; at least ten years older than me, to judge by the lines around eyes and mouth; an old-fashioned dress that was at least two sizes too small. If she wanted to draw my attention, she had succeeded. Not that she needed any devices; like I said, anything without a beard could have drawn my attention without the slightest effort.

"Isn't that a Probal badge?" she said, her voice tense with nervosity, but I did not notice then. I glanced down at my lapel with the small blue-and-green badge. Very discreet. Nobody ever notices it; nobody, except this woman. She stared hungrily at it.

"Sure," I said. "What about it?"

"Do you . . . work in there?" She indicated the pockmarked façade.

"If you call that 'work.' I mostly wait for something to happen." I grinned at her, trying for a dazzling, captivating smile and failing miserably. "Anything special?"

She said, still staring at my badge, "Have you been . . ." she hesitated, "Upside?"

"I'm just back down," I said. "Half an hour ago, I sat in a steel box and didn't have the foggiest idea of when I'd be let out." I shivered. "Look, let's get away from here. I have been Upside for two months and I want to get away as far as possible. That place gives me the jitters." I started to walk down the steps to the plaza, diffuse memories from that plaza forming behind my eyes. I looked away. She fell into step with me.

"Is it that bad?" she said.

"Some of it." I looked down and noticed that she had been talking to my badge. Obviously it was not me that interested her, just the badge. I said, "Excuse me, but I have had a rotten time and I'm on my way somewhere. What is this about?"

She walked beside me for several minutes without saying anything. Finally, "I'm interested."

"Well, I'm not. I've had enough of that place for a long time." I was deliberately rude; I was in desperate need of a drink and female company, but primarily as a means to get away from the Probal business and the things that tried to crawl up from my subconscious as we crossed the plaza. This just wasn't worth it.

"A personal interest," she said, looking straight ahead.

That figured. I looked down at her, the nervous mouth, the darting eyes. I said, "How long have you been waiting here?"

"A long time."

"And it just happened to be me?"

She nodded.

"Most people at Probal," I said, "never leave the building. When they have been at it long enough, they don't seem able to stand the outside anymore. They just stay indoors like the world doesn't exist." I nodded at the dark building. "No windows," I said. "Hardly anyone ever leaves the place."

"I know," she said.

"So?"

"Sometimes," she said, "Probal people take things from Upside. I'm interested in that."

"Nobody takes anything from Upside," I said, momentarily taken aback. Nobody ever took anything from Upside, not because it wasn't possible—it was—but because everyone knew what would happen if they did. It just wasn't done.

She shrugged. "How long have you been there?"

"Three years."

"Perhaps it was before your time, then."

"Never," I said.

She switched the subject. "Where were you going?"

"A drink somewhere." I shrugged. "And something else."

"Let me buy you one." She smiled suddenly. "To make up for all this. We could talk about something else."

We went somewhere and had a few drinks and the kind of dinner I had been dreaming of for two solid months. She was very nice, smiling at the right places, laughing at the right places. Three drinks and two months' isolation made her first pretty and then ravishing. I started giving her hints about my exalted position at Probal. She ate it up, just as I had expected.

Which was curious, to say the very least, since nobody is very interested in Probal and the kind of work it does. I myself was decidedly indifferent before I got the job there. I knew it was some kind of Government agency doing research into Probability Lines—whatever that could be—and that the big, ugly building contained a large number of scientists and assorted personnel, most of them actually living there. There was nothing secret about it—who would be interested in "Probability Lines" anyway?—and to me it was just another ugly building until I graduated and went jobless until I got down to *P* in the Yellow Pages and called them up. That was a long, long time ago.

I'm not a scientist, I don't know much about the theories behind the Probability Line Search, and most of what I know I don't understand. I just press my buttons and sit tight in my steel chamber while everybody's beards get longer and shaggier and pressure builds up until I start having wet dreams. Most of the time it isn't too bad, a quick trip Upside and then back with the computer loaded with readings. Once in a while you might draw a two-month graveyard shift, but apart from that it isn't too bad. One gets used to it with time, I suppose. Or rather, one learns to live with it. After a few years you don't want to face the outside world anymore, hence the windowless apartments in Probal Building. There are TV monitors in the steel chambers, and you see things.

We were sitting in a back booth at the restaurant, well away from the windows, and I said, "Look, I don't know much about it and that's the truth. Not my line of job, that's for the scientists. All I know is, we step into a steel chamber and go off along a Probability Line somewhere, and I don't do the settings, I just go along."

"But why do you call it Upside?" she asked.

I shrugged. "I don't know. That's what it's called. We go along a Probability Line to a version of this world that didn't happen or could have happened if something had been different, and then we sit there and check the place."

"Check what?"

"Damned if I know. Humidity, traces of radioactivity, visual search . . ." I shivered despite the heat. "Some of these Probability Worlds are nasty. Nothing to write home about. Others . . . are not so bad."

"Better than here." It was a statement, not a question.

"Much better, some of them." I drank, lost in thought.

"What if you should go out through the door?" she said.

"Locked," I said.

"But if you unlocked it?"

"Then out I'd go."

"So it is possible, then?"

"Sure, it is possible, no trouble at all, if you could . . ." I checked myself. "I don't know about that. No one ever went out, so why ask?"

"So you just sit there?"

"Yep. Sometimes for a couple of hours, sometimes for a couple of months. It all depends on conditions. I don't know why, but sometimes you can go back whenever you want, and sometimes you can't."

"Sounds primitive," she said.

"It *is* primitive. Probability Lines were discovered less than ten years ago; they are still searching in the dark. Anyway, that's not my stuff. I just press the buttons and watch, that's all I do." I rose. "Let's go somewhere."

We went to another place and had another couple of drinks. By that time, she was more than ravishing. I wanted her so much that it hurt. Two months of frustrated youthful masculinity throbbed in my loins, screaming to be let out. I was prepared to do anything, literally anything, to get her. We sat in an all-night café and she said, "How come they never have brought anything from Upside to here?"

I shrugged, my mind caressing her thighs.

"Perhaps they did, once," she said. "When that project started."

"Perhaps," I said indifferently. "They know what happens if you do, so I guess . . ." Then I caught myself. "Look," I said, "nobody is supposed to know about that thing."

"About what?"

"Nothing." Damn it, if I had been less shy, I'd have walked out on her and gotten me a girl somewhere else. I had the money and I certainly had the inclination. But I was shy, and besides, I felt I had a right to her by now, for having listened to her for so long.

"They did experiments when they started with this Probability Line Search," she said. "They did experiments, and they brought home things from Upside."

"Sure," I said. "They brought home things and then they realized what they were doing and dropped the whole thing. What do I know? I only work there!" I was beginning to get mad. "Isn't there anything else to talk about? I'm off duty, for God's sake!"

She looked down into her glass. "I'm sorry," she said.

"Never mind." I felt ashamed. "I'm sorry I blew my top like that. But I've been locked in that steel chamber for two months now, looking at the same damned scene in the monitors all the time and never knowing when conditions would let me return home again. Right now all I want is to forget about it."

She looked straight ahead, eyes hidden in the shadows. "Imagine what it would be like if you were thrown out into that without a chance to come back." She bit her lip. "I'm sorry," she said again.

"Let's forget all about it." I slipped an arm around her waist. She stiffened momentarily, then relaxed and even smiled. "Let's go somewhere."

"Where?"

"I have a place. We can talk there."

She said, "In the Probal Building?"

"I'm not that far gone yet," I said. "I have a place of my own a few blocks away from Probal. Nice and quiet."

She hesitated. Then, "Okay." She rose and quickly walked out. I followed her out into the night, slipped an arm around her, drew her close to me. She walked stiffly, staring straight ahead.

"I don't know what you think of me," she said. "Coming like this and talking about your job all the time, you must be tired by now."

"Not that tired," I said. My fingers dug into her waist, her body warm and full of promises in my arm, swaying against me with every step. I could barely breathe.

We came to my flat. A small, cramped room with a bed and not very much else, heavy curtains before the window. She took in the room with a quick glance. "It's small," she said.

"I'm not here often," I said. "I don't need much."

She walked up to the window. "Don't!" I said sharply.

She turned. "Don't you like the view?"

I sat down heavily on the bed. "Just keep the curtains as they are," I said. I hesitated. "Look, I have been sitting for two months, looking at TV monitors showing the plaza outside the Probal Building. It looked exactly like the plaza, it *was* the plaza, but a plaza on another Probability Line. There were . . . executions there, night and day, things you couldn't imagine. I was scared as hell when I came out today; I knew this was another Probability Line but I was screaming all the time when I crossed the plaza. This whole city scares me. A year or two from now I won't be able to go out at all, so please leave the curtains, I don't want to see what's out there."

She came over and sat down beside me. "Is it that bad?" she asked.

"You don't understand," I said. "No one who hasn't experienced it understands. Look, most of the time the city is exactly as the one we are in now, only with subtle differences. People dress differently, the cars look different, things like that. But sometimes people act differently, too, they do things you wouldn't think were possible. Sometimes there's no city at all, just meadows or woods, once there was nothing but water, and at one line there's nothing at all, literally nothing at all, nothing but a sort of whirling mist that tears at you even via the monitors. Don't you see?" I said desperately. "How can I know what is reality and what is not? Every one of those Probability Lines are as real as the one we are in right now, and after a time you don't know which line is the most real, which one you really belong to, which one you will step out into when you leave the chamber. When you step out, it's just like stepping out into another line, and if you come from one of the beautiful lines you can't stand it here, you just count the days until you can go Upside again, and all the time the ground heaves under your feet because you don't know what's reality anymore, you'll never know, only everything scares you and you can't stand it anymore." I leaned back in the bed, closing my eyes.

She put a cool hand on my brow. "I didn't know that," she said.

"Forget it," I said morosely.

She was leaning against my shoulder, soft and yielding and smelling of bottled roses. I embraced her like a drowning man, dragging her down onto the bed. She whispered, "No!" but at that point I was way past arguing. She resisted at first, then subsided and went through the motions. I relieved myself groaningly of three months' accumulated sex urge and then rolled over onto my back beside her, groping in the dark for cigarettes. I felt warm, satisfied, and somewhat drowsy. And as that throbbing yearning lost some of its edge, I also felt a bit ashamed. She went out and washed herself, then started the coffee percolator. She moved silently, a dark shadow in the dusky room.

"Are you sore at me?" I said.

She returned with the coffee, sitting down on the bed with the tray between us. She said, "No."

"Disappointed?"

"I should have known. Ten years ago, I would have been terror-stricken, screamed, cried. Now it doesn't matter much one way or the other." She looked at me, eyes gleaming dully in the darkness of her face. "You could have done it more slowly."

"Empathy with other people," I said, "is among the first things that go in this job. When you get to the point when you can't discern between what is reality and what is not, you don't care much for other people's feelings."

"I know," she said.

"You don't," I said. I sipped at the coffee. It was bitter, strong, and with more than a hint of—what was it? Salt? I made a vile grimace. "What *is* this?"

She looked at the cup. "I'm sorry," she said. "I forgot." She went away to the percolator and returned with a new cup of coffee, sweet and strong. "After all these years," she said, "I still forget. Here." She handed me the cup.

I said, sipping at the coffee, "Where do you come from?"

"You wouldn't know the place," she said.

"Try me."

"Somewhere around here," she said. "Not more than a kilometer from here."

"You don't sound like you were born here," I said. "That funny accent, for instance, you sound like someone who came to the city fairly recently."

"When I was born," she said quietly, "there was no city here."

I grinned at her. "Sure," I said. "And this city is more than five hundred years old. You don't look that old to me."

"I was here ten years ago," she said, "and there was no city here then."

I suddenly felt chilly. "What do you mean?" I said.

"There was a small village here," she said. "And a few kilometers away was a kind of feudal stronghold. No cars or rockets, just a few dirigibles now and then. Very peaceful, very rural, very isolated."

I was conscious of a cold, growing spot in my stomach. "Sounds like something out of a fairy tale," I said.

"You wouldn't understand," she said tiredly, as if she had been telling and retelling this until the words came out by their own free will. "I was taken from there."

"You're joking," I said. "How?"

"You know. The steel chamber."

I sat up so violently that I almost spilled the coffee. "You're crazy," I told her. "Nothing and nobody can be taken away from one Probability Line to another. It just can't be done!"

"That's what everybody tells me," she said quietly. "I have been waiting here for ten years, and everybody tells me it is impossible. They told me that in the Probal Building when I was brought here, and when I talk to the men who come out from there they all tell me the same thing." She looked away. "I have been asking everyone for ten years," she said. "I have been waiting outside that building for ten years, and everyone tells me the same thing."

I said, "What do you want?"

"I want to go back."

She stayed two days. She was cool and remote but very obliging. She did not talk much about that fantasy of hers after the first night, but I wondered. The second day I went to the Probal librarian and asked him. He seemed uncomfortable and said he didn't know. I checked on my own, and found that the relevant data dossiers were restricted, out of limits for people like me. When I returned, she smiled tiredly and wrote down a code number for me.

"I got this once," she said, "from a computer technician who had access to all the classified material. He said I wouldn't have much use for it anyway. But this is where I came from."

"I can't help you," I said.

"I know," she said. "I didn't really believe you could. I hoped against all hopes that you could, but I never hope much these days. I just wait and wait and hope that I'll have luck someday, but I don't really believe it anymore."

"I'm just a technician," I said. "I press the buttons and go Upside and handle the machinery and look at the monitors, that's all I do. I'm just a small cog in the machinery, that's all."

"I know," she said. "I'm sorry I've bothered you."

The next day, she was gone. A few weeks later I spoke to a guy at the Probal office about her.

"Sure," he said, "I've seen her. Everyone here has seen her at least once. Always waits outside. She's crazy, thinks she comes from one of the Probability Lines and wants to go back. There's lots of crazy people in the world. Forget her."

"She said it happened ten years ago," I said. "That could have been when the project started and no one knew what would happen if something was taken out from its Probability Line. They know now, so they must have found out one way or another."

He shrugged. "What do I know? Anyway, even if it's true, she can't go back now."

Never. There is some kind of mathematics to explain that, but I'm not a mathematician. All I know is that the door in the chamber is locked from the outside while it is Upside. Under no circumstances must anything be taken from or added to. . . .

Someone must have found out the hard way.

I saw her now and then, standing on the steps of Probal Building, waiting without any real hope while her shoulders sank and her face hardened into frozen lines. The first years, some of the younger technicians picked her up when on leave and took her to bed. She did anything for the ones who were willing to talk to her. But then she wasn't so pretty anymore and they hurried past her, looking the other way. I seldom went out anymore, the city scared me, everything outside the building scared me, I thought of Probability Lines more beautiful and more horrible than any man's imagination, I saw the ever-changing worlds in the monitors, all of them as real or as unreal as my own, and I was scared. I moved into a windowless flat in the building. I never went out again.

Many years later I found the piece of paper with the code number, the code number of her Probability Line. During a test run, I fed the number into the line selector and went Upside.

I leaned down over the monitor and looked down into the whirling emptiness of the world that had been hers before she was taken from it and I saw nothing.

Nothing.

Round and Round and Round Again

by Domingo Santos

Translated from the Spanish by Mae Strelkov

We think of Spain as a languid country, somewhat backward, and rather colorfully quaint. Obviously, it does not look that way to the Spaniards. In fact, this account of modern highways and ultramodern traffic jams is the kind of tale we would expect to find written by a denizen of Los Angeles or greater New York, not by a citizen of Iberia. But there you go, preconceptions again!

It was really my fault, I realize that. I know I was warned: they told me not to be crazy, to leave the car some hundred kilometers from Cosmopolis and take the subway thence. But I was in a hurry, and besides I planned to spend only a couple of days there to settle some official business, and I did not believe any city could be that congested!

Never was I more mistaken.

I entered by the Northern Highway. It's a fabulous entrance—fifty kilometers of highway piercing the city, with those towering buildings on either side. The eight lanes were crowded with vehicles, reminding me of trucks jockeying for space on a flowing stream. But I laughed at my friends and their fears, certain it would be easier even than I imagined.

Then suddenly—as matches spill forth from a matchbox opened the wrong way around—the cars began going their own separate ways as we reached a cloverleaf crossing in three levels, which distributed the vehicles throughout the city. I needed to reach the eastern sector myself, and was riding along the second file on the right, and here my difficulties began.

When I realized that to take the bifurcation to the east, I must get into the first file of the left, it was too late. I must try it at the second cloverleaf. Certainly—and purely theoretically—the five cloverleaves at the end of the highway were linked in such a way that from any one of them you should be able to reach any other. But in practice, I did not manage it. Either the other cars got in my way, or a policeman obliged me to take a route I did not wish to take; at other times I misread the signs placed just fifty meters before the turnoffs. After two hours of circling—somewhat dizzily—I decided to get off wherever I could from that three-level, five-cloverleaf way, supposing that once I was inside the city it might be easier for me to find my way to my destination. Frankly, one doesn't definitely lose hope till the last hammer blow.

As the office where I must solve my official business was in Cosmopolis-East, I'd reserved a room in a hotel in that area. So I drove into the city and the first thing I did was stop before a bookstore to buy a map of the town. The fellow showed me a heavy volume containing 343 partial maps.

"Haven't you got a map that shows all the city at once?" I asked.

"Certainly!" said he. "What are the dimensions of your wall?"

His question surprised me but I understood what he meant when he showed me the smallest example of this type of map—its size was two-and-a-half-by-four meters, yet the city squares had to be examined through a magnifying glass that was included in the price of the map. I gave up the idea; my car is not exactly a compact type, but neither is it big enough for *that*. So I bought the volume with the subdivisions.

When I stepped out, a man in a blue uniform with a cap that contained the legend "Policeman No. 13428 in charge of levying fines" was writing out a slip for me. I tried to protest, but he showed me in the distance a sign warning the public: PARKING IS PROHIBITED.

"And what about all those cars already double parked?" I asked.

He smiled dryly, and answered, "Well, one has to be a little tolerant, don't you agree? But parking three deep is just too much!"

I paid with no further protest: two thousand credits. I thought to myself that for that amount I could have stayed a day at the Imperial Hilton. And the pig had the cheek to tell me he'd cut the fine twenty per cent because I was paying at once!

I continued driving along tentatively (this business of driving while trying to study a map is not easy) in the direction in which I wished to go. And please don't imagine that this was easy. The map indicated the one-way streets, yet I soon found myself on one such, going in the opposite direction from the one that map indicated. This demoralized me, since it canceled out all my gains so far, turned me backward.

I stopped before the first traffic cop I glimpsed, who'd been watching from one side the flowing traffic, with a look of resignation, and I mentioned this flaw of the map. He smiled wearily. "You didn't read the instructions of that volume of maps, did you?"

I confessed I had not.

"So I supposed! Look: the black arrows indicating a one-way street mean what they say: 'one-way traffic.' But those that are in red mean 'one-way traffic, alternatively,' in other words, 'one way, mornings' and 'the other way, afternoons.' Get it?"

"But why all this?" I asked, not seeing any sense in it at all.

He smiled in a Machiavellian way, while studying a car that had just jammed into another car till they were crushed together; then he took out a notebook and wrote: "Two less," and the license numbers of both. He then put the notebook away and added to me:

"It's simple, sir! How—do you suppose—can we control the vagaries of this indecent flow of cars and more cars that invade us, coming and going, unless we do this?"

I abstained from arguing that point. In a way, it made sense . . . these changing directions of the one-way streets took care of the morning influx of cars and their exit each afternoon similarly. But I did wonder what would happen if a distracted driver got onto one of those one-way streets, thinking it was still the morning when it was already the afternoon, and the direction of the traffic had changed.

I asked the policeman and his eyes shone with a sudden gleam as he assured me this happened frequently.

Well, I continued my slow peregrination. As per the map, I calculated that some twenty kilometers still separated me from my hotel; when I finally reached it I was astonished to realize I'd done a hundred and forty kilometers. I left the car and dragged myself toward the reception desk and asked for my key.

"Where shall I leave my car?" I asked.

The receptionist stared at me in horror. "Did you come all the way here in your car?"

It was then that I began to realize that I'd certainly done something wrong. But it was too late to fix it. I nodded.

The receptionist put his hands before himself as though to ward off a ghost.

"Put it wherever you like, put it wherever you like!" he growled. "But don't involve us: your car is your own worry. We only rent rooms for *people*. Or do you imagine we'll provide places as well for those luckless, infernal machines, with space so scarce in the city?"

"Very well," said I, feeling somewhat annoyed. "Don't you worry. I'll go and park it somewhere and return."

I turned to go, but the receptionist called me back with a hiss.

"Sir," he said, "to your left, in the cafeteria, they sell snacks. I'd recommend those of sirloin—they're delicious."

I thought I detected in that remark a certain gloating sadism, and ignored him. Later I would repent for having failed to follow his wise and experienced advice.

When I reached the car, which I left quintuple-parked, a man in a blue uniform with the same sort of cap as the other, containing a legend "Policeman No. 27,342, in charge of levying fines," handed me a slip for my new parking error. I paid up with a resigned sigh. He

studied a little screen—as I later learned, connected to headquarters
—which lit up with the information of my other traffic error, for
which I'd already paid up.

"This is your second misdemeanor today," said he dryly.

"I know," I said.

"Remember! The next time you break a rule today they'll take
away your car."

"Well, let them," I muttered, martyrlike. "Where shall I have to go
to get it back?"

He looked deeply surprised.

"Get it back? Sir! They'll not give it back to you." And he put his
portable screen away and walked off in great dignity.

I got back into my car. I was already sorry not to have followed
the advice of my friends, but now it was too late to bewail this, and
little could I do to rectify the error. I must find a place to leave the
car and get back to the hotel. I felt exhausted after the many hours
behind the wheel, and there was nothing I longed for more than a
shower and to get to bed.

So I began circling.

An hour later I was still circling. Two hours later, three hours later
. . . still circling! And these circles kept getting wider and wider. I
kept getting further and further away, till I had no notion left of
where I might be.

I saw a fellow walking along the sidewalk and called to him. He
came over to me.

"What's the matter, brother?" he asked.

I asked him hoarsely: "Listen to me. I'm a stranger here and am
crazily seeking somewhere to leave my car. Do you know of any
such place near here?"

His expression grew luminous, like the face of Joshua when he
glimpsed the Promised Land.

"Don't ask me," he replied gaily. "Ha! I don't have a car
anymore."

And off he went.

I saw someone in uniform who seemed *not* to be a policeman: I
called to him and asked the same thing. With great condescension,
he studied me and said, "Look, friend! In all Cosmopolis, understand? In all the city, there's no free parking space."

"But there has to be someplace somewhere!" I sobbed. "Perhaps
some parked car will drive off and leave a place?"

"You're a stranger, aren't you? I understand why you'd ask such a
thing. But truly, the way things are, do you suppose that anyone with

the great good fortune to find a space to leave his car in, would give up the space again so another car would usurp that site?"

I had to agree, he made sense.

"But isn't there anywhere, any private parking lot, where I may leave my car?"

"Look, friend," said he, leaning comfortably on my car's window-sill, "this is the city with the densest population in all the world." He gestured toward the towering buildings. "With all those people living therein, do you really think they'll all find parking spaces for their cars?"

And off he went, leaving me sunk in discouragement.

I spent all that night circling, and circling still more, in the neighborhood of the hotel, never finding any free space. It was dawn when, defeated and exhausted, I stopped the car relatively near the door of the hotel.

Certainly, I'd not found a place to leave it well parked. However, all I wanted by then was to tidy myself up a bit, take a shower, and shave. I felt I had a right to this and imagined that for those few minutes nobody would say anything. I left the car, locked it, and turned toward the hotel entrance. But I'd not taken four steps when I saw a man in a blue uniform who appeared from amid the cars where he'd been lurking, and he came toward me with his miniature screen in view. I hurriedly got back into my car.

"You can't park your car here, sir," said he respectfully.

"I'm waiting for a friend," I lied. "It'll just be a minute."

"As long as you don't leave the wheel, it's all right, you can stay," said he. "But don't try to fool me—I'll be watching you."

He stalked off but I could see him return to his lurking place to continue spying.

I ran my fingers through my hair desperately. Something I must do —somehow or other I simply had to get into that hotel. Then suddenly I thought of a solution. Slipping a coin for five credits into the hands of a passerby, I begged him to send me a bellboy from the hotel. When the latter came, I showed him a bill of fifty credits.

"Listen, boy! I've got to go in there to change and tidy up a bit. Will you sit here at the wheel for a minute till I get back?"

"I *can't,* sir," said he, staring avidly at the bill.

"Why not?"

"The syndicate forbids intruding, sir."

"Which syndicate?"

"The Wheelers, of course."

I blinked. My grandma always said there were new things to learn, indeed!

"Wheelers? Explain!" I begged.

This he did. The syndicate in question had two hundred thousand members devoted to this new profession, and any intruder who was not a member would be severely punished.

"Very well," I said. "Can you fetch me a Wheeler?"

"For fifty credits, yes, sir."

"And for ten?"

He sneered.

"Well, if I have to . . ." said I, paying up.

Five minutes later I had a Wheeler at my side. He was young, he seemed dynamic, and he showed me—before I could open my mouth —his identification plate of the syndicate, with his name and photograph. Below was this fluorescent notice: DO NOT ACCEPT THE SERVICES OF ANY WHEELER WHO DOES NOT FIRST SHOW THIS PLATE. IF YOU HAVE ANY COMPLAINT TO LODGE, TAKE NOTE OF HIS NAME AND HIS MEMBERSHIP NUMBER.

"Fine, son!" I said. "Take over. I shan't be long."

"It doesn't matter how long you take, sir," he answered. "It's two hundred credits an hour."

I whistled softly but made no comment. I reached the hotel, and showered, changed, and shaved as quickly as I could. I glanced wistfully at the immaculate bed, but the hour was passing. When I went back down, I caught the sardonic glance of the receptionist, which I ignored.

I paid the Wheeler, he went away, and I started to drive off. The uniformed fellow was still spying from his place and made an obscene gesture at me when I passed. I smiled back calmly, pleased with myself for the first time so far.

But things weren't going that well.

In the first place, no sooner had I turned on the ignition than a terrifying fact became apparent: I had barely any gas. I'd started off with the tank well filled, but when one drives throughout a night, circling, one finally does use up the gas.

I remembered now that in all my circling through the city I'd not seen a single gas station. And such stations are so vital!

I took out the volume of maps—the guide book! To my horror, I now learned from it that in all Cosmopolis there were but five such stations.

Feverishly I went in search of the nearest. It was thirteen kilometers away down those streets going the wrong way for me, and I'd never get there.

I glimpsed again a man in a blue uniform. I grabbed at him as though he were a lifebelt thrown to me as I sank.

"I've got to find a gas station!" I howled. "Where can I find one anywhere near?"

The fellow, despite his uniform, was a good fellow. He glanced at my license plate, saw that I was a stranger to the city, and took pity on me. He leaned on my windowsill in a friendly way, saying, "Look! Gas here is quite a problem. New gas stations cannot be put up—it's been forbidden, hoping that this will help to solve the influx of cars to the city. There are only five gas stations in all Cosmopolis . . . and they almost never have gas."

I felt myself paling. "But then—how do the cars in this city get the gas they need?"

"Well, there's a flourishing black market. It is calculated that there are some eighty thousand clandestine stations that supply gas. You're a nice guy! For a hundred credits, I can give you the addresses of the five nearest of these."

I gave him the money eagerly. He took the map, pointed out the five places as promised, and even told me how to get to them. Only after having done this did he tuck the money into his pocket.

"But that's a *lot* of clandestine stations!" I told him. "Doesn't the Law prevent this black marketeering?"

"Ha, ha! It is the Law itself that provides gas for them all."

"But why? What does it gain?"

He laughed at my ingenuity.

"Naturally, it can thus charge a special high tax!" He put his face nearer to mine, confidentially. "Do you know?" said he. "With this extra tax, they finance the new superhighways for discongesting traffic."

Only much later did I learn—and in a terrible fashion—what is meant by those "superhighways for discongestion."

When I reached where I was going, there wasn't, of course, any place to park, so I had to take on another Wheeler to sit behind the wheel for me. At once he warned me the tariff was four hundred credits an hour.

"Has the price gone up?" I asked.

"No, sir," was the answer. "But this region is classified as a commercial zone: there's a surcharge."

I left the car and went up to the offices. I had to have an *official* interview, as you know, one of those stupid, completely unnecessary interviews without which you can't solve certain legal red-tape—by-products of bureaucracy. And—as always happens in such cases—I was greeted with a "Come back tomorrow." Worse, the man listened to me attentively, then gave me a hundred good reasons why he couldn't attend to me right now, and he gave me a presentation slip for another official office, adding that to solve my problem it would be absolutely necessary for me to go there at eight o'clock that same evening. If I did this, he assured me, patting me affectionately on my back, I'd find *all* my problems solved.

I hoped so, fervently!

So I went back to the car. Before letting the Wheeler go, I showed him the slip above mentioned and asked:

"Where can this address be?"

His whistle was long and demoralizing.

"Wow!" said he. "That's in the *Center!*" And the way he said it gave me cold shivers.

"When do you have to be there, sir?" he asked.

"Eight."

He glanced at his watch.

"You'd better get started at once," said he. "It's already almost too late. You'll barely make it, and I'm not sure if you'll get there in time."

I glanced at my watch: it was ten-thirty in the morning.

"Is it that far?" I asked.

"No, sir: it's only thirty kilometers from here. But I've told you—it's the Center."

As I didn't know Cosmopolis, I decided to take his warning seriously. If anyone knew how long it would take, surely he did. I thanked him. He gave me his hand but made a disgusted face when I squeezed his hand effusively.

The series of partial maps in my guide book grew more and more complicated the nearer I got to the Center, but there was a wide avenue that went from one end of the city to the other right through that self-same Center. This is it! thought I, making for it at once. It wasn't easy to get onto the avenue from a sidestreet, but I managed it at last, only to find myself amid a host of cars rushing after me like a herd of furious bison.

I quickly got to the side, feeling the hair all over my body standing on end in my terror. At last I sighed with profound relief when they passed safely by, though almost scraping me. Again I studied the maps feverishly: I was sure I'd seen a double arrow, signifying a two-way street.

Yes, there was a double arrow but it was printed with yellow ink.

A man in a blue uniform came toward me with a mean look in his eye.

"Don't you see that you're holding up traffic?" he barked.

"I was studying the map," I apologized. "What does this yellow arrow mean?"

"The instructions on page three are there for some reason," said he.

I turned to page three. Yes, there were the instructions, which explained: "A matter of alternating directions. Yellow arrows signify a change of direction each half hour; with a blue line in the middle: every hour; with a red line: every twenty minutes."

I closed the guide book with its maps, feeling that I was caught in a mirage somehow.

"Right now is the half hour for *coming*," he explained. "You'll have to wait half an hour for *going*."

"But how?" I asked, knowing I couldn't just stay there to wait.

"Keep circling," he said. "What do you suppose everybody does?"

So I circled. I discovered that all along the length of the avenue were special streets that seemed to have been made for this very purpose. More, there seemed to be any number of drivers doing just this same circling, along with me, there. So much so that I found myself alongside another car going in the same circulating way, and got into conversation with the driver, and so found that our problems were identical. And thus began a fine friendship, cemented by our mutual desperation. I asked him:

"Why don't they have elevated crossings to avoid all this?"

"They did. And what do you think happened?" he murmured sorrowfully. "The day they opened these raised crossings, seventeen cars were pushed over the edge, while everybody rushed to cross. There were forty-three dead, what with the people in the cars and the people upon whom the cars fell. So they closed the crossings, took them down, and forgot it."

"And what about underground crossings?"

"Also! They tried that, but the first landslide of cars filled the tunnels completely. They've still not managed to haul all the debris away."

"Then why not simply forbid wheeled traffic in urban centers?"

"Are you nuts?" He flinched. "Don't you care about the country's economy? It is based on car-making and connected industries! Do you want the whole nation to be ruined?"

At that instant rang the changeover from *come* to *go*. We rushed to get back onto the highway, racing other cars which would not manage the sprint in time. Once again now we were on the wide avenue the name of which was Avenue Eternity, and eternal indeed it was. Before we could reach the Center, the half hour was over, and we again had to make our escape to the Circular Route (as same were termed), before the avalanche of waiting cars going in the other direction could shatter us. And thus we continued circling.

"I have never been able to make it in just one period," my new friend told me in a defeated voice. "I've always had to wait out two or three changeovers."

"But why these changes? Wouldn't it be better—" I began.

He cut me off with a strange gesture of his hand, saying, "Remember that people not only need to *go,* they have to *return.* And there simply isn't room to have two avenues!"

I remembered just then (my stomach reminded me) that I'd not eaten since the day before. I asked my new companion:

"Is there anywhere where we can eat around here?"

"But of course," he said. "In all these Circular Routes there are places. I feel like eating something also. Let's go. I'll show you the way!"

I followed him. We entered a sort of short tunnel, pleasantly lit. In the center there was a sort of counter opening onto the tunnel itself. As we approached we could see the menu printed up—just one menu: concentrated soup, concentrated chicken, concentrated peach; a ration of nongaseous mineral water; all for two hundred credits. I found it a bit expensive, but my hunger was devouring. At the counter, I deposited my two hundred credits and a girl most lightly garbed gave me a quadruple bottle of translucent plastic with four valves for sucking linked with their four independent containers full of the translucent liquids. The stickers pasted on same indicated the contents: from first to last, soup, fowl, peach, water. I made a disgusted face.

"Hey!" I told the girl. "This menu doesn't please me much. Haven't you anything instead—solid?"

"Solid?" she cried, alarmed. "Are you crazy? This is all that is legally allowed to be eaten when you are driving."

"When driving?" I was astonished. "Oh, then—can't one eat here?"

"Of course not, sir; there's no place. Where would you leave your car while you eat? Keep circling, please; there are others waiting to your rear."

So I went on and got back to the Circular route. I was finishing up my dessert when again the half hour rang: I threw the quadruple bottle of plastic aside, and pushed into the Avenue of Eternity before those behind me could get there first. I managed to reach the turnoff marked CENTER four seconds before the half hour sounded anew and the cars in front of me would drive me back by force.

From that site, and after turning to the left, as per my guide book and map, I must reach the street that would take me to the very Center. But a magnificent, shining disk signaled that it was prohibited—

exactly there—to turn to the left. Don't ask me why—someone later told me it was part of the plan of rulings issued to discongest the Center. Much against my will, I must now turn to the right.

And that was when I lost myself.

I believe it was all done purposely. For an area of some two kilometers around there, the signs multiplied till the place seemed a veritable forest of signs. If I tried to turn right, a sign ordered me to turn left. And on every side I glimpsed men in those blue uniforms, spying, ready to pounce.

After so many turns that my head seemed no longer firmly fixed on my shoulders, I tried to find my way somewhere, but was totally disoriented. I tried to find the name of some street so as to learn where I was, but the street signs were always placed where they could not be seen by a car driver . . . or, simply, there were no signs. I tried to find my way by guesswork, but all I managed was to get still more lost. I was aware that inexorably I was getting further and further from my destination, and it was a matter of anguish to me to realize there was nothing I could do. As a last resort, I tried to find my way by the sun, but I've always been a city dweller, and never learned to study nature. And besides, who can find their way by the sun amid such enormous buildings?

I must have spent a couple of hours circling along some forty kilometers of tortuous and Machiavellian traffic signs, when I thought I saw my way clear at last. Before me was an arrow pointing to the left, with the legend ROAD OF RAPID CIRCULATION.

I clutched at the opportunity as a drowning man might clutch at a worm-eaten board, for salvation. There were arrows now on every hand, the road-sign system now was perfect. Too much so, I should have realized. I blame myself for that now.

Soon I turned into the entrance of a highway. The signs now had changed, informing me this was AUTOPISTA X-332: HIGHWAY FOR RAPID CIRCULATION: MINIMUM SPEED: 150 KILOMETERS PER HOUR. FIRST EXIT AT 320 KILOMETERS.

I tried to escape from that flagrant trap but it was too late: there was no possible exit . . . I was already on the new *autopista*.

I swear I never wanted to be there . . . I swear by God and all the saints. But at that entranceway there was no cloverleaf, no sideroad, nothing. They'd left us without any chance of escape. Only the *autopista*.

I kept going—what else could I do! I'm sure I was as pale as death itself. I thought about those three hundred twenty kilometers ahead of me. Dear God, what had I gotten myself into? Every five kilometers a sign reminded me: MINIMUM VELOCITY, 150 KMS. PER HOUR.

Photoelectric cells would register those breaking the law. I stepped on the accelerator, sobbing.

Some fifty kilometers ahead, I came to a rest area, with parking space, a service station, and a restaurant-bar. It had been announced by a sign five kilometers in advance, and there was a special road branching off to it. I drove in as though it were my last chance for salvation.

The parking lot was in shade, a real blessing on that suffocating day. They sold there packaged food for taking with one; food for eating there; tidbits. I thought I glimpsed solid edibles, recognized same as food, and my stomach gurgled. I asked for a hamburger with plenty of bread and plenty of meat and a liter of beer. I leaned against the counter with a sigh of gratitude.

"Hey!" said I to the waiter. "How will I get back to that devilish city?"

His professional smile was the best you could expect of him.

"Oh, did they throw you out too, huh?"

I nodded sadly.

"It's the new plan for urban order, to discongest the Center," said he, as though that might comfort me. "For the moment they've been set up only along the entrances to the Center, in an experimental way . . . a labyrinth with signs set up by expert psychologists, and at the end of the labyrinth a long and rapid highway leading away. However, it's so successful that they're going to install the system in other places too."

I grunted noncommittally. The truth was that I didn't feel up to commenting.

"The cars these days have turned into a veritable nightmare, you know!" the fellow went on. "And I don't think it's a bad idea. You have to think that if they manage to take a car driver—through muddling him scientifically—to a rapid exit that removes him to a distance of three or four hundred kilometers, a good percentage of drivers will stop trying to reach the city and won't return. And that's a fact—the checks they've made demonstrate that only eighteen per cent of these cars that thus leave the city by the Rapid *Autopistas* do return."

"Yes, but those labyrinths will only fool strangers," I risked saying. "No matter how complicated, they'll not fool local folk, who'll learn the turns at last."

"You think so?" He laughed. "They change the labyrinths each fortnight!"

I was sunk. I ate the hamburger in silence, drank my beer, and thought, THE WORLD IS ROTTEN! Only when my inner man was comforted did I recuperate my morale. I set my teeth and stuck out my chest. If there's one thing I cannot stand, it is to be cheated.

"I shall return," said I, as though pronouncing a sentence of doom.

He shrugged indifferently. "As you wish!" said he. "If you want to face it all again, go right ahead." He stuck his hand into a pocket and pulled forth a card. "When you return via the other side of the *autopista,* I advise you to return to this parking lot . . . it's at the same height as this: THE PLACE OF JOE THE BIZCO. He makes some quick suppers that are delicious. Take it: if you hand him this card, he'll give you a good discount. He's a relative of mine, you see."

I took the card and turned it over. "Supper, did you say?" I inquired.

He glanced at his watch.

"Yes! I think that if you go quickly, by the time you return it will still be in time for supper. He closes late, you see."

I did not see, but the hamburger inside me was like a lump of stone.

So I returned. Despite an inner voice within me screaming not to be such a fool, I returned. I reached the PLACE OF JOE THE BIZCO just as they were closing up, but they let me in. I longed to keep right on going, but something stronger than myself prevented it. I felt exhausted, I felt sharp pains in my arms and my right leg. I needed to rest.

There, while I chewed at a rather rubbery steak that kept me busy for a good while, I thought over my problem carefully. I had to go to the Center—this was imperative. The date for the interview had already passed, but I supposed my excuse would be valid enough to justify my failure to keep the appointment. Surely, in a city like Cosmopolis, a delay as considerable as mine could be excused.

But there was this problem of reaching the place. After a lengthy meditation, I came to the conclusion that it would be too risky to wait till the morning to continue the journey. Therefore, I decided that the best thing would be to set off right now. By night, or rather by the dawn hour, I presumed, by the time I got there, it might be easier. And surely I'd find a parking place near my destination where I even could sleep. The car had reclinable seats. In due course, that morning, I'd look not very presentable; unshaven and untidy; but at least I'd be *there*.

Which is what I did. . . .

When I say I did it, I cannot now avoid a shudder. The truth is it cost me plenty to manage it. Don't you imagine that it's easy to go to the Center of Cosmopolis, not even by dawn light. It's for this very reason, as I understand, that all the important businesses are more and more setting up their public-relations and information offices in the outskirts of Cosmopolis, in the new blocks rising more and more near the exits of the *autopistas,* leaving only the fiscal offices in the Center, as it's well known that only the Ruling Powers can remain traditionally in their inaccessible shells. But I got there, though to do so I had to fill the tank twice—and at shocking prices.

And then I began hunting a place, a corner. It didn't take long to convince me that the situation here was the same as the one at the hotel, made the graver here because it was absolutely, positively, and irrevocably prohibited (save in very rare cases) to park anywhere there. It was at one o'clock in the morning when I began to be really worried. By two, I grew nervous. By three I was becoming desperate.

I then decided to stop the car anywhere, in any corner: if I remained in it they couldn't fuss, they couldn't fine me, and I might even manage a quick nap. My eyelids were already closing, more and more. So I drew up at a place that seemed discreet enough—when all's said and done—dropped back my seat, and closed my eyes.

I don't know how much time had passed—probably just a few seconds—when I heard blows on the window glass, a constant tapping.

"This deserves a fine!" said the man, threateningly.

He was wearing the classic blue uniform. I blinked sleepily, glanced at my watch—thirty seconds since I'd reclined in the seat.

"I'm sorry," I murmured. "I'm just worn out."

"I'm sorry too, sir. And I'm worn out too! Have you no idea how exhausting it is to keep after all these people who think they're brighter than oneself and try so shamelessly to fool me? It's not easy, sir."

He glanced at the license number.

"You're a stranger, are you?" said he. "Only because of that, I'll not fine you. But don't you do it again. Next time you'll not be so lucky."

"Listen!" I begged, pointing toward the building where I must show up in the morning—the same place I should have reached at eight of the night before. "I've got to go there. I've got to stay here till the morning." I glanced again at my watch. "Well, it's morning, now!" I found myself mumbling nonsense about "but now yesterday's today" and so on. "Listen," I tried again, "tomorrow I'll contract a Wheeler to take care of the car and I'll go up there, solve the problem that brought me here, and off I'll go definitely from this infernal place. I'll go back to my own beloved town. There, at least, one has parking space."

He grinned, his yellow teeth appearing. "You shouldn't have said that to me," he murmured sadly. "But I'll ignore it, seeing you have this problem. I'll ignore it, provided you contract a Wheeler for the night ahead. You cannot be here sleeping inside your car, sir. If you're before the wheel, you must be watchful—awake!"

I sighed.

"Oh, very well, I'll look up a Wheeler to stay awake for me, if that's what you want."

"You don't have to hunt one up, sir," said he, sweetening up a bit. He put two fingers to his mouth and whistled deafeningly. At once I found at my side a young fellow who hastened to display to me his syndicate card. "Here you have one. You can trust him, sir," said the policeman. "He's my son."

I gave up my place before the wheel, and reclined in the other seat, making myself comfortable.

The boy studied me. "Sleep well, sir," said he. "I'll see that everything's fine."

And what did he do but put back his seat also and go to sleep at my side.

That morning, I left the bleary-eyed lad in charge of the car and went up to the office at nine sharp. I was very aware of how untidy I looked, but soon realized that the majority of people going about around me in the offices and halls of the building looked just as bad. I glanced briefly into a mirror. Well . . . probably we all were facing similar problems.

But I'd better make sure that I solved the business now, once and for all. I wanted never more than now to get back to the peace of my own home and my own town. So I marched very decidedly now into the office. A secretary stood up and came to meet me.

"What do you wish, sir?"

"I must speak with Mr. Gonzalez," said I, handing her the card.

"Mr. Gonzalez isn't in, sir," said she quickly. "Have you an appointment with him?"

I pointed to the card. "Yesterday, at eight P.M."

"He wasn't here yesterday at that time either, sir. He went out that morning and still hasn't got back. We suspect he's *trapped*."

"Trapped?"

"Yes."

I couldn't take it in. I suppose my face showed my surprise and she must have realized at once that I didn't live in Cosmopolis. She explained:

"That happens quite a lot, sir. Particularly so when one has to go to places which can be reached only by car."

I nodded understandingly. "And you don't know where he is now?"

"Well . . ." She hesitated for a brief moment. Then she gestured me to wait and went back to the interoffice phone, red in hue, and dialed a number. She spoke briefly, then hung up.

"Come, please." She waved to me. She took me now to a huge map of the city occupying all of one wall, and, with the aid of the squares, pointed to a spot. "I've just been told he's exactly there right now," said she.

"Is he at some office there? Some meeting?"

"No, sir. He's in his car, trying to get back."

I studied the map. The site was really far from the Center.

"And did you just now speak with him?"

"Yes. You see, all who have to use a car frequently, like Mr. Gonzalez, have a special telephone installed in it so that they can be localized and rescued. It's the only way to find anyone at any moment, if an emergency comes up."

"Will it take long for him to get back?"

She gestured ambiguously.

"He's been trying since noon yesterday. He says they've changed one of those devilish labyrinths, and it took him three hundred fifty kilometers away: it's their newest labyrinth, just inaugurated, you see? It's taking him almost all night to get back."

"But now he's relatively near," said I, looking at the map.

She grinned at me as though I were a little baby who'd just wet his pants.

"Don't forget today's the day for the Fiscal Audience," she observed.

"And?"

"This means thousands of persons will be coming toward the Center at the same hour. The obstructions usually last till dawn."

I felt myself paling. Things were getting worse and worse.

"Then, is there no solution?"

"Of course there are solutions," said she brightly. "Experience has some value, doesn't it? He told me just now that since he can't get here, why don't you try to reach him there? He's waiting for you on Circular Route S-33," and she pointed it out on the map, "till you get there."

"But I'll *never* get there!"

She seemed to understand my problem.

"No, of course you won't," said she. "Though the going is always the easiest. But there are Wheelers of Circulation specialized in getting rapidly to such sites. Of course, they're rather dear, but if you really want to see Mr. Gonzalez . . ."

Yes, of course I did. Minutes later, I had at my side a young man of a sporty appearance and with a dynamic way to him. The first thing he did, after showing me his syndicate card, was ask what sort of car did I have. I told him and he frowned: a bad car for racing in, said he. Well, I said good-bye to the secretary and thanked her, and off we went, back to the street.

The Wheeler taking care of my car frowned at the sight of his competitor and went off growling between his teeth that he'd "tell daddy." I paid no attention. The new Wheeler sat before the wheel and turned it experimentally, started the car, revved the motor, listened to the sound of it, and shrugged his shoulders.

"Hold on, brother!" said he, and started off.

The trip was *really* short, though it seemed to me eternal, for I lived through twenty years of driving experience right then. That fellow must have belonged to some suicide club; he went scraping by other cars, got ahead in a kamikaze way, and caused by spontaneous generation a good handful of white hairs to appear on my head. But he did the impossible: he took me to Route S-33 in less time than seemed believable. When we reached destination, he studied the speedometer, then the watch, and muttered:

"Three minutes and thirty seconds less than my urban record. Not bad, for this car. That's one thousand two hundred credits, sir."

I paid up without a single remark, because a fellow capable of driving so vilely will be capable of worse things still. And I went on to hunt up Gonzalez.

It wasn't too hard to find him, because he had on the roof of his car a placard that said in bright lettering: I'M GONZALEZ. And now I understood something that had struck me as queer, glimpsed on other cars heretofore in Cosmopolis: the fact that many a car had a sign of this sort on its roof. What surer and quicker way could there be for two people in cars to find each other in the streets, since they couldn't meet anywhere else?

We placed ourselves side by side, I introduced myself, we shook hands symbolically, and I began to explain to him my problem. Gonzalez, like all good citizens of Cosmopolis with cars, had his car well equipped; he now connected the tape-recorder to capture our chat, and took out a notepad on which he could write with just one hand. He listened to me attentively, took some notes, checked up some details on a luminous screen connected to the consulting files of his office via a TV circuit, as he explained to me, and finally frowned deeply.

"Your case is going to be difficult," said he. "I see a grave problem."

"What?"

"You'd better examine it more deeply. Why don't you see me some other day . . . what about tomorrow?"

"Isn't there any other solution?" I ventured, recalling all my past sufferings, and shuddering.

"I'm afraid not. I've got to consult with the minister. Look, your case has nothing to do with Circulation: it therefore has no priority. And I myself am only a third delegate. Can't you get in touch with me—even if only by phone—tomorrow afternoon? I do hope to get back to my office somehow by dawn, and tomorrow—once I've napped a bit—I'll take care of you. I do think I can fix things."

I agreed with a sigh.

"Very well," said I. "I was hoping to get home tonight, but . . ."

He smiled.

"Don't you worry. Tomorrow I'll have things ready. And now I must be hurrying along. I've lost a lot of time circling right here along this Circular Route, and it's prohibited. And today I've been fined twice. . . ."

He gave me a phone number so that I could call him there the following day, we again shook hands symbolically, and off he went. I decided to get back to the hotel. Taking up the guide book and set of maps, I began my peregrinations. This time it wasn't so bad; it seemed as though I was beginning to learn my way around by much practice. And then, when I was still a good way from the hotel, I saw something I'd imagined I'd never get to see—a parking space! At the same time, I saw another car like myself making for it. I'm quick in my reactions: I jammed on the accelerator and shot in while the other car charged after me. It scraped the entire side of my car, but I didn't care. I turned off the motor and got out.

The other fellow was right by my side. He was enormously pale as he stopped the car and got out. I got myself ready for anything that might occur, fists clenched. But he was no fighter. He merely stopped before me, studied me with eyes of hate, and said:

"Sir, you're a pig."

"I know I am," I agreed, happy for the first time since I'd reached Cosmopolis. I watched him go off again, defeated, and putting my hands in my pockets without a care for the kilometers I yet must walk, set off whistling toward the hotel.

Upon reaching it, I went up to my room, stopped before the bed, and without bothering to undress spread my arms out in the form of a cross and flopped onto it. I slept fourteen hours without a break.

The following midday, I washed and shaved parsimoniously, changed, packed my bags, and went downstairs. Imagining that it was very likely I'd have my problems definitely solved that afternoon, why keep the room longer? I paid the bill and on the way out saw the receptionist, to whom I said sardonically:

"I found a parking space for my car." Not satisfied with this, I repeated, *"I have the car parked."*

And I laughed as I saw that my words had been like a stab in the heart of the receptionist.

So I reached the car, and shoved the luggage into it. At once various passing cars crushed their way toward me, then when the drivers saw that I wasn't going, they glared at me like assassins. I went into the nearest bar. From there I phoned Mr. Gonzalez. His secretary told me he wasn't in and her voice sounded as though she'd been crying.

"When will he be back?" I asked.

"Never . . ." I heard another broken sob at the other end of the wire; and then she screamed wildly, "He'll never return!"

I felt myself shuddering icily. I didn't understand it at all, but was terrified.

"Did—something happen?"

"Yes!" moaned the voice at the other end. "They fined him for the third time yesterday."

"Well, but . . ."

"Oh, don't you understand?" sobbed the voice. "Mr. Gonzalez really loved that car. *He refused to abandon it!"*

And she hung up suddenly.

For a good while I didn't know what to do. I called the waiter, and asked him:

"Listen, when they fine you for the third time in the same day, they take away your car and don't return it, right?" He nodded. "And what do they do with the car?" I also asked.

"They turn it into scrap, of course. There are too many cars." He gestured with his hands to show how this was done . . . the car crushed into a compact hunk of metal.

At last I understood. I felt myself growing giddy, and went out to the street. I thought of my car, my beloved car, I thought of my town, my beloved town, of my family, my beloved family—of everything. I thought that I must get back to rescue my car, and I shuddered in terror. I began to laugh, in the throes of a nervous attack.

I laughed still louder when they took me away in a helicopter.

Two months have passed since I entered this asylum. They've tried to cheer me up, give me hope; they've assured me mine is not the only case of its sort, that they calculate that some five or six thousand cases have occurred just like mine, to date. They speak of symptoms and possible therapy. The doctor says that within a week I'll be allowed back on the street.

But something has changed deeply in me. I know that once I'm out I'll never manage to take a car again in my life. And of course my own car is still where I left it . . . now that I've got that parking space there, nobody's going to take it from me. But I fear the idea of how I'll ever leave this frightful city. Other sick folk—citizens of Cosmopolis, all of them (including one that ends up here regularly each year)—have spoken to me of the exits from the city.

They tell me that all the roads now surrounding Cosmopolis are an inextricable tangle or network from which one may never escape. They tell me that between ten to twenty thousand cars are constantly "lost" along this Secondary Network of Highway Discongestion, as it's termed by the authorities. I know that the day I try to leave the city, I can find myself deep in that labyrinth and never escape, *never*. No, I'm not going to try!

I likewise know that the problem that brought me to the city is no longer solvable. Gonzalez vanished, and the only thing I could do would be to start from the beginning, all over again. But how shall I do that? My God, how can I ever start it all again? I've just been reading the newspaper. They're going to create a new law that *absolutely* prohibits any parking throughout the urban sectors of Cosmopolis. The authorities feel that if the law is passed, it will solve all the circulatory problems of the city. And now the doctor after examining me has said something about a relapse on my part. . . .

I have nightmares of crushing machines wearing blue uniforms. I see blocks of twisted metal from which rise laughter and screams. I see cars . . . cars . . . cars. I never cease from seeing them. I even suspect my own bed is one. *I'm* a car. I can't stop, because if I do they'll fine me. . . .

Planet for Sale

by Niels E. Nielsen

Translated from the Danish by Sam J. Lundwall

The good solid imagination of old-time science fiction is at its best in this tale. Niels Nielsen has in his novels written of future wars, of wandering cities, of geographic disasters and the remolding of the world, and here he plays with an idea that only a few have handled in science fiction, such as Theodore Sturgeon, and Nielsen handles it very well.

"No planets!"

Tim O'Shaugh raised his large, ruddy face from the radio telescope. "Not one single planet near Betelgeuse!"

His powerful Irish voice grated with disappointment. Maggio Forlini, the dark Italian, rose, graceful as a cat, against the gravitation of the rocket. "Are you sure . . . quite sure?"

Tim snapped, "As sure as I am that Angelo's grandmother was a Comanche squaw in a flea-ridden village in the godforsaken country New Mexico!"

The quadroon Indian, Angelo del Norte, the oldest of the men aboard the *Black Stallion,* en route to the red giant Betelgeuse, was silent. Nothing in his brown leathery face showed that he had noticed the insult. He knew well enough how much willpower was needed to stay four years in a cramped rocket . . . so much time would the return trip from Betelgeuse take, even with this, the first rocket from Earth, with its faster-than-light speed. Besides, Tim's insult was mostly the result of the bitter disappointment.

"Try again," suggested the fourth crew member, the German Egge Kerl. His angular face was noncommittal.

"Try? Try?" Although Tim at least nominally was captain for this small group of prospectors, he was the one who let his disappointment show most. "Haven't we circled Betelgeuse? Have we seen as much as the shadow of a planet? No! This whole trip, six hundred light-years, plus a bonus of ten million dollars for every discovered planet, has been a fiasco."

He glared at them. Their immobile faces irritated him. Sure, prospectors had to take chances everywhere, be it on Earth or in space. But his hot Irish temperament always made him lose his temper.

For a moment all were silent, thinking about the long journey home. They stared out through the windows at Betelgeuse, which hung aport as an enormous burning gas cloud in the black depths, a furnace in the well of darkness. The light-magnetic engines of the *Black Stallion* worked at one fourth their capacity as it tumbled on in its elliptical orbit around the giant sun. Softly singing, the large rocket fell through eternity, and far, far away astarboard, an almost invisible spark flashed in the darkness—the home sun.

The rocket was launched by the Panama Cosmic Trade, Ltd., one of the international cartels that had sprung up following the discovery of twin relativity ten years earlier, 2088, which at last had made faster-than-light travel possible. Earth capital could now concentrate its enterprising spirit on the neighboring stars, the planets in the solar system having long since been turned into lucrative Earth branches. For a fantastic payment plus bonus for every discovered planet, these four adventurers undertook to go with the *Black Stallion* to Betelgeuse, a four-year trip. Now they had arrived, after seven hundred thirty days of meteors, magnetic storms, and cosmic neutron storms. Their greed was overwhelming. Nothing less than a new empire could satisfy them. And now Betelgeuse appeared to be nothing but a lonely golden star that never had given birth to a single planet out of its red flaming womb! Oh yes, disappointment hurt even behind Angelo's impassive face.

"You try!" Tim glared at the cold German and kicked at the radio telescope. "I have been looking so long my eyes hurt!"

He fell silent, tired. He walked heavily over to the computers, punch cards for the long journey home prepared. "Just think—travel more than two hundred light-years and not even get a single planet!"

Kerl leaned down over the radio telescope. Tim sniffed scornfully. Angelo and Maggio stood behind Kerl, clinging on to a diminishing hope.

Angelo stared out at the red sea of fire aport. In millions of years it had flung out its titanic energy into the emptiness, without lapping one single planet with its life-giving light! Why? He was enough of an Indian to wonder. For him, a sun was almost a god. Why did this red giant god wander over the heavens with no soul to adore it, with no one to be born, grow up, and die beneath its incredible cosmic fire?

"Planet astern . . . thirty degrees aport," Kerl said quietly.

"What?" Tim O'Shaugh stiffened. "Impossible! I should have seen it even if it was no more than ten miles across!"

Kerl arose. "Look for yourself," he said coldly.

Tim glued his face to the eyepiece, stared and stared. Finally he rubbed his stinging eyes. "Yes . . . it is there! With atmosphere, seas, clouds . . . everything! How could I have missed it. . . ."

He looked humbly at them. One after one, they looked into the eyepiece. A small obvious disc, a drop of dew shimmering in the black depths, a living planet face that breathed, apparently as yet very distant, hardly larger than a coin but obviously a planet. And it even had atmosphere! A valuable rarity.

"Ten million dollars!" Maggio whispered reverentially.

The others nodded. Their lips became thin and hard, the face of the hunter as the prey comes near. Now a run close to the planet while the instruments made the routine analyses . . . air, water, mass, minerals; then they could return home and get their money, and still later a rocket fleet would be launched to pacify and exploit with clouds of nerve gas and load precious stones and metals. Ten years from now, the Panama Cosmic Trade, Ltd., could pay its shareholders fantastic dividends!

The *Black Stallion* turned and swept down toward the planet, which, according to visual analysis, ought to be millions of miles away. Then, suddenly, alarm lights began to flash at the radar console. Object on collision course! Brake rockets automatically ignited. Only the antigravitational field saved them from being crushed by the braking.

A meteor? They stared at the radar screens. In the emptiness ahead the small spheroid still hung, somewhat larger than before but apparently as distant. There was nothing else to be seen.

"But . . ." Tim's chin fell. Slowly they realized the truth: the alarm had sounded for the planet. It was the planet they had barely escaped colliding with. But, if so . . .

"It is hardly a hundred fathoms from us," Angelo whispered. "It's apparent size is its real size. . . ."

"Ten meters in diameter!" Kerl already stood at the instruments. "Well, perhaps ten-point-two," he added with German exactitude.

"It can't be true," Tim groaned. "Look . . . look at those small crystals . . . cities, by God! And the white lines . . . roads! And the rectangular fields . . . cultivated land! But no larger than . . ." Astonishment made him temporarily mute.

"If the size of the inhabitants bears the same relationship to the planet as ours bears to Earth . . ." Kerl made some quick calculations. "In that case, they are about two thousandths of a millimeter long!"

He looked at them. A quiet amusement glittered in his cold blue eyes. "Like germs . . . typhus, tuberculosis, cholera!"

"Do you mean that this planet is inhabited by . . . typhus germs?" Maggio's chin with the blue stubble trembled.

"Not quite . . ." Kerl regarded him smilingly. "Germs don't build cities or cultivate land. Besides, that problem is only theoretical, since . . ."

"Since this dwarf planet is completely worthless!" shouted Tim.

"For us!" Angelo looked at the infinitesimal planet that quietly rotated before them, a blue butterfly, a valuable toy, dropped from the hand of God in the moment of creation.

"Yes . . ." Tim was about to rebuff the calm quadroon Indian.

Suddenly his surly eyes lit up. "Sure, Cosmic Trade won't pay a single dollar for a ten-meter planet. But . . . London's Astrophysical Museum?"

"Right!" shouted Maggio. "A real, inhabited planet in a glass jar . . . what a sensation! Ah, people would run to the museum! They will pay us ten million for an exhibit like that!"

"Spacesuits, immediately!" Tim sent them running. His eyes were hard. "Dress up! We'll take the magnetic crane along. Hydrogen tank two is empty. We can put it there. The tank is pressure-proof . . . for the sake of the atmosphere!" He screwed on his helmet.

"Exactly." Kerl smiled.

"Ten million!" Maggio shouted. "That is, if we can get those germs home alive!"

They stormed out from the air lock with the help of their oxygen guns. Kerl, who almost never lost his head, held a microscope under his arm. Angelo came last, silent and thoughtful. Billions, he thought, held by a curious fear. There might be billions living on that planet . . . mothers who right now are wiping their children's running noses. Men who steer ships over the seas. And then . . . incredible shadows in the sky, signs, cosmic trolls . . .

They moved in on the planet, four men in clumsy spacesuits. They made a circle around it. Their shadows fell over the mountains, darkened the seas. They pointed fingers at it, and laughed in their suit radios.

"Lilliput!" shouted Maggio. "The planet Lilliput!"

Lilliput hung between their greedy hands, following its eternal orbit around the red sun, an infinitesimal relative to the giants of the universe. But not a dead asteroid without atmosphere, a golden, frozen stone. It hung in space surrounded by a shimmering halo, an air tiara; a whirling water-gray and plant-green planet, a smiling, living child of the sun.

"A miniature Earth," Kerl muttered. "Probably with quite different gravitation. A unique specimen in the cosmic scale of size . . ."

Angelo stared at the dwarf planet, swallowing heavily. He saw the day march on over it, saw snow-covered mountains glow like rubies, saw mighty light-gray oceans in which the red mother sun reflected, saw curious crystal growths here and there on the continents, big cities, saw the winding lines of rivers, the glittering lights of lakes, a planet face, showing the marks of millions of years but still alive, young and ruddy. . . .

"Let it be!" His partly superstitious Indian wonder overcame his greed. "It is theirs. They are a people. They may have souls like us!"

"Souls . . . ?" grunted Tim. "Sure! If germs have souls . . . what then? That's good! I'll get the magnetic crane."

He floated back to the ship, whose shimmering steel body burned bright red in the light from the giant star. The oxygen gun described a hazy line after him.

"The cities are bursting with life!" Kerl mutteringly examined the cities with his microscope. "Small black dots . . . obviously scared . . . probably panic. They can see us in the heavens. . . ." He methodically pointed the microscope at place after place. Sailing ships, small as fish-scales, dikes, and forests passed in the field of vision like things seen in a drop of water. A swarm, life, flight, struggle, death . . .

The small silvery planet quietly went on in its orbit. They followed, not noticing the movement. With the tranquility of the true scientist, Kerl saw a mountaintop shudder and crash down. He laughed. "Our body mass affects the revolution. Earthquakes. Just wait until we arrest the rotation, that will kill them by the millions!"

Tim came back with the magnetic crane trailing after him. "We'll make fast the cables to the magnetic pole field."

He quickly swam forward, turning like a free-style swimmer in the darkness and the emptiness around the planet. He closed in on it like a giant from a fairyland universe.

"Look at him!" Maggio shouted. "What do you think those germs say about him? Ah, they can frighten their kids with him when they don't want to go to bed! 'Tim will get you if you don't go to bed!' "

Kerl smiled. There was an odd, trembling tension in his voice.

"I can see them! There are millions of them down there! They must think we are archangels with flaming swords!"

"Hey!" Tim laughed, dropping his cable. "Archangels, not bad! Come on, boys! This is the first and last time in our lives that we can be archangel Michael!"

They were gripped by a kind of intoxication. They were cosmic gods! They held on to one another's hands. Even Angelo was carried away. Using their oxygen guns, they drew nearer to the planet, and danced around it, faster and faster. They laughed and shouted, a truly Homeric laughter. They were giants, their brows touched the stars. Their dance in and out of the atmosphere of the dwarf planet created cyclones, dark spirals in the cloud cover that stormed on over ships, coastlines, cities. Every triumphant step cost ten thousand lives.

"Stop . . . stop!" Angelo withdrew his hands. He remembered a few words from a bygone age . . . his grandmother, who pointed up at the stars over the dilapidated village, an old, trembling voice: "Every star is a soul, one of God's angels, little Angelo. . . ."

The small planet whirled courageously in the dark veil of eternity. Northlights blossomed over the poles, the clouds spewed out rain. It spread out its silvery wings, it praised its Creator, it gave birth to life and defended it as well as it could.

"Don't do it!" he whispered into the radio. "Don't you see . . . it is sacred, it is a ray of light shining in through the door of life. The punishment will be horrible if we steal it. Someone could come to our planet just like we came to Lilliput. . . ."

Laughter. "Cries over a bunch of germs!" gasped Tim. "Some dust on a palm. Only a superstitious Indian could do that!"

He gripped the dangling cable. "Now look here! See how I take ten million dollars!"

He fell down toward the dwarf planet. Like a serpent's throat the crane claw yawned at the revolving sphere. The strong cable strained with a soundless whine of steel. . . .

The *Black Stallion* hurtled toward the Earth, a shining lightning, a gray line of light that went right across the universe. They traveled away from Time, they conquered the wastes of space with tiger leaps, the conquerors. And down in the hold of the rocket, Lilliput hung, an imprisoned blue butterfly whose glorious wings were broken.

Kerl and Tim had been very careful with the valuable thing. Using the antigravitation generators, they created a weightless field in tank II, in which the dwarf planet could float like a blue humming-bird in a cage. They pumped in oxygen, nitrogen, argon, steam, and carbon dioxide so that the beings could breathe. Yes, they even put up a small hydrogen sun. They did everything one reasonably could expect for ten million dollars.

And they were rather successful in keeping the "dust" alive, the dust, the germs, or the living dots the microscope showed them—the millions that had survived the floods, the earthquakes, and the cyclones that stormed over the surface as the crane ruthlessly halted the revolution of the planet, as the infinitesimal crystals disappeared beneath red clouds and volcanoes yawned like dragon's jaws, cosmic catastrophes that occurred on areas the size of a hand.

The journey home was not bad. They spent many fascinating hours in tank II, using magnifying glass and microscope. They scraped up living, crawling dust with delicate tools and put it under coldly glittering lenses.

"This is much better than a flea circus," Tim said often with a good-natured laugh. "Look how they run! Heh-heh, one millimeter per hour! They don't understand what's happening. They just can't realize there are super beings like us!"

"Perfect objects for genetic research," Kerl remarked. "They multiply faster than drosophilaes. They must live by a faster time rate. One of our hours could be a year for them. Just think what that means! A scientist could inoculate a whole nation with cancer, keep it in a matchbox, and follow the progress for a hundred generations . . . resistance, propagation, dying out!"

"It might not be such a good idea to sell it to the Astrophysical Museum," Maggio said thoughtfully. "We could open a kind of hatching business and sell them by the thousands! What do you say? One thousand dollars per million! They might grow by tens of millions per day. And no costs for food and nursing!"

"Just scrape off Lilliput ten thousand dollars a day!" Tim slammed his hand against his thigh. "Beautiful. One million for instructive demonstrations in schools! Ten million for the war game the strategists are playing with! They could people a whole planet and see what happens to them in an atomic war!"

"One might be able to train them to handle the micro-mechanisms in spaceships—that should be cheaper than transistors!" Kerl aimed his magnifying glass at the planet. "Look . . . they are already building up their cities again. You can see the crystals changing. They are very viable." He smiled.

"Yes." Maggio got another idea. "You could put a few thousand of them into the artificial diamonds the women have in their eardrops! Diamonds cut like lenses! Beautiful talking pieces! One could see the people running around inside!"

Yes, there were happy hours in the tank with Lilliput. They built castles in the air and made countless millions in their dreams. They launched an entirely new industry: the Lilliput Syndicate!

Only Angelo was quiet. He looked at the small planet that hung in tank II, light as a blue bubble. He looked at the shattered continents and the burned cities from which new streets radiated. And he imagined millions of eyes staring out into the darkened universe around the planet, the rusty walls of tank II where no stars burned. He lost his appetite, he could not sleep; he got sick, pale, and haggard.

"It's his damned Indian imagination," muttered Tim now and then. "He's thinking about those germs! He believes they can think and talk. *Germs!*"

"Which they probably can," Kerl said coldly.

"What?" Tim looked uncertainly at him.

"That's just it." Kerl's eyes glowed. "That's what makes it fantastic: sentient germs!"

He raised his hand and let the shadow fall over the cities, mountains, nations. "They're beautiful! Don't you see?"

"Well . . ." Tim saw the raised hand hover like a hawk over the dwarf planet. "Yes! That's it!"

Angelo could hear their laughs as he lay on his bed, tormented by a nightmare that undoubtedly only sprang from a too vivid imagination.

"Your ship must be sterilized!" the official said coldly. "You know the regulations: all ships returning from deep space must be treated to a heat of one hundred degrees centigrade for twenty-four hours in order to kill all potential alien germs."

"But don't you understand?" Tim shouted. "This planet in tank II, it is alive! Inhabited!"

"A kind of microscopic beings," Kerl added. "About two thousandths of a millimeter high. A unique race, very suitable for scientific experiments!"

"A planet?" the official said indifferently. "You mean that mineral specimen, that . . . eh . . . asteroid you have brought with you?"

"A living planet!" protested Maggio. "We saw it in orbit around Betelgeuse, with northlights and clouds and everything!"

They stood at the Panama interplanetary air field. Outside the building, the *Black Stallion* reared its meteor-scarred hull, back from the longest journey in the history of man. Technicians were pulling up a gigantic hot-air blower to the hold hatch in order to sterilize the ship. Tim, Kerl, and Maggio fought stubbornly and unsuccessfully for their castle in the air, the Lilliput Syndicate. Alas! How could a dull official understand such a thing?

"You can talk how much you want about nations in drops of water and micropeople at a thousand dollars each. I don't care."

The official tapped lightly at the opened regulations book. "Regulations are regulations! We can't risk letting these . . . eh . . . bacteriological races loose on our planet! That would be irresponsible, gentlemen, ir-re-spon-sible!"

They protested. They waved their arms and shouted. They did not even see that an ambulance drove up and drove away with poor Angelo, who insanely babbled about "blue angels" and "the poor stolen butterfly"!

The electric hot-air blower started with a deep growl. Waves of scalding-hot air swept into the *Black Stallion,* going from room to room. The three spacemen were resigned and quiet. An accomplished fact could not be argued with. The official closed his book and looked after them, shaking his head. A mild case of space jitters . . . all spacemen experienced such a thing upon returning home! It was certainly not easy to be an official at the Panama interplanetary air field!

The trio hesitated for a moment by the rocket, outside tank II. They listened through the deep growl, not knowing exactly what for. Inaudible screams? The roar of burning cities? The rushing of boiling seas?

"People are stupid," Maggio said sincerely.

"Right," muttered Tim. "We could have made millions . . . millions!" He repeated the word like a lament.

"We were gods to them . . . gods." Kerl's gaze was wistful. "And then . . . sterilizing!"

Twenty years later, an official found something that looked like a large round stone in one of Panama Cosmic Trade's warehouses. He did some discreet checking, but no one appeared to be interested in it. Spacemen always dragged home meteorites like this as souvenirs. He bribed one of the crane operators to transport the stone to a place outside the city at evening. He knew what beautiful splinters these meteorites made. He blasted it with aerolite and built a beautiful rockery from the pieces in his garden.

Soon flowers glowed over this architectonic masterpiece and he admired it many times with his wife.

"Just think," he always said, "just think . . . to get a rockery transported all the way from Betelgeuse, three hundred light-years from here, for only ten dollars!"

Ysolde

by Nathalie-Charles Henneberg

Translated from the French by Damon Knight

The by-line is a compound signature for a husband-wife team, that of Nathalié and Charles Henneberg. But after the death of Charles many years ago, Nathalie continued the delicate and colorful fantasy writing that made their by-line the French equivalent of Merritt and Zelazny. We do not know, therefore, whether this story was written by both or by Nathalie alone, but in any case the effect is memorable.

I

When he embarked for Nyx, the seventh planet of the Spike in
Virgo, with his daughter Iza, a blind and deaf child, enclosed in her
immobility like a little mother-of-pearl idol with white-golden hair,
Ross the Technocrat knew he was doing a senseless thing. He had
scoured the galaxy in search of an impossible miracle. He had consulted the physicians, the healers, and the wise men of innumerable
planets. In vain.

All confessed themselves powerless. Iza had been born of an all-
but-dead mother, crushed in the wreckage of a spaceship, and death
had never quite released its grip on the cells of her body. Nevertheless, they had kept her alive for years. Ross would not give up—
he would not have been what he was, a Technocrat IV, if he were
capable of weakness or despair.

Somewhere between the Herdsman and the Whale, fate had given
him one last chance: a traveler had told him about the strange quality of Nyx.

"Don't bother telling me that it's an improbable world," said the astronaut. He had the graven waxy mask of those who have stared too
long, through narrow screens, at infinity and the stars. They were sitting under the climatized dome of a federal station, on an artificial
satellite, waiting for the next ship. It was an unforeseen accident that
had brought the great Technocrat to rub elbows with the mob. He
congratulated himself on it. And it was a station like many others beyond Pluto, with its Plexiglas bubbles for differing gravities and
atmospheric pressures, its humidifiers for the Over-Plants, and its iridescent artificial suns. One was surrounded here by the fauna of a
hundred universes: the gritty purplish cones of Foramen and the
Spider-Flowers of the Hyades, the threadlike Capellans and the
crystalline intelligences of Alpha Bootes.

With a sweeping gesture, the explorer took in that whole mass.
"We've grown used to them, haven't we? But the first sight of them

made me feel pretty small. And their worlds are the same: sometimes dazzlingly beautiful, sometimes disconcerting and almost absurd. Why should this fiery abyss be inhabited by creatures made of translucent quartz? Or why should that frozen black globe have its caverns full of the most fragile orchids? You know, there are whole phyla that are alive, in the organic sense of the word, only one year out of every thousand—but then, what a dazzle of colors. . . . What was I saying?"

"You were talking about Nyx," said Ross.

"Ah, Nyx! That's something else again. Everything is real there, but time flows backward. Is it an effect of the planet's rotation, or of its sun, Spica? It's an enormous one, you know. There are a hundred and ten stars in Virgo, and it's the most brilliant of them all, a supergiant that you can see from Earth with the naked eye."

"How do you mean, it flows backward?" asked Ross. He was taller by a head than the spaceman; he was tired, in a hurry to get back to Iza, and he hated to waste his time.

"Oh, well, for instance, take Terra. She ages gradually. She has her ruins, her mountains erode away, certain gases escape from the atmosphere. The same things happen in the same way everywhere else in the universe. But on Nyx, it's different. It's a planet that was inhabited, civilized; now it's returning to its origins . . . and so rapidly! Two hundred years ago, apparently, the atmosphere and climate were like Earth's. Now you have to wear a pressure suit there; it's a hotbox, swept with cyclones and floods, and the instruments register as much cosmic radiation as in our ionosphere."

"Curious," said Ross. "Any other peculiarities?"

"Well, there isn't much more to tell, except that human connective tissue seems to reconstitute itself. Paralytics walk there, no doubt, and the blind see. The only thing is, there's another danger. The ship's doctor explained it to us as we were passing. All the dead cells revivify and proliferate; in time it degenerates into a sort of cancer. Nyx is uninhabited today."

Sirens summoned the passengers; a crowd separated the two Terrans, and Ross never saw the astronaut again. But as soon as he got back to Earth, he visited the Cartographic Office, its galleries hung with star charts, its armored towers of filing cabinets and its implacable electronic brains which knew precisely everything about the universe. The functionaries of this important service had an unctuous and sacerdotal majesty—and they came from every part of the galaxy.

Because of Ross's rank, he was received by the deputy director.

"Someone mentioned Nyx to me," said the Technocrat, seating

himself across from this faintly mauve personage in his purple miter. "How does it happen that this planet doesn't appear on the astrogational maps?"

"Ah!" said the other. "Nyx? It was formerly in our atlas. It was—how shall I put it?—effaced. Yes, by order. You see, in the early days of galactic exploration, the scout ships put pretty nearly everything on their charts—unimportant asteroids and hell-planets. Later on, the authorities began to put some of these places off limits—the really intolerable ones—but they realized that would only attract swarms of adventurers to them. To people like that, a forbidden planet is necessarily crammed with gold or peopled with sirens which the federal government reserves for itself. There were quite a lot of casualties. There was only one solution left: to obliterate the dangerous planets. That's what we did."

"That carries a danger with it—a pilot might land there by mistake."

"Most of them are off the regular routes. Like Nyx."

"Why is Nyx dangerous?"

Somewhat reluctantly, the cartographer pressed a button. A microfile opened; a tiny screen lit up on the opposite wall. The metallic voice of a robot told the improbable history of a world which had thousands of years of civilization behind it, a planet covered with the ruins of megalopolises, immense deserted landing strips, proud monuments, falling apart under the weight of the temperature, the flora, and the general conditions of a carboniferous age.

"It seems," said the deputy director, "that we're dealing with a phenomenon brought about by the recent enormous nuclear explosion of the furnace Spica: an old sun which must have returned to its primitive state. Nyx, in any case, is also returning to its genesis. It should be interesting to see where this devolution will stop. The origins of life might be studied there."

"By whom?" Ross asked.

"Oh, scientists from terrestrial stations."

"There is a laboratory on Nyx," the robot responded obligingly. "Two prize-winning biologists are conducting local observations: Dr. Lorris Nevel and Dr. Marina Nevel. Certificated. Married. On Nyx for three years."

"And they're still alive?"

"So far, yes."

The cartographer was able to turn off the loquacious machine: Ross had no more questions for it. His stellar-propulsion ship was waiting for him at Marsport. He left the next day, taking Iza with him.

II

Marina Nevel passed the electron microscope to Lorris. Her hand trembled slightly. They leaned together over the experimental tank in which the atmosphere of Nyx was being bombarded with various radiations. They were trying to re-create in the laboratory the exact conditions which had produced organic life on Earth.

Above the prefabricated dome, which sheltered their precious apparatus, yawned the terrible sky of Nyx, studded with enormous diamonds. The hundred and ten stars of the Virgin filled the vertiginous emptiness, and that dome of dark gold was striped with coal-black shadows of tree-ferns.

From the moment they set foot on the retrograde planet, the two scientists had approached their experiment as a great adventure. They knew, without the need of words, that they would never again see the gentle Earth, its mild oceans, its regular seasons, a stable and familiar world about which they knew everything save its origins. They knew also that their time on Nyx would be short. They had taken as their point of departure the old twentieth-century hypothesis of Dauvilliers and Séguin. It was known that these two pioneering scientists had re-created the primeval conditions in a sealed environment. Their postulate was that the sun's ultraviolet rays, working on the oxygen and carbon dioxide in the atmosphere, and the ammonia in the seas, had created nitrogenous matter and given birth to the evolution which was to culminate in Man.

Nyx itself offered a medium for genesis; and the cosmic radiation and interstellar gases at the Nevels' disposal completed the action of the ultraviolets.

Today, the primary phase of the experiment had reached completion.

Lorris trained the microscope on the tank, which seemed empty to the naked eye.

Nevertheless, on the tiny screen, bathed in a colorless flood, something moved among the vibrations and luminescences. It was impalpable and thin, visible only at high magnification, and for just a moment. Nevel thought that they had lost the game.

But Marina extinguished all the lights, except for the black-light screen, and in that half-darkness the thing glimmered feebly, hardly more than the luminous spark of an electron. It must have possessed senses, or some extrasensory perception, for it immediately fled to the bottom of the tank, exactly like a frightened animal, and for a second Marina felt herself watched by an unwinking gaze. Not hostile—but terribly insistent and curious.

She shivered and drew Lorris aside on the platform that surrounded the lucite globe. "Well," she said, "have we found it?"

He hesitated. "It looks like it. The invisible quantum, the spark of life in its pure state . . .

"Of plasma?"

"No, radiant energy, I think. A form of light, in short. It's strange that no one has ever associated the two ideas. Even though all the ancient scriptures speak of light and life together. Let's not get carried away, we've got a lot of analyses to do. I'll start on them now."

"No you won't!" Marina protested, wiping her narrow white forehead under the fringe of blue-black hair. "Spica will be rising any moment—it will be unbearable outdoors, and our airsuits are in the house. Come on, we've been up all night; it's time to have something to eat, like normal people. Let her irradiate herself awhile longer, little Lumen—we'll call her Lumen Nevellia."

"All right," he said. "You go ahead, I'll cover the globe."

She left him, with a possessive smile and glance. In spite of everything, this tall blond man, with the gray eyes of a dreamer, often seemed terribly far from her. In other times, the lords of Lorris had worn a cross on their breastplates or had been riders of chimeras. On Earth, Marina had had to submit to an unusual treatment, to cure her of jealousy. But on Nyx, all was well. Nyx was the vast dreamed-of prison for a spirit that fled always toward the unknown and the invisible.

While Lorris covered the globe, she went down to the house, which was climatized like all the rest. She hurried; a glow of light, first blue, then purple, already rimmed the horizon; huge Spica was about to rise, heating the retrograde planet's atmosphere to a fantastic degree, causing spores and seeds to burst. All the molds would come to life, the water in the ponds would begin to boil. Each new dawn found this world changed, more terrible. Not to mention the storms! Marina paused before the big Plexiglas window which formed one wall of the house. The city was silhouetted against the uncertain light, drowned by the jungle: towers, domes, colonnades, these ruins had a quality of colossal harmony. Her eyes went to the thing she loved best: a temple, carved and pierced. At the corner of an intact balcony, looking out over the forest, a statue devoured by moss was still beautiful—like a Valkyrie.

"But not when you see her close up, surely!" Marina had said, the day when Lorris had pointed it out to her. "See how she's powdered with green. Under that veil she must be hollowed out, tunneled. Every pore in the stone is a nest of terribly active molds. . . ."

"Well, then," Lorris had said, "she's half alive."

It was only a statue. Marina gave a smile to her inoffensive rival, then went out on the terrace. To her surprise, Lorris was standing there, looking absently toward the already incandescent sunrise.

"What's wrong with Lumen?" she asked abruptly. She recognized that strained, obstinate expression. Lorris turned his distorted face to her.

"Lumen? It's living energy, all right, as I thought. But mutable, intermittent—it needs to be fixed in matter; I think that was the role played by Dauvilliers-Séguin's amino acids. Otherwise, as a quantum, indivisible, it exists for the shortest possible length of time."

"Meaning?"

"That there's no more Lumen in the tank. Don't get excited. I can make another one at will."

"And then you'll give it an acid breakfast."

"Yes . . . no. Let me think." His face lighted up. "Why should we stick to classical methods and tie ourselves down to the frightful slowness of nature? Our lives wouldn't be long enough, working with animated plasma. We could try a more daring experiment—introduce Lumen into a complex biological organism."

"You want to create a chimera, a monster?"

"We're not talking about fables, Marina."

"And when I say *monster*," she interrupted, "I know what you're aiming at. First you want to reanimate a dead frog—then a saurian. A man is out of the question, luckily, unless you start working on anatomical pieces. But even with a frog it would be dangerous, because we know nothing about Lumen's characteristics. Do you want to turn a batrachian with an atomic brain loose on the universe? Enough atrocities. Come have your breakfast."

He did not seem to hear. Inside, he put on his airsuit.

"Where are you going?" Marina demanded.

"There's a heaviness in the air," he said absently. "That means a storm. I'm going to turn on the cosmic-ray projectors. The experiment ought to be interesting, if—"

The rest was lost in the hissing of the thick steam that rose from the ground, the furious crackling of bursting sepals—the whole prelude of a terrible symphony. Nevel walked away like an automaton, and at the same moment Spica rose in an orange mist that concentrated its fires. Sky and earth took on the color and almost the consistency of lead, and the forest was no more than a hideous backdrop, placed there centuries ago, for a tragedy. When the young scientist came back, violet tornado shapes linked the sky with the plateau. Nearby, the ocean boomed. The Nevels knew the hurricanes of Nyx, compared to which terrestrial cyclones were mere breezes; they hurried to seal the doors and close the shutters, transforming their house into an airtight unit, as closely sealed as a spaceship.

Just as the last shield slid into place, a giant fern shattered itself on the roof. Marina turned on the periscopic screen: she loved storms. Out there it was an inferno, madness unchained. Purple balls of lightning were bounding under the horsetails. The enormous sun was only a pale spot among the cataracts and whirlwinds, and tresses of vines lashed the screen like floating hair. Finally a new tornado arrived, whirling giant saurians and the trunks of mimosas three meters off the ground, and the screen suddenly stopped working. In the abrupt darkness inside the house, the last note of a record Lorris had put on trembled for a moment in the air—a music that spoke of a ship scudding before the storm, of a hyperborean ocean, and of two lovers linked by fate. Silence followed. Then, with terrible distinctness, the Nevels heard a tapping in Morse on the shuttered door:

S.O.S.

Instantly they were on their feet. A living being was struggling there, in torment! A human cast away on Nyx was calling for help. Quicker than Lorris, Marina was in front of the door.

"Don't open it," she cried, "it may be a trap!"

As always, she interposed herself between him and the unknown, between him and the hostile, dangerous world. . . .

"Remember, we hardly know this planet at all. Remember the stories the explorers told—all those living sands, the plants that kill—"

The signals were growing weaker.

"You're crazy," said Lorris. "Our first duty is to help any intelligent being in danger."

"Intelligent? How do you know?"

"It uses universal signals."

She clung to the man's shoulders, trembling, "Don't open it! I'm afraid—I don't know why!"

As suddenly as it had begun, the tapping stopped. Tearing himself away from the too-soft arms, Lorris slid back the panel. A purple flash of lightning lit up the landscape.

It was a terrible moment, the calm at the heart of the storm. In full daylight, the mad planet was shrouded in darkness. Amid the whirlwinds and electric discharges arose a Nyx of the Tertiary, fantastic, with its mud aboil. Cataracts tumbled down the mountains. Against the pale blotch of Spica, the megalopolis held up its haunting profile.

At the doorsill, Nevel ran into two bodies. The man, burnt, unrecognizable—a black and red mask, convulsed with pain—had fallen full-length. Even in death, his arms were tightly clasped around a child, a silhouette of wax and mother-of-pearl, covered with a mantle of long golden hair. She did not seem wounded, but Nevel, bending over her, could not hear her heartbeat. He lifted her: she was heavy and already cold. The charred dead man seemed to stare at Lorris with reproach—this dead man who, after a stellar shipwreck, had made his way through the Neozoic jungle and all its traps, with his child in his arms.

Nevel was seized with remorse.

At that instant, the cataclysm broke out anew. An immense line of fire cut the firmament in half, and the lightning struck the dome of the laboratory. Picking up the young body in his arms, the scientist threw himself back into the house and closed the panel.

"She's only a child," he said. "And I'm afraid she's dead."

They did everything they could for her. In the end they had to give up. The girl, who might have been fifteen, wore a bracelet with her name: *Y. Ross.* It was a name everyone knew. The Technocrat's ship had landed on Nyx, to be met by the hurricane. But why had he come to this demented planet? No one could give them the answer; and, bending over the lovely corpse, Marina and Lorris gave no thought to their own disaster or the destruction of the laboratory.

III

The storm lasted twenty-four hours and ended as suddenly as it had begun. Nevel went out and surveyed a scene of desolation. In two days and nights, Nyx had regressed a geological age. The ancient ruins were flattened. Only a few edifices of indestructible jade or onyx were still standing, here and there—and the green statue on the roof of the temple.

"Stay here," Nevel said to his wife. "I'll go and see if there's anything left worth saving." He pointed to the laboratory, which was virtually obliterated. "Afterward, we'll have to bury those two. . . ."

It was impossible to preserve the bodies. Lorris had no idea what condition the electronic installations were in. Probably everything had been broken, ripped apart. He left, and Marina was alone with the young dead girl. This time she had not protested. She felt strangely humble and guilty, and she searched for excuses. "Actually," she told herself, "we couldn't really do anything for them: the child was already dead when the man arrived, only to die himself. . . ."

Then, once more, she put aside these useless rationalizations: the past was the past; they had to live and face the future. What were their own chances of survival?

"We have this house, intact, and the provisions in the cellar; we have our airsuits, a light rifle, a disintegrator which I don't know how to use. The rifle has a radioactive bead a little too large; the other day, I shot at a saurian that was carrying off a moufflon. I killed a big lizard, but the flesh of the moufflon was radioactive, unfit to eat. I've got to ask Lorris to fix the bead. . . . If we manage to repair an interplanetary transmitter, we'll have to try to reach Earth. They'll evacuate us, probably. I won't like that at all."

She was happy on Nyx, with Lorris. She didn't mind the storms.

She made her rounds as usual, corrected an excess of ozone in the air, turned on the climatizers, and inspected the storeroom. Everything was apparently in order. But when she went back to the living room, a strange, oppressive feeling came over her: a feeling she had had once before, as if someone were watching her, withdrawn and curious.

She turned mechanically: the child's body, which they had placed on a folding bed in the corner of the room, had not moved. But the sheet that covered it had slipped down, revealing a face as white as cherry blossoms, as snow, as the abyss—and immense, wide-open eyes.

They were strange, those eyes, between their long lashes like fringes of black velvet; they were vast and clear like the spangled sky of Nyx, and they were certainly not human. "If the elements could see, they would look like that," thought Marina, stunned.

Automatically she moved forward. But suddenly the girl's body under the sheet made a sinuous movement of withdrawal—like a supple and flexuous animal retreating. *Exactly that kind of motion.*

"I'm losing my mind," said Marina to herself. "Lumen! At the instant the lightning struck the laboratory, was there a Lumen under the cosmic-ray projector? A quantum of life that escaped, settled elsewhere, in this corpse?"

Even her thoughts stopped, frozen with horror.

Call Lorris? She had always tried to shield him from the outside world. Besides, she was not sure how he would react.

No, she preferred to solve the problem alone. She straightened, and walked toward the child.

Then without a breath, in a single squirm, the slender body rolled off the bed and flattened itself against the wall. The fixed, terrible eyes stared at Marina, eyes in which wavered the original light; and through the tunnel of that stare, she entered the world of genesis, fabulous, a prodigiously ancient life—dating from before all morality and all differentiation.

Marina understood that a new species had appeared on Nyx. She did not know her own powers as yet, not all her muscles obeyed her, probably she did not even have a voice—but all that was a matter of development, of acclimatization.

For she could no longer doubt. Escaped from the shattered laboratory, Lumen had sought a host—and she had instinctively chosen the most complex organism.

From that moment, two forces struggled within Marina: scientific curiosity and terror born of repulsion. The second had all but won. Her human hands were already stretched out to destroy the horrible fascinating creature, when Lorris came back. His first words were:

"She's alive!"

Impulsively he threw himself down toward the cot behind which swayed the huddled form. Marina wanted to cry out, "Don't touch her. That isn't a human child. . . . It's I don't know what kind of horror that we've created by accident, and we ought to destroy it before it begins to do harm. . . ."

But her frozen lips did not move. Mute, immobile, she watched Nevel bend over, lift the radiant little idol and her riches of golden hair.

He laid her down on the bed and examined her, uneasy.

"She fell," he said. "How did that happen? Her eyes are open, but can she speak, can she hear? She's all stiff."

As if in response to these anxious questions, the body lost its rigidity, it shivered, the fragile arms unfolded, rose like wings, and settled in a cool collar upon the shoulders of the leaning man.

Marina cried out—at long last: "Kill it! It's a monster, without a soul or a mind!"

Without a mind? . . .

From the instant when the spark of primitive life glittered in the cosmic darkness, Lumen had perceived and assimilated the universe.

In her fashion.

Could the term "mental process" be applied to the slow concentric waves—the circular movement of electrons around their nucleus? *Cogito, ergo sum.* Turning the ancient Terran wisdom to her own use, Lumen lived, therefore she thought.

It was not a monologue. Neither time nor space existed as yet for the unfinished creature. An occasional datum or image sprang up from the primal source. Little by little, a logic took shape. Beyond that was the darkness, the absolute void.

(Marina would have been chilled with terror, if she could have entered that abyss peopled with amorphous figures, vague ideas—formless monsters, still lost in a chaos as old as the universe.)

Lumen's thought:

I am. I have always been. Or at least I've been part of something . . . primordial, eternal. It was like an ocean into which endlessly flows all that is essentially life: light, matter, and motion. An infinitesimal atom, I was lost in the universal symphony.

I was taken out of my environment, hurled into the darkness. I was cold. And also . . . I don't know the word—when one retracts before an opposing principle. Yes—fear. Then the world exploded. It was horrible. I wanted to diffuse, dissolve myself, but something captured me, like a magnet.

It was suffering a terrible agony. Hot, red energy was pouring out of it in torrents. I fell aside, but then it grew cold. I labored in that ice, in that darkness. . . .

Now there is light again. A narrow container condenses and restrains me—me, limitless, diffuse, a nebulosity. There are things I can't grasp. I haven't succeeded in moving this matrix of fragile flesh. But that will come. I can feel it.

The contrary principle takes on a shape, too. The negative pole. I see it ("they" call that "seeing"). There is a word also for this bundle of intuition and nerves: "a woman."

Silence. Hide. She wants to destroy me. Why? She is large and powerful. Run. My body does not obey me. Slip down, fall . . . The positive principle enters. When he is there, all is well, our two energies communicate. But there must be a contact: he must come closer. I manage to loosen my rays . . . or are they tentacles? I cling to him.

The woman cries out. She wants to kill me. . . .

Marina had screamed at him. Now she realized that Lorris had never looked at her so coldly. She stepped back involuntarily, put her hands to her bleeding mouth.

"You're crazy," he said, as he had said once before in the uproar of the storm, while a hand stiffening with approaching death rapped at the door of their shelter. "The child has just come out of a coma; think of the shock she's been through!" His voice softened. "You're suffering from shock, too, I think. Take a sedative and lie down. You'll see, nothing nicer could have happened to us: now we've got a little human sister. You won't be alone anymore, when I'm away. . . ."

"No!" Marina cried. "It's Lumen!"

He looked at her uneasily. "By heaven, I wonder if the shock hasn't affected you more than I thought! Listen to me, Marina. The lab was struck by lightning, then flooded by rain—everything is damaged, burned, or waterlogged. The experimental tank is full of muddy water. There's no more Lumen. And no possibility of reconstituting the environment. Does that satisfy you?"

With her back against the wall, Marina had managed to take down a corroded hatchet Nevel had brought back from the megalopolis. She brandished it, trying to strike the light-creature. Quick as lightning, the creature slid away and huddled against the wall. The weapon flashed through the air. Lorris had not had time enough to intervene: a little blood spurted from Lumen's temple; she fell back, motionless, in her glory of golden hair.

Nevel strode forward. He was pale with anger.

"If this is how it's going to be," he said, "I'll lock you up."

"I'm your wife, Lorris!"

"Yes, and an attempted murderer. A dead man left this child on our doorstep; we have a responsibility to her. Come on."

He led her into their room. She went without protest, inert, emptied of her rage. Her act seemed to her odious and grotesque. Nevel closed the door on her and locked it, without a word. When she was locked in, she wanted to explain; she cried out, banged the wall. No one answered. Then she came to her senses, went to the medicine chest and took out a sedative.

Lorris had returned to the girl, who seemed to have fainted. He looked frantically for a glass, some wine in the refrigerator, and finally settled for a short, squat flask of crystal in the shape of a wine-skin, containing a golden liquor which he tasted as a precaution. Yes, it was just right for a child: a sweet Terran wine, thyme-scented, "a sort of herb wine," he thought, pursued by a vague recollection, a legend or a few piercing notes of music that spoke of a green ocean. This couldn't harm anybody. The one mouthful he had swallowed was cool as autumn air, but deep within it there was a hidden fire. Lorris knelt beside the girl's still body and forced the liquor drop by drop between her teeth. Lovely and terrible, the creature surged up in blood and gold, and he found himself staring into a charming inverted face, the spangled ocean of her eyes, and her lips like a fruit waiting to be bitten. A strange fire was in him, an insinuating warmth—it seemed to Nevel that he was coming home to the world for which he was made, a distant shore, a forgotten country.

He bent down. The flowing hair smelled like honey. The mouth had the salt taste of spray.

IV

Marina awoke with a start. Damn that sedative! Or had she taken an overdose? She had slept as if she had been poleaxed. Her memory was blurred, but her hand automatically explored Lorris's vacant place on the pillow. Then that awful day came back to her, in all its details, with an intolerable clarity. She got out of bed and ran to the door. It was no longer locked: Nevel must have come in to make sure his wife was asleep.

The living room was empty.

It was the pleasant hour before Spica's rising. The air, freshened by rain, smelled of seaweed, of the jungle. No doubt Lorris had gone out to prospect in the ruins, without his airsuit.

And Lumen had disappeared.

Lumen . . .

Suddenly Marina felt terribly weak. Her hand reached for the crystal flask that had contained an ancient liquor, a wild elixir given to her by her grandmother. There was a legend attached to that wine, but she had forgotten it.

The flask was empty.

For an instant Marina had a sharp, terrible sense of aloneness. She knew she had lost Lorris . . . had he ever really existed, that blond rider of chimeras? He had come into her life, carried her off beyond the void, the stellar eddies, nebulas, then he had disappeared again into nothingness. And Marina was left alone on a demented planet, where mysterious life roamed among the tree-ferns.

She had to make an effort to control herself. Moving as if in a dream, she put on her airsuit, took down from its rack the light rifle, useful in spite of its too-large radioactive bead. It felt comforting in her hand. She left the house and followed her instinct, or rather a subconscious strain of music, evoking another flat beach, a greener ocean. The path under the horsetails descended toward the ocean, glittering with a thousand stars. Marina came to the shore.

This was the place.

They were lying on the white sand; she, covered with the flowing, sparkling mantle of her golden hair. (How had they ever mistaken her for a child?) Long and slender, she gleamed like a pearl. Never had Lorris gazed at his wife with such dolorous rapture. He had laid his disintegrator between them. Their hands did not touch.

The waves died at their feet in a silken murmur, and the whole world was mysterious and pure, as at the dawn of its creation, when life emerged from the sea.

Marina bit her wrist to suppress a convulsive shudder; she leaned against a boulder—aimed—fired.

She knew the secondary radiations had not spared Nevel. For the moment, that made her task easier. On the sand, the dark trace of a slender body faded away immediately. Marina sighed with relief: that was the last of Lumen!

Lorris was only stunned. She hunted up an intact carrier and took him back to the house. When he revived, she claimed total ignorance.

Lumen? But he knew perfectly well that the tornado had destroyed their installation. There was no way of re-creating the essential conditions of the experiment, and they could not contact Earth.

Yes, a cosmic storm had swept Nyx. No doubt that accounted for this abrupt change in evolution; they must take that into account in future experiments. Yes, a ship had crashed, and they had found the bodies of Terrans. One of them was even buried under the giant horsetail in the clearing. A man. Afterward? Nevel had been sick. That was all.

Bitterly, tirelessly, she wove around him the veil of forgetfulness. Lorris was very weak and could hardly get up. One day when Marina had gone out, he slipped, as he often did, into a state of semi-consciousness. His hand, dangling off the bed, brought up a long golden hair, clotted with dried blood. He heard a piercing melody and glimpsed the icy sparkle of the stars on the sea.

When Marina came back, he asked, "Was someone wounded here? I found this near the bed."

Marina turned away, pretending not to hear. There was a certain cruelty in her action, but he had been cruel first. Time was on her side. Time . . .

In the ruins of the laboratory, she found an interplanetary transmitter, almost intact, and destroyed it.

Meanwhile, she took devoted care of Lorris and led the primitive life of a pioneer. Since the hurricane had ruined the cultivable area of the camp, she had to hoard their stores of food. Out hunting, or fishing, she took the path to the ruins. A strange, relentless youthfulness drove her to climb the eroded walls of buildings, leap into the pits that had been cellars, swim across ponds that had been swimming pools. She learned to go by night, with a spear, for big purblind fish that shunned the light of Spica. Nevertheless, certain street corners, certain fishing ponds made her uneasy: a dim glow wavered there.

She had never felt so light, so brisk. Except for stabbing headaches, accompanied by a slight swelling of the eyelids and temples, she seemed to have grown habituated to the climate of Nyx.

In her longer and longer expeditions into the jungle, she formed the habit of taking the temple as her reference point. Built of green and white jade, almost veinless, it was probably the most ancient structure in the city, and the one that had best withstood the assault of the elements. And the statue of the goddess was always there. Marina smiled at it each time she passed.

Until one time.

At one of those Nyxian dawns—one of those rare moments when the world lived between the heavy darkness and the intolerable glare of day—Marina was coming back across the megalopolis. Her bag was empty. Her rifle had begun to jam, and she still could not manage the heavy disintegrator. (Without her realizing it, everything was falling apart at the station. Machines were out of order, rusting to pieces; she had restored the electricity, but there were short-circuits in the electronic brain; a tenacious mold covered the walls; and Marina took all this with astonishing lightness, as if she too were returning to childhood.)

Finding herself before a basin strewn with waterlilies, whose smooth, dark waters trembled gently, she thought perhaps she could spear some of the huge batrachians that swarmed among the green leaves. She leaped up onto the curb, and the surface of the water reflected her with pitiless precision: ragged clothes, her body strangely thickened, but endowed with a savage agility, and childish face with an unsightly tumor on the forehead.

She had not even realized that the cells had proliferated. She felt only the sharp pang: this was how Lorris saw her.

Indeed, she must have become a horror to him!

At the same moment or nearly, under a sky of gold, her contracted pupils met the gaze of the goddess on her jade pedestal, lit by the green glow that penetrated the undergrowth.

She was always there, immovable and victorious; the sheath of microorganisms had not succeeded in destroying the perfect harmony of her features. Great eyes opened in the touching softness of her face, like gulfs in which wavered a dreadful living glow. She had seen the birth and death of worlds; and she had survived them.

She was . . . life.

In the uncertain glow of dawn, Marina thought she saw a faint smile curve the full lips.

She fled, because the thick hammering of blood in her temples was taking on a form, a meaning. Scattered through the night, emitted by all that trembles, lives, breathes—mosses, algae in the marsh, wills-o'-the-wisp—she sensed the thoughts of the creature she had vainly tried to destroy. . . .

Lumen's thoughts:

She is there. She wanted to kill me. She succeeded, or almost. I've lost my host again, and it's all the more dreadful because I'm differentiated. She has taken me away from *him*—the positive pole toward whom I yearn, with whom I must melt together to form a whole.

Cast out into the icy darkness, my need to expand and disperse myself draws me toward the abyss. But then, I know, I would lose *him* forever—our one contact was so brief. So I stay here, clinging to the infinitely small, to plants, to certain minerals which they penetrate. Chained. Trapped by the matter which holds me. I exist.

I will not die unless it is with *him*.

I exist. I will not die except with *him*.

My siblings, my sisters (for we are born spontaneously, now that the laboratory has been destroyed) do not know *why they are*. They wander with the phosphorescences over the eelgrass, they sway with the seaweeds in the depths. . . . I cling to stones devoured by moss. It is black and cold. High in the sky, I am immobile and cannot lift my limbs of jade and onyx.

But I am still beautiful. And I love *him*.

V

Marina's wild flight had taken her toward the pools she normally avoided, to the left of the camp. For a moment, she thought she felt an enormous, hostile presence. A monster was at her heels. Reeds crackled in the marsh, and immense jets of water spurted. She would not let herself look back. She ran.

It was when she emerged into the clearing, across from installations, that she saw the ceratosaur.

A walking mountain, preceded by a little head, flat and malevolent, horribly fanged. Marina fired her rifle with trembling hands. A feeble spark sprang out; the charge was exhausted. She screamed.

What occurred then, in the old days, on Earth, would have been called a miracle. The door of the house opened, and Lorris sprang out, armed, clad in his iridescent breastplate. The knight of legend had returned. Leaning against the wall to mask his weakness, he raised the disintegrator to his shoulder and fired.

For a moment, at the edge of the empty clearing, Marina believed that Nyx had shown its power, that time had really turned backward. . . . She was saved, Lorris had never been struck by the radioactive discharge, her wonderful, impossible life was about to begin again! But Lorris, having destroyed the ceratosaur, let the weapon fall.

He said, "I'm going to die. Marina. Where is Lumen?"

She had the strength to say, with swollen, icy lips: "Who is that?"

"You know very well. Life. *Our life*—animating that child."

Marina chose her words with cold cruelty, like a little girl who breaks a toy deliberately: "I burned the body she stole. She has no more form. She can't see or hear. Even if you called her, she wouldn't come!"

"Ah," he said, "that's what I wanted to know. . . ."

Then he bent his knees and, slowly, like someone who has long ago taken the measure of his death and of the earth where he will sleep, he laid his temple on the sill and stretched out. For a long instant, Marina remained motionless and mute. The satellites of Nyx, as they set, cast an iridescent light on the pale form, lying across the sill, and suddenly the Terran woman heard a heavy step—a crackling of mimosas and ferns that no ceratosaur could have made.

The purple sun of Spica rose over the horizon, and in its diffuse clarity, Marina, inexorably diminished, saw that enormous thing she could never understand: a stone, a figure of jade—worn, covered with green moss—that emerged from the forest and walked toward the dead man.

That bent its knees and lay down beside him, mouth to mouth, motionless forever.